Little Eden

Book One

A Magic Book opens the heart and expands the mind.

Thank you to everyone who made this book possible.

KT King was born in 1973 in East Yorkshire, England. Having suffered with Chronic Fatigue Syndrome (CFS/ME) for over 25 years she hopes to help raise awareness for the millions of sufferers worldwide. CFS is currently misunderstood, stigmatised and incurable.
A healer, psychic and ascension coach for over 20 years she has put some of her experiences into fiction & created Little Eden as an escape place for the kind hearted & curious!

ISBN: 978-1-9164296-1-1
Little Eden - A Magic Book

KT KING

Little Eden

Book One

A Magic Book

MAP OF LITTLE EDEN. LONDON, ENGLAND

Not to scale

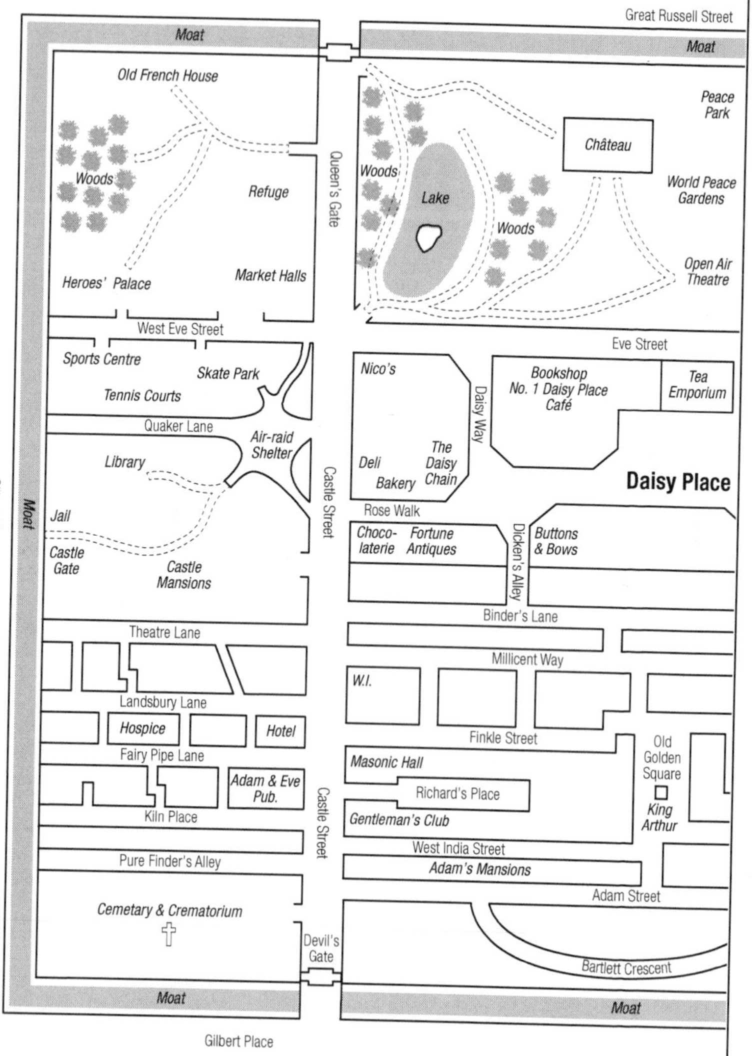

Great Russell Street
Moat
Old French House
Woods
Refuge
Heroes' Palace
Market Halls
Queen's Gate
Woods
Lake
Woods
Château
Peace Park
World Peace Gardens
Open Air Theatre
West Eve Street
Sports Centre
Skate Park
Tennis Courts
Quaker Lane
Air-raid Shelter
Library
Jail
Castle Gate
Castle Mansions
Gilbert Place
Eve Street
Nico's
Daisy Way
Bookshop
No. 1 Daisy Place Café
Tea Emporium
Deli
Bakery
The Daisy Chain
Daisy Place
Rose Walk
Castle Street
Choco-laterie
Fortune Antiques
Dicken's Alley
Buttons & Bows
Binder's Lane
Theatre Lane
Millicent Way
W.I.
Landsbury Lane
Hospice
Hotel
Finkle Street
Fairy Pipe Lane
Masonic Hall
Old Golden Square
Adam & Eve Pub.
Richard's Place
King Arthur
Kiln Place
Gentleman's Club
West India Street
Pure Finder's Alley
Adam's Mansions
Adam Street
Cemetary & Crematorium
Devil's Gate
Bartlett Crescent
Moat
Gilbert Place

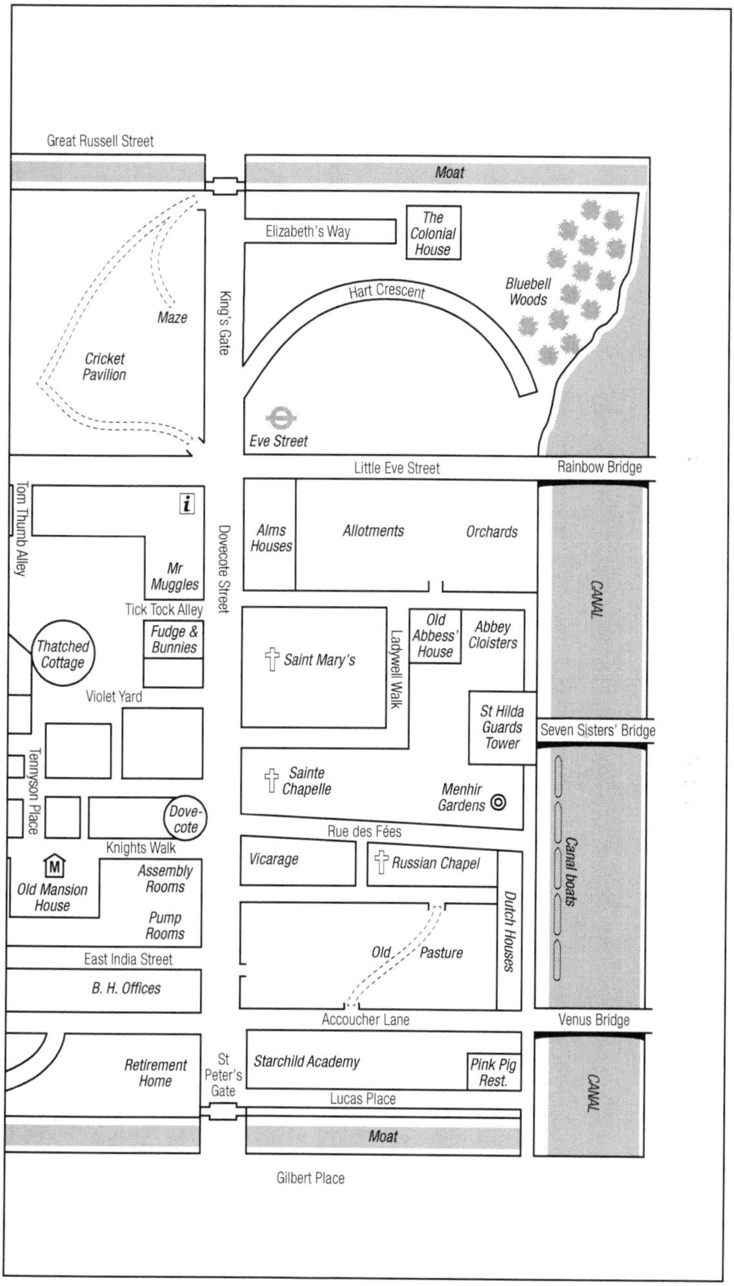
Great Russell Street
Moat
Elizabeth's Way
The Colonial House
Hart Crescent
Bluebell Woods
Maze
King's Gate
Cricket Pavilion
Eve Street
Little Eve Street
Rainbow Bridge
Tom Thumb Alley
i
Dovecote Street
Alms Houses
Allotments
Orchards
Mr Muggles
CANAL
Tick Tock Alley
Fudge & Bunnies
Thatched Cottage
Saint Mary's
Ladywell Walk
Old Abbess' House
Abbey Cloisters
Violet Yard
St Hilda Guards Tower
Seven Sisters' Bridge
Tennyson Place
Sainte Chapelle
Menhir Gardens
Dove-cote
Rue des Fées
Knights Walk
Vicarage
Russian Chapel
Canal boats
M
Old Mansion House
Assembly Rooms
Pump Rooms
Dutch Houses
Old Pasture
East India Street
B. H. Offices
Accoucher Lane
Venus Bridge
Retirement Home
St Peter's Gate
Starchild Academy
Pink Pig Rest.
CANAL
Lucas Place
Moat
Gilbert Place

London Gazette 29th December 2011

Obituaries

Lillianna Rose D'Or
Beloved Aunt and Little Eden Trustee, passed away peacefully, after a short illness, 21st December 2011.

Best known as Lilly Rose singer and stage actress, Lilly will be much missed by all the residents of Little Eden and by her fans from around the world. Lilly will be remembered for her loving kindness, her outstanding musical talent and for her lifelong charitable works within the town of Little Eden.

A public Memorial Concert will be held at The Peace Gardens outdoor theatre, on 21st February 2012, in aid of the Little Eden Charities Trust.

Advance tickets are available at
www.littleedenlondon/concerts.com

A private funeral will be held on January 1st 2012.

The much loved No.1 Daisy Place Café-Bookshop, Little Eden, will continue under the management of her nieces, Lucy and Sophie Lawrence.

Chapter 1

~ * ~

It was a sad beginning to 2012 for the residents of Little Eden, and as it would turn out, it would not be a good year for the rest of mankind either - but more about that later!

First things first…

New Year's Day was almost over as Robert Bartlett-Hart sat alone in his library sifting carefully through the mounds of newspapers which were strewn all over a capacious mahogany table. The sombre shadow of dusk began to seep into the clear blue January sky, and all at once multifarious reading lamps, scattered randomly amongst the furniture and piles of books, turned themselves on, in perfect unison. Robert poured another cup of tea from his Kyushu and sighed. He fought, ineffectually, with the oversized, dry, rustling broadsheets, trying to tame them by folding and flattening them the best he could. For posterity, Robert attempted to glue the numerous obituaries into the Little Eden archive (a huge, slightly musty, leather-bound book), but the scissors kept losing themselves amongst the unruly sheets and little scraps of paper kept sticking to his hands; no matter how much he tried to shake them off, they just re-stuck somewhere else!

Robert's silent contemplation was suddenly shattered by the brusque opening of the library door and his mother's voice slicing through the peaceful air.

"Did you find the obituary I asked Lancelot to put in the Kolkata Times?" Jennifer Bartlett-Hart asked him. She went straight to the large mirror which hung majestically over the sideboard and began adjusting her black, feather-laden hat. She caught sight of a picture of Lilly on the front page of Tatler magazine which lay amongst many others on the table. The magazine was running an old photograph of the glamorous stage star, Lilly Rose, from 1964. Lilly was posing in a 'Vivienne Westwood', wearing white go-go boots, long curling fake eyelashes, and her blond hair was peeking out from beneath a jaunty velvet cap.

The headline read:

"A celebration of the life of a Parisian Diva who became a very English Rose. Lilly Rose D'Or. Her life in pictures: pages 10 - 14."

Jennifer turned away to look in the mirror again. “Lilly hasn’t been Lilly Rose, star of stage and screen, for decades!” she huffed. “I doubt she even has any fans left who remember her! All this fuss and for what? She owned a Café for most of her life for goodness sakes and put on far too much weight eating all those afternoon teas. I don’t think that is much of anything to shout about.”

Robert sighed and ran his fingers through his brown tousled hair. “Thousands of people come every year to her charity concerts, Mother, you know that,” he replied. “And she has been a Trustee with us for over twenty-five years, and a friend to us - all my life at least. I don’t know what we would have done without her all these years.”

“I was the most beautiful woman in London once upon a time,” Jennifer replied, tilting the brim of her hat this way and that to make the most of her features. “I don’t suppose I will be on the cover of a magazine when I die. I had to give up any chance of fame to marry your father and have you boys.” Absently, Jennifer picked up a couple of newspaper clippings and added, “I hope you are nearly ready to go? Collins will be here any minute. Did you hear me Robert?” Jennifer looked admiringly at her long, manicured nails. “It’s just one funeral after another these days. It could just have easily have been me.”

“They say only the good die young,” Robert said under his breath, trying, in vain, to get the glue off his hands.

Jennifer took off her hat and rearranged her hair again, scowling into the glass. “I don’t see why your father insisted Lilly be buried with our family. Lillianna Rose D’Or or whatever she wants to be called this season is not family and never will be, and it is embarrassing for me! Your cousin Lancelot insisted on it. He can find a legal loophole when it suits him - but not when it suits me it seems.”

Robert sighed again. “It was in father’s will, Mother; you know there was nothing anyone could do. We have been over and over it.”

Jennifer grimaced, and wiggled her hips to prevent her black skirt from riding up her long, slender legs. “Your father went on about Lilly endlessly whilst he was alive; I never understood it. We always had to do whatever he wanted! What did he ever care about Little Eden? Off he goes to America with that floosy, Christabelle, without as much as a by your leave! Well! I am not going to go to this sham of a ceremony. The whole thing is just to embarrass me!” With that, she launched herself out of the room and slammed the door behind her.

Robert shrugged, and raised a resigned eyebrow as he dolefully drank the rest of his, now cold, cup of tea, and continued to cut and paste.

After the stomping and the banging of doors had finished, he could hear the sound of his brother, Collins, calling jovially from the hall, "Are you ready?" he called, "Varsity says we'll be late if you don't hurry."

"Varsity can wait!" Jennifer shouted down from the landing. She came tottering back down the stairs wearing a different hat and stiffly kissed her son on both cheeks. "Whoever thought of a memorial service in the evening? I ask you!" she complained.

Jennifer stood on the bottom step of the stairs and started to rearrange her son's clothing, brushing fluff off his black suit. "This is off the peg!" she said, in disgust. "Where did you get it? The fit is terrible!"

"It's 'Lanvin', Mother," Collins replied. "Varsity picked it out."

"I don't care!" Jennifer replied, straightening his tie. "You have perfectly good bespoke suits. Go upstairs and change. You left an Anderson-Sheppard here last week. Go and put that on. If only Robert had your looks and you had his sense of style - I would be less embarrassed to be seen with you both!"

Collins smiled, and kissed his mother. "The fit is perfect, Mother. Only you would ever notice, no one else will."

Jennifer snorted. "Well those Lawrence girls certainly won't notice such details. Lucy dresses dreadfully! They were far too self-confident when they were little girls and I don't see much improvement over the years." Jennifer fussed with Collins' mop of blond hair and he tried to get away from her, afraid she might pull out a hanky and start dabbing his face at any moment! "Robert tells me Sophie isn't feeling well and is staying at the Café indefinitely. She has some sort of fatigue. I ask you! Tiredness is an illness now, apparently! As if we are not all tired all the time! They are as bad as Lilly and your father with their freedom of speech and their women's liberation and all that environmental nonsense. Robert's in the library. There's caviar on the sideboard - your favourite."

Collins nonchalantly kissed his mother again, flung open the large panelled door into the library and headed straight for the champagne and canapés. Collins admired his appearance in the mirror and then, turning to the table, he poked at the papers whilst he munched his aperitifs.

"What's all this?" he asked, in his usual casual manner.

"The obituaries," Robert responded, without looking up.

"What all of these? Good god! You would think the woman was a saint." Collins laughed, nearly choking on a piece of crostini.

"I think she was," Robert mused. "Or she should be!"

Collins smirked, and looked at Robert in the mirror's reflection. "I suppose I quite liked the old girl myself," Collins admitted. "Baked a damn good cake! Shame she's dead."

"Shame?" Jennifer retorted, marching through the doorway whilst pinning her third choice of hat on her head. "It's no shame!" she said, pushing her son aside with her hip. "Move, Collins, I need to look in the mirror! Now, perhaps we can have some of the family money to spend for a change?"

Collins downed another quick glass of champers and said, "Talking of money, Mother, I'm a bit short this month."

"So am I, my dear. Ask your brother! He holds the purse strings around here. He is the one who won't let us have our own money! Always spending it on the poor or giving it to a charity. Well! Charity begins at home!"

Wearily, Robert pulled on his long cashmere overcoat and replied soberly, "This is not the time to talk about money."

"Oh come on Bobby, old boy!" Collins said. "With Lilly out of the picture you can hand out the family fortune a bit more. I promised Varsity she could…" Collins paused and grinned, "F**k! Varsity! I left her in the car. She is probably steaming by now!"

Jennifer surveyed herself in the full-length hall mirror. She smiled at herself again in the looking glass but only until she caught sight of Varsity, who was walking up the front steps wearing a magnificent silver fur coat and looking as if she had just finished a photo shoot for Vogue. Collins rushed out onto the porch, put his arm around his wife's tiny waist and hastily ushered her back into the car.

Robert escorted his mother to the Bentley. Jennifer slid onto the leather seat and into her best finishing school position. She greeted Varsity with a 'good evening' and a 'you look awfully nice.' She couldn't help pouting at Varsity's youthful beauty. To comfort herself, she checked that her finger nails were still in perfect condition.

As the car passed by the end of Adam Street, the ice on the road was treacherous and Dyson, the chauffeur, was taking it slow. By the time they had reached the old Assembly Rooms, on the corner of Knight's Walk, Jennifer had run out of things to say, so she began rooting about in her handbag for her hanky, pretending she was unable to find it, whilst Varsity occupied herself by refreshing her lipstick.

Eventually, the car pulled up outside the gates of the graceful gothic Sainte Chappelle. It was a dark winter's eve, but the street lamps gave a cosy glow to Dovecote Street and softened the harshness of the icy chill in the air. As Jennifer stepped out of the car she cockled over on the curb. Robert caught her just in time before she landed face down on the cobbles! She had expected to see some famous guests outside the Chappelle, but looking anxiously around she was relieved that no one was there. She took Robert's arm and paraded up the lantern-lined path, to be greeted by the singular Reverend Sprott, who was looking rather chilly, but who had been determined to wait outside, in the high and very ornate porch, to meet and greet the Bartlett-Harts. Robert gladly gave his mother over to the Reverend Sprott's care.

The Chappelle was full of shadows - peppered with sudden bursts of flickering candle light. The glorious gold leaf of the majestic pillars seemed to be on fire, and the towering cobalt blue windows shimmered in a heavenly dance. The delicate, sweet scent of pale pink roses played amongst the deeper, muskier odour of beautiful bright white lilies. The melange of ancient church odours - a faint dampness of stone, wood polish, and carnal fresh flowers - invoked a shiver of ancient memories in the mourners.

Tonight, this holy and most sacred palace of light played host to the friends and family of Lilly D'Or. Not least, to her two beloved nieces, Lucy and Sophie Lawrence, who were standing by a small table which was covered in flowers, bottles of water and a mound of pink crystals. The sisters had been greeting the many mourners for at least half an hour already.

Jennifer air-kissed both girls and put on her best funereal face. "I am so sad," she said. "Lilly was a great friend. I don't know how I shall organise things without her. I know you are both grown up now, but I always think of you as little girls when you came here for the holidays..." Jennifer paused as she caught sight of the crystals and added in alarm..."Are you sure you should have those in here? Reverend, what do you think?"

Sophie glared at her and turned to greet Robert, who gave her an affectionate hug.

Lucy handed Jennifer a rose-coloured crystal and said, smiling, "God made the crystals too. These are rose quartz; the gentlest of all the crystals, the very best for grief and overwhelming emotions. We have one for everyone who wants one, and there is Bach Flower Rescue Remedy®[1] in the bottles of water."

Jennifer tried to complain to the Reverend Sprott again about the blasphemy of using crystals in church, but he had already turned to talk to some of the other guests. "Well, I suppose it won't do me any harm," Jennifer conceded, reluctantly. "But I don't want any funny water!" She turned away, looking for any guests from Hollywood or Broadway.

Collins smiled at Sophie, "Well now, what are these things? Calm the nerves, do they? I use a bit of the old whisky myself!" He tapped his jacket pocket - revealing the sound of a metal hipflask underneath.

Sophie offered them both a crystal. "It's like a worry stone; something to hold during the service and to take home as a comfort," she explained.

Varsity took the crystal, and leaning forward out of earshot of Collins, she whispered to Sophie, "I have one of these at home and a purple one too, but I don't remember what it's called."

"The purple one is amethyst," Sophie whispered back. "It's good for healing and protection."

"You must miss your aunt very much?" Varsity whispered again.

Sophie frowned a little and could only manage to nod in agreement. She could feel tears welling in her eyes. Varsity was about to say something else when Collins suddenly grasped her around the waist and exclaimed, "Come on sexy! Mama wants us down the old family pew."

Robert bumped his shoulder gently against Sophie's, and handed her his silk handkerchief to wipe away her tears. He was about to ask Lucy where her boyfriend, Jimmy, was, but before he could, a mountain of bouquets came crashing through the Chappelle doors.

It was Linnet Finch, who, hidden behind a dozen wreaths and bunches of flowers, had burst through the doors, followed by her daughter, Alice, who was also laden down with armfuls of posies and baskets of flowers. Sophie managed to dive forwards and save a few bunches as Alice began to lose control of them. "Alice, be careful!" Linnet exclaimed. Alice's hands, even in mittens, had succumbed to the cold.

"Whoops a daisy!" Sophie said, gathering bunches of multicoloured flowers to her chest. "Good job there wasn't any holly in these ones!" She smiled at Alice, who was looking distressed as she picked up several stray flowers off the floor.

---

[1] RESCUE REMEDY®, A Nelson and Co Ltd

"I have never seen so many flowers - except in your shop. You're doing a wonderful job, Alice!" Sophie told her. "Why don't you keep this one?" Sophie offered. "It's so pretty! A bouquet of gossamer butterflies instead of flowers, how wonderful is that? It'll match your bedroom perfectly, and when you look at them you can say, 'Lilly is sending me butterflies from heaven.'" Alice beamed and held the posy gently, as if it had suddenly transformed into real butterflies which might fly away at any moment.

Alice, at the age of seven, still had all of her imagination firmly intact.

"Where's Tambo?" Alice asked meekly.

"He's with Jack. Go and see if you can find him!" Sophie smiled, and Alice skipped off up the side aisle. She was met halfway by Tambo who was dressed in his gospel choir robe, but missing his usual big smile. Alice gave him one of the butterflies from her bouquet and he held it carefully in his hand.

Only two years older than Alice, Tambo still had some of his imagination left to play with!

They sat down together in the front pew, and whispered to each other under their breath in the secretive way that best friends do.

"Sorry these flowers are so late!" Linnet said, still panting a little, and placing the bouquets around the doorway as decoratively as she could. The orders just keep coming in! I ran out of lilies hours ago. The Hospice and the World Peace Centre will be glad of them afterwards and the Women's Refuge too. I never expected so many - did you?"

"Never in a million years!" Lucy replied. "It's amazing; it's as if all the flowers in London have turned up here to be with Aunt Lilly. I knew she knew a lot of people, especially from the old days on the stage, but some of the people who have sent them - I have no idea who they are! They obviously thought a great deal of her though."

"I know! Linnet replied. "She was one amazing lady! Luckily, I had a few of the fabric flowers left, and Minnie had some butterfly and button posies in her shop. Have you seen Minnie? I thought she would be here by now - she went on ahead of us."

Minnie appeared from the shadows carrying several handmade paper and button flower posies, and smiled at her friends.

"Oh, they're lovely!" Sophie said, as Minnie arranged them around the font.

"Aunt Lilly did like those!" Lucy giggled. "Do you remember when we both made one for her, Sophe? Mine fell apart and Mr T's dog ate it! He pooped glitter for a week!"

"Crikey, that was years ago!" Sophie recalled. "I remember that! Wasn't that on your first craft workshop Minnie? Do you remember all the bunting we ended up with? Aunt Lilly went bunting bonkers! That was before it came back into fashion, mind you; when shabby wasn't actually chic." Sophie looked around the Chappelle and smiled. "That's what we should have had - bunting!"

Lucy giggled. "What with all the stained glass, the flowers, the candles and the people, it might have been going a little too far - even for Aunt Lilly!"

Minnie couldn't hold back her tears when she thought of Lilly who had been like an aunt to her too, and such a good friend to her own mother; God rest her soul. Linnet held her hand. "Come on," Linnet said, kissing away a tear from Minnie's cheek. "Let's go and sit down."

As they glanced down towards the altar they saw the tall and effervescent Jack Fortune strolling up the central aisle.

"Here comes Sir Walter Raleigh!" Collins murmured to Varsity as they watched Jack heartily shake hands with various guests as he passed by their pews.

"Why do you call him that?" Varsity asked.

Collins chortled and replied, "Because, if there was anyone in history he would have been, it would have been Sir Walter Raleigh; the handsome, globetrotting, arrogant devil!"

"Is he the man who invented the bicycle?" Varsity asked thoughtfully.

"No!" Collins laughed. "The potato!"

Jack came to the Bartlett-Hart box pew and shook Collins' hand whilst he winked incorrigibly at Varsity. "Good to see you, old chap," Jack said and paid Varsity a compliment which, unusually, made her blush. "Robert with you?" Jack enquired.

"Bobby's up the top end with the Lawrence girls," Collins replied.

Jennifer leaned over and coughed, so that Jack would notice her.

"Ah! Mrs Bartlett-Hart, you are looking as beautiful as ever!" Jack said.

Jennifer smiled and replied, "Call me Jennifer, silly boy! How many times do I have to tell you? I hear you had to cut your trip to Mexico short to come back for this. That must have been very inconvenient for you."

"Not at all, Mrs...Jennifer...not at all! I would have come back from the ends of the earth to be here for Sophie and Lucy, and Tambo, and for Lilly too, of course."

"I thought you would have been too busy with all that you have to do!" Jennifer grimaced.

Jack winked and smiled. "I am never too busy for my friends."

"Well!" Jennifer muttered to Collins, when Jack had gone up further up the aisle to greet others. "He didn't come to your Aunt Elizabeth's funeral! Where was he then? Somewhere like Kathmandu probably, digging up treasure, as usual. I suppose he considers himself a better friend to those Lawrence girls than to you and Robert, even though you went to school together!"

When Jack finally reached the table of crystals he embraced both Lucy and Sophie at the same time. They melted into his chest, and his energy sent a wave of relaxation through them both. He didn't say anything; aware that the agreement earlier that day was to say as little as possible. He just made a gesture by touching them both gently under the chin and smiling. They knew his meaning was 'chin up - you can get through this - I see your strength'. He held Robert's shoulder and shook his friend's hand as they exchanged understanding looks. Jack took a bottle of water and said, "All present and correct? Shall I close the doors?"

Sophie nodded, but knew Lucy was still waiting for Jimmy to show.

Sophie squeezed her sister's hand and whispered, "He must have got delayed in traffic."

Lucy shook her head, "I just got a txt a few minutes ago. He can't make it! They had to delay filming again, and he couldn't get away."

Sophie put her arm through Lucy's. "Why didn't you say something?"

"I couldn't! Linnet arrived." Lucy frowned.

"Honestly, I could throttle that Jimmy…" Sophie began to say, but Lucy put her hand on her sister's arm to stop her.

"Don't start on him, not now!"

Jack put his arm around Lucy. "Okay, old girl?" he said smiling. "Where's J…" Sophie caught his eye and started shaking her head and mouthing "No". Jack looked confused for a moment, looking round as if expecting to see Jimmy somewhere in the shadows. It was incredible that he had not come to support Lucy on such a day. But he diplomatically said nothing more and took her hand saying, "Come on, old girl - let's give Lilly a send-off she would be proud of!"

Chapter 2

~ * ~

When everyone was seated, and the gospel and church choir had assembled themselves in the chancel, Jennifer sniffed loudly into her hanky as the Reverend Sprott sombrely climbed the winding steps of the resplendent pulpit to make his address. The golden eagle lectern was so high that if his oversized hat had not been so large he would have been barely visible to the congregation. What he lacked visually, however, he made up for in oration. He cleared his throat several times, awaiting complete silence, before commencing his address.

"Now we are in for a long haul!" Collins murmured, and sat back in the pew as if getting comfortable for the evening.

I will spare you, dear readers, Reverend Sprott's sermon, as it was long and laborious and had little to do with Lilly and more to do with himself. But, Robert's speech was, thankfully, a great deal shorter. Robert genuinely thanked and praised Lilly for all she had done for Little Eden and for his family; and he ended his heartfelt address with Lilly's favourite version of The Lord's Prayer:

Our Father who art in Heaven;
Hallowed be thy Name.
Thy kingdom come, Thy will be done
On Earth as it is in Heaven.
Give me this day all I need to survive;
Forgive me my trespasses as I forgive those who trespass against me.
Lead me from temptation and deliver me from evil.
For thine is the kingdom, the power & the glory of
Love.[2]

As the prayer came to an end - suddenly - everyone jumped! The organ had let out a wretched screech, followed by a long howl and a deep penetrating moan. Eventually, the searing noise gave way to the tune of Jerusalem* and the notes, naturally amplified by the high vaulted ceiling, sent a physical thrill through everyone. Rustling hymn books and the general murmur of 'what page is it?' led into a rousing rendition of the old English hymn.

[2] *KT King 21st Century Prayers*, KT King, 2015

Lucy and Sophie felt too emotionally wobbly to sing and left it to Robert and Jack to let rip in their deep baritone voices. Jack deliberately sang out of tune at times to relieve the tension, raising a smile from the girls and Tambo - for which they were very grateful. Alice wasn't sure if it wasn't a bit naughty to sing out of tune because they were in a church and at such a formal occasion. But she noticed that the Reverend Sprott sang out of tune too, (though not deliberately) so she decided that perhaps one should just sing no matter what one sounded like!

The Little Eden Gospel Choir soon took over the musical delights for the evening and soothed the hearts of the guests with their angelic voices, including a joyful rendition of 'Get Happy.'

Then it was Tambo's turn to sing in memory of his great-aunt Lil.

Tambo had been singing since he was a toddler, and whenever he had felt sad he and Lilly would sing together. He had learnt that music cheered people up, and he liked to be able to 'spread the happy' as he called it, whenever he could. Tambo bravely stepped up to the front and Ginger, the choir leader, introduced him. He had chosen to sing, 'Swing Low, Sweet Chariot' which was one of Lilly's favourite gospel songs.

Unexpectedly, Tambo suddenly lost his nerve, and stood, shaking, in front of the congregation. Ginger gave him a microphone and winked encouragingly at him. Tambo could feel his hand shaking, and he felt his heart beating faster. There was an awkward silence. Everyone waited for him to begin. Tambo was afraid that he wouldn't be able to find his voice. His mind went blank. Stage fright paralysed him for the first time in his life. But then, he could swear he heard Lilly's voice in his head saying, When in doubt, let go, let Goddess! Those familiar words rallied him now, and within seconds he had found his courage!

With the gospel choir supporting him, he began to sing with confidence, but after the first verse, Tambo's voice faltered again and tears replaced his song. The choir continued with the chorus as Lucy's heart pounded with the desperate need to get to her son. She stood up in haste and tried to get out of the pew, but before she could, Alice had jumped over the wooden partition and in a flash she was holding onto Tambo's hand, singing as loudly as she could. Tambo's tears subsided at the sight of his friend. It was as if the whole Chappelle was suddenly ignited! A tangible wave of love flowed through hearts of the audience; causing some to smile and some to weep with a heady mixture of sadness and joy. Lucy sat back down in relief, trying to fight back her tears. Jack put his arm around her as she let a mixture of pride for her son and grief for her aunt wash equally through her chest.

As Tambo finished the last line the congregation were enfolded within a deep sense of complete and utter peace…

If I get there before you do, I'll cut a hole and pull you through…
If you get there before I do, tell all my friends I'm coming too…
Swing low sweet chariot.
Coming for to carry me home…[3]

Then all at once, everyone stood up and applauded loudly! Tears streamed down Tambo's cheeks. He needed a hug, which he got, first from Alice and then from the whole choir who gathered him up in their embrace.

The Reverend Sprott muscled his way to the front again and effusively thanked Tambo and the choir, then he launched himself into another lengthy sermon, which gave everyone time to recover their emotions, with the flower remedy in the bottles of water going down a treat!

During the Reverend Sprott's second sermon, Lucy snuck Tambo outside into the cloister gardens. The frosty night air had left sprinkles of icy dust on the trees, and the neatly mown grass in the Abbey courtyard looked as if it had turned from green to white in the moonlight. They walked over the crunchy carpet and amongst the cluster of silver birch, which seemed like elegant pearlescent elves, guarding the sacred Little Eden spring. Mother and son sat together on the ancient menhir, just listening to the water singing with the stones. All of sudden, they felt the fleeting chill of an unseen breeze rippling towards them through the trees. With a whoosh it tickled their noses and fluttered through their hair.

"Did you feel that Mummy?" Tambo whispered.

"Yes," Lucy whispered back, rubbing her nose. "The angels are amongst us!"

As quickly as it had arrived the breeze was gone. "I don't think Aunt Lilly is far away," Lucy said with a smile.

"You think she is still here in spirit?" Tambo said excitedly, looking around, as if expecting to see Lilly as an apparition rising from the waters. But there was nothing to be seen. He wanted Lilly to visit him from the other side and hoped he wouldn't be too scared if she did. Just to see her

---

[3] *Swing Low Sweet Chariot*, Wallace Willis, Circa 1860

one more time, he was sure that would be enough to fill the chasm that had been gauged out of his chest. "Lilly said she would come and see me from Heaven if she could. Do you think she will be a ghost?" Tambo asked his mum.

Lucy laughed. "No, a ghost is not the same as an angel. If she were a ghost, I would be very sad."

"Why?" Tambo asked.

"A ghost is energy that is stuck. We want Lilly to have reached the Heavenly Realms, don't we? Or, as Dr G would say - the Pure Lands."

"Jimmy goes looking for ghosts on TV, doesn't he?" Tambo asked. "But they never see any, do they?"

Lucy sighed and replied, "Yes, that's what he does. But you are right, they never actually see any ghosts on camera. The technology isn't advanced enough yet."

Lucy shivered. She was starting to feel the cold. "Do you want to go back in the Chappelle or shall we just go home?" Lucy asked him.

"We can go back in," Tambo said, looking serious. "Aunt Sophie will need us."

Lucy squeezed Tambo's hand. "You're always thinking of others. I'm so, so, proud of you. You sang beautifully today, and if we are lucky…" she paused and giggled…"Reverend Sprott might have actually finished by now!"

As they reached the Chappelle door, Tambo stooped down to pick something up off the mat in the porch way. "Look, Mummy, a white feather! It wasn't there when we came out. It must be from Aunt Lilly!" he exclaimed.

Lucy felt overwhelmed with grief, and tears rolled down her cold cheeks and into her big woolly scarf. Tambo looked up into the night sky and saw another pure snowy white feather floating down from above, and yet there was not a bird to be seen. "He caught it gently in his hands. "Here, Mummy," he said, "This one's for you."

Without warning, they were startled by a loud clatter! They nearly jumped out of their skins! The wooden door opened towards them with a loud creek. It was Jack, come to look for them.

The service was over.

Back inside the Chappelle, Lucy and Sophie said goodbye to the guests, and invited most of them back to the Café for the wake.

"I thought we might go with Lilly's ashes to the crypt now," Robert told Lucy as he ushered his mother towards the car.

"The crypt?" Jennifer said sharply. "You didn't say! Robert? Why didn't you ask me about this?"

"It was very kind of your husband, I mean ex-husband, I mean Melbourne…Mr Bartlett-Hart…to allow Lilly to be buried with the family," Lucy stuttered.

Jennifer ignored her.

Robert opened the car door. He could smell the scent of warm leather waft into the ever more freezing air outside. "You won't like it down there in the crypt, Mother, it's dark and dusty, and you know how claustrophobic you get."

"It's my family crypt as well! Why shouldn't I go?" Jennifer replied curtly. "I should be there, and besides, your father would have wanted me to represent him."

"The passageway may have flooded due to the rains last week. What about your shoes?" Robert added. "And, it's not a formal ceremony, Mother, just Lucy, Sophie, Jack and myself."

"Oh! Goodness me! I know when I am not wanted!" Jennifer replied, and pulled the car door shut.

Robert sighed as he returned to his friends who were huddling together in the Lych Gate to keep warm. He looked at Lucy and Sophie saying, "Are you sure you're happy to go now? We could go in daylight if you'd rather?"

"It makes no difference, old chap," Jack chortled. "It's always dark down there! You're not scared of the dark are you?"

"Boys, don't start!" Lucy giggled, and put her arm through Jack's. "Come on, it won't take long! I would like to get Aunt Lilly settled in before bedtime. Then we can get back to a nice warm cuppa."

They wound their way through the Abbey courtyard and down the peculiar covered passageway, which separates Hilda-Guards Tower and the Abbess's house. There, they reached the charcoal grey and much smaller church of St Marys, where they came upon a concealed oak door in the north wall of the chancel. Robert gave his phone to Sophie to hold as a light and rooted in his pocket for the key.

"This phone is a bit sticky!" Sophie grimaced.

"Mmm, so is the key," Robert mused. "Oh, that will be glue! I was sticking the…never mind…let's go in!"

He opened the door and switched on the antiquated electric light inside. The single bulb was dim due to age and general muck. They followed Robert to another door: this one, not much larger than the first, was crossed with a rusty metal bar. It opened out into an even narrower passage where steep, well-worn stone steps, led down into pitch darkness. Robert turned on his phone again to light the way. There was a disturbing damp smell and they could hear the distant sound of rushing of water.

As they descended, the roar of the water became louder, and they found themselves walking next to an underground and very fast-flowing stream. Suddenly, they could feel a biting cold around their feet. The water was lapping a little over the uneven walkway as it gushed through the tenebrous channel alongside.

"Ow!" Sophie exclaimed.

"You ok, old girl?" Jack asked, from behind.

"Yes! It's just the water!" Sophie replied. "It's colder than any water I've ever felt before."

"Nearly there!" Robert said reassuringly.

"Not sure 'nearly there' helps much!" Sophie replied. "It's where we are going that I don't want to go to!"

The entrance to the crypt wasn't very far. The pathway took them away from the stream and onto dry ground. They soon reached a highly decorated iron gate, which was not locked. A few more steps down took them inside the crypt.

"It smells of old pianos" Lucy remarked.

"It's the smell of death!" Jack said in her ear and grabbed her from behind. She screamed! Turning around and hitting him playfully on the shoulder, she nearly dropped the small box she was holding, that contained her aunt's ashes.

"Sorry, old girl! That was in bad taste," Jack admitted.

"Yes, it was. But then, you usually are!" she replied, but smiled.

Robert lit one of the huge, half-used, church candles which lined the walls of the dank mausoleum. As he lit more of them, the darkness receded and the chamber began to transform from an eerie pitch black to heavenly shining white. Sophie lit the candles on the other side of the wall and tomb after tomb was slowly revealed, each one more beautiful than the last. Glowing white marble sepulchres and alabaster angels were unveiled from the shadows, and blazing medieval effigies were born into the light. Twinkles of candle flame danced and sparkled over the multitude of brass plaques, making the whole room shimmer, as if it had come alive with angelic light.

"Wow," Sophie murmured, as she bathed in the lustre enveloping her. "This is amazing!"

"Not so scary now?" Lucy asked Sophie. "Are you okay? Do you want to go back?"

"No! It's okay." Sophie replied. "It's not in the least scary in here after all, is it? It's as if all these ancestors are friendly - not one of them isn't glad to see us! Why didn't you ever bring us here as kids Robert?"

"We came down here once," Jack said. "Do you remember, Robbie? You wanted to impress that girl - what was her name?"

"If memory serves, old chap," Robert smiled, "She was more impressed with you than with me or my ancestors!"

Jack laughed, and shrugged nonchalantly, "Can't help my natural charm, old boy!"

The friends started to walk between the tombs. Some were very close together, but others seemed to have their own little space, as if saying, Look at me! The girls stroked their hands over the cold yet seductive glimmering marbles and read some of the inscriptions.

"I love this one!" Lucy said. She was standing next to one of the largest tombs and placed her little box down upon it. Two translucent alabaster angels were devotedly bowing over effigies of a husband and wife who were holding hands. The carving of their features was so exquisite - they looked as if they could wake up at any moment and carry on with their lives. "Not only is it divine to look at but there's a poem," Lucy said. "Listen…

Once the breath of her life was gone, I could no longer breathe. Once the sound of her voice was gone, I could no longer hear. Once the touch of her love was gone, I could no longer feel. Once I am buried by her side, I shall live with her eternally.

And then it says…

Here lyeth the bodye of Henrietta Bartlett-Hart 1739-1801. Adored and much-loved daughter of Lady Nancy Franklin-Grey and Rt. Hon Mr Elliott Bartlett Esq. At eternal rest beside his loving wife, devoted husband Mr Owen Hart Esq. of Tara, Ireland 1738-1802."

"That is so sweet!" Sophie said. "Perhaps some people do love each other for a lifetime? At least he only had to live a year without her. Weren't they the ones who started the Little Eden Trust?"

"Yes," Robert answered, looking on. "Henrietta and her twin brother Jeremiah put the whole of the town into Trust in 1799. Jeremiah was a Quaker and a philanthropist. Henrietta remodelled a great deal of Little Eden. Most of Castle Street was rebuilt, as well as the theatre, and she opened the Chateau parkland to the public for the first time. She built Hart and Bartlett Crescents too. Her legacy has certainly lasted, just as she had hoped it would."

"Oh!" Sophie exclaimed as she read the effigy for herself. "So, they were the ones who put the two surnames together! I remember now - that you were not always double-barrelled! You were just Bartlett once."

"We were just Bartholomew to start with when we first came over from France," Robert explained.

"You have quite a collection of relatives down here, old chap," Jack said. "I like this one…

Robert "Bobby" Bartlett-Hart 1801-1879.
Here lie my bones and those of my beloved wives, Miss Bettina French, des' 1824. Lady Patricia Dumpling, des' 1841. Miss Charlotte Montgomery with our dear children, Henrietta, Georgina & Roberta des' 1862.
My faithful mistresses, Nana O'Donnell, des' 1826, Idumanti Ishwari, des' 1866.
May we be family for Eternity.

…now there is a man after my own heart!" Jack laughed. "How many women?"

Lucy frowned. "I don't think its decent putting them altogether like that, if you ask me."

Sophie sighed. "I think they will be quarrelling over who gets to marry who in the next life and probably for eternity! Till death us do part is written into marriage vows for a reason. To swear eternal love is always a huge mistake. There's no escaping them in the next life!" She looked around again and asked, "What's the oldest tomb, Robert?"

"It's hidden." Robert replied. "Father showed me it once. I can't remember exactly where…er…yes…here, it's hidden behind this big one!" He squeezed behind a stupendously monumental marble and disappeared from view. The others peered, the best they could, around the imposing tomb, and tried to catch a glimpse of the concealed grave. Robert hovered a candle over an almost perished, life-sized, wooden effigy of a long-forgotten woman. She was wearing (they could just make out) what seemed to be a nun's apparel, and in her hands, she was holding a large open book, which was resting on her chest. A delicate crown sat upon her head, which was now covered in cobwebs and dust. There were still some golden flakes of paint just glinting in the deepest carvings. The imposing lady had a broken sword and a half-rotted shield by her side, and her feet were still resting on a sleeping lion.

"Meet Alienor Bartholomew!" Robert said. "The founder of Little Eden way back in 600 AD."

Sophie felt a sudden chill up her spine, which caused a wave of nausea to ripple through her whole body, and her face drained to a deathly pallor. The others looked at her in alarm! She began to shake her hands as if she had too much energy running through her, and she began to tremble.

"Oh, crikey," Lucy said. "I know that look! What? What is it Sophie? What have you seen? Did you hear something? Is there something or someone here with us?" Lucy looked around in fright.

"No! Yes! I mean, there is something here with us!" Sophie said. She paused again and looked, transfixed, at the empty space in front of her. Jack and Robert looked anxiously around too, although they didn't really know what they expected to see! The temperature around them had dropped at least a degree and they all started to shiver. Robert moved uneasily out of his hidden place to join the others. He started to feel the hairs on the back of his neck rising up.

Lucy reached out for Sophie's hand. "What happened?"

"Can you feel that?" Sophie asked.

"The cold? Yes, it's gone icy in here," Lucy nodded. "Is it a ghost?" she asked - hoping to God that it was not!

The candles suddenly flashed and began to burn brighter. The subterranean room became effervescent with an unnatural light that seemed to sparkle and hum. Sophie shuddered again and closed her eyes.

"Who can you see?" Lucy whispered.

Sophie regained her composure, and opening her eyes she looked around the glittering room. The others watched and waited. They saw her smile slightly and then frown, as if trying to focus on something. She began to laugh a little and then grinned. She nodded, "It's okay folks! It's not a ghost - it's a spirit guide."

"Well!" Lucy said, still petrified. "That's okay then!"

"But, who is it?" Robert asked.

Sophie smiled and replied, "It's just Alienor Bartholomew come to visit us, or, depending what time frame you are in, it's also Aunt Lilly!

Chapter 3

~ * ~

Sophie beamed at her friends and was excited now! The others couldn't see any spirit or apparition, but they could still feel the icy cold chill. Robert stepped sideways and suddenly realised that they were in a genuine cold spot. It was most definitely a degree or so warmer just a few paces to his left and to his right, and he kept shifting about to check that he wasn't imagining it!

Sophie closed her eyes again and pointed towards one of the ornate sepulchres. "Alienor Bartholemew's spirit is standing round about…there!" she said. "I can see her with my third eye, but not with my eyes open. Can anyone see anything? Robert can you?"

Robert looked thoughtful and replied, "I can't see anything, but we are definitely in a cold spot.

Jack shrugged his shoulders. "I can't feel or see anything! Are you sure there's a ghost?"

"It's not a ghost!" Sophie replied. "It's a visitation! Alienor is acting as a spirit guide."

"Oh, well!" Jack chuckled, none the wiser. "That makes all the difference!"

"I'm bloody freezing!" Lucy said. "I can't see the spirit, but I keep seeing little flashes of white and blue light, like tiny bubbles, that ping away almost as soon as you look at them. Who can you see?" Lucy asked her sister. "Is it Alienor or Aunt Lilly?"

"They keep switching from one to the other like a hologram," Sophie told her. "But now you have asked that, Alienor seems to be staying. You know me - I get the psychic information in pictures, like a movie in my mind, so bear with me whilst I work out what's going on. Wait!" she said suddenly. "Hang on! Alienor is showing me something. She's taking me into the past." Sophie screwed her eyes up tight so that she could shut out the candle light from around her and concentrate on the vision inside her mind. "I can feel a time-portal opening out at my feet."

"Oh!" Robert unexpectedly exclaimed, and they all looked at him wondering what he was going to say. "I feel as if I am standing on boggy ground and I'm wearing riding boots. I can actually feel them!" He looked down at the dry stone floor and at his handmade brogues. To his normal eyes the floor and his feet were exactly as they should be. But, with his eyes shut, the strange dream-like sensations that the sixth sense conjures in the mind, gave him the impression that the lower half of his body had disappeared and been replaced with someone else's legs and feet. He realised however, that they were not someone else's. This was not a possession. They were his own, past life, legs and feet!

"Yes!" Sophie responded. "I can feel that too! In the past we are in a boggy field: there's grass and water everywhere. I can see fields that seem to go on forever and an expanse of pale blue sky shot through with a sunset of pink clouds. Oh! I can see a standing stone too. I'm right next to it!" She put out her hand and Jack watched in disbelief as she patted the air and said, "It's not very large. It's mossy and wet. Oh! There are more of them - I'm standing inside a circle of stones."

"Is Alienor showing you Little Eden, but in the past?" Lucy asked. "Is it when she was here in 600?"

"Yes, I think it must be!" Sophie nodded. "I think we have been taken back to the time before Little Eden became a village or a town. I can't perceive anything else that makes it look like the Little Eden we know today. There is no castle, no Chateau. In fact, no buildings of any kind."

At this point Robert interjected: "I feel as if, in the past, I'm leading a white horse and I'm wearing leather riding clothes. I am getting the impression that there is a woman with me and she is riding on the horse."

"Yes, I can see that too," Sophie agreed. "The woman is Alienor. I can see more people on horseback too. The horses are amazingly decorated; one has a huge feather on its head and it looks as if the bridle has jewels inlaid on it. There are a few ladies on horseback, in beautiful dresses, and men too, all dressed in leathers!"

Sophie hurriedly jumped to one side and exclaimed in alarm, "Crikey! What was that?" She focused her third eye downwards, away from the horses, to see what it was that had brushed up against her leg. "Oh, it's a dog!" she said with relief. "It seems friendly enough, but it's all soggy and muddy! Ooo, it smells like wet dog too!"

"I can smell that!" Lucy said, wrinkling up her nose in disgust. "What else can you see or sense?" Lucy was eager to get more of the psychic picture that was unfolding for Sophie and Robert. "Tell us!"

"The scene is moving on…it's moving forward in time," Sophie told them. "Yes! Yes! Now I can see a moat has been made and the boggy land has been drained. There are sheep, and pigs, and newly planted trees to make orchards. There are chickens, deer, and doves - and flowers, thousands of flowers! Sophie nodded to herself as she made sense of each picture that came into her mind. "The people here sell flowers - there is a big flower and bird market where the old market cross is now."

"I feel dizzy!" Lucy said all of a sudden, and steadied herself against a marble pillar. Jack took her arm and held her close to him. "What else can you see? What is she trying to tell us?" Lucy asked her sister.

"I think we've had enough of all this!" Jack said, a little concerned that Lucy looked so pale in the candle light. "You okay, old girl?" He was starting to wonder whether his friends were not slightly mad.

"I'm okay!" Lucy told him. "I can't see psychic things like Sophie but I can feel them. I got dizzy, that's all - like being on uneven ground."

"Oooo, that's weird!" Sophie remarked. "I can sense the whole crypt is changing and I'm surrounded by wooden walls, not stone! The floor is made of planks too. They're sort of raised up like a pontoon." Sophie felt the floor with her feet, and moved a little from side to side, and then bounced up and down a few times.

Jack just raised an eyebrow in wonder. He really didn't know what to think!

"I know why I thought it felt like a pontoon - because it's a floating floor. There's a spring right underneath where we are standing and it's bubbling up right here!"

Everyone looked down at the floor, but to them, in the present time, it still looked like solid stone, and as dry as a bone! The only water was outside the crypt, flowing down the underground stream in the passageway beyond.

Suddenly, Robert sneezed and made everyone jump! "Sorry!" he said, as Lucy put her hand to her heart, trying to catch her breath. "Something made me sneeze!" Robert reached for his hanky, but then he remembered that he had given it to Sophie earlier at the Chappelle. He hoped they did not notice him wipe his nose on his sleeve!

I can smell smoke!" Lucy said, as she sniffed the air.

"I can smell that!" Jack exclaimed. "Although, it smells more like hashish to me! Where is it coming from? Is someone coming up the passageway?" Jack went to look through the gate, but the passageway was pitch dark and he couldn't hear any footsteps.

"They are burning herbs in the wooden church back in the 600's," Sophie explained. "They use it like incense to cleanse the space. It's sage - that's why it smells a bit like hash."

"Is it real smoke?" Jack asked, looking around him trying to figure out why he could smell something that didn't seem to be there in reality.

"No, of course not!" Sophie replied laughing. "You're picking up a spirit-smell coming through a time portal. It's called clairolfaction. It's like clairvoyance only instead of sight, it's smells that you pick up. It's actually the most common of the clairsenses. People smell the past a lot - pipe smoke, and baking, perfume too!"

"I thought clairvoyance was seeing into the future?" Jack said.

"Past, present, future," Sophie replied, "It's all the same really!" She put up her hand to stop anyone saying anything more, and cocking her ear to the air, she added, "Listen! I can hear prayers being said. Can anyone else hear that?"

They all listened carefully, pushing their ears up and putting their heads on one side, as if that position might help them hear better; eventually they all shook their heads. They couldn't hear anything except the faint rush of water and the odd flicker of a candle flame. "I can smell the past but I can't see or hear it!" Lucy said, with a frown - wishing she could see it in her mind's eye as Sophie could.

Sophie could see people entering the simple wooden chapel. "I can see a group of nuns praying; they are Sisters of the Rose. Robert! Alienor wants to talk to you. She is right beside you. Can you feel or hear her?"

Robert closed his eyes and concentrated. "I can sense what she is saying, but it's telepathic rather than audible. Tell me what you think she is saying and see if we are getting the same message?" he suggested to Sophie.

"I can't hear her speaking out loud either," Sophie replied. "But I know what she is saying…she says; The dark forces are gathering in greed. We are all at a crossroads. In the year of our Lord Twenty Thousand and Twelve the planets will change their course to re-shape the future of mankind. Robert must learn to use his sword. The dragon portal must be defended. Robert must make the choice."

"Yes!" Robert replied. "That is the message I got too! What's a dragon portal?"

"No idea!" Sophie replied.

"Well, that makes perfect sense then!" Jack said, teasingly.

Lucy pushed against his shoulder. "Shhh, it's important!" she scolded him lightly.

"Just before you mentioned the sword," Robert said, "I felt someone was handing me one. I mean, not really, but astrally. I can sense it! It's rusty and old. It's finely engraved and the hilt is magnificently carved in gold. I can't explain why, but I feel as if it is mine. As if I have used it in battle in a past life. It feels almost real!" He had his hands out in front of him, as if he was holding up an invisible sword, "I can almost feel its weight. It's jolly heavy." Everyone looked at Robert but saw nothing real in his hands.

"The vision is fading," Sophie said. She made sure the time portal was closed down and opened her eyes to look at the 2012 world again; and tried to get her mind orientated with her usual five senses.

"How do you see it? Spirit I mean? Past lives?" Jack asked. "Did you really see all that? I knew you did these psychic-type things, but honestly, from here, it just looked as if you were making it up and waving your hand about a bit. And Robert, you looked like a crazy person with your invisible sword!"

"It looked and sounded crazy to me too, once upon a time," Sophie laughed. "It always does when you don't experience it yourself. I remember seeing someone on the TV, years ago, talking to spirit, and thought they were a complete nutter! I couldn't believe it then either. The thing is, the sixth sense and psychic stuff takes place inside your mind, not externally, so, to someone observing you, you just look as if you are making it up! But, it feels very different when you are in the trance state. When it happens to you personally, you have no option any more - you have to believe it!"

"What did Alienor look like?" Lucy asked. "Does she look like the lady on the tomb over there? Did she have a book and a crown?"

Sophie looked thoughtful for a moment and said, "Pretty much! She was wearing a cardinal red and royal purple cloak with a splendid ermine collar, and she had a small, very plain, but beautiful gold crown on her head. But I didn't see any books!"

"And no lions at her feet!" Jack joked.

"No! No lions!" Sophie smiled. "Just a wet dog!"

"Let's put Aunt Lilly's ashes in their place and go back to the Café!" Lucy suggested. "It's getting late and it's all got a bit too creepy for me!" As Lucy turned to pick up the small box containing her aunt's ashes, Sophie held her hand up and said, "Wait a minute, it's not warming up in here as it should. It feels as if there is something still happening in the spirit world. Let me look! I thought I had closed it all down." Sophie closed her eyes again and tears began to roll down her cheeks. Lucy put her arms around her in concern, but within a few seconds Sophie smiled and her eyes shone with joy. "It's okay, Luce, it's Aunt Lilly again! She looks so beautiful - like a shining angel! She wanted to say goodbye properly."

"Where? Where?" Lucy said eagerly. "Oh, I wish I could see her!" Lucy sighed, exasperated at not having the ability of clairvoyance.

"She is giving you a hug right now!" Sophie smiled.

"Oh, my god, I can feel it!" Lucy replied, and she too, started to cry. "It's so strong! It really is the feeling of being hugged! Aunt Lilly, if you are there, can you hear me? I love you!" Lucy said out loud.

"She can hear you," Sophie reassured her.

"I will take good care of the Café and the Bookshop and of Sophie and Tambo. I promise! Tambo wanted to see you earlier; did you leave us a sign at the Chappelle door?" Lucy asked her aunt.

"She's showing me white feathers!" Sophie declared.

"That was it! Yes!" Lucy smiled. "We found two white feathers in the doorway when we were outside during the service. It really is her! Oh, Sophie, describe her to me! What is she wearing?" Lucy urged.

"She's wearing her favourite dress, the vintage one; you know - her black and white 'Grace Kelly' dress.

"I can smell her perfume!" Lucy said with delight. "It's her! Sophie! Oh my god! It's really her!"

All of a sudden, Robert jumped backwards and let out a (very manly) scream! "Good grief! It felt as if someone just brushed passed me! I felt it on my neck!" Robert brushed his clothes down as if he were covered in some invisible dust.

With that, Jack followed him with an unexpected, "What the f**k!" A ghastly breeze shot through him, violently blowing out the candles along the wall next to him. Jack couldn't help himself and he exclaimed again, "F**k! I saw that!"

"Saw what?" Lucy asked him urgently, holding onto Sophie in fright.

"That!" Jack said, pointing at nothing. "That! There! Damn it! It's gone! It was, well it was a woman! I mean a ghost! Didn't you see it too?"

"Really?" Lucy said. "You really saw a ghost? What did she look like?"

"Like a woman!" Jack repeated, still a little dazed.

"No, I mean did she have long hair? Short hair? Dark? Fair? Short? Tall? Was it Aunt Lilly or Alienor?" Lucy quizzed him.

"Enough with the twenty questions!" Jack replied a little snappily. He was actually shaking and was shocked at how his body had reacted so violently and involuntarily to the ghostly presence. He was not usually easily frightened. "Good god, I'm actually shaking here! My heart feels like it's going to burst - it's beating so fast! Give me a mo'!"

Lucy put her hand over his chest to calm him and he began to regain his composure. Jack took a deep breath and finally, in a softer tone said, "Well, err…she, it, her…whatever it was…it wasn't either Lilly or Alienor. She had long, red hair and bare feet. She looked like she was wearing one of those old-fashioned white night dresses, sort of came off the shoulder, sort of baggy!"

"Yeah, she would be half undressed, knowing you!" Lucy teased him, trying to lighten the fear she felt racing through him.

"No! I'm being serious!" Jack insisted, pointing towards the west wall of the crypt. "She went right through me and disappeared into that marble!"

"That definitely doesn't sound like Alienor or Lilly! Who was that?" Robert asked, and they all looked at Sophie for answers!

"I don't know?" Sophie said, nonplussed. "I didn't see her, but if you hold on, I'll ask my guides, see if they know!"

"Ask who?" Jack asked Lucy, cocking his head in Sophie's direction.

"Her spirit guides!" Lucy replied. As if it was perfectly normal to ask spirit guides for help in general.

Sophie concentrated for a few seconds. "It was…hang on…oh dear," she said and wrinkled her nose. "I'm hopeless with getting names! It's Mel… or maybe Annie…or both?"

"Maybe Melanie?" Lucy suggested.

"Yes, that's it!" Sophie replied. "But, wait…uh oh…I don't know if I should say this, but I get the strong feeling that whoever Melanie was in the past, she is Jennifer in the now!"

"My mother, Jennifer!" Robert exclaimed. "Good grief! But Mother isn't dead!"

"No! But Melanie is!" Sophie said.

"How can someone be more than one person at once?" Jack asked. "Robert was riding a horse in 600 but he is standing here right now! His mother is a ghost called Melanie and Lilly was once a Bartlett-Hart ancestor called Alienor? This is too confusing!"

"That's reincarnation for you," Sophie replied and shrugged.

"It's suddenly warm again!" Lucy said. "It must be over now. Robert, are you okay? Sophie, are you okay?"

"Yes, I'm ok now." Robert said. "I feel everything is normal again."

"I'm okay." Sophie nodded.

"Did your father know that Aunt Lilly was a reincarnation of Alienor; and that's why he made her a Trustee and why he let her ashes be laid down here?" Lucy asked Robert.

"He never said anything like that to me!" Robert declared, looking a bit shaken. "But he did believe in reincarnation. I don't understand? Why would Alienor come back as your Aunt Lilly rather than a member of the Bartlett-Hart family?"

"When it comes to past lives we don't always stay within the same family, but often we stay close by," Sophie explained. "Some people are reincarnated hundreds of thousands of times! And who knows who she was before she was Alienor! She could have been born into different cultures, lived in different countries - been a man even! She has been several of the people buried here, I can feel it!" Sophie said.

"Who else has Alienor reincarnated as down here then?" Jack asked, looking around as if expecting to see words appear on tombs saying;

'Alienor was 'ere too!'

"Well," Sophie began, and then paused as she let the answers come to her psychically. "I get the impression that she comes back into the Bartlett-Hart family when she is needed. I get a strong feeling she was Henrietta - the one who started the Trust." Sophie pointed at the tomb with the two angels on it and shrugged her shoulders. "I don't know why she came back as our Aunt Lilly and I am too tired to work it all out now."

"It's possible that we could all have been a Bartlett-Hart at one time or another then?" Lucy said, looking around to see if she felt affinity with any of the people buried in the half-lit crypt. She hoped she would have one of the grander tombs. "Would you know, Sophie? Who we all were in past lives - if we were any of these people down here?"

"Past lives are so complex!" Sophie said yawning, fatigued from so much psychic work and from such a long day. The chronic fatigue was starting to wash over her like a wave and she sat down on a low tomb. "Sometimes, it's helpful to go back into past lives to heal trauma, and when used as a therapy it can be very effective. But you have to be careful with it! Knowing what you have done in a previous incarnation can change the way we see each other in the present. For example; if I had killed you in a past life would you want to know that?"

"Mmmm…yeah….not sure I would want to know about that, old girl!" Jack laughed. "By the way, who is this mysterious woman in white who just ran through me? Melanie? Is she one of the ancestors? Is she buried down here too?"

"I'm not sure," Robert said. "I wish I had paid more attention to the family tree now. I would have to look it up, but the name doesn't ring a bell. I don't remember a Melanie on any of the tombs in here. Everyone have a quick look around - see if you can see Melanie anywhere."

Sophie stayed sitting down. She really just wanted to lie down and go to sleep! She felt weak and had a terrible headache, but she waited patiently whilst the others all took candles and looked around; but there was not a Melanie to be found on any of the tombs or plaques.

"I think we should go," Lucy said, realising that Sophie was looking rather peaky. "It's getting damp and proper chilly now, and besides I need a wee! Let's get Lilly's ashes settled and go home."

Lucy carefully picked up the small box containing her aunt's ashes and took out what looked like a Fabergé egg.

"That's not real is it?" Jack said surprised, looking at the egg in the candle light.

"No, of course not! You should know that - Mr Antiques Dealer that you are!" Lucy laughed.

"Besides, if it were real wouldn't it have some sort of surprise in the middle?" Robert asked.

"Well, it has now!" Lucy giggled. "If anyone opened this at Easter they would get a surprise, that's for sure! There are some of Lilly's ashes inside it!"

"It's a jolly good copy!" Jack said. "Those are real diamonds and the enamelling is exquisite. It would still sell for thousands. Where did you get it?"

Lucy pushed his hand away playfully. "Don't get any ideas! I can see pound signs in your eyes!" She giggled again. "Stella Dew gave it to us.

Apparently she promised it to Lilly when she died. Obviously, she imagined that she would die before Lilly - being so much older." Tears welled up in Lucy's eyes and she held Sophie's hand.

"Stella said Lilly should have it anyway," Sophie said in a faint voice.

"It seems a shame to hide it down here, it's so beautiful. But it sort of goes with all these fancy tombs doesn't it?" Lucy said. "Aunt Lil won't be disgraced with this as her resting place. Even if she was not technically an aristocratic Bartlett-Hart this time around!"

"Knowing what we know now, should we put her with Alienor?" Robert suggested. He reached behind the sepulchre again and placed the egg on the crease of the wooden pages of the book. It sat proudly in the fold, as if it were a ready-made nest.

"Oh, yes!" Lucy said, peering round. "It looks perfect!"

They said a few words of goodbye, and took a minute's silence, before Jack said, "Well, this will be a night to remember! I understand why Jimmy Pratt goes ghost hunting now. Bet he wishes he had come tonight after all, and brought his camera with him, his loss on all counts!"

Sophie shrugged as Robert helped her to her feet. "Psychic and paranormal experiences like this wear off very quickly and the logical brain soon kicks back in. What you saw, felt or even smelt with your intuitive brain becomes just a whisper and dream again within a few hours. I bet you, tomorrow, you will be rationalising it all away!"

"Come on folks!" Lucy smiled sadly. "Let's leave the spirits to sleep and go have a hot cuppa cha!" She turned and led the way back into the passage, taking one of the candles with her.

Robert blew out the remaining candles and followed behind Sophie. He took one last glance at the crypt, wondering if he would see something supernatural flash through the air, but it was now as silent as the grave should be!

Chapter 4

~ * ~

Meanwhile, back on the surface, the freezing night air had sent forth a crystal shower. A crisp carpet of virgin snow smothered the Abbey walls, roof and courtyard. The large stone lions, guarding the gates, looked as if they were wearing thick, white, velvet cloaks upon their backs, and huge saucer-sized flakes were falling as the friends emerged from their subterranean tomb. They set off towards Daisy Place Café, going up Dovecote Street where the multicoloured, solar powered, Victorian style street lamps shone out, creating a sparkling rainbow along the whole length of the street. The road and cars were engulfed in frosty icing and not a soul had walked upon the smooth and untouched expanse of newly fallen snow. Sophie and Lucy couldn't resist making patterns with their feet.

Jack started a snowball fight which somehow ended up being boys against girls. As they made their way along the road they took refuge behind whatever they could find. Jack hid behind the statue of Friar Tuck, who greeted all those heading down Lady Well Walk. The affable monk was sporting a white hat and had extra froth on his flagon of beer! Jack gathered a heap of snowballs so that he could pelt the girls as they dodged past him to their next hiding place. In Violet Yard, the girls managed to ambush the boys by hiding behind the old thatched cottage, the roof of which was now so heavy with snow that the straw cockerel was completely submerged and looked like a blob of whipped cream on the top. Some local teenagers, who had been walking through from Binders Lane, joined them, and for several minutes it was open warfare, with snowballs flying in all directions across the Yard. A truce was called when Lucy got snow down the back of her coat, and when Robert slipped and fell off the wall by the Juice Bar landing face down in a heap of snow!

The girls sat for a moment on a wooden bench against the wall of the tiny one roomed thatched cottage. The overhanging neatly cut straw created a natural shelter from the biggest flakes. Jack rescued Robert, who was having trouble standing back up as he couldn't get a foothold in the thick powdery snow.

"Listen!" Sophie said to her sister in a hushed voice.

"I can't hear anything." Lucy whispered back.

"Exactly!" Sophie replied. They sat for a few moments, and the absolute silence was awe-inspiring. In the heart of London, not a voice, not a siren, not a car, not even an alarm could be heard for a few seconds together. Peace pervaded the magical night, and it was as if a cushion of tranquillity surrounded them. "Imagine." Sophie mused. "In Alienor's day it would have been so quiet here. There wouldn't have been a city - just woods and fields as far as the eye could see. On a night like this in Little Eden it would have been like being in Heaven itself!"

The silence was soon shattered by the loud cawing of a black crow as it flapped overhead. Then, in the distance, a police siren could be heard, and a car alarm went off. Immediately, the city returned to its usual jumble of cacophonous noises.

"Didn't last long!" Lucy said. "If only the old walls around Little Eden could block out the noise of the city, it would feel as if we had our own world here. A village far from anywhere, where nothing bad ever happened and where only lovely people lived."

"I suppose the walls keep lots of things out; but yes, it would be good if they were sound proof too!" Sophie smiled at the idea. "The walls have kept out the rest of the city, the plague, and even the Great Fire; but as for the people - I reckon evil gets in everywhere, just like sound does!"

The large crow landed on the snow-laden White Rabbit statue, perched high on the wall of Mr Muggles' Clock Shop. It called loudly, three times, as if to draw attention to its presence. Sophie grimaced. "Something isn't right! That crow is making too much of a show of itself. It means there's witchcraft somewhere abouts."

"Now come on, old girl, that's just superstition!" Jack chastised Sophie, as he approached the bench, having finally hauled Robert to his feet. "I may have been converted about the paranormal somewhat, tonight, but crows and witchcraft are going too far!"

"Of course they are," Sophie said sympathetically. "We can only accept that which we are ready and willing to accept. *'There are more things in Heaven and Earth'*[4] as they say. Most of them you may never need to know about, but it doesn't mean they are not out there!"

"Not everyone understands the difference between Holy Spirit and just spirit," Lucy told him.

"Spirits are just ghosts aren't they?" Jack asked. "Nothing holy about that!"

---

[4] *Hamlet*, (1.5.167-8), Shakespeare, Circa 1607

"Aunt Lilly isn't a ghost, she's a guardian angel. There's a huge difference!" Sophie replied.

Jack smiled. "Go on then. Explain it to me. I know you want to!"

"I don't want to explain anything, if you don't want to hear it," Sophie replied, yawning. Her mind was becoming fuzzy, and her thought processes were slowing down to a crawl, as fatigue started to crush her body. She had pushed herself too far that day and should have gone for a lie down hours ago; but she was often stubborn and did not heed the signs in time. Besides, now she was past the point of no return and the adrenalin was taking over. She knew she would not sleep tonight due to sheer exhaustion.

"I do want to hear it, old girl. Honestly. Go on. Tell me the difference between a ghost and a guardian angel!" Jack said, trying to hide an air of mild amusement.

"Mmm, I don't know!" Sophie replied. "You're taking the piss now."

"I'm not, honest, old girl, please tell me!" Jack tried to stop his cynicism from creeping through. Part of him did want to know, but another part of him just thought it was all ridiculous.

"Okay," Sophie said half-heartedly, "A ghost is a residual part of a deceased person's consciousness that did not pass over at death and is stuck in the astral realms. A spirit comes through a portal from another level of consciousness deliberately, and it will come and go when it needs to. A guardian angel is usually a spirit guide who only comes to help and do good. An ordinary spirit can act as a guide to humans but it can be anyone and they may even cause harm.

Jack nodded as if he sort of understood, but he didn't really.

"So, what is this Melanie, Jack saw? And come to that, what is Alienor aka Lilly?" Robert asked.

"I don't know what Melanie is yet - she could be a ghost or a spirit," Sophie replied. "I believe both Alienor and Aunt Lilly are spirit guides and that they are angels. She and Lilly are sending their consciousness as close to the human realm as possible, to be of help to us."

"Well, that makes perfect sense! Not!" Jack laughed.

"Jimmy might be disappointed that he can't add Lilly or Alienor to the local ghost walk!" Robert smiled.

"Jimmy will have to be content with the headless highwaywoman, Genevieve Dumas, who rides her horse up and down Millicent Way, wailing over her lost lover, Henry Bashingbrooke, who disappeared one night without a trace!" Lucy giggled, and then in a hushed tone and with a dramatic turn of phrase she added, "She is said to walk the old castle walls looking for her stolen booty!"

"Or, Mr Muggles' grandfather who walks Daisy Place asking people what time it is!" Sophie laughed and then frowned. "Mind you, I don't like ghost walks. They create fear and give the other worlds a bad name."

"You are starting to put me off this place!" Jack laughed. "I presumed the ghost walks were just a load of old hooey to attract the tourists." Jack pondered some existential ideas for a few seconds, but he couldn't quite get his thoughts in order. "Are you are telling me we have resident spirits? I mean, ghosts, or whatever they are? Have I been living with lots of people I can't see?" He looked around but could see nothing but blankets of snow. "Can they see me?"

Sophie smiled. "We are surrounded by spirits and ghosts all the time, nice and nasty. Like invisible txt messages flying through the air, or digital signals! Not just in Little Eden, but everywhere on the planet. I wouldn't worry about it. If you've not noticed anything yet, in your mind these things do not exist for you, so why worry about them."

Lucy giggled and said, "If Genevieve can't even find Henry or her booty after two hundred years, I reckon she won't be finding you in a hurry!"

"You are not the type of person a ghost or a spirit would bother with much anyway," Sophie reassured him.

"What's that supposed to mean, young lady?" Jack said, raising an eyebrow.

"If they want to be seen or a message passed on they will chose someone who is likely to be able to see or hear them, it's just common sense really," Sophie said. "You are not overly sensitive to emotional and psychic energy in general, so they'll leave you alone."

"Is that a compliment?" Jack smiled.

"Built like a brick shit house, is what she means!" Lucy laughed and threw a huge snowball at the back of his head. Jack tried to grab hold of her, but she managed to get away from him. He caught up to her just outside the No.1 Daisy Place Café.

The Café was lit gaily from within by twinkling crystal chandeliers which sprinkled speckles of light across the glistening snow outside; the sound of Jackie Wilson's 'Your Love Keeps Lifting Me Higher' came dancing its way, joyously, through the door. As Lucy opened it, a warm blast of air rushed over them, and their friends greeted them effusively. They were met by a boundless sea of hot tea and half-eaten finger sandwiches; and many of their friends were gathered together around the piano, on which Tambo was playing with gusto! As he spotted his mum he stopped playing and jumped up shouting, "Mummy, look!"

Tambo pointed to the long glass serving counter. "Look what Mrs B has made!" He gave his place at the piano to Ginger, who launched everyone into a rendition of 'Love Train' by the O'Jays. Tambo led Lucy to the polished mirrored counter and there, on the marble top, stood a majestic and huge, five-tiered cake. It was enrobed in opulent white fondant and bejewelled with fresh roses and lilies. It towered above everyone and was crowned by a magnificent angel made of glimmering gold chocolate.

"Wow!" Lucy exclaimed. She turned to see Sophie and Robert come through the door and waved them over to come and look at the delicious looking cake.

"I made it for you, my loves," a soft, kind voice said from the kitchen doorway. They turned to see their dear Mrs Bakewell, beaming at them. "Devlin made the Angel - bless him. There is a surprise inside too!"

"That's so lovely Mrs B!" Lucy said, giving her a huge hug.

"What's the surprise?" Tambo asked, trying his hardest not to touch the cake. "Can we cut it Mummy?"

"Yes, of course, although it seems a shame to spoil it!" Lucy said. "Can I have a cup of tea and take my coat off first?" Tambo nudged Alice, who was standing eagerly next to him. He motioned for her to go and get a cup of tea, then he pulled his mum's coat off for her as quickly as he could.

"Okay! Okay!" Lucy giggled. "Come on then, tell everyone to come and see! Where's the knife?"

Robert dinged a spoon against his tea cup and called for the rest of the guests to watch the cutting of the cake. "Everyone! Everyone!" he announced. "Lucy and Sophie would like to cut their splendid cake, made by our very own celebrity baker Mrs B, in memory of our great friend Lilly."

Everyone was hushed, and watched in anticipation, as Lucy cut into the bottom tier. The icing gave way to reveal a stunning three layers of luxurious vanilla sponge and soft, fluffy, butter cream. Tambo stared at the slice and then peered into the tier. "What's the surprise?" he said, a bit disappointed.

"The surprise is in the Angel," Mrs Bakewell said, with a magical twinkle in her eyes! "Get a chair, Tambo, so you can reach!"

Tambo hurriedly hopped up onto a chair so that he was as tall as the cake on the counter. "Should I just break it, Mummy?" he asked, unsure what to do.

"Just lift it up!" Mrs Bakewell replied.

With that, Tambo lifted up the chocolate angel, and hundreds of tiny pink sugared hearts and edible glitter cascaded down the cake, like a waterfall of confetti. The guests exclaimed in delight and spontaneously applauded!

Alice picked one of the hearts up off the counter and licking it, she said, "Ooooo, they're candy, you can eat them!"

"The tiers are all different flavours, my loves, all of Lilly's favourites," Mrs B explained.

"Can I have a slice of all of them, Mummy?" Tambo asked hopefully.

"It'd be rude not to!" Lucy giggled. "Help me hand it out though, won't you?"

Sophie was falling asleep on her feet, and Mrs B, seeing she needed to rest, said kindly, "Come in the kitchen, my love. Sit with me while I bag up the Arval bread for everyone to take home."

Sophie gladly put her slim arm through Mrs Bakewell's large soft one. Mrs Bakewell always looked like a well-risen cob wearing an apron and a light dusting of flour! She bustled Sophie away from the party into the peacefulness of her culinary world. "Sit down there, my love," Mrs B said, offering Sophie her comfy chair by the Aga, which she used during her tea breaks.

Sophie closed her eyes and felt herself feeling calmer as Mrs Bakewell chattered on whilst she tied black ribbons around the parcels of Arval bread and made neat little bows. "It's a shame your father is too ill to have come to the funeral."

"He isn't too ill," Sophie replied in a matter of fact way. "You know him! He doesn't like gatherings and he doesn't even like travelling further than his allotment or the local pub. To be fair, he thinks going out of East Yorkshire is going abroad."

"The simple life is often a happy one," Mrs Bakewell mused, as she laid out the fruitcake parcels on a tea tray. "Families are not always made up of those who gave birth to you - that's a fact and no mistake."

"That is very true," Sophie said, yawning again. "Aunt Lil was our mother really, and you have always been like our granny!"

"Get away with you!" Mrs Bakewell smiled. "That's very nice of you to say so, my love! Although, I wasn't old enough to be a granny when you first started coming here as babies. I was only in my thirties you know! Doesn't time fly?"

"I wish Aunt Lil could have seen your lovely cake," Sophie said to Mrs B.

"She'll be looking down on us, my love," Mrs B reassured her.

Just then, Linnet popped her head round the kitchen door. "Lucy asked if you could come out - Tosha wants to make a speech."

"Right ho!" Mrs B said, wiping her sticky hands on her apron and carrying out the tray of breads with her.

The Café had gone quiet. The rabble rousing and singing was put on hold as chilled glasses were filled with champagne for the toast. Tosha was standing on a table so that everyone could see her. "Dank you. Dank you!" Tosha said (in her soft Polish accent) as she gave a little bow and nearly fell off the table but was pushed back on by her sister Tonbee. "As da new manager of the notorious No.1 Daisy Place Café-Bookshop, the rest of staff ask me to say few words, or rather dey volunteer me to say few words! We would like to say huge dank you to Lucy and Sophie for all love and care they show us since Lilly passing. And, we dank Silvi Swan for offer of free grief counselling." She raised her glass towards Silvi and fought back her tears. "We very grateful for extra pay, when Café closed last two weeks, and we want you know we are 'all hands on deck' for next few months." Her voice was filled with emotion as she carried on. "We all start here as temporary staff and we stay so long we lose count of years. Daisy Place seem to get under skin, become part of us! We miss Lilly every day but we continue her vision into future. So, we raise glass to Lilly - our boss, our friend and our guardian angel!"

"Hear, hear!" Everyone rejoined and drank the champagne.

Tosha nearly got off the table but Tonbee pushed her back up. "The song!" she whispered.

"Oh! I nearly forget!" Tosha giggled. "We would like to sing one of Lilly's favourite songs, 'One Love'." And with that, Ginger took to the piano again, and the Café was blessed by music and song which helped wash away the sadness and the grief they all felt at the loss of their friend Lilly.

The party continued with more singing and a few more random speeches. The sugar rush from the cake was over and most of the kids were taken home to bed. Due to the champagne, there were some tears, but also lots of laughs; and about midnight even some of the adults started to crash.

Everyone eventually left; braving the snow, which was now coming down in tiny, but slightly crazy, flakes. It was filling up the streets at a pace. It draped itself heavily over the trees and snuck into all the nooks and crannies between walls and eaves. It balanced precariously on window sills and clung to all it touched.

Robert walked home with a small group of friends, and one by one, they reached their respective homes. He continued, alone, through Old Golden Square, from where he could see, albeit snow-covered, the very first mansion house built by his ancestors in 1242. The wattle and daub had been restored but most of the crooked wooden beams were original. In the other direction he could see his own house, a grand Georgian pile, standing majestically at the centre of Bartlett Crescent.

Since 600, Little Eden had grown from a marsh land into a sanctuary hamlet. In the time of King Alfred its new stone walls had isolated it from the rest of the London area, keeping it safe from plague, fire and crime - the town, even today, keeping its own laws. It had developed into a thriving medieval place of pilgrimage, when a relic of St Hilda of Whitby was brought to the Abbey, and later it became an Elizabethan centre of printing and trade. It then grew into a Georgian masterpiece: home to political activists and social reformers. During Robert's father's time, Melbourne Bartlett-Hart, had moved out of the Chateau, and in the 1960's gave it over to a Buddhist Centre. Since then the town had flourished with artists and artisans, and it had become a refuge for those who wanted to live in a community of peace, mutual respect and support. In recent years it had become a unique experiment in 21st century eco-technology and heritage preservation. The place was ever the same in essence, yet ever changing with the times.

In the tranquillity of the midnight snow, not a soul was stirring, and it felt like a peaceful and very ancient sanctuary again. Robert paused for a few moments at the foot of the life size statue of King Arthur. He wiped the snow from the plaque which reads:

'Where lay the mighty bones of ancient men.'[5]

Robert sighed, his breath visible in the crisp English air, and he looked up at the grey, snow-filled sky. Robert didn't think of Little Eden as an experiment - he thought of it simply as home.

~ * ~

[5] *Morte D'Arthur*, (The Passing of Arthur), Idyllis of the King, Alfred Lord Tennyson, 1856

Back at Daisy Place, up on the roof terrace of the Café, Jack, Lucy and Sophie were all wrapped up warm, and sheltering under the wrought iron porch of the conservatory, watching some belated New Year fireworks, which had exploded into the sky just after midnight. The night before, on New Year's Eve, London had been set alight by the pyrotechnics, wowing tourists and Londoners alike, who had gathered in their thousands, in Trafalgar Square and beside the Thames.

"I wish Jimmy was here," Lucy said. "It's silly, I know, but I don't like to sleep alone at the moment."

"I thought he was only filming in London?" Jack said. "Surely the tube is working, in spite of the snow?"

"Well, it can't be can it," Lucy said, a little sharply in her frustration. "I don't know where he is. I don't think he can have a signal on his phone. I hope he's alright."

"You don't have to worry about Jimmy!" Jack told her. "He is big enough and ugly enough to look after himself. It's you who needs taking care of. Why don't I sleep on the sofa again tonight?"

"Would you?" Lucy asked. "That would be a comfort to know you were here." Jack put his arm around her. "I can stay as long as you need me," he reassured her.

Lucy looked out across London and sighed. "I used to love Little Eden at New Year. Everyone dancing and singing in the streets, going around to all the different parties! Do you remember that year when we went to ten different houses and Robert passed out in the park?"

"I remember that!" Sophie giggled. "He woke up in the maze and couldn't find his way out!"

"And, what about that New Year we went down to the Thames and Sophie got arrested for trying to climb that lamp post!" Lucy reminisced.

"And Robert had to pull his 'diplomatic immunity act' to get the constable to let you go!" Jack laughed.

"I didn't get arrested for climbing a lamp post!" Sophie protested, with a smile. "It was what I said to the policeman that got me arrested!"

"And what about you?" Lucy said, turning to Jack. "You are not so innocent Jacky boy - with all your New Year's shenanigans!"

"Ah, New Year's Eve is when anything goes!" Jack laughed. "A night of madness and mayhem - the usual rules do not apply! What can I say?"

"We have had some laughs!" Lucy said. "Aunt Lilly said last year was the best New Year she had ever had. But now it will never be the same again. It will always be tinged with sadness."

They watched a few more fireworks and finished off the champagne. When the sky grew silent again Sophie said, "London looks amazing in the snow - eerie almost - as if everyone were contemplating what to do with the year to come. I wonder what this year will bring?"

"With Aunt Lilly gone, it feels as if the world has lost its sparkle," Lucy said sadly. At moments like this she felt dry and crackly inside, and she could feel her heart physically aching, as if part of herself had died along with her aunt. "It's going to be a hard year without her."

"Anything could happen." Jack said. "Life is full of unexpected events, and some will be good ones!"

"I hope this year will bring only good things!" Lucy wished.

"I have a feeling that something bad will happen," Sophie replied shaking her head. "After what Alienor said in the crypt about dark forces, I have a sense of foreboding in the pit of my stomach when I think about the year ahead."

"It's just your grief talking, old girl," Jack said. "I wouldn't put too much store in a ghost story. All will be well, you'll see."

"I think," Sophie sighed as she looked up into the sky. "This could be the last New Year any of us see in Little Eden."

Chapter 5

~ * ~

Next morning, Tambo was outside playing in a fresh layer of snow with Jack Fortune, Minnie Fig, from Buttons and Bows Craft Shop across the Square, and Alice. They were building various snowmen and snow animals around Daisy Place. Lucy called down to them from the roof terrace of the Café, "Tambo, honey, can you go over to the restaurant and ask Nico if he has a spare lasagne and garlic bread? I completely forgot, the new headmistress, Miss Huggins, is coming for lunch!"

"Right ho!" Tambo shouted back up to her. "Look Mummy! Alice made an owl and I made You! This is Aunt Sophie and we made an angel - which is really Aunt Lilly!"

"Who is that?" Lucy said, pointing at a snowman whose enormous head was perched precariously on top of a very tiny body.

"That's Jack!" Tambo shouted up. "Minnie said he had a big head – so we made him with one!"

"You can't win 'em all," Jack laughed. "Hey Luce - can I meet this new headmistress?" he added with a pleading smile.

Lucy grimaced and then, reluctantly, nodded in consent. "Okay, but hands off! She will be trying to settle in, and by the sounds of it, the new school will take up most of her time, so she won't have much time for romance."

"Who said anything about romance?" Jack chuckled and winked. He blew a kiss to Lucy and smiled again.

"Minnie, why don't you and Linnet come to lunch with Alice?" Lucy called down again. "It might give poor Miss Huggins a buffer to Jack-the-lad here! Robert's coming too, so actually, thinking about it - Tambo - you'd better ask Nico for two lasagnes."

After a while, Minnie came in from the cold, and found Linnet in the Café kitchen already helping Lucy prepare the lunch - or at least they were taking Nico's bubbling hot lasagnes out of the oven and chopping up some crisp green salad.

The Cafe kitchen is a spacious and usually, a very bustling place. There is always the smell of fresh bread wafting in the air and in spite of the shining chrome, steel, glass and bevelled white ceramic tile, it always sends a cosy and welcoming sensation through all who enter there. Fridges and freezers of different sizes and colours hold all manner of delicacies and delights inside them. Shelves are laden with jars of homemade jams, tins of flour, baskets of fresh fruits, and delectable pots of golden syrup and runny honey. The ceiling is hung with utensils, copper pots, and different-coloured enamelled pans, whilst an eclectic mix of fine china cups and saucers are carefully arranged on a colossal Welsh dresser, which almost fills the back wall, and a prodigiously long marble-topped oak table graces the middle of the room. A king-sized stove stands next to a queen-sized bread oven, from which Mrs Bakewell produces a festival of scones, cakes, cookies, muffins and boundless other sweet delicacies on a daily basis.

Most days it is a hive of activity, but today was Sunday and there was just Lucy, Linnet and Minnie in there, chatting away and preparing lunch.

"What do you suppose Miss Huggins will be like?" Minnie asked Lucy as she picked up a cucumber and started chopping. "I think, with a name like Miss Huggins, she must be nice and bouncy, don't you think? Very cuddly and chubby - you know - carrying a few extra 'huggy' pounds! A matron sort! That's just what the kids at the new school will need."

"I bet she's a middle-aged woman wearing some nice knitwear and carrying an umbrella wherever she goes!" Lucy giggled.

"She isn't Mary Poppins!" Linnet laughed, as she put some hot garlic bread in a basket.

Miss Huggins arrived at the Café at exactly twelve noon. Minnie saw her first through the window. "Erm…as far as Miss Huggins goes… girls…" Minnie said…"We couldn't have been more wrong! Look!"

Miss Adela Huggins was not carrying any extra "huggy" pounds or an umbrella. In fact she looked more like a Hollywood goddess. She was immaculately dressed for a Californian winter and she tottered up the alleyway from Eve Street, keeping upright the best she could in her high-heeled boots, dragging her suitcase behind her; whilst her son Joshua, awe struck by his surroundings, fell over a mound of snow that Alice had shaped like a goose.

Tambo and Alice ran into the Café and threw their coats onto the floor. "They're here!" Tambo shouted as he pulled Alice's wellies off for her, and chucked his own into the shoe basket at the bottom of the stairs.

"Shall I go wake Aunt Sophie? I want to show her what we made," Tambo asked his mum.

"No, sweetie," Lucy said. "Aunt Sophie is exhausted - best leave her to sleep."

"Why does Sophie get so tired?" Alice asked, pulling on her enormous, fluffy, tiger-feet slippers.

"Because she has an illness called chronic fatigue," Lucy explained. "It means...well," she paused a moment to think of the easiest way to describe it to Alice. "Imagine we all have a charger inside us like a mobile phone, and when we go to bed or meditate, we recharge, so that we can do all the things we want to do whilst we are awake - like build snowmen or eat lunch! Sophie's charger doesn't always work properly, so she can't recharge like we can. She could sleep and sleep for days and it wouldn't make much difference. Sometimes her battery works fine for a while and then goes flat again."

"Can't we buy her a new charger?" Alice asked, thinking that must be the simplest solution.

"No sweetie!" Lucy replied, trying not to laugh.

"What if Sophie doesn't wake up, like Lilly?" Alice asked, helping Lucy fold some dotty napkins into triangles. Lucy felt a little alarmed that Alice would fear such a thing, so said kindly, "Oh, no, that won't happen, don't you worry about that, sweetie."

"But Mummy said, 'Lilly went to sleep and woke up in Heaven'," Alice replied, and looked at her mother, Linnet, who had just come into the Café carrying a bowl of salad, and who looked rather embarrassed.

"Oh! I see!" Lucy replied. "I promise you Sophie isn't going to die in her sleep." Lucy looked at the sheepish Linnet and tried to do some damage limitation. "There are different kinds of sleep, Alice. Sophie's sleep is extra sleep; we all have normal sleep, and then there is the special sleep called death that means you wake up in Heaven. But that won't be happening to anyone again for a while."

"Can death sleep happen to me?" Alice asked, looking concerned again.

"Oh! What a question!" Linnet said impatiently; but with that, the Café door opened and their two, very cold and tired, new guests walked in.

A warm blast of air welcomed Miss Adela Huggins and her son Joshua into the Café, and it was followed by hearty greetings and introductions. Alice took the opportunity to ask her new headmistress about waking up in Heaven as soon as she could. Linnet looked mortified, but Miss Huggins just smiled and said, "Well now, Alice, that is a big question for a little girl! I like to think of it this way; you are only human for a very short time - just a few years - maybe a hundred at the most; the rest of the time you are an angel and you live in Heaven. You live there for eternity with all your angel friends! Being human is a bit like going on holiday. So, when you are not human any more you wake up where you started from - in Heaven!"

Alice looked satisfied with that answer and Miss Huggins changed the subject before Alice could ask any more 'difficult to answer' questions!

"Now!" she said. "You tell me all about yourself; and I want to know all about Tambo too! How old are you both, and what do you like best at school?"

Everyone chatted merrily as they ate lunch, and Miss Huggins found out that Tambo was quite the musician, and requested he play the piano for her when the main course was finished. "What can you play?" Miss Huggins asked him.

"Anything I have heard before," Tambo replied, going to the white baby grand piano, which sat in the corner of the Café under a multicoloured crystal chandelier. "What is your favourite song, Miss Huggins?"

"Well, I don't know!" Miss Huggins replied. "Perhaps, 'Close every door to me' from Joseph and the Amazing Technicolor Dreamcoat."*

"I know that one!" Alice piped up. "We did Joseph at school last term. I'll sing it and Tambo will play it!"

With that, Alice transformed the cheerful mood in the Café into a melancholy one as she began her lilting song…

Close every door to me
Hide all the world from me
Bar all the windows
And shut out the light
If my life were important I
Would ask will I live or die
But I know the answers lie
Far from this world.[6]

Alice had a magical voice which transported the listener into another world. When she had finished, no one spoke for a good few seconds. It was as if their hearts, and the clocks, had stopped for a moment. Everyone felt suspended in time. Suddenly, Jack began to applaud and the others joined in.

---

[6] CLOSE EVERY DOOR from JOSEPH AND THE AMAZING TECHNICOLOUR DREAMCOAT, Lyrics by Tim Rice, Music by Andrew Lloyd Webber, 1970

"This Café is heavenly! It's so beautiful," Miss Huggins said, sighing in a relaxed and happy way. "And so full of talent too!" She looked around at the quotes on the walls, at the fine china, the glistening mirrors behind the glass counter, and the multitude of cookie jars, cake stands and beautiful teapots. "It's so traditionally English yet with a hint of the Parisian! It was a lovely lunch as well. We are very glad you still invited us. I mean, I was sorry to hear about your aunt."

"It's best to keep busy I always think. And, isn't company the best medicine? Or is that laughter?" Lucy replied, welling up at the thought of her Aunt Lil.

"Play something upbeat Tambo. Cheer us all up again, buddy!" Jack suggested. Tambo grinned and joyfully played 'Happy Feet' whilst Alice and Joshua did a silly dance, making everyone laugh again!

"I know!" Lucy said smiling. "What about something sweet? We have loads of cake left from last night."

"Can we go and play?" Tambo asked, when they had finished their desert.

"Yes? Can we can show Joshua Little Eden?" Alice asked.

"Don't take him too far!" Lucy said, as she brewed some tea and coffee. "Stay in The Peace Gardens, then there won't be any traffic. Go and see if Blue wants to join you, and you can introduce Joshua to Dr G. Oh, and you can show him the Christmas tree on the lake too. They will be taking the lights down in a few days. Joshua, you can borrow some wellies and gloves."

"Be careful near the water and do not stand on it if it is icy! It will be wafer thin and won't take your weight!" Linnet told Alice sternly. "Are you listening? Did you hear what I just said about the lake?"

"Yes, Mummy!" Alice replied, putting on her outdoor garb as quickly as she could, and in a wink, off the children went, out into the fading light of an English winter's afternoon.

The adults began to get to know each other as the kids went out to play. Miss Huggins was quizzed rather a lot about her life but didn't seem to mind talking about herself.

"How is it you are related to Robert again?" Lucy asked her. "He did explain it, but I never can get my head around second cousins twice removed and such like."

Adela laughed. "Oh, it's a long story," she replied, "I am one of the

American Bartlett-Harts, descended from Henri Bartlett who went to the colonies in the 1600's with his wife and family. They were some of the first settlers in Massachusetts. Henri was younger brother to Robert; not your Robert, but the 1600's Robert, who inherited Little Eden back then. My paternal grandmother was a Bartlett, she married my grandfather, Christopher Huggins, so we lost the family name then."

"Do you have any brothers or sisters?" Minnie asked.

"My brother moved to Sedona a few years ago, and I have a half-sister, she is a veterinarian in Venice Beach."

"Sedona?" Lucy interrupted. "Oh! How exciting. Sophie and I have always wanted to visit that place. They say it's the Glastonbury of America!"

"My brother seems to think it is an important spiritual site." Adela nodded. "We don't see much of him now. He is a shaman and a writer."

"Oh! He would love our Bookshop at the back of the Café here!" Lucy said. "After Watkins, it's the biggest bookshop of its kind in London! Mr T and Titch are experts in ancient manuscripts and such. They sell over the Internet - to all over the world!"

Lucy was always enthusiastic about the Café-Bookshop.

"The books go up four floors! Mr T has a precious collection of ancient books and manuscripts down in the cellar as well; but you have to have an appointment to see them and only millionaires can afford to buy them. We may have your brother's book on the shelves. Is he a Huggins too?"

"No, he's called Cooper Stone," Miss Huggins replied, sipping her coffee. "He changed his name for spiritual reasons."

"Are you sure it wasn't for legal reasons!" Jack chuckled but stopped when he saw Adela Huggins flash him her best headmistress look which let him know that she was quite serious and that she didn't consider it a joke.

"Cooper Stone?" Lucy exclaimed. "My sister, Sophie, has read all of his books! She will be so excited that he's your brother. Let's take our coffee into the Bookshop. There are sofas in there. I will show you your brother's books on our shelves." Lucy led the way and the others followed, carrying their drinks with them.

They went into the Bookshop through the back of the Café where the two meet (although, you could say that the Café is at the back of the Bookshop, depending on how you look at it). The bookshop frontage gives out onto Eve Street. Large windows are filled with the latest titles, and heavy wooden shutters open upwards to make canopies, under which, cheaper second-hand paperbacks are arranged in old tea chests, and placed on the pavement on fine days. Inside, just as Lucy had described, towering shelves cling to the walls as they rise up a full four stories high to greet a regal stained glass skylight above. Wooden balconies seem to unfold from the walls, as if suspended in mid-air, providing galleries for each floor. A grandiose spiral staircase descends into a crescent-shaped sales counter, which is bathed in patterns of multi-coloured sunshine at certain times of day from the skylight above. It is a veritable Gothic cathedral of consciousness!

"Wow!" Miss Huggins said as she gazed upwards into a sky of books. "Now this is what I call a bookshop! It's marvellous! Gee, even the chandeliers are made of books. This is extraordinary! I could live my whole life in a palace of books like this." She smiled and walked around, touching the books with reverence, as she soaked in the all-embracing ocean of knowledge. "Can I take a picture on my phone? I have to send Cooper a picture of this. He will love the idea of his books being in here!"

Lucy switched the balcony lights on low, which gave the whole place a soft and mysterious glow; whilst the scent of caramelising sugar and freshly ground coffee wafted through from the Café.

The bookshop really is one of the most relaxing places to spend an afternoon! It is possibly the neatest and most orderly riot of colour and wisdom ever seen! Real palm trees, in large Chinese ceramic pots, clean and clear the air. The usual musty smell of first editions and antique folios is enclosed in a series of enticing cubbyholes, beyond the main area of the shop, down a narrow corridor, which takes you behind Sumona's Tea Emporium next door. The corridor itself is constructed out of stacks of books, and above one's head is a mysteriously self-supporting archway, made from parcels of novels. To go down into the private and elusive cellar you have to know which bookcase conceals the secret doorway. Only Mr T, Titch, Robert, Lucy, Sophie (and Lilly of course), know which one it is!

Lucy looked up Cooper's name in the ledger. "Your brother's books are on the third balcony," she told Adela. "They should be on…shelf number ten… under the section marked 'S'. Mr T arranges the books by subject, alphabet, and also by level of knowledge. The higher up the books on the shelves or floors, the higher the level of consciousness contained within them. So, beginners start here, on the ground floor, and work their way up. I haven't read any of your brother's books myself, I'm afraid to say. But Sophie is onto level three and above now. I am still on the ground floor," Lucy added.

“I’m not sure I’ll ever leave the ground floor,” Minnie said.

“You have read The Celestine Prophecy,” Lucy reminded her. “That’s one of the best ‘awakener’ books there is for opening people’s minds. You have made a start!”

Minnie shrugged. “Well, yes…but to be honest…” she whispered to Adela and Linnet...“I didn’t really understand most of it!”

“You don’t have to understand true spiritual books for them to open your consciousness,” Lucy said kindly. “It’s the invisible energy inside the book that matters. Words can be like keys that open a door of consciousness in your mind without you even being aware at the time. Well, that’s what Sophie says anyway. She calls them Magic Books!”

“I don’t really understand that idea either!” Minnie laughed. “But, I will keep trying!”

“Here, let me guide you to your brother’s books,” Jack said to Adela and led her up the spiral staircase. They wove their way around to the third floor, where Jack offered to climb the polished mahogany ladder, which is attached to the top shelf and slides along a brass rail in the floor of the balcony. But Miss Huggins insisted she climb up herself in order to reach her brother’s books.

“What level of spiritual consciousness are you on Mr Fortune?” Miss Huggins asked Jack, as she took some photos of the shop from the top of the ladder.

“Oh, I’m not sure what to believe.” Jack smiled. “It’s much simpler just to think there is one life and this is it. And, that we should enjoy it as much as we can.”

Miss Huggins smiled down at him from her vantage point. “Well, that is one way to cope with life’s trials and tribulations, I guess. Yet, it puzzles me that you are surrounded by so much esoteric knowledge but you are not interested in it?”

Jack grinned. “Just because it’s written in a book doesn’t make it true, now does it?”

“Gee, I can’t argue with that!” Miss Huggins laughed as she came back down the ladder. Jack took the opportunity to hold her hand as she stepped back onto the balcony floor. “I find the written word is very powerful indeed, don’t you?” Miss Huggins said. “For good or bad! Look at some of the philosophies that have taken hold through literature - Nazism, Communism, Existentialism - to name but a few. Written and spoken words create spells and beliefs that can take us over like a virus in the mind. One has to be very careful not to find oneself brainwashed by fear."

Jack shrugged. "Meditation, praying - all this spiritual stuff - that's brainwashing too though, isn't it?" he suggested.

Miss Huggins nodded in agreement. "Of course it is! Everything is brainwashing when you think about it! Whether it's watching television, listening to the radio, surfing the net, or even reading a newspaper or a magazine." She looked out of the window across the square to a 19th Century illustration painted on the side of one of the old buildings, depicting a monk holding a bucket full of suds, advertising Friars Soap. She nodded towards it and Jack glanced over. "Advertising can capture you very easily, play on your desire to be better thought of by others. Does it matter which brand of soap you use if it gets the job done? No, of course it doesn't! But we humans make it matter, and we spread that belief through words and images every day. We cannot escape brainwashing. We wash our brains with information every day and we don't even think about what we are washing it with. Most people just go with the flow, never thinking about what they are hearing or seeing." Adela looked at the books around her and caught sight of the Dalai Lama smiling on the cover of one of his books. "I would rather wash my brain with love and compassion."

"Well!" Jack laughed. "I can't argue with that I suppose!"

Back down on the ground floor, the friends were sitting on the sofas in the window, enjoying their hot drinks and some of Devlin's handmade chocolates. He, handily for them, had his Chocolaterie just across the square, in Rose Walk.

"Jack is a smitten kitten!" Minnie giggled, lifting her feet up into a moon-shaped easy chair and hugging her mug of ginger tea.

"I don't think he stands much of a chance though," Linnet said, as she sank into some large cushions scattered on a deep pink leather Chesterfield sofa.

"Why not?" Lucy asked. "She would be the first woman to say no to Jack in a very long time!"

"She is too intelligent!" Linnet replied.

"Jack isn't exactly a dunce!" Lucy rebuked her.

"I am not saying he is!" Linnet said. "But, she is…" Linnet paused for a moment whilst she thought of the right way to describe her new acquaintance. "She is one of those women who needs an exceptional man -

you know - a really confident man! Not arrogant, but who is intelligent and caring. One who knows how to share his life without taking more than he can give in return."

"Well, that explains why she's single!" Minnie laughed.

"What about Robert? She might fancy him!" Lucy suggested.

"No! I know! What about Devlin?" Minnie giggled, sampling one of his delicious chocolates. "He's very intelligent and good-looking too; if a little younger than her perhaps?"

Linnet protested. "I don't know why we always presume everyone is straight and in want of a man!"

"That is true!" Minnie agreed. "She may prefer you, Linnet!"

"Don't be silly Minnie!" Linnet replied. "Why do you always have to suggest I may not be faithful to you when it is much more likely it's you who would go elsewhere?"

"Oh, Linnet!" Minnie said, kissing her. "You are so insecure it's kind of sweet! I wouldn't worry! I think with a figure and a face like that, Miss Adela Huggins may break a few men's and women's hearts during her time in Little Eden!"

"Shhh," Linnet said. "They're coming back down!"

"Did you find them?" Lucy asked Adela as she came to join them on the sofas.

"Yes, thank you," Adela replied, smiling. "I sent my brother the pictures. He will think this is the British Library!" She sat down, and looking around again said, "I think I bought a book from here once. It must have been about eight years ago, online. I am sure I did! Do the books come wrapped in brown paper and string with a label that says:

Thank you for purchasing your wisdom from Daisy Place

"Yes!" Lucy replied with a grin. "We still wrap them all up like that. Oh! How much fun that you have already been here in spirit!"

"How could I not remember?" Adela said. "How small the world really is! I remember the brown paper because it seemed so old-fashioned and traditional."

"You may find most of Little Eden a little old-fashioned and traditional for your taste!" Linnet said. She couldn't help wondering if Minnie did fancy Adela after all, and now felt a tinge of suspicion about the new addition to their party!

"But that's what I like about this whole place!" Miss Huggins replied. "I felt a sense of deja-vu the moment we stepped off the underground at Eve Street."

"Robert likes to blend the best of the past with the best of the future, together," Lucy said.

"Robert is almost a revolutionary in the way that he sees the world! I think he must have been Benjamin Franklin, or some such person, in a previous life," Adela said. She looked around at the friends. "Sorry, I'm presuming you believe in reincarnation?" They all nodded - except for Jack, who just shrugged.

"He came here apparently." Minnie said.

"Who?" Linnet asked.

"Benjamin Franklin!" Minnie replied. "They say he came to the Café here in Daisy Place to discuss the politics of the day. Or, so the stories go. Forward thinking is a thing Little Eden is used to, and equality too. Suffragettes used to meet in this very Café, and in fact, this was the first coffee house in London that didn't exclude women. Although, I do have a sneaky feeling that when it was the old coaching inn in the 1400's it may also have been a brothel!"

"This is why I am going to love it here!" Miss Huggins said.

They all looked at her in surprise.

"Oh, not because it was a brothel!" She laughed. "But because of the history and the legacy of Little Eden. I believe we need to build a future on firm foundations. Not on the foundations of a brothel of course!" She laughed again. "We must build on the best parts of the past. US history shows us that it is not a good idea to just sweep the past away without regard or understanding. But, it is also time for a new start. I feel it, don't you? 2012! There is something exciting in the air. Something big is about to happen.

Chapter 6

~ * ~

The friends sat around talking, in the Bookshop, for the rest of the afternoon. They had decided that they liked Miss Huggins very much, and she felt as if she was one of them already. They quizzed her about the new school that she'd come to set up in Little Eden.

"It's exciting to think that we'll have the first Star Child Academy in the world here in Little Eden," Lucy smiled, "The old school has lain empty for thirty years and now it's coming back to life again."

"You have a huge task ahead of you!" Linnet told Miss Huggins. "When will the school be ready?"

"I hope to have the new staff settled for the Easter intake," Miss Huggins replied.

"I'm rather sceptical about this star child stuff myself." Linnet professed. "Too far-fetched if you ask me! I'm going along with it because of Lucy and Lilly really. I don't see that Alice is much different from any other child her age. But they tell me that she is a star child, or crystal child or indigo; whatever the fashionable labels are these days. They say she needs a different type of schooling if she's to flourish. I admit she struggles with aspects of her schooling, but who doesn't?"

"There is a lot of nonsense written about such things, this is true!" Miss Huggins admitted. "One must be careful not to be dragged into wild conspiracy theories. Star children are only different from other people because their consciousness vibrates at a higher rate than others. Instead of feeling human, they feel the Earth is a foreign place, and often they want to 'go home'. But they don't always know what they mean by 'home'. They can get lonely and confused in a human body. To some of them it can feel like being trapped in a very small, dark room, which is full of evil words and violent deeds; and they cannot get out!"

"Alice says that sometimes," Linnet nodded, "That she wants to 'go home'. But I think she means where we lived before, in Hampstead."

"You know she doesn't mean there!" Minnie said, a little impatiently. "She doesn't even remember where you lived before - she was too young. She's said to me a few times that home is up where the stars are; and she says that everyone is green where she comes from, but most other people from the stars are blue. She thinks humans can be very mean to each other;

and she doesn't understand why."

"Earth is a scary place for some star children," Miss Huggins agreed. "Their chakras and meridians do not fit their physical bodies as they should do. For them, it can be like being a round peg in a square hole - and they can really feel like aliens sent to Earth."

"You're not going to tell them all they are little green men are you?" Linnet said, rather horrified.

"Of course not!" Miss Huggins replied. "If the children at the school need to talk about 'home' they can, and if not - then they do not need to. And besides, not all the children at the school will be star children. We welcome any sensitive souls. That's why the philosophy behind Little Eden Star Child Academy is: 'nurturing, compassion and confidence'. I believe happy children learn better than unhappy ones, and everyone should learn to get along together - no matter where their soul might have come from originally. We all need to stick together for the common good, to think globally and to be inclusive. It's not a new philosophy. It's as ancient as Moses going up the mountain or Buddha sitting beneath his tree. Compassion and respect are at the core of everything, or at least, they should be."

Linnet frowned. She had imagined the Star Child Academy would just be for sensitive or gifted children and not be quite so 'out there'. She looked around the Bookshop and felt as if she was the alien there!

"How do you know what type of soul someone is?" Jack asked, confused by the whole idea. "Isn't a soul just a soul and that's that?"

"Why should it just be so simple?" Miss Huggins replied and smiled. She looked at Jack quizzically and then added, "You, for example, are a white knight soul, that is obvious."

"Is it?" Jack said, not sure if she was serious or not. He wanted to ask what a white knight soul was but wasn't sure he really wanted an answer.

Miss Huggins elaborated for him anyway, "A white knight soul is a cross-breed of angelic and elemental mixed together." She interlaced her fingers to illustrate the point. "They were created to fight evil, and when necessary, to go to war with other humans who have been taken over by evil. Of course, the whole 'knight thing' got corrupted, just like everything else does down here. It lost its true purpose and became an excuse to slaughter people in the name of God."

"Oh, I see," Jack replied.

He didn't really see at all, but when he thought about it later on it made sense to him that he would be a white knight. He felt as if his purpose in life was to protect others from harm, and he felt an affinity with the idea of fighting evil.

"Well! I am excited about teaching the children arts and crafts," Minnie said, trying to change the subject, as she could see Linnet was getting more agitated and unhappy with the way the conversation was going.

"I don't suppose you would like to be a teaching assistant would you Lucy?" Adela asked her. "I need two more before term starts."

Lucy shook her head. "Too busy I'm afraid."

"What about Sophie?" Jack suggested. "She would make a great TA. If we can get Sophie some work here in Little Eden she may consider staying here with us permanently."

"She can't work full-time though, and we mustn't push her into thinking she has to work at all," Lucy replied.

"Yes," Linnet agreed. "But you know how proud and independent your sister is. Even if she thought she could contribute to her keep, even a little, she would be more comfortable with staying."

"It's criminal that she can't get any Disability Living Allowance for chronic fatigue. There's no help out there." Minnie sighed, feeling very sorry for Sophie, and a little afraid of what might happen to her should she fall ill as Sophie had done. Her shop was all she had, and all her shop had, was her!"

"What did your sister do before she became ill?" Miss Huggins asked.

"She trained as a lawyer, but her ill health meant she couldn't work full-time, so she never really got a career going. Every time she was getting somewhere she would get a severe bout of chronic fatigue; and a few months ago she had to give up her job and her home completely and come and live with us. It comes and goes, you see, the fatigue. It's like a virus that just never goes away. She's an empath and she's a bit psychic too."

"I look forward to meeting her!" Miss Huggins said.

"Sophie would be an asset wherever she was," Jack said. "Although, don't go into any crypts with her! I learnt my lesson last night."

"And Mr Fortune, are you interested in teaching our children something?" Miss Huggins said, turning to him.

Jack grinned. "All I know about is antiques, I'm afraid, and not much about that really!"

"Antiques?" Miss Huggins asked. "You mean old tables and chairs?"

"Jack has the antique shop across the square. Fortune Antiques. It was his mother's," Lucy told Adela. "He doesn't sell tables and chairs; although he can get those things if you need anything like that. He gets us our vintage china and plates for the Café. But mainly he sells ancient things, like Roman figurines and Greek pots, even fossils and dinosaurs."

"That sounds perfect for children!" Miss Huggins exclaimed.

"Oh! I am not that good with children really," Jack replied, grinning and leaning back in his chair.

"Nonsense!" all the girls said in unison.

"Don't listen to him!" Lucy said. "He is like an uncle, big brother and best friend to my Tambo, and he has taught both Tambo and Alice to climb, swim, dive, fish and goodness knows what else. That's when he is with us, mind you! He goes all over the world looking for treasures. He's quite the Bear Grylls of Little Eden."

"Well, I would rather teach the children how to survive in the wilderness than about antiques," Jack said, smiling at Miss Huggins. "How about I take you out for dinner sometime? Perhaps we can discuss it?"

"Oh, I don't mix business with pleasure Mr Fortune," Miss Huggins said, smiling. "I will send you an application form and I hope to see you at the general meeting in a few weeks' time!"

The girls couldn't help smiling too!

~ * ~

Just as it was getting dark, about three o'clock, the kids all came back from their snowy adventures. Miss Huggins said her thank yous and goodbyes, and ventured out into the frosty white air again.

Adela and Joshua made their way through the snowy streets to their new house, which Robert had provided for them. It was just a few streets away on Accoucher Lane, behind the varied collection of old school buildings which had once been a foundling hospital.

Joshua had already fallen in love with Little Eden, the snow, and his new friends. He didn't stop talking about his afternoon all the way home. He talked incessantly from Daisy Place, all the way down Dovecote Street. He kept pushing snow off the tops of walls and railings as he trudged. When he found a particularly deep patch, he would jump into it with both feet. He was so intrigued by the coloured street lights and all that was around him, that he didn't even care about his soaking wet trainers and jeans. He kept checking if there really were cars buried under the piles of snow by pushing it off their bonnets. Their noses and cheeks were burning red and huge snowflakes started to float out of the almost invisible sky, but it didn't faze Joshua who just kept on talking! This is a snippet of what he had to say:

"Momma! You should have seen the size of the Christmas tree! There's a huge lake with a massive turtle-shaped island in the middle. Tambo says you can take boats out in the summer and go and sit on it. He said it's a god called Atishu."

"I think you might mean Vishnu?" Adela smiled.

Joshua shrugged and continued, "There's a big open-air theatre. Tambo says they have awesome concerts there and he sings in them sometimes - in public! He's like a real pop star! How sick is that? Can I have a new drum set this week? Tambo says we can start a band. Can I Momma? Oh, Momma, you must come and see the big house. It's epic! There were people in orange robes, like at Long Beach. They gave us lemonade but I couldn't have the cookies 'cause they had wheat in them. They'd made a big Buddha out of snow. Alice said that the little boy, Blue, can't eat wheat. He's a Tulku. What's a Tulku, Momma? Is that someone who can't eat wheat?"

"It is someone who is very special," his mother explained. "It's a Buddhist thing. Blue has been born especially to help others with their enlightenment, but I don't think it has anything to do with not being able to eat wheat."

Joshua nodded. "Alice said he was special. He doesn't speak English very well yet. He's only been here a few weeks. He's new - like me! Alice says she lives in a shop that sells flowers and her daddy's in prison. That's the English word for jail, but we've got to keep that on the down low."

Joshua paused to make some snow balls, then continued, "Tambo says I can sing in the gospel choir with him...oh, Momma, look!"

Joshua suddenly stopped talking and pointed in front of them. He was rarely speechless but this was one of those moments! They had just turned the corner into Accoucher Lane. On one side of it was a long terrace of Georgian, three-storey houses, rendered with smooth plaster and with Venetian shutters hung at each window.

Joshua gasped. "Awesome! The houses are all different colours! Is one of them for us? I want to live in the red one, no, the purple one! Is ours the green one? Look at that one - it's pink!"

"It's number twenty-one," Adela replied, looking at her phone to double-check the details. Joshua ran as fast as he could to find their new house. "Momma! It's a yellow one! Righteous!" Joshua peered inside through the small panes of the tall window. He couldn't resist pulling the metal rod beside the front door which rang the bell. He was rather shocked to find that someone actually opened the door from the inside!

"Well now, you must be Joshua," a jolly lady said to him with a big smile. She was standing on the other side of the door wearing a flowered print pinny and yellow 'marigolds'. "And you must be Miss Huggins, to be sure!" She greeted them warmly. "Welcome to Little Eden!" she said.

Iris ushered them into the hall and beyond. "Come on in my dears, you must be freezing! This snow was unexpected, so it was. Down it came, day before yesterday, without a by your leave! I'm Iris - Iris Sprott - the Vicar's wife and W.I. chairwoman. We always like to welcome our new residents. I came earlier to clean and air the place, and I put the heating on."

Joshua walked into the large living area and felt the warmth of the fire; it made him realise he had gotten very cold after all. He stood by it, warming his legs, as his mother tried to keep up with what Iris was telling her but with Iris having an Irish accent, and a very fast way of speaking, she only caught parts of it!

"Take off those wet things, my dears, before you catch cold!" Mrs Sprott told them, as she helped them off with their coats and continued to tell them what she wanted them to know.

"I have put you some bits and pieces in the fridge, so I have. Milk and such like. If you need anything, anything at all, you just let me know. I've left my number by the telephone and I'll pop in again tomorrow to see you've settled in. I thought Mr Robert might have brought you?"

"Mr Bartlett-Hart was detained, I think," Miss Huggins told her. "Mr Fortune offered to bring us, but I thought we could find it. Thank you so much Mrs…?"

"Sprott, dear - Sprott with two 't's, but call me Iris, to be sure. Now, you have everything you need, do you? You know how to dial the emergency services here do you, my dear? We have our own Little Eden Fire Brigade. Volunteers only, you understand. So, call 899 for them or for our security services. Although I hope you never need them, to be sure! We don't have much crime here, thank goodness! Everywhere is safe enough. We had CCTV installed five years ago on each of the gates. We like to keep ourselves apart from the big city, so we do. It's our village inside these walls and has been for over a thousand years. This is the best of all possible worlds, to be sure. We all look out for each other here..."

Iris did actually pause for a moment, but it was only a moment!

"...The local doctor's number is on the pad by the telephone. The surgery is over in Theatre Lane, you can't miss it. The Shakespeare Theatre's on the corner. Do you like the theatre, my dear? We get all the new shows before they go to the bigger theatres in the West End! Oh, and before I forget, the caretaker won't be back on the school grounds 'til Wednesday, so if you need to get into the school at all, the keys are with Noddy Harroldson. He lives on the first narrow boat you come to after the Dutch houses along the old canal. It doesn't lead anywhere these days, mind you, but we had one of the old rivers come up this way, once upon a time. Noddy was on the streets for six years before he came here to the Little Eden Refuge - turned his life around, so he did, but I think this town has a little magic in it for everyone who lives here, so I do. Now! I must be off! The Reverend will wonder where his dinner is."

"Thank you Iris," Adela said, when she could get a word in edgeways. Adela was a little bewildered by Iris, but glad of her kindness and all she had done for them. Coming into a warm house, with food in the fridge and the beds made, was enough to make Adela want to shed a tear. She realised she was exhausted after the long journey, and just wanted to put on her pyjamas and sit by the fire.

"No trouble at all, my dears!" Iris replied. "You'll settle in here in no time, to be sure. You must come and have lunch with us at the vicarage next Sunday. We have a roast joint every week. You must meet my son Elijah. He is about your age, Joshua. We adopted him as a baby from Romania, so we did. I don't know about him being a star child, like Tambo and Alice, mind you, but he will be coming to the new school. My husband, the Reverend, is quite angry at your little venture, though I probably shouldn't say so. It was Lilly's - god rest her soul - idea; the Academy. But, I think my Elijah is something a little bit special. He has a way of speaking to the saints as I have only ever seen back home when I was a girl. I said to the Reverend, 'If being at the new school will help him, well, far be it from us to stand in his way, I am sure!' The Reverend doesn't approve of talking to the saints, but I would rather hear it from the horse's mouth than from a book written two thousand years ago by goodness knows who! I can't say I know what a star child is exactly, but new things are not always ungodly now, are they? I mean, Jesus was new once too, wasn't he? Although, I prefer Mother Mary myself."

Adela nodded but didn't know quite what to say. She thought Iris was going to leave them as she had started putting on her coat, but they had her for a while longer yet.

Iris smiled and picked up a map of London. She waved it at them enthusiastically. "If you want to take your boy to see the sights, well, there's a bus that'll take you into Covent Garden. It goes every fifteen minutes from just outside the Old Pump Rooms on the corner of East India Street, but it's only a ten minute walk to the main market anyhow. I left you a map of Little Eden as well, my dear. We have a lot to see here inside the walls, so we have! Ever so many tourists we get here nowadays. Joshua might like the skate park over on West Eve Street. I can't keep Elijah away from there these days, and there is a swimming pool and you can play tennis over there too. There's cricket in the park in summer and if Joshua can ride a horse he could learn polo on the old pasture. I hope we'll see you in church during the week. We have a family service every Wednesday at six o'clock. The gospel choir always sings - it's very popular! Although my husband, the Reverend, he took some persuading. He likes his music traditional, so he does; but I said to him, so I did, I said, 'Gospel is traditional too - it's just not our tradition, is all!'" Iris thought for a moment and added, "But perhaps you are of another faith - or perhaps none at all? Well, well, we have so many different types of worship inside the walls. Why, if we don't have Quakers and Buddhists, and Hindus and goodness me, so many others...I'm sure God gets confused with himself, trying to keep track of who's doing what, but I believe all the true paths lead to the same place. Although, don't tell my husband I said that! He likes his way best, to be sure! Well, I had better let you get yourselves settled."

Iris was nearly out of the front door when she came back and popped her head back around, saying, "Now, promise me you'll ring me anytime if you need anything, won't you? I can see myself out, to be sure!"

When they were sure Iris had really gone, Adela and Joshua looked at each other. "I think we have found someone who talks as much as you do, Joshua!" Adela laughed, and they threw themselves down onto the sofa giggling.

"Welcome to Little Eden indeed!"

Chapter 7

~ * ~

You may be wondering, dear readers, why Robert had not turned up to his lunch meeting with Miss Huggins? He was not usually so unprofessional or forgetful, but this was an unusual day for Robert. He had been called to an impromptu family meeting at eleven o'clock that morning.

In the well-stocked and imposing library of his family home in Bartlett Crescent, Robert's mother, Jennifer, his brother, Collins, their solicitor, Lancelot Bartlett-Hart and their business manager, India Fitzroy were all gathered together anxiously waiting for him to come downstairs.

The meeting did not go well!

Only five minutes into it, Robert slammed his fist on the table and pushed his chair so violently that it shot across the room and hit the wall, crashing to the floor. Without saying anything, he grabbed his coat and stormed out of the house in a state of all-consuming fear.

Lancelot and India looked at each other in shock and then in dismay.

Collins shook his head disparagingly as he drained the last drops of his whisky on the rocks.

Jennifer (who always had something to say on all occasions) remained silent, and then she sedately arose from her chair, leaving the room without saying a word.

After a few moments of awkward silence, Collins feigned a cough and got up to leave saying, "Well, that's that then!" He held out his hand to Lancelot and added, "See you in court, old chap. No hard feelings! Just business and all that, you know!"

"Quite!" Lancelot replied, and reluctantly, but politely, shook Collins by the hand.

"Be a good girl now won't you, India dear?" Collins said and winked.

India smiled sweetly and replied, "Oh, Collins, I am always good - some say too good." She paused for a moment and stared directly into his bright blue eyes. "At business that is! See you in court."

Collins grinned. He wasn't really listening. He was thinking about what he was going to have for lunch and he left to go to his club.

"F**k!" India said, sitting down in a daze. "I can't believe it! It seems too incredible! Impossible! Ridiculous even!"

Lancelot gathered his papers together and didn't reply straight away. He was too shocked to say anything, and he was not a man to be easily moved. "I had better go and find Robert," he said finally. "I have never seen him so angry! He hardly ever even raises his voice."

"His face drained so quickly he looked almost grey!" India said. "I thought he was going to have a heart attack on us, right here in the library. He will have gone to the Café to see…"

"To see Lilly?" Lancelot suggested, raising an eyebrow.

India frowned. "I forgot what I was saying for a moment. If Lilly was here we wouldn't be in this mess! I can't believe what just happened has just happened. We should have seen this coming Lancelot. We should have seen the precarious state her death would leave us all in!"

"No one could have ever foreseen this, surely?" Lancelot replied, helping himself to a quick shot of Glenfiddich. He offered one to India but she shook her head. Her eyes looked slightly glazed over.

"Do you know - I feel as if I might be dreaming? If I am, wake me up for god's sake!" she said. As she felt panic rush through her body, she took the glass of whisky out of Lancelot's hand and downed it. The shock made her cough and she nearly choked. Lancelot thumped her on the back.

"I think that just woke you up!" Lancelot said. "It's very real, I'm afraid."

"Over a thousand years down the drain in one fell swoop," India said sadly.

"I think the whisky was only fifty years old!" Lancelot replied, trying to make a joke; but even he couldn't do any more than raise a sad smile at this moment.

India went to the window overlooking Adam Street. The fountain in the front garden was frozen over. Not a single drop of water flowed from the vase of Isis. Carved over three millennia ago, the statue of the goddess had been brought from Egypt, and she had graced the gardens of the Crescent for over one hundred and fifty years. Her presence felt majestic and immortal. Yet today, she seemed a solitary and pallid figure, perched upon her cold marble pedestal and plagued by snow.

"Well, I won't let it happen, even if you're resigned to it!" India blurted out suddenly, her blood beginning to boil with anger; or maybe it was just the whisky!

"It's not that I want it to happen either," Lancelot said, putting his coat on. "But right now, I can't see any way in which we can legally stop it. You have to keep a level head in legal matters. I have told you that before."

"Oh, I know! I have a lot to learn about legal matters! You remind me of that on a daily basis!" India frowned. "I may be years younger than you, but I have turned this town around since I took over from Papa, and I have made it viable concern. She sighed, and looked over to Adams Mansions, where Bartlett-Hart and Fitzroy had had their legal offices since 1805, along with a publishers, accountants and investment house.

"There is so much more to do!" India added. "I haven't poured my heart and soul into this place to feed a good-for-nothing, low life coaster, like Collins Bartlett - bloody - Hart, or to keep his vapid excuse for a wife in Jimmy Choos and Chanel f**king Number 5!"

"Come on, that's not fair!" Lancelot smiled. "Varsity would never wear anything that inexpensive!" He winked. He was always slightly amused by India's passionate outbursts.

He joined her at the window. "You know I think you have done an amazing job here," he said to her, nudging her shoulder with his arm in a friendly gesture. "I just meant for you to keep a clear mind. Getting stressed and angry won't help. We must trust in God. If a way can be found, we will find it and if not…"

"What? Let go and let God?" India erupted. "You know what? God doesn't give a damn about anyone and you will never convince me otherwise!"

"I'm not trying to convince you of anything, India, but God isn't about fixing stuff to suit an individual's needs or wishes." Lancelot sighed.

"Damn right, He's not! That's quite obvious!" India said angrily. "Although, He seems to like Collins and Jennifer rather a lot right now!"

Lancelot put his hand on her shoulder. "God isn't a man on a throne, waving a magic wand around, sorting out all the problems. If he was, do you think the world would be full of famine and war? Having faith in God is about finding the courage to move through our immediate pain and find a way forward with compassion for everyone concerned. We must seek justice, but we do not maliciously harm those who wrong us."

India didn't look at him. She was still seething inside.

Lancelot continued his lecture anyway. "When we have faith, it's like wearing a raincoat in a storm, but you cannot always stop the storm from happening. I always find my faith…"

"Everyone has faith in something around here!" India interrupted. "My god! There are enough religions around here to sink the Ark, but when it comes to Collins and Jennifer, all those religions are powerless!" India went to put on her coat. "Well!" she said, as she buttoned it up. "I believe we make our own luck! Hard work and intelligence - that's what counts! All the praying that goes on around here didn't get us out of debt and make Little Eden a viable concern again. Me, Lilly, you and the rest of the team did that. The amount of European and Lottery funding we got over the last ten years - you think God sent that? Oh, I know, don't tell me! Your Quakers have poured millions into the pot as well. I know. I know. Well, if you want to: let go and let God. But in this case, it will be more like…let go and let God destroy everything that is good in this world and that hundreds of generations have given their lives to create and even died to protect. Well, you know what? I won't let Him!"

"That's fighting talk, my girl!" Lancelot said, smiling sadly. "By the way, you buttoned your coat up wrong!"

As they walked through the Crescent gardens, a grand old willow tree shuddered suddenly and shook off its heavy snowy blanket. An urban fox, startled by the sudden avalanche, darted out from under the trees and straight across their path. Lancelot felt a chill go up his spine. He felt as if there was evil in the air. Instead of angels around, he sensed dark entities floating on the wind, just waiting to catch hold of everybody's anxiety and feed off it, so that they could multiply like spawn and shower the whole world with fear. He prayed for the protection of the Holy Spirit to dispel his agitation. Then, he said, "You want some help in that fight against Jennifer and Collins, or are you going it alone?"

India pouted and reluctantly let go of her anger. She smiled up at Lancelot. "Help would be nice, yes!" she replied, nudging his shoulder with hers.

"Well, then," Lancelot said, as they crossed the street. "Let's keep a cool head, stay calm and pray for a goddamn miracle, so I can find the loophole in the loophole!"

~ * ~

The subject of this morning's very brief meeting had been decided after the funeral, whilst Robert had been at Lilly's wake. On their return from the Chappelle, Collins, Varsity and Jennifer had lounged in the living room, drinking champers, and this is a snippet of the conversation they had:

"Well, I'm glad that is over and done with!" Jennifer moaned, as she warmed herself next to the open fire. She looked at herself in the palatial, mirrored overmantel and frowned.

"It was a lovely service," Varsity said, taking a chilled glass of champagne from Collins.

"If this room wasn't so large I would be warm for a change!" Jennifer complained, rubbing her hands together over the flames. "Why we can't get a modern sofa, I don't know! It would be much more comfortable than these rigid old things!"

"They are called antiques, Mother," Collins laughed. "This one belonged to the Duc D'Orleans or some such person." He put his feet up on the chaise longue as if to illustrate a point.

"I don't care if they belonged to the Queen of Sheba!" Jennifer said with venom. "But, I suppose I shall have to put up with them 'til things change! I think we should tell Robert what we have decided tomorrow!"

"Are you sure this is what you want, Mother?" Collins asked. "You will lose him! He will never agree."

"He will agree!" Jennifer replied, sitting down on one of the damask covered chairs. "He has no choice in the matter! Lose him? Honestly Collins! Robert will do exactly as I tell him to do. You are sure your cousin Lucas is agreed?"

"Yes, I spoke to him again yesterday. He will vote with me." Collins sighed.

"I wonder if there is another way?" Varsity began to say. "I was thinking…"

"This is nothing to do with you, Varsity!" Jennifer interrupted. "I will make you a very rich woman and you can thank me for it later! As for now, I suggest you say nothing about it to anyone. This is a family matter and will stay as such. Collins will do as I tell him, and Robert will too."

"Well, if you want to go ahead, Mother, we will. But you may find Robert is less of a pushover than you imagine," Collins went to make himself a whisky chaser.

"It isn't a case of being a pushover!" Jennifer snapped back, holding her glass out to him for a refill of champagne. "He will do as he is told and that is all. Your father left this place to you boys, and we can do as we want with it now that that interfering do-gooder Lillianna D'Or is gone! That woman and your Aunt Elizabeth stood in our way for far too long, both of them lording it over you boys as if Little Eden belonged only to them. Well, your Cousin Lucas agrees with me now. He's not like his grandmother, thank goodness! That's an end to it. Tell Lancelot and India I wish to see them in the morning and tell your brother to join us as well."

~ * ~

Having stormed out of the meeting, Robert didn't have a plan as to where to go, and he found none of his usual comfort in walking around Little Eden. He suddenly remembered that he could not go and talk to his friend Lilly any more, as he always had in times of trouble. His heart ached as he thought of her and he longed for her to be alive again. Alone and afraid, he marched quickly towards Devil's Gate and across the moat bridge into London's Gilbert Place. He just kept walking amongst the slush and the crowds down Drury Lane, and he found himself in the midst of the bustle of Covent Garden. The sides of the roads were piled high with grey and black speckled mounds of snow. Some of the cars were still buried deep, but Londoners were still about their business, none the less. Robert hardly noticed anyone, even when he nearly collided with some of them! He apologised automatically, seeing nothing except his internal rage. He didn't even try to shake it off. He fed it with anxious and angry thoughts, which whipped up more and more fear.

As he reached the Thames he found himself standing next to Cleopatra's Needle. The water, silvery and thick, like liquid mercury, reflected the low and heavy sky, overcast with mink grey clouds. He stood for a while, feeling the icy chill rising off the water and the sharp bitterness of frosty air which seemed to emanate from the snow on the Sphinxes' faces. His anger suddenly vanished, leaving an empty, aching darkness, churning in his stomach. His breath began to fail him. He felt nausea creeping through his veins and he steadied himself against the frozen wall. He couldn't sit down - the steps were covered in ice and the benches had blankets of white over them, three inches deep. His body and hands felt hot and cold at the same time. He needed to get inside and sit down somewhere! He looked around and he could hardly get his bearings. His mind was sweeping and swirling - no thoughts could find a place to rest. He found himself turning, automatically, to the only place he could think of. He hurried down the street to Craven Passage - to Shilty Cunningham's house.

As he reached Shilty's abode, a diffident Clive Basildon was leaving the house. He was kissing Shilty goodbye at the front door. Robert walked up the steps and they greeted each other as old school friends do.

"Barty, old chap!" Clive said, shaking Robert's hand vigorously and slapping him on the back. "What brings you out here? Just off myself! Had f**king grand Yuletide with this one!" he added, winking at Shilty again. "Lucky I got her off you, old chap!"

Robert couldn't raise a smile, fake or otherwise, but he shook Clive's hand.

"Coming to the wedding aren't you?" Clive said, going down onto the slippery pavement. "F**k!" he exclaimed, as he nearly went arse over elbow into a snow covered car. He grabbed the railings and laughed. "That's if I get to the altar alive! All the old chums will be there! Grand day out it'll be! Au revoir!"

With Clive out of sight, Shilty looked at Robert, and Robert looked at Shilty. She was wearing a short silk kimono which didn't cover much of her long tanned legs. She smiled welcomingly, and opened the door wider, beckoning him inside. Without a word Robert grabbed hold of her waist, spun her around and kissed her. His strong hands cradled her head as her long dark hair cascaded through his fingers; and before she could think what was happening, he had thrown off his coat, spun her round again and pressed her up against the wall. The emotional confusion twisting in his heart had turned to lust and Shilty felt the ripples of his desire racing through her body, igniting her own. As he pushed himself deep inside her, the thundering and whirling in Robert's mind transformed into a potent physical force. Shilty gasped. She was swept up into his uncontrollable passion. Suddenly, he was overwhelmed and his frustration was broken - shattering his former anger into a million tiny pieces. He pulled her back against his chest, trying to catch his breath, and held her tightly.

"F**k! I'm so sorry," he whispered, as he gently kissed the nape of her neck.

"What for?" she asked, turning around in his arms and keeping her body tight against his. Her eyes were bright and her heart was racing beneath her breasts. She smiled up at him.

Robert half smiled and said, "Because I don't have the right to do this anymore. To just walk in and…"

"Sweep me off my feet?" Shilty laughed, interrupting him. She looked into his eyes and could see fear, not love; sorrow, not joy, and it dawned on her that his passion was not from his desire for her, but due to something else entirely.

“Something ghastly must have happened?” she said to him. Robert winced as if her words had cut him. She took his hand. “Come upstairs and tell me,” she said, and led him to her bedroom, which was still dark, the shutters drawn. He let her undress him and they slid into her unmade bed, still warm - always inviting.

Not more than a few words passed their lips for the next two hours. Robert felt it was time to leave when she began to ask him questions again. He was aware he had used her purely for his own needs, and he felt a little ashamed about cheating on his friend Clive, but Shilty just lay back against the pillows, naked as you please, and smiled, saying, “That’s break-up sex for you! I wondered if it would ever happen!”

Robert let his guilt slip away as he ventured out onto the cold streets again. Within minutes he had forgotten he had even been with Shilty and he was consumed by thoughts of Little Eden again. Anger still breathed within his chest, but it was quiet for now, like a sleeping dragon rising and falling just beneath the surface.

Crossing the bridge at St Peter’s Gate he looked down at the old moat, which is now only a stream with pathways and cycle tracks on both sides. In the spring it is a river of tulips, and in the summer it transforms into a multicoloured ribbon of flowers. But, in the frozen grip of winter, the shallow water was as smooth as glass and the water lilies lay captured within its icy embrace.

Robert tried to bring his mind to order. What would Lilly do? He remembered the escapades in the crypt after the funeral, the night before. Her ephemeral presence had brought a warning which now seemed suddenly very real. All he could think was: *Lilly had brought a warning - maybe she would bring the solution too?*

~ * ~

Five-hundred-year-old oak trees have grown into the masonry of St Mary’s Church, creating living pillars, which flank the entrance and breathe life into the ancient edifice. The nave is always open to all who need to go in, and fresh flowers charmingly cascade from the font and on either side of the altar. A narrow and exposed staircase winds its way up into the bellcote at the far end, and from the vestry one can travel down into the crypt, where the friends had had their supernatural adventures the evening before.

Robert paused for a moment in the tiny chapel of St Katherine and prayed for guidance:

St Katherine, St Katherine, St Katherine.
Sit with me a while in peaceful contemplation, whilst I listen to the divine guidance from within my heart.
Create with me a sacred space in which my mind is quiet and my heart is still.
With your strength, dear sister, I am refreshed and renewed.
As we become one in tranquil solitude.[7]

Robert had never been much of a churchgoer. He was bored by the sermons, and sometimes even offended by them, but Iris Sprott often reminded him that a great deal of good had been done by Christians in Little Eden over the centuries. He had come to realise that the true heart of Christianity was older than its namesake. His father had taught him that at the core of both Christianity and Buddhism was an incorruptible well of unconditional love - even if organised religion had often become 'twisted by knaves to make a trap for fools!'*

Lilly, as well as writing songs, had also written some new prayers, which had been adopted by the Little Eden congregation. She had always felt old prayers were clutching at her heart instead of opening it. Lilly always said she could tell which prayers and hymns inspired the soul and which tried to take it from you.

He asked earnestly for help from St Katherine and St Hilda, and he felt an urge to go down into the crypt, alone.

Robert took the back stairs, through the vestry, and down into the dark crypt. He lit a couple of the candles and sat a while in the shadows, amongst his ancestors. He didn't feel afraid, but he did feel oppressed. He could sense a crushing pressure inside his chest, as if every person entombed there was crying out for him to help them. It was silently deafening. He asked for Alienor or Lilly to appear before him. A few minutes passed, and he nearly gave up; but just as he got up to leave, he felt the familiar chill of a spirit beginning to take form.

Closing his eyes he could see an apparition of Alienor rising from her hidden tomb. She walked through the marble edifice in front of her as if

[7] *KT King 21st Century Prayers*, KT King 2016

it was not even there. She stood before Robert and he could see that she looked just as she did in her effigy; wearing a cowl and a cape. A sword hung in its scabbard at her side, and she was holding a thick set of papers bound by string in one hand. In the other, she held Lilly's Faberge egg; as Alienor blew gently on it, it opened up like a puzzle box.

A white light suddenly shot out of the egg and almost blinded Robert, to the point that his eyes actually started to water. The white light faded into a rich purple and then into a soft lilac. In this violet flame he saw a vision of Lilly appearing. She became a silvery ephemeral figure, with graceful snow-white wings which seemed to fold perfectly behind her. Her angelic-like form grew taller until she shimmered and shone, life-size, beside the regal Alienor. The two women stood smiling at him. He reached out his hand, but there was nothing to feel in reality. He tried to keep his concentration, attempting to hold the apparitions in his mind; but he was not an adept (this was his first major psychic vision without Sophie by his side) and before long, the delicate light of Lilly began to fade, leaving only Alienor standing in front of him.

All of a sudden, her countenance changed. She looked powerful and stern. She pushed aside her velvet cloak and drew her sword in a quick deft motion. Its shining blade vibrated as it moved, and a deep, tenebrous, sweeping sound, resounded in his ears. She offered it to him, but he dared not take it from her. He could feel her willing him to take the sword into his own hands, but a force, stronger than her, stronger than him, prevented his hand from accepting it. Without warning, she threw her book at him, and he ducked, as if it were real and about to hit him. "Whoa!" he cried out loud. Its pages fell around him like a pack of cards. His concentration was broken.

Robert tried to refocus and find Alienor's image again with his third eye. He finally caught sight of her kneeling at his feet as if in prayer. She was weeping. At first he could not see why she was crying so. But, as his vision panned out from her recumbent position, to his horror, he could see dismembered human bodies strewn about the floor of the whole crypt. Looking upwards, he saw a foggy grey cloud hovering over his head. He tried to back away from it, but the whole place was filling up with dark forces and there was nowhere to hide. Black, writhing, slithering snakes came up from the cracks in the flagstone floor and squirmed their way between and through the dead bodies. He lifted himself up onto one of the tombs to get away from the squirming reptiles. He knew that the snakes were not real, but he was filled with such a feeling of unholy dread, he knew that whatever this darkness was, it was having a very physical effect upon him. The supernatural had come to feel very real indeed!

Then, from nowhere, he heard a disembodied, guttural and maliceful laugh. Its monstrous echo cackled amongst the sepulchres. It set his teeth on edge. Robert felt a gelid shiver race down his spine as a freezing blast of air ran through him like a knife. He saw, for a fleeting moment, the miasma of a red-haired woman, dressed in a white night gown, run through the north wall of the crypt. She left only a vapour of mist behind her and the putrefying stench of death. He thought he was going to be sick! He started to say the Lord's Prayer, and for the first time in his life, he was grateful for having been made to learn it off by heart at school. It came up from his subconscious like a wellspring that had been closed off for many years.

The creeping darkness cleared away in a flash, and the smell of corpses was replaced by the odour of roses. As he turned his attention back to the floor, the bodies were all gone, and so was Alienor. He felt the temperature returning to normal again. His odious nausea abated and he breathed a sigh of relief. He quickly blew out the candles, and made his way, as quickly as he could, back up the steps into the nave, and back to his sanity.

As he came out into the graveyard Robert pondered for a moment. A flashback of Alienor throwing the book at him kept replaying in his mind. It made him think of Mr T and the books in the basement of No.1 Daisy Place Café-Bookshop. Perhaps Mr T would know more about Alienor? Robert immediately took himself off to Daisy Place.

Chapter 8

~ * ~

Mr T is so called because he looks like a faun! He is a veritable Mr. Tumnus.[8] His real name, however, is Avery Goodfellow. Mr T's history goes something like this:

After his university days, Mr T took a job at the British Library. His love of books, history and languages is insatiable. He can speak a dozen languages, including many ancient ones, and can read and translate even more than that! His life, however, has been limited by his inability to recognise his strengths and to improve his weaknesses; so he really is the same man at sixty two that he had been at twenty two; and he has never changed or grown up a day since. His concession to human feelings has found its outlet via his Lhasa Apso, called Cedric, who is now so ancient a dog that he looks as threadbare as his master.

Unfortunately, Mr T did not last very long at his first job. After a rather unpleasant debacle involving some Gorgonzola and an illuminated manuscript, Lilly gave Mr T the Bookshop to run. It is debatable whether Lilly had done him a favour by providing such a sheltered life, or whether, if he had had to make his own way in the world, he might have grown up and into himself. But, the 'what ifs' of life are always impossible to know for sure, and it is just as likely that, without the surrogate care of Lilly, he would have withered away years ago; perhaps dying alone somewhere amongst the stacks of the British Library - being found several days later, by a wandering curator drawn towards his corpse, only due to him starting to smell!

Over the years, Mr T has amassed a large personal collection of books, for which he has become quite famous amongst a certain clique of scholars. Few other people know that Mr T's cavern of treasures exist beneath their feet. Mr T's secret cellar ventures under Sumona's Tea Emporium, next door to the Café. It then continues beneath Tom Thumb Alley (where you can find the smallest shops in London) and finally, underneath the tourist information shop, which holds pride of place in the only remaining section of the 14th Century wooden balconied coaching inn.

Robert arrived at Daisy Place and entered via the secret door at the end of the alley. He did not want to be seen by the others just yet. He found Mr T where he usually was, amongst his most adored and prized manuscripts.

[8] *The Chronicles of Narnia*, C.S. Lewis, 1949, Harper Collins

This cellar is not a dank, cold, dark place as cellars often are, but a technological marvel of temperature control, humidity stabilisation and dust eradication! Each book has its own glass case, powered by electricity to ensure perfect storage. Some of the folios are two thousand years old, dating back to ancient Sumeria. One of the walls is a sea of scrolls, each carefully rolled and neatly placed in small tubes which are immaculately labelled and dated.

Years ago, Robert's father, Melbourne Bartlett-Hart, had given Mr T the task of preserving, cataloguing and storing the Bartlett-Hart family archives. Papers, books, legal documents, family letters, newspaper cuttings - you name it - if it related to the family it was down here in the B.H Room.

Whilst the girls and Jack were entertaining Miss Huggins in the Bookshop above, they had no idea that beneath them, Robert and Mr T were going through the family archives from the last thousand years.

Robert and Mr T found the Deed of Trust which had been drawn up by Henrietta Bartlett-Hart and her twin brother, Jeremiah, in 1799. It protected Little Eden and all property therein from ever being sold. It gave a personal stipend for trustees but forbade the family members from profiting by the sale of any part of the town, no matter how small.

Mr T also produced a prodigious parcel of letters written by family members regarding the setting up of the Little Eden Trust, and many newspaper cuttings from that time.

It had been quite the talk of the town when the news first broke! At least one journalist thought that the Trust was a good idea, and had this to say about it in June of 1799:

London Chronicle

I have the pleasure to report to you of a happy sojourn I spent in the small walled hamlet of Little Eden, on Wednesday evening last. Despite the general move in our metropolis to sell land for new tenements, the noble family of Bartlett-Hart believe in holding onto their property, as well as building new sanitary dwellings for the benefit of their residents. The Rt.Hon. Jeremiah Bartlett, a Quaker, sets a rare example of generosity and kindliness, endeavouring to selflessly aid the able bodied and impotent poor alike. His twin sister, the most celebrated Mrs Owen Bartlett-Hart, made an eloquent speech in the lately renovated Dovecote

Street Assembly Rooms. Her evening gown was greatly admired, being made of the finest blue French silk and cut into the Arabian style. In her speech, Mrs Bartlett-Hart declared that the ethics of Little Eden are: tolerance, personal responsibility and community. By continuing to hold the ownership of all the land and property within the walls, the family believe they can better control the moral character of the residents therein. There is to be an application of rent control, allowing the current residents to remain within their abodes without fear of eviction; a present predicament so rife in London at large. In order to maintain the legacy of the family, a trust has been drawn up which prevents any land or standing property from being sold to third parties by future generations. A letter from Her Royal Highness, Queen Charlotte, was read in her absence, in which it was declared that Little Eden is "a place worthy of its name" and assured the continuation of the Royal Charter, given by King Alfred, which allows many legal concessions to continue within the sanctuary boundary and for it to remain outside of the reach of the prescribed assizes. I found myself quite saddened to leave such a prestigious event at the end of a delightful and inspiring evening. If there is a place on earth so happily situated and gaily inhabited as Little Eden, it is yet to be discovered!

One of the letters in the bundle was from Queen Charlotte. In 1799, a royal seal of approval meant a great deal indeed! So here it is, dear readers, for your perusal:

My dearest Henrietta

What can I say, but that I regret most deeply, that I am unable to attend your soiree on Wednesday next. I so enjoyed the pleasure of visiting with you last year, and your dear little hamlet is such a favourite with me. I will visit your rose gardens again this year if I may, as I am collecting a great many for Frogmore. As to more pressing matters, I have the pleasure of assuring you that Mr Pitt ensures the full respect given to the Peace of St Hilda and the Liberty of Little Eden, as testament to the legacy of charity and generosity that your family uphold to this day, and now safeguard for future generations to come.

I declared to my dear brother Charles that, upon my honour, there is no place in England more befitting and worthy of its name than Little Eden.

Always yours, Charlotte

It seemed that, back in the day, everyone who was anyone, had an opinion on the matter!

Some people, however, found Little Eden to be quite the opposite and could see no reason for preserving such a tedious place:

Thames Tide Courant

There is not a prison in all London worse than finding oneself inside the walls of Little Eden. Temperance and Charity are order of the day. A drink of coffee or chocolate is all one can expect for no gin is consumed within the gates. A man cannot find the usual supply of japes in this part of London. The streets are patrolled, from morning 'til night, by men in uniform bearing the coat of arms of the Bartlett's. As for the new Pleasure Gardens, they are far from providing any real pleasure. There is not a pretty young girl for hire to be found. There is talk of this Holy Hamlet being taken into Trust to preserve its Christian morals for future generations. I do not think that a soul of any wit would care to dwell in such a place in which only the strictest of puritans will find themselves content.

As they gathered together a box of what seemed to be the most likely sources of information, Robert didn't tell Mr T why he wanted to research the Trust and kept his anxieties to himself. He took his leave around five o'clock but he didn't want to go home, nor did he want to see his friends at the Café, for fear of blurting the whole thing out. He felt fragile and slightly ashamed. He didn't know whether to tell anyone what had been said that morning or not. He needed more time to think! He followed his feet again and this time they took him up to Hart Crescent, in the north-east corner of Little Eden, and to Stella Dew's house.

Stella Dew lives in the central house of Hart Crescent. Black and gold painted railings enclose a half-moon shaped lawn which is surrounded by a walnut grove. Where there had once been a deer park, these days, the only harts to be seen are pretty wire statues, dotted about the manicured gardens. Robert knocked on the door and rang the bell. Stella, although in her seventies, is sprightly, and her eyes still twinkle with a childlike innocence, even after all her years on Earth. Opening the door, she beamed at him, but immediately felt a whoosh of great sorrow wrap itself around her, which made her frown. "My darling boy, come in, come in!" she said, puzzled as to why he looked so pale and grey. "You look and you feel dreadful!"

On entering the marble hallway Robert felt at ease immediately, and he could see through into the inviting living room, which had an open fire burning merrily in the grate. Stella helped him take off his coat and took him through. "Sit, sit!" she said, and stoked the fire. "Now, what will it be? Tea? Coffee? Or something a little stronger? Or something a little stronger in your tea?" She laughed, but could tell that Robert was not in a laughing mood. "You sit there and I'll get you both tea and a brandy, how's that?" Robert nodded and was glad he had found Stella home alone. He sank into her comfortable sofa and sighed.

In Stella's Victorian-style kitchen the cupboards are always full of delectable treats. She seems to attract a great many hampers each Christmas, from all over the world. Perhaps, it is because at her age and with her affluence, there is little left to buy her that she would want or does not already have. Taking some carrot and ginger cookie muffins from one of them, she mulled over Robert's strange mood. Perhaps he is just missing Lilly, she thought.

"Now then, my darling!" she said, as she returned with a tray to find Robert standing by the fire, poking at the coals. "Tell me all about it!"

And he did.

When he had finished, Stella frowned. "Well, what's to be done?" she asked him and herself. "We need a management meeting. The more heads the better on this one, I would say!"

"I don't know if I should tell anyone," Robert moaned. "I shouldn't have told you. I'm afraid everyone may panic!"

"Tut, tut, my darling," Stella replied. "You mustn't carry this alone. No, no! I agree to some extent that the fewer people who know the better for now, but I suggest you tell the girls and Jack, at least. And you must work with Lancelot and India. There are none so loyal to you than those two."

Robert swirled his brandy and gazed into the fire. "There is nothing I can do. It's over, Stella. It's over."

Stella tutted. "Now you listen to me! It is never over 'til the day you die! Not 'til your last breath is spent, is it over. Never give up! Never give in!"

"It's hopeless!" Robert sighed and felt as if he might cry. "Little Eden is finished and there is nothing I can do to stop it! Without Lilly…" he paused and kicked the coal scuttle with his foot.

Stella missed Lilly terribly and felt her own grief rise to the surface. She knew Robert's propensity to dwell on his darker thoughts and considered encouragement rather than consolation would be the best course of action right now. "This is your time Robert!" Stella told him. "Your time to stand up to your mother and your brother, and to fight for what you believe in!"

"I am not sure what I believe in," Robert mused, putting another log on the fire.

"Then we must help you find out!" Stella smiled. "Come and sit by me." She patted the cushions and invited him to sit back on the sofa again. "Do you remember when you were a little boy, how you used to love the stories of my ancestors in Russia? Why do you think you liked those stories so much?"

Robert shrugged. "They never gave up, no matter how terrible it got?"

Stella smiled. "Exactly! Love triumphs over hate and good triumphs over evil! They are grand and wonderful tales! Now, what story would you like your great-grandchildren to hear about you?"

Robert looked surprised. "I have never thought about that."

"Well, perhaps you should!" Stella suggested.

Robert didn't know quite what to think. He felt as if his thoughts were not his own. One minute he was angry, the next he was resigned. One minute his predicament seemed like an avalanche hurtling towards him, and the next it didn't seem real at all.

"Now, are you staying for dinner or not?" She grinned, as she knew his answer would be a yes. "I have lobster, oysters and blue mussels from our cousin Jessica in Maine. I send her a haggis for Burns Night every year and she sends me the most delicious seafood. I always think I get the better end of it!"

"How could I refuse?" Robert replied, and sighed as he lent back against the soft cushions. "And you can tell me all about great-grandmother Princess Provotski again."

Robert relaxed during his time with Stella and was reluctant to leave. On his way home he decided he would go and see Lucy, Sophie and Jack after all, to discuss the escapades in the crypt from the night before. He was not sure that he would tell them his secret just yet mind you!

~ * ~

Robert went to fetch Mr T and they both walked across the roof terrace to No.1 Daisy Place, trying not to slip on the snow and ice whilst laden down with books and boxes. Mr T's dog, Cedric, followed behind them, wearing a hand-knitted jacket and little booties to keep his paws off the cold snow. Sophie let them in by way of the conservatory doors, and as soon as Cedric felt the warm air wafting out from the living room, he rushed forward between Roberts's legs, sending the books and boxes hurtling to the floor with an almighty crash.

Lucy rushed in from the bathroom, wrapping her dressing gown around her as she did so. "Oh my god, what's happening now?" she exclaimed.

"Sorry! Sorry!" Robert said, gathering up the books and papers which had shot all over the floor and sofas.

"Where have you been?" Lucy said sternly, as she scooped her dishevelled blond hair up into a pony tail. "We've been worried sick about you! Close the door, Mr T - it's freezing!"

Robert looked at her in amazement. "What do you mean, where have I been?"

"Today! Lunch with Miss Huggins! The new headmistress!" Lucy reminded him.

"Oh, good god, sorry!" Robert replied earnestly. "I forgot!"

"Damn right you did!" Lucy scolded him, with a smile. "And went into hiding too! None of us could get hold of you. Not even Jack! Lancelot rang several times to see if you were here."

Robert shrugged.

"Where did you get to anyway?" Sophie enquired. "Jack reckoned you had a hangover and were probably sleeping it off."

Robert looked for somewhere to sit down, and Mr T made himself comfortable, nearly disappearing into the cushions of Lilly's favourite chair.

"I'd better ring her and apologise." Robert sighed, and looked deflated.

"Don't worry about it right now!" Lucy told him. "We made an excuse that you'd eaten something dodgy at the wake and it had given you the runs!"

"You didn't!" Robert exclaimed.

"She kept calling you 'Mr Bartlett-Hart' in a very regal way, and actually thought you were a proper aristocrat," Sophie giggled.

"We thought it would demystify you somewhat if she knew you pooped like the rest of the commoners!" Lucy added, with a serious face.

"Tell me you didn't?" Robert said aghast.

"Don't be daft! Of course we didn't," Lucy said laughing. "I said you had urgent family business, and that you would ring her when you were back in the office."

"I wouldn't worry. I think Jack is going to be taking care of her in your absence!" Sophie told him, with a naughty smile.

"I am sure he is!" Robert said, raising an eyebrow. "Is that a fresh pot of tea?" he added, looking at the teapot on the kitchen work bench in the corner.

"I am finished making tea for the day!" Lucy said, and sat down on the sofa with Sophie.

"Well, I will make my own cup of tea seeing as the servants are on strike!" Robert smiled. "What will it be, girls? What can I tempt you with this evening?"

"I need the anti-cold tea - honey and lemon please," Lucy said. "I think I might be coming down with something."

Mr T sneezed and got out his hanky. "I hope you're not coming down with a cold too, Mr T!" Lucy said, and kindly handed him a box of tissues.

"I'll have peppermint tea, ta," Sophie said, yawning. Her tired eyes were watering from trying to stay awake, and she thought it might keep her going for another half an hour or so.

"Sorry! I am being rude," Robert said suddenly. "I haven't even asked how you two are today?"

"We are ok, I guess," Sophie replied. She was lying of course. The two sisters felt as if they had been run over by a bus, and Sophie could not bring herself to eat, whilst Lucy could not stop eating. "We are more interested in you! Where did you get to that you couldn't answer your phone? Enquiring minds want to know!"

"I went to Shilty's," Robert said in a blasé manner, as he made the drinks.

The girls' jaws dropped, and they didn't reply for a moment or two. Cedric looked at him too, as if he just as surprised at the reply!

"Oh," Sophie finally said, trying not to sound shocked, and she winked at Lucy.

"I thought you weren't seeing her anymore?" Lucy said nonchalantly.

"Well, no, not technically," Robert replied, and came to sit down. "That's not important! I spent the afternoon in the cellar looking up Little Eden documents, and I've just been with Stella. I want to talk about what happened in the crypt with you all. I want to know who Melanie was or is, and what Alienor meant when she warned us about the future. Is Jack here?"

"I think he went to do laps at the pool," Lucy said. "Oh! Here he is now!"

Right on cue, Jack came in from the roof terrace and shook the snow off his boots at the door.

"Close the door!" Sophie and Lucy said in unison. "We were just wanting you, and here you are! Good timing!" Lucy smiled.

"As always!" Jack grinned. "Robert! Mr T! What's going on? What are all these papers for?"

"I was hoping we could have a search party for Melanie," Robert said.

"Who?" Jack replied.

"You know - the woman you saw in the crypt!" Lucy interjected.

"Good grief! I had forgotten all about that!" Jack replied, as he took his coat off and made himself a coffee.

"Put the big light on, would you, Jack?" Sophie asked him. "And can you turn the heating up a bit too?"

"I was thinking about what happened in the crypt after the funeral. In fact, I can't get it out of my head. Things have happened since which make Alienor's appearance and warnings seem more real now," Robert told them.

"What happened in your family meeting this morning?" Lucy asked. "Lancelot said you stormed out. He was worried about you!"

"I can't tell you, exactly, right now," Robert muttered.

"What are you keeping from us?" Lucy urged.

"I don't want to tell you yet - it may come to nothing," Robert stalled.

"Come on, old chap!" Jack said, sipping his hot drink. "Out with it!"

"It may panic you all. I don't want to worry you with something that may turn out to be nothing!" Robert replied, with a sigh.

"You're scaring me!" Lucy said. "I feel all funny inside now you have said that - as if something really bad is about to happen. If it's that bad you should let us help you! Share it with us."

"That's what Stella said," Robert sighed.

"Then tell us too, old boy!" Jack urged him.

"You have enough to deal with right now!" Robert replied.

"Come on!" Lucy said. "We don't keep secrets from each other!"

"It would be better we hear it from you rather than on the grape vine," Sophie suggested.

"Look, for god's sake!" Robert said, exasperated. "If you really want to know - my brother and my mother have decided to sell Little Eden, lock, stock, and barrel. That's what has happened!"

They were all aghast for a good few moments and nobody spoke. They all looked at each other in turn as if hoping someone would break the shocked silence. Cedric awoke from his snooze and looked around. He looked as stunned as everyone else!

"But, that's not possible!" Lucy eventually exclaimed. "Little Eden is in Trust! They can't sell it!"

"You got that right!" Robert replied, pacing up and down in an agitated manner. Cedric jumped off Mr T's lap and followed him up and down at heel, as if coming out in sympathy. "That was the point of the Trust, yes - to stop the future generations cashing in or gambling it all away. It also meant that we avoided high death duties and could keep the place intact!"

"I don't understand!" Sophie said, bewildered. "I need some chocolate!" She opened a box of Devlin's handmade chocolate truffles which was on the coffee table.

"Since Lilly died, and having lost Aunt Elizabeth a few years ago, we are down to three trustees. The Trust can be disbanded if a unanimous decision is made by all of the trustees," Robert explained.

"But that's not unanimous!" Jack said. "That's just two against one. Just don't vote with them!"

"I don't really have a choice!" Robert said. "They can take me to court apparently, and claim I am being unreasonable! And they will probably win. According to Lancelot, they have the best lawyer in England."

"Don't tell me!" Lucy said. "Not your mother's 'boyfriend', Robin Shaft?"

"The very one!" Robert replied.

Sophie couldn't hold her emotions in any longer and burst into tears.

"You see!" Robert said, going over and sitting with her. "This is why I didn't want to tell you. It's too much for you all. What with Lilly dying and you being so ill. I shouldn't have said anything."

"Sorry, old boy," Jack said. "We shouldn't have badgered you when you said you didn't want to tell us. We just wouldn't let it lie!"

"This is serious!" Sophie said, wiping her eyes. Cedric bumbled up and sat on her knee, licking away her salty tears. She cuddled him close and buried her head in what was left of his soft fur.

Lucy looked dazed and thought for a moment. "This is really serious!"

"I mean," Lucy said out loud, "We will all have to move out! We couldn't keep the Café or the Bookshop! We couldn't afford to buy the flat! We would lose everything!"

"So would everyone single person in Little Eden!" Robert sighed angrily. "No! You just wouldn't let it lie!" Robert said, trying to smile. "You must promise not to tell a soul outside this room about it. There might be riots in the streets, people leaving and even some attempted suicides."

"Good grief!" Lucy said. "I hadn't thought of that! What about Mrs B and all the staff?" Lucy exclaimed. "What about Linnet and Minnie? Sumona, Devlin, Stella? They couldn't afford to keep their shops without the Trust! All our friends and neighbours? People who have lived here all their lives, inherited their shops and homes from their ancestors? All their hard work! Their dreams! All down the drain."

Lucy could see in her mind's eye everyone she loved packing their bags and walking, tearful and grief-stricken, out of Little Eden, pushing trolleys packed with their belongings. Cars, queuing up to leave through the gates, filled with suitcases and precious things. Everyone having to leave overnight, never to return. It felt almost like an exodus to her.

"F**k, you're right!" Jack said. "I couldn't afford to buy my apartment, none of us could! What, with rent control and financial support from the Trust, I doubt there's anyone living in Little Eden who could afford to buy their own place? I mean, I presume all the buildings would sell for market value and London prices?"

"Oh, I assure you they would!" Robert replied. "The estimate of selling the whole of Little Eden is currently at eight billion pounds!"

"How much?" Lucy said stunned.

"It's the charities I feel worst about," Robert said, with a heavy feeling in the pit of his stomach.

"They can't sell the charity buildings as well can they?" Sophie asked. "I mean the refuge, the hospice, the retirement home, Heroes Palace - where are they supposed to go? What would happen to them and all the people they help?"

"All to be sold from under them!" Robert replied. "The charities don't own the buildings. The Trust does. I've managed to give them a peppercorn rent over the years, but I won't be able to save them from being turned out now."

"No way! This isn't fair!" Lucy exclaimed angrily, and she burst into tears. Mr T handed her a tissue and held her hand. He sniffed a little himself, but no one was sure if it was his cold or if he was crying too.

Cedric didn't know who to comfort first, so he made his way around everyone, snuffling into each of them in turn.

"Can't you save any of it?" Lucy said, patting Cedric's head. "The chateau? The World Peace Centre?" Sophie said, concerned.

"Gone!" Robert nodded.

"The new school?" Sophie asked.

"There will be nothing left. Nothing!" Robert repeated. "None of the buildings have a preservation order on them or listed status. We never needed to protect them with a law - everyone just knew preserving them was the right thing to do. But, once they are sold to arms and drug dealers, nothing will remain except a few facades. Nothing, nada, nil...all gone!"

"OMG!" Sophie exclaimed. "I saw it!"

"Saw what?" Jack asked.

"Oh god, yes!" Lucy exclaimed. "What you said on the roof last night - after the funeral! You said it might be the last New Year anyone spends in Little Eden!"

"What did you see?" Robert quizzed Sophie sternly. "What and when?"

"In the crypt, after the funeral, I got a feeling of dread!" Sophie explained. "I felt sick and just for a moment I saw dead bodies everywhere. I saw Little Eden razed to the ground as if a nuclear bomb had been dropped and everything was burnt to ruins. The vision was just for a millisecond and then it passed and Jack yelled out about Melanie and, well, I wasn't sure what it meant."

"What does it mean?" Lucy asked.

"I can tell you exactly what it means!" Jack said. "Arma…f**king… geddon. That's what it means!"

Chapter 9

~ * ~

The friends sat in silence for a while. Each one was letting the news sink in, and its far-reaching consequences took root in their minds. They realised that the idyll of Little Eden was about to be lost forever. It was the end of the world as they knew it. Where would they all go? Where would they all live? The future held nothing but bankruptcy and poverty for most of the residents.

The beautiful historic buildings of Little Eden would be razed to the ground to make way for skyscrapers and multi-storey car parks. The ancient woods would be burnt down; multinationals would sweep away the quaint artisan shops. Perhaps, part of the 9th Century walls might remain in ruins, as a little nod to a long forgotten past.

"I suppose we should have seen this coming," Sophie said, breaking the lingering silence at last. "This place was too good to last forever. It's been like living in a dream world. It's not the real world."

"If Little Eden isn't the real world then I don't like the real world!" Lucy replied. "Pass me the chocolate truffles, Mr T. I need a box load right now!"

"Community never wins over individual greed," Sophie mused. "Only in fairy stories do we really get a real happily ever after. Little Eden is the last place on earth where love still comes before money, but that is not the way of the world. A few mega rich people own us all and what they say goes. No one will support us, I can see the fat cats all waiting to pounce."

"Don't get too sentimental - it's just bricks and mortar!" Jack said.

"Little Eden isn't just bricks and mortar!" Lucy retorted. "It's who we are! It's our home! They don't just want to sell the land; they want to sell us!

"It's not just the buildings - it's people's lives that are at stake," Robert agreed. "But, we are powerless if there is money to be made. It is a miracle we have lasted this long."

"Jennifer has no shame!" Lucy said. "She's never understood how important Little Eden is, and now she's shown that she never will!"

"Dr G always says that any form of security is a temporary illusion created by humans," Sophie mused.

"That doesn't seem to comfort me right now!" Lucy replied, biting into another truffle.

Robert nodded, but said nothing for a few moments. "We need to find out more from Alienor," he said finally.

"What can a ghost do for us now?" Jack asked. "We need to act legally! Get Lancelot on the case. Not go looking for spooks!"

"I think Robbie's right," Sophie said. "Perhaps the spirits can help us? They may have more to tell us."

"Yes." Lucy agreed. "Aunt Lilly can still help us from beyond the grave. If only we could find a way to communicate properly with her. God, I wish she was here. She'd know what to do! Shall we go back to the crypt?"

Jack frowned. "I was thinking about the crypt, and to be honest, it all seems too fantastical in the clear light of day. I think we were all carried away by the atmosphere and the emotions of the funeral, and I'm not even sure what happened now - if anything happened at all!"

"You did see the spirit of Melanie though," Lucy chided him. "You were the only one who did! You saw a woman in white nearly pass straight through you!"

"Did I?" Jack replied half-heartedly, as he went back to the kitchen area to refill his coffee.

"Yes!" Sophie, Lucy and Robert all chimed together.

"Well, if I was the only one who saw her - maybe I didn't see her!" Jack replied in a huff.

"Are you saying you lied? That you made it up?" Lucy quizzed him.

"No - not exactly!" Jack frowned. "I just mean that, maybe, in that atmosphere and with all the talk of ghosts, I may have been suggestible! It was frightfully dark and gloomy and actually rather spooky, remember?"

"It wasn't!" Sophie rebuked him. "Once all the candles were lit it was beautiful! And if you are that suggestible I wish I'd known before. I could have gotten you to do all sorts of things with a little light hypnotherapy over the years!"

"Very funny!" Jack replied. "All I mean is, there were shadows and candle light, and you were talking about seeing things…"

"What about the cold spot?" Robert interrupted. "You felt that!"

"The temperature down there must be always changing," Jack said emphatically, and was about to hand a cup of coffee to Mr T, when he realised that he had nodded off in his chair, with Cedric snoozing on his lap. "There are bound to be drafts and breezes in a place as old as that."

"What about the smells?" Lucy suggested. "I smelt Lilly's perfume and you smelt smoke remember?"

"I was thinking about that too," Jack responded. "There were probably just wafts of incense coming down from the church above."

"There wasn't anyone in the church above!" Robert replied.

"Well, maybe we were standing underneath where they keep the incense," Jack argued. "I don't know! Maybe they keep it in a cupboard in the vestry or somewhere like that."

"Are you going to deny the whole thing just because it was supernatural?" Sophie sighed.

"All I know is - there is always a rational explanation for the paranormal or supernatural, if one looks hard enough, old girl!" Jack said with conviction, as he sat on the arm of the sofa. "And, I don't think the supernatural is a helpful line of enquiry when we are all facing eviction!"

"I definitely smelt Lilly's perfume," Lucy said, offended at the suggestion she was lying, and she poked Jack in the ribs. "I may not be clairvoyant like Sophie but I often smell spirit odours, don't I Sophie?"

Sophie nodded and agreed with her sister. "She does!"

"You are the only one who smelt Lilly's perfume, so maybe it was all in your head. Maybe, you just thought you could smell it because you wanted to," Jack responded.

"I don't have the start of dementia if that's what you're implying!" Lucy remarked.

"I'm just saying that maybe this woman in white was just in my head!" Jack continued. "And maybe, the cold spot was just in Robert's head, and as for the rest of it, sorry old girl, no disrespect, but maybe the rest of it was in Sophie's head."

"That's a lot of maybes, and a lot of heads," Sophie giggled. She was finding it amusing watching him tie himself up in rational knots.

"Charming!" Lucy exclaimed, and shoved him off the arm of the sofa. "Listen here, buddy boy! I felt the change in temperature! I felt Lilly hug me! I smelt her perfume and I don't appreciate you saying me and my sister are lying!"

"I didn't mean it like that!" Jack said, picking himself up off the floor.

"Then what other way do you mean it?" Lucy demanded indignantly.

"It's alright!" Sophie said, and smiled. "I told you he would start to rationalise it! It's the classic behaviour of someone who is sceptical and doesn't want to believe."

"So, I have to agree with you two, do I?" Jack replied.

“No, of course not!” Sophie said. “The human brain is designed to block out sound and light frequencies outside of the range of the five senses. It keeps us sane. The brain naturally snaps back into place after a psychic experience. If it didn’t, you’d be seeing auras and ghosts all over the place; and you’d not know what century you were in, or even what planet you were on; and you’d have a mental breakdown! Even for a seasoned psychic it can be hard to remember what happened during an episode a few days later. The weirder the experience - the harder the brain fights to forget it and rationalise it.”

“I suppose,” Jack mumbled and went to find something to eat.

“You believe though, don’t you Robert?” Lucy asked him.

“I suppose the more it happens, the harder it is to come up with other explanations,” Robert replied. “I would trust Sophie whatever she said, even if I didn’t feel or see it myself.”

“My rational mind tells me there has to be a different and rational explanation,” Jack called from the kitchen area.

“Your ‘rational’ explanations, so far, seem to be cupboards full of incense that don’t exist and that we are all doolally!” Lucy retorted, throwing a cushion at him, but missing him completely and hitting Cedric on the nose, who yelped in surprise, waking Mr T from his reverie!

“F*ck it! Alright!” Jack acknowledged. “I don’t have any explanations - rational or otherwise!”

“It’s easier to dismiss it than to believe it!” Sophie agreed. “Don’t be too hard on him Luce.” She turned to Jack and added, “Just think of a dog whistle!”

“Eh?” Jack replied.

“A dog whistle!” Sophie repeated. “A dog can hear it, but a human can’t. Does that mean the dog whistle isn’t making a sound just because a human ear can’t pick up that frequency?”

“I suppose not!” Jack said, starting to get a bit tired of arguing. “But even that doesn’t mean one can’t have a healthy degree of scepticism!”

“Of course we should all keep common sense as our first port of call,” Sophie replied. “You can only trust those people you can trust! If you believe any Tom, Dick or Harry you can be led up the garden path. Some people who get into ‘so called’ spiritual stuff become mentally unstable, having lost all grasp on this reality.”

“I need something to eat!” Jack said, changing the subject. “There’s nothing in your cupboards!”

"I haven't felt like going shopping," Lucy told him, unwilling to get up from the sofa. "There's pizzas in the freezer - put them in the oven for us? That's if you believe the pizza is real and not just a figment of our imagination that is!"

Jack smirked and went to find the pizzas. He was confused, which he didn't like as it felt uncomfortable, but he couldn't really be bothered to figure it out either! It made his brain hurt when he tried to make sense of things. He wanted to believe his friends, but he just couldn't get his mind around how the paranormal/supernatural could work. He shrugged and decided to just trust them. If his three closest friends in the world understood it, then that was enough for him! He relaxed and began to feel at ease again.

Robert still wanted to talk about what had happened in the crypt. He waited till everyone had taken a loo break, and then broached the subject again. "Can we talk about the message Alienor gave us, without getting sidetracked as to whether it was a real message or in our heads? I need to get some clarity on it. If I can find out more about why Alienor said what she said and who this Melanie is, I will feel better."

"I can't remember word for word," Sophie replied. "As usual the whole experience begins to fade nearly straightaway, but it was something like: Dark forces are gathering. We are at a crossroads. In 2012, the planets will change their course to reshape the future. Or something like that."

"I think she actually said, reshaping the future of mankind!" Jack interjected.

"Who said that Jack?" Lucy giggled. "There was no message, according to you - it was just in our minds, remember?"

Sophie nudged her sister and looked over at Robert who was pacing the room. "Be serious. I think Robbie is a bit distressed," she whispered.

"Why are psychic messages always so vague?" Robert pondered.

"I don't really know why that should be," Sophie mused. "We have to use our own minds as the receiver, and we don't always have fibre-optic or broadband."

"Ah! Ha!" Jack exclaimed. "You just said it is all in your mind!"

"Well, of course it is!" Sophie replied. "It's like having a very sensitive radio receiver in the mind. The receiver is our pineal gland which triggers our psychic brain, and it can pick up different stations from the spirit realms. But it's not fool proof technology!"

"I remember Alienor said, Robert must learn to use his sword, and then you said that you had a sword in your hand," Lucy interjected, trying to refocus the conversation again.

"The message doesn't tell us much really, does it?" Robert sighed.

"Wait!" Sophie said, "I am sure she said the dark forces were gathering in greed."

"Well, they are certainly doing that!" Robert replied angrily. "All I know is that my ancestor from 600AD comes back from the dead, she turns out to be the same soul as Lilly, and that I have to find my sword and beware dark forces gathering in greed because its 2012!"

"Seems straight forward to me!" Jack said suddenly. "Alienor was warning you about Jennifer and Collins' plan to sell Little Eden, and you have to kill them both to stop them!"

"This isn't the Middle Ages," Robert replied. "I can't put them in the Tower and cut off their heads!"

"More's the pity! It would be so much simpler!" Jack smiled.

"What do you know about the history of Alienor already, Robert?" Sophie asked him. "Maybe the rest of the information lies in these books and papers, and she just wanted to pique your interest enough to get you to investigate further?"

"Well that isn't a bad theory!" Lucy agreed. "I mean, who's to say that the spirit world has to tell us everything? Maybe, it's just a prompt sometimes. A sign post. Not the full story."

"Lancelot always says: We are the hands of God; without our hands, nothing can be done," Sophie said. "I have usually found that we don't get any more information until we start participating."

"I've found out bits and pieces about Alienor this afternoon, with the help of Mr T," Robert told them.

This is what he recounted to his friends about her:

"Alienor was a noble woman of the Bartholomew family from Poitiers, France. The urban myth goes that she was supposed to marry a Merovingian prince but ran away to England to escape being prostituted out by her family. She was a Virgin Queen, in the sense that she had her own fortune and was royal in her own right. When she got here to England, she was granted this piece of land by her cousin, Queen Bertha of Kent, to set up a Christian abbey…"

Jack put the pizzas on the coffee table and Robert helped himself to a slice and then continued…

..."Apparently, the land was an ancient, sacred, pagan site of healing.

The power of the water here was famous throughout Europe. Once Alienor took ownership of the area it became a mile square of sanctuary land. That stone seat you see in the Abbey, near the altar, is a Freidstool, and anyone sitting on it was supposed to get a fair and open trial; even the King couldn't overrule the justice of the Freidstool. Little Eden has remained politically neutral ever since, even through the period of Danelaw. When Alienor died in 641, records show that Little Eden passed to her cousin, Constance, and from then on, female cousins or nieces kept developing the place as a sanctuary for healing, charity and learning, until one of her descendants married and had children. Robert Bartholemew married Maria D'Aquataine and started a family estate here. That's when you get the start of the Little Eden we know today."

"So, to Alienor, Little Eden must be like her baby, and is a sacred site. No wonder she has come through now! She wouldn't want you to sell it. She must be trying to get you to save it," Sophie said.

"But, who is Melanie?" Jack asked. "What does she have to do with anything? Is she a Bartlett-Hart?"

"Remember, Melanie is Jennifer from a past life!" Sophie reminded him.

"But, Melanie is dead and buried," Jack said.

"That doesn't make any difference," Sophie replied. "We are all motivated by our past actions and beliefs - for good or bad. Jennifer is a vindictive and greedy cow for a reason. Maybe the dislike of Little Eden stems from when she was Melanie?"

Robert shrugged. He just could not equate his mother with what she was doing. He knew she was not the most loving or the most generous, or even the most considerate of people, but she was his mother and he wanted to think the best of her.

"Melanie must have come back from the dead to help Jennifer destroy Little Eden. It may even be Melanie who put the idea in Jennifer's (well, her own) head in the first place!" Sophie suggested. "If we could find out more about what happened to Melanie in her lifetime, maybe we can stop her. Past lives carry karma through the centuries and feed all sorts of present actions and ideas. When a past life is cleared of its emotional karma, it is usually rendered harmless."

"You mean like getting closure on something that happened lifetimes ago?" Jack asked.

"Exactly!" Sophie agreed.

"How's that even work?" Jack asked - then wished he hadn't.

"We are not just a human body made of static physical cells," Sophie explained. "We are an ever changing ball of consciousness that expresses itself through a physical body. Our DNA programming goes back even as far as Adam and Eve. We are human, but we are also multi-dimensional. It's complicated. You wouldn't understand any more right now."

"No, I don't suppose I would, old girl," Jack said, quite happy not to hurt his brain again.

"Why don't we look through these documents and see if we can find any reference to a Melanie, and see if that triggers some more information?" Lucy suggested, aware they were getting off track again.

"It's a good a place to start as any!" Robert replied.

They all looked through the books and papers, eating pizza and drinking homemade wine.

Nearly an hour went by before Sophie said triumphantly, "I think I may have found Melanie!" She handed Robert a faded and yellowed scrap of paper that had been folded inside another letter. The note read:

My own darling Bobby

Some news has reached me at which I am greatly distressed. I am writing to you urgently, eager for your reply by return. The Colonel tells me you are to marry Captain Shaftsbury's ward, Miss Melanie Humphreys. This I cannot believe to be the truth. Reply at once, my heart will not be still until you yourself deny this pernicious rumour.

It wasn't signed.

"Gosh! So, there is a Melanie in the family after all!" Robert said, turning the note over, but there was nothing else written on it. "A Melanie Humphreys, ward of Captain Shaftsbury. There isn't a date though."

Mr T grinned and pulled at Robert's sleeve. He handed Robert a ledger he had put down about half an hour ago, but now rooted out again from under his pile of documents. Robert read out loud the relevant bit:

"Aug 4th, 1870. Received from Captain Edmond Shaftsbury the sum of twenty thousand pounds. Due dowry of Miss Humphreys...then in brackets it says...(Humphreys B.H dpt 1878 with issue 3 Aus.)"

"Was she married to that chap in the crypt, Bobby?" Jack asked. "I remember him. He's the one who had all those wives and mistresses buried with him. It wouldn't surprise me if he had a secret wife as well. He was certainly one for the ladies!"

"Did Melanie die in 1878?" Lucy asked. "I wonder why she wasn't mentioned on the tomb with Bobby and his other wives?"

"Maybe she died after him?" Jack suggested.

"No, Bobby died in 1879," Robert said.

"Wait!" Sophie exclaimed. "I found something a minute ago that had the *dpt* on it! I don't think it means deceased. It means deported! Look!" She held up a document on which was written:

Samuel Smith, Hall Boy, Little Eden, dpt to colonies for theft, 13th day of October, the year of our Lord, 1866

"No wonder Melanie wasn't mentioned in the family tree or in the crypt!" Lucy said. "She must have done something pretty bad to be deported - quite the scandal in the family!"

Robert shook his head. "It doesn't make sense. As far as the official records go, Bobby's last wife was Charlotte and she died of syphilis. He eventually died of it himself."

"I don't see how knowing about Melanie and Bobby's antics in the bedroom will help us save Little Eden?" Jack asked. "What does all this tell us?"

"It means the woman who ran through you in the crypt might have had syphilis!" Lucy laughed. "Let's hope it's not catching!"

"Very funny!" Jack responded.

"But, if Melanie died in the colony of Australia, which we assume she did, and she isn't buried in the crypt, why is her spirit here in Little Eden and not wandering about somewhere on the Gold Coast?" Lucy asked.

"And, I don't understand how Robert's mother, Jennifer, can be alive and in spirit at the same time!" Jack said.

"I told you already!" Sophie replied. "Our consciousness is not static! Time and space are not an issue."

Jack sighed. "Never mind. Don't bamboozle me again Sophie!"

"Basically, all we need to know right now, is that Melanie must be have been really pissed at the B.H family in 1878, and she has reincarnated as

Jennifer in this lifetime, so that she can get her own back for being deported," Sophie said. "I suppose selling Little Eden is the ultimate revenge."

"Well, they say revenge is a dish best served cold, but waiting over a hundred years and several lifetimes - that's positively frigid!" Robert said, half smiling.

"But, why now?" Lucy asked.

"I suppose it might have something to do with 2012." Sophie mused. "If we are going to stop Jennifer and Melanie we need to deactivate that past life and separate them from themselves - if that makes sense!"

Jack laughed. "You mean Jennifer is a bad influence on herself?"

Robert was not so amused. "How do we neutralise Melanie?" he asked.

"We could use past life regression, but I don't think Jennifer would agree to that!" Sophie replied. "But, if we could research what happened, maybe we can dispel the karmic energy."

"You mean if we find out what really happened to Melanie, maybe we can help her to let go of the past?" Lucy suggested.

"Precisely!" Sophie replied. "If Melanie was deported and was actually innocent, we can give her some justice, and then perhaps, she will rest in peace and leave us all alone."

"What if she is guilty of something?" Jack asked. "Wouldn't it be opening a can of worms to go digging?"

Sophie shrugged. "It might. But it's a risk we need to take. I suggest you get onto Silvi Swan in the morning, Robbie, and book yourself a past life regression session. You, being a blood relative means that you will carry the ancestral history in your DNA. You'll be able to recall what happened to Bobby - with a little expert help!"

That's possible?" Jack asked. "Isn't that time travel?"

Sophie shrugged. "Yeah, sure! We can all time travel - we can't take our physical body with us, but we can go anywhere with our mind."

"So, you are going to travel back in time to see what happened to this Melanie, in the hope that you can stop Jennifer wanting to sell Little Eden?"

"That sounds about right!" Lucy nodded.

"We must not let Melanie's spirit out of that crypt!" Sophie said. "Until we can deactivate them both, it'll be best if we can contain her spirit in there."

Robert looked rather alarmed. "Er...I think Melanie's spirit might have vacated the crypt already."

Sophie looked at him in surprise.

“When I was in the crypt this morning, Melanie showed up and she ran through the wall and disappeared. I didn’t close the portals down. I forgot!”

Sophie sighed and shook her head. “That’s just what we need! Double trouble!”

Chapter 10

~ * ~

Robert was reluctant to return home after being with his friends, but it was now the early hours of the morning, and he knew he had to go at some point. He walked back to Bartlett Crescent under the ever-falling flakes of snow, which were now becoming more like sleet. When he came close to his house, he could see a light on, on the ground floor, although his mother's room was in darkness on the third. He entered as quietly as he could, but he was met by a surprise in the hallway.

Shilty Cunningham stood by the door into the snug. She was wearing a deep cut, electric blue satin, evening gown and was holding a martini in her hand; she slid the olive seductively off its cocktail stick.

"What are you doing here?" Robert asked impolitely, as he shook the wet snow from his trousers.

"Well!" Shilty laughed. "That's a nice greeting I get - especially considering earlier!"

"Sorry," Robert whispered and ushered her into the snug. He glanced up the stairs to make sure his mother was nowhere to be seen, and then closed the door behind them. "It's just, I didn't expect to see you again, so soon."

He went to fix himself a drink. "I was worried about you!" Shilty told him. She took the decanter off him and handed him a brandy from the warming tray instead.

"Why have you come here, Shilty?"

"I told you," she smiled. "I was worried about you!" She sat down on one of the chairs, letting her dress fall a little from her shoulders. She looked up at Robert with wide eyes, but she could see he was not being very responsive to her seduction technique. "And I wanted to know what had happened this morning," she added. "After all, it's not every day your ex turns up and shags your brains out before you even have chance to close the front door, now is it?"

Robert looked embarrassed, but Shilty was never embarrassed about anything, and continued to talk. "I've been having a little chat with Collins. He tells me you left this morning's meeting without a word and all he wanted was…"

"F**k, Shilty!" he exclaimed. "I don't want to talk about it! Not with you anyway." He rested his hand on the mantelpiece and stared into the fire.

Shilty looked hurt and he saw the expression on her face. "I didn't mean that the way it sounded," he said. "It's just…it's a family matter… and I shouldn't have come over to yours this morning. I'm sorry! It was a mistake."

"That's just the kind of thing a girl likes to hear," Shilty replied. She was smiling, which disconcerted Robert slightly. "Well, I'm here now and I don't fancy going out in that snow again tonight, so why don't you invite me to stay? I'll be a married woman soon and that means you can never have me again!" Shilty downed her martini and put her arms around him. Her lips were soft and her body was enticingly warm. Robert was tired. He really couldn't be bothered to say no to her. He let her lead him, by the hand, up the stairs.

~ * ~

Shilty had had a little chat with Collins before Robert had gotten home, just as she said she had; only, she had left out some minor details! She had been greeted at the door by Collins, who was staying over on the orders of his mother. Mrs Bartlett-Hart had been in a 'frightful state' all day. Varsity was already in bed, having caught the same headache as Jennifer, so Collins had lounged away the rest of his evening in the snug; enjoying himself by making various cocktails and reading the newspapers.

"Well! Hello!" he exclaimed, as he opened the front door. "If it isn't Miss Shilty Cunningham. What a lovely surprise. Come in! Come in! Robert isn't here. Come to think of it, we don't know where the f**k he is!" Collins laughed. He took her coat, revealing her slinky dress from under the dark fur. He looked longingly at her pert round bottom that danced as she walked, smoothly outlined under its satin sheath. Her perfume was intoxicating and Collins wanted her to stay a while, for his own amusement. "Cocktail?" he asked her.

"Robbie came over to mine earlier," Shilty told him, taking Collin's martini out of his hand. "I'll have this one," she said, smiling. "He was in a strange mood. Not that I minded."

Collins looked her up and down as he made himself and her another drink. He had always liked Shilty Cunningham and been rather envious of Robert. Collins had picked up his wife, Varsity, off the New York catwalk two years ago. She was considered one of the most beautiful women in the world (by the media), and Collins had wanted her; so, he got her. But Varsity lacked the curves and reckless bounciness of Shilty Cunningham. Shilty was buxom and bubbly, and there was nothing she liked better than to flaunt it! She never wore more than she had to and was proud of her inner, and indeed her outer, goddess.

"Can you stop staring at my breasts, Collins, and tell me what is wrong with Robert?" Shilty pouted.

"If you don't want men to window shop - you shouldn't put them on display!" Collins laughed.

"They are my breasts and I can do what I want with them!" Shilty replied, standing sexily by the fire place.

"I can think of a lot of things I would want you to do with them!" Collins grinned.

Shilty giggled and put her hand on her hip in mock annoyance. "Why, Mr Bartlett-Hart, are you trying to seduce me?"

"Perhaps I am!" Collins confessed, gently brushing back her long dark hair to reveal her bare shoulder. He stood so close, as to almost kiss her. "How about an exchange?" he suggested.

"An exchange?" Shilty replied. She knew that glint in Collin's eye. She knew it, because she had it too!

"You put your window dressing to good use, and I will tell you what you want to know!" Collins said, smiling.

"I think I will just wait for Robbie, and he can tell me himself!" Shilty replied, with a smirk. She turned away from him, ever so slightly, so that he could see her figure to its best advantage in the fire light.

Collins sat down and leaned back in his chair. Undeterred, he continued, "I have a proposition for you, Miss Shilty Cunningham. One which I doubt you can refuse!" Shilty turned back to face him with a look of curiosity on her beautiful face. "If you can make Robert do what I need him to do, you could be a very rich woman indeed," Collins laughed. "And I know how much you like money!"

"I have plenty of my own money. Thank you very much!" Shilty replied, finishing her second martini and going to help herself to another one from the drinks cabinet.

"Oh, I am not talking millions, old girl. I am talking billions!"

Shilty was suddenly very interested indeed! She smiled, and walking towards him, she slowly took down the straps of her dress one by one. She let it slip to the floor saying, "Tell me what use you want me to put them to, and then you can tell me all about it!"

Collins put down his drink and swiftly pulled her towards him. He couldn't believe his luck, but knew how to take full advantage!

After Shilty had given him what he wanted, he made them both another martini and told her what had happened that morning, "…So you see… if you can persuade Robert to play along with Mama, Lucas and me, you could have the billionaire husband you always wanted!"

"The husband I want is Clive, thank you very much!" Shilty retorted, pretending to pout over her drink.

Collins shook his head. "The husband you have always wanted is Robert, but with money! Think of it Shilty, old girl. Billions to spend on anything you want!"

Shilty sighed as she lay on the soft, deep, shag pile hearth rug. "I see one - no - two problems with your proposal," she suggested, kicking her legs up behind her in an absent kind of way. "One: Robert may not listen to my advice, and two: he is the one who called it a day with me, remember. He may not want me back!"

Collins smiled and handed her a warmed brandy. "Oh, Shilty, Shilty, Shilty! My dear!" he said, kissing the soft curve of her back. "With assets and talents like yours, any man would beg you to be with him; and my brother is no different! If he finished it with you, it was because he knew you wanted a style of living he couldn't give you. He's always sacrificing himself for someone or another." Collins turned over onto his back. "If I wasn't married already, I may even consider taking you on myself, but as it is…"

Collins suddenly stopped talking. He put his finger to his lips to indicate for Shilty to stay quiet. They listened for a moment. They could hear a key turning in the front door. "He's back!" Collins exclaimed. In a shot, he was on his feet. He grabbed his clothes from the chair and whispered, "I'll go out through the library and up the back stairs, you stay here!"

Collins headed out the other end of the snug, whilst Shilty grabbed a tissue or two, rescued her knickers from the fire iron, rearranged her dress and quickly poured herself a martini from the cocktail shaker. She was just in time to greet Robert as he entered the hall.

~ * ~

The next day, Jack, Lancelot and the Little Eden Head of Security, Johnathon Grail, were to be found working out in the gym. The familiar smell of rubber mats and sweat, combined with the rhythmic sound of the machines, relaxed them all. 'I'm Every Woman' was playing in the background just as Miss Huggins arrived. She had come to join her and Joshua as members.

Jack introduced her to Johnathon and Lancelot. One look at her slim figure, long legs, blond hair and full lips, was enough to make them both enamoured of her within seconds.

"She's fair game!" Jack laughed, as they watched her walk away.

"May the best man win!" Johnathon winked.

"I find it offensive the way you talk about women!" Lancelot grimaced, as he pulled down the shoulder press. "Miss Adela Huggins is a woman, not a piece of meat to be hunted down and eaten."

Jack laughed. "I'd like to ea..." but he didn't get time to finish his sentence before Lancelot interrupted him.

"Don't even go there!" Lancelot rebuked him.

"When did you get so sanctimonious?" Johnathon replied, with a smile. "Or, is it that you want her for yourself?"

Lancelot would have blushed, if he was the blushing kind, but instead he calmly replied: "I've grown up and you two are still eighteen years old, that's all. Women like Adela are looking for a man to support them; an equal, who can stand with them. Besides, she's a single mother - she needs someone reliable in her life."

Jack laughed again. "You've been reading Cosmo again, haven't you, old boy?"

"No! It's India's influence on him!" Johnathon smiled. "Strong, independent women - isn't that what they all want to be these days?"

"And what's wrong with that?" Lancelot replied. "I like my women to be women; not silly girls who think a six-pack and money are all that matter."

Johnathon winked. He lifted his t-shirt, admired his torso and laughed. "I was hoping they only wanted the six-pack, seeing as I have no money!"

Lancelot shook his head, and they continued to spot each other, until Robert arrived.

"You're late!" Jack told him, as he changed places with Johnathon. Robert shrugged. "Come on, old chap!" Jack encouraged him. "Nothing like lifting the old weights to shake off the doom and gloom. You coming to do laps after? I've already played squash but we can have a game of tennis later?"

Robert just shrugged again. He shook hands with Lancelot. "Can you do something for me?" Robert asked him.

"Anything," Lancelot replied.

"Can you research the old family legal files and see if there was ever a Melanie Humphreys married into the family. It's a bit of a mystery, but we think Bobby BH might have had another wife after Charlotte Montgomery."

Rather surprised, Lancelot replied, "I thought you were going to ask me how we can stop Jennifer, Collins and Lucas."

Robert looked the other way and pretended to change the setting on one of the machines.

"Don't you want to stop them?" Lancelot said, rather alarmed.

"Of course I do!" Robert replied.

Lancelot and Jack looked at him as if they were not sure that they believed him.

Robert looked sheepish and repeated half-heartedly, "Of course I do."

"What's going on?" Johnathon asked.

The other three looked at each other as they remembered that the possible sale of Little Eden was supposed to be a secret.

"Nothing," Robert replied. "Just some spooky stuff that Sophie wants to know about. Past lives and such. In fact, I can't play tennis, I have to go and see Silvi Swan later, for some past life regression, and I need to pay a visit to Dr G."

"Past life, what now?" Johnathon asked.

"Regression," Robert replied, as if it were perfectly normal.

"What's that when it's at home?" Johnathon enquired.

"Hypnotherapy or some such," Robert replied. Although, he was not entirely sure himself what it really was.

"Ah!" Johnathon smiled. "Did me no end of good that hypnotherapy. Almost cured my insomnia, and for pain relief, it's a godsend! I swear by it. But, not heard of past life regression. Interested to find out about it. Let me know how it goes."

Jack looked at Johnathon in surprise. "I didn't take you for a mumbo jumbo type, old chap!" he said.

"A lot of athletes use hypnotherapy," Johnathon replied. "I'm quite into all that 'mind over matter' stuff."

Just then, Miss Huggins appeared again. She was being shown around by not one, not two, but three male gym instructors. She made her way over to say hello to Robert.

Robert apologised for his missing her lunch and they chatted politely for a while, but he was distracted, and he found it difficult to concentrate on what she was saying. Lancelot had to prompt him a couple of times and fill in answers where Robert was a little slow. After a few minutes, the gym instructors seemed quite insistent that she continue her tour with them.

When she was out of sight, Lancelot laughed. "You need some kind of therapy! Was it her figure that distracted you, or what's happening with Little Eden?"

Robert smiled. "I can't think straight today, and no, it wasn't her 'figure', as you put it; fine as it is. She's family anyway; I could never think of her like that!"

"I would say that takes you out the running as well, old boy," Jack said, to Lancelot. "Seeing as she's family."

Lancelot threw a glance at Jack and replied with a smile, "She's a distant cousin and removed enough to not make it matter. Besides, she is closer related to you than me. She's the American branch of the family and you are one of them, remember?"

Jack frowned.

Johnathon laughed at them all. "Seems like that just leaves me in the running then!" he said and admired his six pack again.

Chapter 11

~ * ~

After the gym, Robert made his way to No.1 Daisy Place for lunch, and found Sophie awake, but Lucy in bed asleep instead.

"Shh!" Sophie said, as she let him in. "Lucy is having a nana nap. I think it's all getting to her today."

"I need some advice," Robert admitted. "Would you come to the chateau with me? I thought Dr G's wisdom might be of help."

Sophie nodded, got her coat and put her winter boots on.

"It's still freezing out there, but it's stopped snowing at least," Robert told her. "Don't forget your gloves."

Robert and Sophie walked through the wrought iron gates at the corner entrance to The Peace Park. Blades of green grass were poking through in patches where children had rolled away the snow to make snowmen, and by the side of the open air theatre they could hear shouts and screams of delight, as kids raced down the slopes on sledges. Although the lake was no longer frozen solid, irregular pieces of silver ice floated gently upon the waters, crashing into each other from time to time. Robert took Sophie's arm to make sure she didn't slip as they crossed the wooden bridge, which was treacherous with compacted snow. As they approached the walled gardens, the lack of bird song was slightly eerie. Sophie suddenly shivered, as if someone had walked over her grave.

They were glad to get into the warmth and welcome of the chateau; a beautiful yellow stone edifice in the French style, and former residence of the Bartlett-Harts. Robert opened one of the dark blue double doors, and the scent of delicate incense surrounded them immediately. Sophie felt calm again.

They took off their shoes and made their way into the Altar Room to wait for Dr G. Sophie walked around on the warm, soft-pile carpet and gazed at the gruesome looking and outrageously colourful buddhas, mounted in glass cases on both walls. She was always fascinated by them. The soft sound of OM chanting drifted in and out from an IPlayer in the corner - the room seemed almost otherworldly.

Dr G did not keep them waiting long. He entered from his private meditation room where, from a rotund bay window, he had a view of the lake and a sunny aspect. He greeted them with a smile that lit his eyes up from within and offered them some hot butter tea. Sophie took it gladly - if only to warm her hands around the bowl - she did not really like the taste, but Robert didn't seem to mind.

"We have come to ask your advice," Robert began to say as they all sat down on large floor cushions.

Robert explained the situation about the sale of Little Eden and waited for Dr G to speak.

Dr G sucked air through his teeth, but he did not reply. He simply smiled and sipped his tea.

Robert looked at Sophie and frowned. He wasn't sure whether to say anything more or not. There was an awkward silence for a few seconds, then, finally, Dr G spoke. He shook his head slowly. Then, very softly, he said, "This is not what you have come to ask me. You wish to know what lies beneath the Abbey."

Sophie looked at Robert, who raised an eyebrow.

"We have had an extraordinary experience, Dr G," Sophie admitted. "The thing is…the thing is…it turns out that Aunt Lilly is a reincarnation of Robert's ancestor, Alienor, and they have both come to speak to us from the other side. It's rather odd. They are separate and yet they are the same. Anyway, they are telling us that Little Eden is in danger and that Robert must do something about it; and I don't think Robert knows what to do about it exactly."

Dr G sipped his tea again and did not reply.

Robert looked at Sophie.

Sophie shook her head and shrugged.

Do you remember, dear readers, that at the beginning of this story I mentioned that 2012 would not be a good year for the rest of mankind either? Well, here goes…

"Okay, Dr G," Sophie said at last, "This is what I really want to know! What is a dragon portal exactly, and why is there one under the Abbey? And what has 2012 triggered? I keep seeing flashes of Armageddon that are somehow linked to Little Eden, but I don't know how."

Dr G nodded and smiled. He was happy to reply when the question was the right question! "This year, for your Christian calendar, is 2012. But for the Earth calendar - this year is the end times."

Sophie looked a bit horrified.

Dr G smiled. "Endings are beginnings. A global clean-up of old human karma begins. The dragon lines are clearing."

"What are dragon lines?" Robert asked.

"Ley lines," Sophie whispered to him.

"Ah, okay!" Robert nodded.

"Do you believe in all that New Age stuff about the end of the world?" Sophie asked. "I know there are a lot of books about it out there - some are quite outlandish!" She was a little surprised that Dr G would take notice of conspiracy theories and the like.

"No, no, no, indeed!" Dr G replied gently. "But the dragon lines are emptying out their corrupted energy - like sewage flows into the Ganges. This energy is invisible to most humans. It is fear and spells." He shook his head and repeated, "So much fear; so many spells."

"No wonder there are so many yucky energies on the airwaves!" Sophie said. "But, where is all the energy 'sewage' going to? Surely it isn't all flowing under Little Eden. Is it?" She shuddered at the thought.

"No, no, no. Not all of it." Dr G stood up and went over to the windows. He looked out over the knot garden in a thoughtful manner, and then continued..."Imagine dragon lines are like old telephone wires laid inside the earth. We can send our thoughts along them. Dragon portals are like the telephone receiver. Through the portal you can access other parts of the world, other dimensions and other periods of time. From here, in Little Eden, you can travel to anywhere in the whole universe."

"What does he mean, 'travel'?" Robert asked Sophie, under his breath.

"Astral travel," Sophie replied quietly. "You know - where you travel about in time and space with just your consciousness - in trance or in meditation. You leave your body behind in one place and go elsewhere with your mind. Like in past life regression - you'll be doing that later with Silvi."

"Like Dr Who[9] but without the need for a Tardis?" Robert asked.

"Like who?" Dr G replied, turning around to face them.

"Dr Who!" Robert repeated.

"Who is this Dr Who?" Dr G asked.

"Oh! He is a character off the television," Sophie laughed.

Dr G smiled and nodded. "I sometimes think that I shall teach myself these television programmes, but I have no time."

"Well," Sophie continued, "Dr Who can travel through time and space inside a magic spaceship called the Tardis, which looks, from the outside,

[9] Dr Who, Sydney Newman, C.E. Webster, Donald Wilson, 1963 onwards, BBC

like an old fashioned telephone box."

"Ah!" Dr G smiled. "And he travels through portals?"

"Yes." Robert nodded. "But that's just fiction."

Dr G smiled, took his seat again and poured them all some more tea. "It is in the stories that we find the great spiritual truths. Many people do not wish to believe the truth. It is easier to believe that we are one dimensional beings rather than bundles of multidimensional consciousness."

Robert nodded. "I am starting to wish I'd left well enough alone."

"Why do the ley lines - dragon lines I mean, need cleaning though?" Sophie asked.

"You see," Dr G paused and thought for a moment how to explain. He placed his fingertips together as if to gather his thoughts. "All human experience is recorded in the rocks and in the stones, in the sand and in the water. The whole planet is a library that needs clearing of fear and lies."

Sophie screwed up her nose and thought for a moment. "You mean, whatever happens in human history is recorded in the planet? All the wars, and the sadness?"

Dr G smiled. "And all the joy, and all the laughter."

Sophie mused. "Just like human DNA, we register and store everything. Does the planet have DNA too?"

"Indeed, it is the DNA from which we are all made," Dr G replied. "Now is the time for new DNA."

"I think you're saying that the planet is being defragmented and cleared of viruses just like a computer?" Robert pondered. "A bit like getting ready to upload a new operating system?"

Dr G nodded. "This year, we must gather the guardians together, to protect the dragon portal here in Little Eden. Great and powerful light will be sent to Earth over the next few years. This light is billions of compassionate thoughts. These thoughts must be allowed to flow into the dragon lines. Each dragon portal needs to be guarded and protected. Why else do you suppose they brought you here?" he said, looking directly at Sophie.

"I came back here because I am ill, and I lost my job and my home," Sophie replied.

Dr G shook his head and smiled again, a little sadly, as he could feel Sophie's pain. "You were brought here, just as I was brought here, just as Blue was brought here, just as any of the star children are brought here - to guard the portal."

"How do we guard an invisible portal?" Sophie asked.

"You just do," Dr G replied.

"I can't do anything at the moment, never mind guard some portal or other," Sophie replied. She was getting angry because she was fearful of not being up to the task. "I'm asleep over sixteen hours a day at the moment. I won't be much use!"

Dr G smiled. "In the West you think busy is best. Always busy, busy, busy. Just doing and doing can be very good, but it can also be quite useless. Just 'being' can, sometimes, yield greater results."

"What do you mean, just 'being'?" Sophie asked. She did not understand what Dr G meant. But, she would come to understand a great deal more in the years to come.

Dr G tried to explain. "Your human body, even a broken or ailing body, is anchoring consciousness. That consciousness may be very powerful. What could Nelson Mandela do in prison? He could not 'do' anything; yet his 'being' inspired millions of other people to do something. His 'being' was just as important as everyone else's doing."

"I don't think comparing me to Nelson Mandela is quite suitable," Sophie replied.

Dr G was not to be put off. "Anchoring the incoming compassion through your body means that it can flow into many other people. This requires you 'being' here; whether you do anything else or not."

Robert interjected, "You are valuable to us all, Sophie. Don't ever think that because you are not well that you are less important than anyone else."

"I presume we won't be getting paid for guarding this dragon portal?" Sophie asked. "Spirituality doesn't buy food and shelter unless you are part of a monastery or institution."

Dr G nodded. "When we cannot do for ourselves, allowing others to help us helps them. Their generosity and selflessness feeds their compassion and puts their compassion into action."

Robert was feeling tired and felt as if they were getting nowhere fast. "What does all this have to do with my mother wanting to sell Little Eden?" he asked directly.

Dr G looked at him as if he should already know the answer and did not speak. Robert liked Dr G, but at times he found his delivery of wisdom rather infuriating!

"I think, maybe, your mother has been sent to Little Eden to try and get all the guardians away from the portal," Sophie explained. "If we all have to move out, there will be no one to anchor the compassion as it flows through."

"So, it's not just about the money then?" Robert asked, a little surprised.

Dr G shook his head in agreement. "Your mother is motivated by greed. Greed is her dark side. When we hold attachments to the material world we can be easily corrupted and manipulated by fear. The darkness seeks out fear; it feeds on fear - it is Fear. The guardians must be strong enough to conquer all their fears. Guardians must have pure hearts."

"Who are these guardians?" Robert asked.

Dr G replied. "Sophie, Blue, Alice, Elijah, Tambo and you, Robert. There will be others, when they are ready."

"But, Blue is only five years old, and the others are still children!" Robert exclaimed.

"Indeed!" Dr G nodded. "Star children carry different DNA already and they will slowly change mankind and the planet."

"Do you mean there will be a whole new species of human?" Sophie gasped.

"Indeed." Dr G touched her arm to settle her. He could feel fear coming from her in waves. "Fear creates the wheel of karma. The new arrivals cannot carry karma over and over into lifetime after lifetime in the same way as we do; it makes the energy too dense for them to survive in. Samsara must not be the same for them as it is for us."

"I said it was like a new operating system!" Robert nodded.

"A fresh start?" Sophie shrugged. "What if they just mess up the ley lines too? Fill them with fear?"

"That is for them to decide," Dr G replied.

"I don't think I like the idea of being an extreme cleaner!" Sophie said. "I hope there are plenty of light workers around the world with their etheric marigolds and their astral loo -brushes at the ready. I don't fancy doing this alone!"

Dr G smiled; he was always amused at how prosaically Sophie saw the spiritual world. "Each dragon portal has its own team of extreme cleaners, as you call them. Corruption must be cleared to make way for a new way of thinking. At present, humans align their consciousness to the Sun. This makes them selfish, self-centred and male-orientated. The star children align themselves to Venus. This makes them compassionate, caring and female-orientated."

Robert held up his hands. "Enough!" he said in exasperation. "This is too much to take in! To understand! Why Little Eden? Why us? Why here? I do not understand!!!"

"Why do you create the Star Child Academy here in Little Eden?" Dr G smiled. "Lilly knew the dragon portal here is one of the most important portals in the world. She knew we needed the star children to come here."

Sophie sighed. "It seems unlikely; I mean, there are far more famous holy sites around the world than our little corner of London - Stonehenge, for example."

"Do not be deceived by ordinary appearances!" Dr G reminded her. "Do you think important work is done in the middle of Piccadilly Circus, as you say here. You are using Western thinking again. You think busy places are important places, but they are not the places to do serious work. No, no, no, indeed! One must also have secret places, quiet places, safe places."

"But, shouldn't you be a guardian too?" Sophie asked, rather wishing she had not been given such a job. "You are the most qualified here, after all."

Dr G smiled. "I guard the guardians! You guard the portal."

"But, we don't know how to guard this portal!" Sophie said, exasperated.

"Do what you are guided to do, when you are guided to do it. That is all," Dr G replied.

Sophie half laughed and half wanted to cry. "Well, thanks Dr G," Sophie said sadly, "All you've told me makes perfect sense and has been very helpful! Not!"

"Let me get this straight!" Robert said suddenly. "My mother is being coerced by the dark forces, who are using her past life experiences to fuel her current greed. Selling Little Eden looks like a simple case of money grabbing, but you are suggesting that the real reason is so that this dragon portal, which is apparently under the Abbey, is left without guardians, who happen to be me, Sophie and a bunch of kids. And all this is so that the dark side (whoever they are) can stop this new light from coming in; which according to you is like some kind of spiritual toilet cleaner or compassionate bleach! And, all because there are some star kids being born as humans who have a special DNA inside them, and they want to live in a happier world and do not want to keep reincarnating like we do?"

Dr G just sat back on his cushion, smiling with his whole face, as only a lama can do. His eyes twinkled, and in his usual enigmatic way, he said nothing more.

When Robert and Sophie left, they were a little shaken and forlorn. They stopped at the corner of Little Eve Street and Sophie looked up at the sky to see millions of snowflakes scattering downwards in a haze of grey and speckled white. She held out her hand and they came to rest on her glove. She remembered some of the lines from a poem she had once read:

The rise of human-kind
is not an ascension of some...
...knit with seven billion snowflakes
none the same
connected, geometric matrix
all in hand
Crystalline[10]

Sophie sighed.

"Do you believe Dr G?" Robert suddenly asked her.

"What do you mean?" Sophie replied.

Robert shrugged. "About the dragon portal and a new species of human?"

Sophie smiled a little sadly. "I suppose I do. It would explain a few things about this place and about lots of things actually. Aunt Lilly said something to me and Luce the day before she died, and I thought she was just over dramatizing as she often did, but now I think she knew something was going on."

"What did she say?" Robert asked.

"She said that we were guardians of this place and that we must always respect the Abbey, no matter what we thought of religion. She said the whole town is a sacred place and always has been and always will be. She said people would be waking up and not to be afraid. She said that I was here for a reason and to be brave. I thought she was just trying to be kind about me being ill and her dying."

"I don't understand it myself. I don't see how our little town could be so important to anyone but us. I don't know what it is I'm supposed to do. I understand that star children are special kids, but a new species of human? I think Dr G is going too far this time."

"Why should there not be a new species emerging? It has happened several times before," Sophie replied, stamping her feet to keep warm, as she was starting to feel the cold.

[10] The Rise 2, Rise, Andrea Perry, 2016, Vocamus Press

"Not in our lifetime surely!" Robert replied.

"That's rather arrogant don't you think?" Sophie grimaced.

"How do you mean?"

"Well, humans have developed and changed over millions of years. There have been at least three species of human already. The world does not stop changing just because we think it sounds outlandish. We are living through a massive cosmic energy shift that cannot be easily explained because we don't have the luxury of hindsight, but when it's all over it will become history and we will have been part of that."

"I suppose nothing stays the same forever," Robert admitted.

Sophie sighed. "Something is happening to the planet and to mankind: I can feel it. It's as if the whole planet is wobbling on its axis and sensitive souls are wobbling with it. I feel as if we are gathering speed and are going to be thrown through the ozone layer into another vibration, like a basketball through a hoop."

"Well, let's hope it's a slam dunk!" Robert laughed.

Chapter 12

~ * ~

The next day Lucy had found it hard to get out of bed again!

The Café was due to open the next day and the amount of preparation she needed to do overwhelmed her. She was struck by a strong sensation to run away and started to panic. She presumed she was coming down with something and felt her forehead, which didn't feel particularly hot or cold. She thought the best thing to do was to take a hot shower, but the heat of the steam made her feel distinctively dizzy and with that - she crashed to the floor!

As Lucy regained consciousness, the first thing she saw was her sister fanning her with a magazine. She could hear Sophie's voice calling, "Luce! Wake up! Wake up!" and then she could hear someone running up the stairs.

Jack burst in - breathless and covered in snow. "Is she alright?" he asked, as he rushed to kneel beside Lucy, who was dazed and naked, except for a hand towel that Sophie had quickly draped over her.

If you are wondering, dear readers, if Jack knew that Lucy was in distress via telepathy or something psychic of that sort, I'm sorry to disappoint you, but in this instance it was science that prevailed in the form of a txt message from Sophie, which she had sent immediately on seeing Lucy lying out cold on the bathroom floor!

"I heard an almighty crash from in here and there she was - out cold on the floor!" Sophie explained. "I thought for a minute she was dead! The shower was going. I got soaked before I could turn it off. My heart nearly burst out of my chest with fright! Then of course, I realised she'd probably just fainted - like she did when we were younger. She hasn't fainted in years. "Luce, are you alright? Talk to me, Luce!"

"Did she hit her head?" Jack asked, going into 'first aid' mode.

"I don't think she hit her head," Sophie said, examining Lucy as much as she could.

"I didn't hit my head," Lucy said, trying to sit up. "It doesn't hurt anyway. I just blacked out! I felt weird when I got up earlier."

"Come on, back to bed, little lady," Jack said, carrying her to her room where he laid her on the bed. Sophie dried her down with some big soft towels and pulled the covers over her. Lucy lay there for a few seconds and then sat up in distress, "I can't lie here, there's too much to do!"

Sophie frowned as she wrung out her own pyjama top. "There is a lot to do, but if the Café stays closed another day, it's not life or death!"

"But we are fully booked all day! It would mean ringing everyone, and when could we fit them in? We are fully booked 'til March!" Lucy groaned and lay back against the pillows.

"A victim of your own success, eh!" Jack said smiling. "Don't worry old girl! We can do anything that needs doing!"

"You don't know where anything is or what needs doing!" Lucy replied, feeling as if she just wanted to go to sleep. Her head and heart were thumping. Sophie looked in the drawer of the bedside table for some Rainbow Rescuer but the bottle was empty.

"We don't know exactly what to do, that's true!" Sophie replied. "But I know plenty of people who do! Leave it to us. It will all be done. Just wait and see!" She tucked Lucy up in the duvet and took Jack out onto the landing. "Jack!" Sophie said in a hushed voice. "Call Mrs B and ask her if she can come this morning. She was coming this afternoon anyway, and then call Tosha and tell her to get as many hands on deck as she can! Tell her it's an emergency! Try and get them to come ASAP!"

"Right ho!" Jack said and got out his phone.

Sophie went to make some tea and took it back into Lucy. "Now!" Sophie told her sister kindly. "Drink this and hold this smoky quartz - it will help put your aura back together! I'll go over to the new shop and see if they have any Rainbow Rescuers. Here, I'll put on some wave music - it always makes you feel more relaxed."

Lucy nodded and sighed. If the truth be told, she wasn't very comfortable taking over No.1 Daisy Place Café-Bookshop from Aunt Lilly. She suddenly found herself in the position of matriarch - she was the one at the top of the family tree. She was the person who everyone else would look to for help and advice. It was a daunting place to find herself in so suddenly! She would have to make the decisions, take all the responsibility for the business, the family, and the money. Her admiration for her aunt went up a thousand fold as she realised how much Lilly had taken on her own shoulders over the years. *How did she cope?* Lucy thought to herself. *She took us on as babies, gave up her career and took over the Café to support us; she must have wanted to run away a million times.* After a few minutes, however, she could feel the sounds of the soothing waves retuning her body and mind, and she felt her anxiety and tension fade into peacefulness and relaxation.

Very soon the Café was a hive of activity with everyone buzzing about. There is nothing like a crisis to bring out the best in people and make things work out just fine in the end.

Mrs B popped upstairs to see if Lucy was okay and perched beside her on the bed. Lucy opened her eyes and smiled. "Is there anything I can get you, my love?" Mrs B asked her.

"No, I'm alright," Lucy said. "Is the Café okay?"

"Of course it is, my love!" Mrs B said reassuringly. "There has been a Café of sorts on this site for over a thousand years and hopefully there will be one here for a thousand more. We can cope with everything. We all love this place as much as you do, you know that."

It suddenly dawned on Lucy that the Café staff were as in love with Daisy Place as she was! It was somewhere where they were always welcome, where they felt needed and appreciated, and above all it was a place they could feel safe in. Suddenly, her heart sank as she thought of Little Eden being sold and her friends finding out that their beloved Café would exist no more.

"There is nothing we are given in life that we cannot cope with," Mrs B said. "Have faith."

Lucy sighed. "I struggle to keep the faith, Mrs B, when I see good people, like Sophie, hurting, and poor people starving, and innocent children being abused all over the world, and billionaires buying diamond encrusted cars instead of helping others. Sometimes I just feel overwhelmed by it all."

Mrs B patted Lucy's hand. "Have faith in the saints, my love," Mrs B said and held out a necklace she was wearing which depicted St Therese of Liseaux. "My grandma said to me on her death bed, 'Patricia, she said, never forget the true saints. They are your comfort and your guides through life and through death'. I was only nine years old, but I took her word for it and she was right! No matter how bad life gets, the only wisdom I know, is to accept what life brings, to forgive yourself and others, and to pray for comfort and strength every day."

"But sometimes when I pray, nothing happens," Lucy admitted.

"What is it you hope will happen, my dear?" Mrs B asked her, as she tucked in the duvet.

"I ask for things and they don't happen or I don't get them," Lucy replied.

"You make it sound like God is a mail order catalogue!" Mrs B smiled, plumping the pillows. "Prayer is about finding the comfort and the courage to face what is happening, my love."

"I wonder sometimes, if it's worth praying or wishing at all!" Lucy mused. "The Law of Attraction says if you wish hard enough for something it will happen. But it doesn't seem to be working and only bad things seem to happen." Lucy sighed and looked up at the ceiling.

"I don't know about the Law of Attraction, my love," Mrs B replied, "All I know is that I feel a wave of comfort and joy when I pray, even when life is at its worst. When bad things happen it means I have to pray even harder because I need extra help to cope with them."

"Talking of helpful spirits - have you felt Aunt Lil's spirit around you?"

"Yes, of course, my love!" Mrs B said, as she stood up to leave. "She was in the kitchen this morning - we had a good chat."

"You did!" Lucy's eyes widened. "What did she say?"

Mrs B closed the curtains a little and replied, "Oh, she asked me to keep an eye on you and to help you rest and not over do it! She said she was between worlds at the moment but in no pain at all. She said she would like to stay as your guardian angel but she isn't sure if that is possible yet. Something about Robert making a decision? But she didn't say what. I did wonder what Robert had to do with it."

"Did you actually see her?" Lucy asked.

"No, my love," Mrs B replied, shaking her head. "But I've spent so many years talking to the saints, I know how to chat with the spirit world when the occasion arises. Now, you get some rest and leave the Café to the rest of us." As she went through the door she turned and added, "You are always needed and valued my dear, and we all love you. Don't you worry, Lilly will guide you!"

Later that afternoon, Jack came down into the kitchen to find something to nibble and found Mrs B humming along to the tune 'Lean on Me', which was playing on the radio, whilst she busied herself in her kitchen - doing what she loved best!

"Afternoon Mrs B!" Jack said. "Anything going spare?"

"Come in, my love, I need a word with you!" Mrs B said. The kitchen was filled with glorious odours of fresh baking and the whole delightful room was clouded in warm floury air. "Lucy needs some time off and some care and attention," Mrs B told Jack, as she rolled out some pastry. She kept talking as she made bread, tarts, cookies, muffins and cakes of all descriptions. She had a knack of having several pans bubbling away at once and a hundred and one different things in the ovens, on hobs, on cooling racks - you name it - she had it on the go! "I know you've been staying here with them these last few nights, but can you stay a little longer? I don't like to think of the girls being alone, especially after what happened with Lucy in the shower this morning. And I know Lilly is worried about them."

"Of course I can!" Jack replied, reaching for a rose and vanilla jam tart that was fresh out of the oven and it burnt his mouth!

"They are hot!" Mrs B said smiling, pretending she hadn't seen him spit it out and fan his mouth to cool it.

"Yeah, got that!" Jack laughed. "I don't have to go back to Mexico right now if I don't want. I can stay around."

"Good!" Mrs Bakewell replied and handed him a zucchini muffin. Jack willingly tried anything that Mrs B cooked up!

"What do you think of Jimmy?" Mrs B suddenly asked him.

"Jimmy?" Jack replied, with his mouth full of muffin.

"You know! Jimmy Pratt! Lucy's beau," Mrs B said.

Jack laughed. "I don't think we call them beau's these days, Mrs B!" He finished his muffin and added, "I dunno what I think of him really. These are scrumptious Mrs B. Anything else you need me to test?" Jack thought for a moment. "He should have been at the funeral for Lucy, I know that much!"

Mrs B gave him a tiny cheesecake to try. "Jimmy Pratt is exactly the kind of man Lucy would pick as a beau," Mrs B said. "Whether anyone else would pick him is debatable. Lilly told me this morning that she was worried about his influence on Lucy, but as we all know, if you say anything about her choice of men it will push her towards them, not away. Lucy can never see the faults in people, bless her."

"She can see the faults in me!" Jack replied. "These cheesecakes are tasty Mrs B but rather small!"

"They are for afternoon teas, Jack, they are meant to be delicate and ladylike!" Mrs B laughed.

"Yes, I suppose they are. That's the only thing with this Café - nothing is bigger than an amuse-bouche most of the time!" He shrugged and helped himself to another one. "Wait a minute. Did you say Lilly told you this morning?"

"Why yes! Here in the kitchen. We had a little chat." Mrs B nodded and stirred some custard.

"Why doesn't that surprise me, Mrs B!" Jack said, slipping a maid of honour into his mouth. "Have you met the new headmistress?"

"No, not yet," Mrs B replied, taking some oat cookies out of the oven.

"Adela Huggins!" Jack grinned. "She's amazingly clever and she's one of the most beautiful women I have ever seen!"

Mrs B rolled her eyes and shooed him away from some fresh banana bread.

"Adela has a son, Joshua. We took him with us this morning to the climbing wall. He was good at it too. Quite the outdoors man it seems!"

Jack sneakily stole a warm cookie whilst Mrs B was busy looking in the fridge for some cream and then continued…"Adela rides very well apparently."

"I am sure she does," Mrs Bakewell replied, pretending not to notice the tell-tale crumbs he had down his t-shirt. "It's not my place to say, Jack, but if this Adela Huggins is going to be the headmistress of new Star Child Academy I presume she will be around in Little Eden for many years to come, and we wouldn't want to make things awkward for her now, would we?"

"Whatever do you mean Mrs B?" Jack replied, feigning a frown.

"You know exactly what I mean Jack, my boy!" Mrs B responded, waving her rolling pin at him. "There are plenty of fish in the sea that can swim away as soon as you get bored with them. Those that need to stay around here, well, perhaps you could leave them in peace!"

"Who says I would get bored with her, maybe she is the *one*!" Jack grinned.

"You have no clue who the *one* is and when you realise who it is, well, we will all be thankful for that!" Mrs B scolded him, but she smiled. "Now, go and see what the girls would like for their dinner. I may as well make something for them whilst I'm here."

Jack kissed her on the cheek and pinched another muffin on his way out.

~*~

Earlier, Sophie had hopped across a snowy Daisy Place wearing Lucy's pink wellies and Jack's oversized wool coat. The glittering snow crunched and crinkled beneath her feet as it sparkled in the twinkling fairy lights, which are strewn, all year long, across the shops and balconies of the yard.

She chuckled at the various snow creatures the kids had left behind, half hidden now, under the newly fallen snow and looking rather more comical than before!

The shops across the way are a row of 18th Century bow-fronted establishments. The shop Sophie was heading for had been recently renovated. The wooden pillars around the door were carved into flowers of all kinds, spiralling their way up in garlands towards the new, but vintage-style, shop sign, which read:

Peony Bow
Parfumier Parisian

The old shop bell tinkled as Sophie opened the ornate glass door. Peony Bow was inside unwrapping precious bottles of perfume and aromatherapy. Sophie caught her breath as she closed the door behind her. She was completely engulfed by an olfactory wave of heady scents. The whole shop was aquiver with sensuous and alluring aromas. An exotic frisson of damask rose and patchouli floated in the air, followed by a blissful bouquet of mandarin, bergamot and frangipani. She sighed, enraptured by the enchanting fragrances. As she looked around, her senses were even more bewildered by the luminosity of gleaming glass and gilt, adorning the rich rosewood interior. Exquisite bottles of perfumes, reflected in the mirrors behind them, seemed to go on and on forever into a far-off land. The counters effervesced with sumptuous glass bottles wearing beautifully printed labels in; lavender, candy pink, mint greens and raspberry red. On the central table, grand baroque glass urns, richly gilded, glimmered with mystical liquids, the colour of honey dew and burnished amber.

"Come in!" Peony Bow called to her, smiling. "Sorry it's so cold in here! The heating isn't working yet. I just wanted to get these boxes unpacked." Peony Bow was wrapped up in a pale cashmere hat and scarf and some silver-grey, cable-knit fingerless gloves. She had two super-soft knitted jumpers on, one layered on top of the other, and on her feet she had big furry boots. Peony was petite and naturally slim. Any outfit she wore she seemed to carry off with a certain Parisian charm. "What can I do for you?" Peony asked. "Sophie isn't it? Lucy's sister?"

Sophie was still transfixed by the mesmerising radiance of the scene laid out before her, and suddenly couldn't remember what she had come in for. "Oh, yes, well…Lucy said you were stocking Rainbow Rescuers…I wondered if you had any for sale?" Sophie stuttered.

"I put all the bottles out yesterday. What do you think?" Peony pointed to an alcove, the height of the room, filled with small bottles of coloured liquids which were magically separated into several coloured layers. The display looked stunning. The bottles were reflected in the glass behind them and lit from underneath, which created a rhapsody of colour and light. "I always love the display they make, don't you?"

"Oh, yes!" Sophie replied. "This is the most beautiful shop I have ever seen!"

"Thank you!" Peony replied. "I was sorry to hear about your aunt. That is why you need a Rainbow Rescuer I suppose?"

"Yes." Sophie nodded. "We've run out of the Happy Life."

"Happy Life is so good," Peony said. "But here, try Rest and Repair. It has strawberry which is good for grounding, rose for grief, and tangerine is invaluable when you have been through a trauma. It'll put your aura back together and soothe your emotional body too." She chose a bottle from the middle shelf which was humming with the three magical colours - it was comforting and relaxing just to gaze into it.

"I think we are both still in shock." Sophie admitted. "It's only been ten days since…we keep expecting her to turn up, you know, as if she had just gone on holiday or popped to the shops or something. Everyone says it will get easier and I don't doubt that it will eventually, I suppose, time allows emotions to heal and fade. We will try anything to help us get through it - anything that'll keep us off drink, drugs, too much food and wild bouts of shopping!"

"It's nice to have neighbours who are into holistic health and such like!" Peony smiled. "It makes you feel as if you can talk about things! Little Eden seems like paradise to me. Everyone is so liberal but it's more like Mayfair than Glastonbury - which I prefer!"

"That's one way to describe it I suppose!" Sophie said, laughing.

Peony looked Sophie up and down for moment and added, "I know I have only just met you, but I feel as if I know you already! Do you believe in past lives?"

"Oh, yes!" Sophie smiled.

Do you think we knew each other in a past life?" Peony asked.

"Oh, I think so!" Sophie replied, picking up scent bottles and luxury handmade soaps. “I feel as if I have known you before. I’m getting serious deja-vu in here!”

“Maybe we could do some regression and find out?” Peony suggested. “I had a regression session once. I was a lady’s maid in a big house!”

“Yes,” Sophie laughed, “Many people are.”

“Sorry?” Peony said.

“Oh, sorry!” Sophie replied, putting down a bottle from which the scent had nearly blown her head off. “I didn’t mean to imply that what you saw during regression wasn’t true, or anything! It’s just past life regression is a bit hit and miss. We often retell things we have seen on TV or read in a book, but it feels very real under hypnosis. The amount of people who claim to be Elizabeth I or Casanova is amazing!”

“Do lots of people think they have been maids in stately homes?” Peony asked, a little disappointed.

“It’s a common memory, yes,” Sophie replied. “But then, sometimes we remember our ancestors’ lives in regression, but it’s still kind of personal I suppose.”

“You mean we are just telling stories our family have told us or making up stories based on old photos we might have seen?” Peony asked.

“Not necessarily.” Sophie said, shaking her head. “But the memories of what your ancestors did and witnessed are recorded in your DNA, just as much as the colour of your eyes or the talents you inherit. You know, like being able to play the piano or being able to do maths, being an addictive personality or an extrovert. Most information lies dormant in the DNA until you go inside your mind to find it. Like having a big library inside you but you never read all the books!”

“Like having Wikipedia in your DNA you mean?” Peony suggested.

Sophie laughed. “That’s why so many people feel they have been someone famous in history. Anne Boleyn is one of the most common. It’s like that life story gets into our collective psyche and we make it part of our own story.”

“Really?” Peony asked, fascinated to know more.

“You’d be surprised! Male, female, young, old - from all over the world - say they have memories of being Anne Boleyn or having been at the crucifixion of Christ - that’s another popular one - seems to me there must have been busloads of tourists at that event if everyone who says they were there, was actually there.”

"It sounds awfully complicated. I didn't realise there is so much to it! You will have to tell me more sometime."

"Here, let me pay you for the Rescuer, how much is it?" Sophie asked, rooting in Jack's pockets for some ten pound notes.

"No need to pay, no, no!" Peony assured her. "Your aunt Lilly was the one who got me the shop in the first place, and besides, I will be picking your brains about past lives for weeks to come. I have a feeling all sorts of other weird and wonderful things are bound to happen whilst you are here!"

"That's very kind," Sophie said. She realised that her mind was slowing down and she had to fight to find her words as a wave of fatigue was washing over her. She felt she should leave but she didn't want to go. She let Peony rattle on, glad of the company, not wanting to have to go to bed again, alone.

Peony was enthusiastic about her new venture. "I've rented out the first floor as an old-fashioned barbers and guess what? It only turns out that it was a barbers way back in the eighteen hundreds. We found where the chairs had been fixed to the floor under the linoleum. It's all meant to be, don't you think?"

Sophie was glad that Peony didn't know of the sale of Little Eden and the impending doom. Her new shop might be out of business by the end of year. She felt a pang of sadness for Peony's childlike enthusiasm, knowing that her hopes and dreams maybe over almost before they had begun.

"I hope it wasn't Sweeny Todd's!" Sophie laughed. "Who's the barber going to be?"

"His name is Vincent Piccolo. Perhaps you have heard of him? He is very famous in the world of hairdressing. He has won a lot of awards! Very exclusive."

Sophie laughed. "Oh, I know Vincent! He lived in Castle Mansions as a boy. His parents still do, they owned the fish and chip shop in Violet Yard. He always wanted to be a hairdresser. Good for him!"

"Vincent's up there now, come and have a look upstairs. It's as beautiful as down here! It's all burrwood panelling and mirrors, and the products he uses smell divine.

Peony led a very tired Sophie up the stairs. They were greeted by a sign saying:

Gentlemen are measured by their manners and by the style of their hair.

Two large Georgian-style sash windows look out over Daisy Place and stylish traditional barbers' chairs had been placed in front of each one. Deeply sensuous scents of neroli, sandalwood and clary sage floated in the air and the shelves were stocked with a plethora of gentleman's luxury grooming accessories such as staghorn shaving brushes, vintage tortoiseshell combs, ceramic shaving bowls and soft leather wash bags.

Vincent Piccolo was in the other room and called to them when heard their voices. "I'll be out in a minute, darling!"

Vincent came through double doors, which look, from the outside, as if they belong to a Victorian wardrobe, but once opened they reveal another small and alluring room beyond, which is decked out with luxury tailored shirts, silk ties and exquisite handmade brogues. The quote on the wall reads:

A gentleman wears only that which suits him, not necessarily that which he can afford.

Vincent was sporting a very neat, if rather oversized, beard and well groomed hair. In fact, he was a little too well groomed and looked as if he had just stepped out of an eighteen hundred's time portal himself!

"Well, I declare!" Vincent suddenly exclaimed in a high-pitched squeal. "If it isn't Miss Sophie Lawrence!"

Sophie smiled, trying to take in the spectacle that was an adult and dandified Vincent. The last time she had seen him he had been a rather dull seventeen-year-old in a shell suit. He kissed the air around her four times and Sophie nearly passed out with strength of his aftershave.

"Well!" Vincent said, with a flourish. "What do you think of my new abode? Isn't it fabulous, darling?"

Sophie nodded. "Absolutely fabulous!"

"Isn't it? Isn't it!" Vincent said, as he wiped the counter down with a silk handkerchief. "And isn't our little Peony Bow just adorable?" He smiled so widely that his teeth almost glowed fluorescent white!

"Er, yes!" Sophie nodded. "I wouldn't have recognised you."

"Transformation, darling!" Vincent replied. "That's the name of the game, as they say! I can take any ugly duckling and create a swan before your very eyes! Confidence comes from the outside, you know! I mean, not to be awful, darling, but you do look rather drab and tired. I would hardly have recognised you either. I don't do women but for you I could make an exception! An hour with me and you'd be fixed up for life!"

Sophie smiled - she was slightly amused but didn't reply.

"Vincent!" Peony scolded him playfully. "You'll have to forgive him, Sophie. He says whatever comes into his head! Don't you? Vincent."

"Oh, darling, don't ever be offended by me!" Vincent replied, waving some shaving brushes in the air in a theatrical manner. "I just say what I want, when I want! Being myself, open, and true, that's what I'm about these days! What you see is what you get with me!"

"Yes. So it would seem!" Sophie replied. "It's nice to see you again after all these years. Good luck with the new venture."

"You are such a darling!" Vincent replied. "Well, must get on - so much to do before opening! You'll come to the opening night? Did we send the Lawrence girls an invitation, Peony, darling?"

Peony nodded.

"Well then, we'll all be able to catch up over champers and canapés!" Vincent bowed, and flounced back into the wardrobe.

Peony and Sophie walked back down the stairs, and Sophie couldn't help giggling to herself.

"Vincent can be a bit full on," Peony admitted. "But, I like his honesty. As he says - what you see is what you get with him."

"Perhaps!" Sophie chuckled.

Just as Sophie had opened the front door and was about to say goodbye, Peony said, "Can I ask you a personal question?"

"Yeah, sure!" Sophie replied, closing the door again to keep out the chill.

"Well, it's more about Lucy, really," Peony admitted.

"Oh, don't worry! You can ask us anything," Sophie said, "What you see is what you get!"

"Well, I was wondering - are Lucy and Jack Fortune an item?"

"No! Good grief!" Sophie laughed. "Whatever made you think that?"

"Just the way he is always coming and going from the Café, I suppose," Peony admitted. "He was helping me, the other morning, with a delivery and he mentioned Lucy quite a lot."

Sophie shook her head. "Jack is like a brother to us. His parents died when he was fourteen and he lived with our Aunt Lil 'til he was old enough to take over the antiques shop."

"Oh, poor Jack!" Peony exclaimed.

Sophie smiled at Peony's concern. "It is rather a sad story actually," Sophie told her. "Jack's father, Ace Fortune, was high up in the Government, although no one really knew what he did exactly. He was killed in an IRA car bomb in the eighties, here in London. Jack's mother, Maggie, poor soul, she took an overdose shortly afterwards. Jack was at boarding school with Robert, so Lilly used to have him for the holidays with us." Sophie smiled to herself, seeing Peony's sad face. "I don't suppose you are asking because you fancy Jack by any chance?"

Peony blushed.

"Oh! No need to be embarrassed," Sophie reassured her. "You won't be the first and you won't be the last to fancy the pants off our Jacky Boy!"

"Well, I have only met him a couple of times." Peony admitted. "But, he is, well, very…"

"Annoying, arrogant, too good-looking for his own good?" Sophie interrupted and then smiled. "Just kidding! Jack is a sweetheart really. We trained him and Robert well, from being boys. They know how to say 'please' and 'thank you' at the right times, open doors for ladies and they send flowers on birthdays. We have never managed to get them to really listen, but I think that is asking too much of any man!"

"I met Johnathon Grail the other day as well," Peony said and giggled. "He was rather fit, I must say."

"Actually, thinking about it," Sophie commented, "There is a high proportion of handsome and very nice men here in Little Eden. It must be the atmosphere that attracts them! Devlin Thomas, at the chocolate shop, and Tage Johansen, at the baker's across the alley, they are both as yummy as the things they sell! In fact the only thing that could improve on Devlin is if *he* were covered in chocolate!"

"I bet none of them are single, are they?" Peony enquired. "I thought, with Jack especially, it would be a long shot if he was single."

"Jack is never in a relationship very long. He will tell you he can't be tamed and won't ever marry. I think eighteen months is about his record. All his girlfriends think they are the one who will 'fix' him, mind you."

Peony looked disappointed. "I knew there had to be a catch!"

"Oh, don't let me put you off!" Sophie replied. She looked out of the window and across at the Café. "I believe we don't actually choose who we fall in love with anyway. There is either 'love-karma' between two people or there isn't. That is what makes us fall for each other - karma. It's always karma. Not love!"

"You don't believe in love?" Peony said, a little shocked.

Sophie shrugged. "Personal connections of any kind, work colleagues, family, friends, partners - it's just soul mates reliving their past life relationships for good or bad! And in my experience, romantic soul mates are usually a whole lot of trouble!"

"Well, if you and I have a past life karma maybe I have with Jack too?" Peony said hopefully.

"If you have love-karma with Jack then there will be little choice in how you feel about each other," Sophie replied.

"But, am I his type?" Peony asked.

"Are you definitely female?" Sophie laughed, looking her up and down.

"Of course!"

"Then you are his type!"

Chapter 13

~ * ~

Back over at No.1 Daisy Place, Lucy awoke with a sudden feeling of panic. She didn't know where she was for a moment and her heart was racing with fear. She felt for her tiger's eye bracelet but realised it was not there. Then she remembered, she had left it in Lilly's room on the day of the funeral.

She gently opened the door to her Aunt Lil's room, but at first, she couldn't bring herself to go in. She hesitated. The bedroom was engulfed in semi-darkness. A veil of ashen shadows danced in a solitary shaft of crepuscular winter sun, which stealthily slipped through the half-closed curtains and lay across the bed. The snow on the roof was pressed against the French windows, almost to knee height, creating an icy barrier to the outside world.

Lucy took a few shaky steps inside and closed the door behind her. She stood motionless for a while. A hush pervaded the room with an eerie stillness and Lilly's perfume still lingered in the air. Suddenly, a piercing pain ran through Lucy's chest like a sharp blade. The spectre of grief was twisting in her heart again. She could almost stand the physical pain. Physical pain was a comfort right now. It was a languishing witness to her still being alive, when most of the time she felt so numb.

In a daze, she walked slowly over to the dressing table and there was her bracelet, where she had left it. She sat down at the dressing table and looked around at Lilly's things - now covered in a fine layer of white dust. She picked up a photograph of Lilly holding Tambo in her arms, taken the day he was born. It had pride of place, in an ornate silver-gilt frame, amongst her perfumes and pearls. Lucy hugged the photo to her searing chest. "Oh, Lilly," she said quietly, as she rocked gently backwards and forwards. "What am I going to do without you?" She replaced the photo and wrapped Lilly's pearls around her hand like a rosary. With that, her stomach squeezed itself into wrenching knots and grief began to creep like sickening spiders prickling and crawling through her blood. She felt herself drop to the floor, engulfed by a torrent of tears. She sobbed her heart out, there on the carpet, until she had no energy left to cry any more.

Lying with her cheek pressed against the floor, Lucy, involuntarily, began to pray…

Great Goddess of Love in whom I trust,
Please send your feathers to surround me,
So that, beneath your wings I may take refuge.
Let your faithful covenant be my shield and my castle.
I shall not fear the terrors of the night, nor the arrows that fly by day
For you shall send your angels to guide, comfort and protect me in all my ways.[11]

Under her breath she repeated the prayer over and over. Gradually, she felt a silent wave of comfort and solace flowing through her. The deafening noise of her pain was hushed and a feather-like, floating sensation caressed her senses. "Are you here?" Lucy whispered under her breath. "Aunt Lil, are you here?" Unexpectedly, she began to feel a strength rise within her. It was a mysterious, yet unmistakable, sensation of being supported by an invisible force. She found she could stand up, albeit a little shakily, and pulled herself onto Lilly's ample bed. Cuddling her aunt's cold, soft pillow, which cooled her burning cheeks, her poor wretched body found comfort in the cradle of feather quilts and white sheets. Her mind began to clear, and as she slipped into a half-sleep, she could hear a mellifluous whisper dancing inside her mind...

I am a thousand winds that blow
I am the diamond glints on snow
Do not stand at my grave and cry
I am not there; I did not die[12]

Like a lullaby, the words echoed through her mind until she fell asleep.

Lucy had slept for well over an hour when she was eventually awoken by her sister. "I didn't want to wake you before," Sophie said, sitting on the bed. "Whatcha you doing in here? You feeling any better?"

"Yes, a bit," Lucy replied. "I came to get my bracelet, but I had my first tsunami of grief. I must have fallen asleep. "Oh, my god," she said suddenly, pointing at the floor. "Look!"

Sophie looked down and saw the photograph of Lilly and Tambo on the floor beside the bed. "It's just a photo," Sophie said puzzled.

"But, what's it doing on the floor?" Lucy asked. "It was on the dressing

---

[11] *KT King 21st Century Prayers*, KT King, 2015
[12] *Do Not Stand at My Grave and Weep*, attributed to Mary Elizabeth Frye, 1932

table earlier! How did it get over here?"

"Well, you must have brought it with you and it rolled off onto the floor when you fell asleep," Sophie suggested.

"No, I didn't! I swear. I didn't!" Lucy protested.

Sophie and Lucy looked at each other and felt chills race down their spines!

"Oh, don't!" Sophie said, picking up the photo. "You're giving me goose bumps!"

"It must have been Lilly!" Lucy replied. "She must have moved it whilst I was asleep!"

Sophie shivered. "I don't know. I mean, maybe that is going a bit far? Things that move around by themselves - that's a rare thing and usually there is another explanation!"

"You sound like Jack!" Lucy rebuked her. "You know as well as I do, that old Mr Muggle's ghost used to put all the clocks in the shop back half an hour on his birthday! Or, what about Stella? Her mother's portrait literally jumped off the wall the day of her funeral and landed on the sofa! Don't you remember?"

"I suppose," Sophie said, putting the picture back on the dressing table. "I don't like things that go bump in the night. You're giving me the creeps."

"But, if it is Aunt Lilly, then there's nothing to be scared of, is there?" Lucy replied.

"I guess not," Sophie said. In spite of her regular conversations with spirits she didn't like it when they got too close in the human world!

Lucy rubbed her forehead. "I had the strangest dream. I can't remember it all now."

Sophie saw fear shoot across Lucy's eyes and she shuddered.

"It was about Alice," Lucy recalled. "I remember now. Oh! It was awful." She shivered as she relived it. "Aunt Lil was in the Abbey, but she wasn't dead. She rose out of her coffin and the choir kept singing as if it was perfectly normal! Then, Alice got into the coffin and I kept trying to pull her back out, but Jennifer started nailing the lid on, and Shilty Cunningham started praying as if Alice was dead, and I kept screaming at everyone to save Alice, but no one could hear me, and then (and this is the weirdest bit), a huge hole opened up just beneath the coffin and a massive dragon came up through the floor! Then everyone did notice what was happening and ran away screaming, but I just stayed there and tried to get Alice out of the coffin. The dragon seemed to be friendly to me. Then…" Lucy paused for a moment…

"Then what?" Sophie asked.

"...Then…" Lucy held onto Sophie's hand, "I know it was only a dream, but it was so vivid I thought it was real - which seems silly now of course, but…"

"What?"

"…I looked up and saw that all the kids had been hung from the rafters of the church, and Alice fell into the hole in the ground and I couldn't save her. Robert was there, but he was just a little boy, and I tried to get him to help me, but he just stood there eating an ice-cream, of all things. I really thought all the kids were dead and I couldn't save them!"

Sophie patted her sister's hand to reassure her, but her own heart turned cold with fear. She had not told Lucy about what Dr G had said to Robert and her about the dragon portal. This independent knowledge was confirmation that maybe there was truth in it after all. "It's okay. It was just a bad dream," Sophie said. "It wasn't real."

"No. It wasn't real," Lucy replied. "They are all okay though, aren't they? I hope it wasn't one of my portent dreams."

"All the kids are fine!" Sophie replied. "They're all playing outside."

Lucy sighed with relief. Still a bit shaken, she wanted to change the subject. "I was thinking, let's redecorate in here as soon as the snow clears. We can get Noddy to come and repaint. Then you can have this room as your own and you'll feel as if you are settled here with us. I wondered if you wanted to keep the furniture - we always loved it so! Do you remember? We used to come in here and pretend we were princesses in the Palace of Versailles!"

"I bet we could both still fit in the wardrobe!" Sophie giggled. "Are you sure it's not too soon to move Aunt Lilly's things? Don't most people leave a room for a while before clearing it out?"

"Everyone is different," Lucy said, making the bed. "And we both know Aunt Lil isn't dead to us; she's just in spirit rather than in a body. I know she would want you to be in here where you are safe, and besides, I can't stand to be maudlin. I won't be able to come in here anymore if it feels like a tomb or some kind of shrine. It's too upsetting."

"I would have thought you should have these rooms. They're bigger than yours and have the en suite and the view across London. I can take your room if you like," Sophie suggested.

"No, I want to be on the same floor as Tambo," Lucy told her. "And besides, me sharing a bathroom with my son makes more sense than you having to share with him!" Lucy hugged her sister. "And another thing!" she added. "Aunt Lil left this place to us both! I wish you would stop thinking it's mine!"

"But you do all the work here. You earn the money to keep it going." Sophie sighed.

"So?" Lucy said. "We are a team, and if one team member goes under for a while, well, we don't just walk away, do we? We rally round and help out 'til they are back on their feet!"

"The thing is, I am not sure I ever will get back on my feet," Sophie confessed. "It seems chronic fatigue is a recurring illness for some people, and I am one of those people. Even after all these years, it's not going away. I could be well for a few years and then bam - back to square one - in bed for twenty hours a day, and even if I feel okay, I'd still be sitting on my arse most of the time just trying to stave off another relapse!"

"I don't care if you sit on your arse all day, every day, for the rest of your life, as long as you are sitting on your arse with me and Tambo!" Lucy laughed. "You're not going anywhere!"

Sophie hugged her sister. "What would I do without you?"

"You'd starve in the hedgerows and become a bag lady!" Lucy teased.

Lucy put her hand on the back of her neck - it was aching with sadness and her throat hurt from crying so much.

"Here," Sophie said. "I got us another Rainbow Rescuer." She put a few drops of the coloured oils on her palms and rubbed them into Lucy's temples and neck. "This will take away the sting."

All of a sudden they could hear someone calling from the conservatory. It was Jimmy Pratt, who had finally shown up after days of being offline. Sophie sighed as Lucy went to find him.

He was standing in the kitchen area looking around, as if he had never seen a kettle or toaster before in his life.

"I'm dying for a brew! Make us one, babe. And none of that fancy herbal stuff - proper tea with two sugars," he told her. He tried to embrace Lucy but she pushed him gently away. "I can't stay long," he continued to say. "Van Ike wants to edit the film we took at the Tower. We got some great footage at the old prison. Well, some bits that will look like great footage when we edit them together. It was bloody cold in there! You got anything to eat? I'm starving! Bacon and eggs?"

Automatically, Lucy started to make him a cup of tea saying, "Do you have to edit today? I was hoping..."

"I can't stay, babe!" Jimmy interrupted. "The network want it as soon as. It's the biggest deal Van Ike's ever done. We're changing the title to Haunted or Not. Good eh! I get top billing now! I thought I would change my name - *James Hollywood* - how does that sound, eh, babe? You've got a famous boyfriend now."

"Well, it's better than Pratt!" Lucy said, sighing and handing him his tea. "I am fine, by the way, thanks for asking."

"Come on, babe!" Jimmy replied, coming to her side of the kitchen worktop and putting his arms around her from behind. He nudged himself playfully against her round bottom. "Come on, you know I love you; even if you are getting a little tubby these days. Why don't I show you how much I love you! Come and have a quick cuddle in the bedroom, eh?" He spun her around and was about to kiss her when his phone started ringing. "Got to get this, babe!" he said.

Before Lucy had finished whisking the eggs, Jimmy told her he had to go.

"But your eggs?" Lucy said, slamming the spatula down on the worktop in frustration.

"Come on, babe!" Jimmy replied, looking like a hurt puppy. "You know how important work is to me! Opportunities like this don't come round very often. I thought you understood? I can't be in two places at once, now, can I? You said you would support me. You want me to do well, don't you? Make lots of money, so I can buy you nice things? Don't wait up. Love you!" He kissed her, and then he was gone out of the conservatory into the snow, disappearing across the roofs and elevated walkways.

Lucy sat down in despair and started to cry again.

Sophie came through and made her sister a cup of tea. She sighed to herself. *Bloody love-karma!* she thought. She looked at Lucy and felt compassion welling in her heart for her sister. She tried to change her anger towards Jimmy into compassion as well - to the best of her abilities anyway - she couldn't help thinking he was a f*ckwit just the same.

Chapter 14

~ * ~

That evening, Robert had been summoned to the Little Eden Hotel for another family gathering. There he found his mother, his brother, Varsity, India, Adela and Lancelot, already seated in the à la carte dining room. Robert was surprised to see Shilty sitting there as well.

"This is a merry party!" he said sarcastically, as he sat down next to her. "What are you doing here Shilty?" he added under his breath.

"Collins invited me," she whispered back, "He thought you needed some moral support."

Lancelot caught Robert's eye and nodded to him in a gesture of solidarity.

No one said anything for a while until Jennifer began to ask Adela for some Hollywood anecdotes, but she was sorely disappointed. Adela's father, albeit a sound man for Universal Studios, had very little social contact with the stars, and preferred the company of his technical colleagues to celebrities. The table fell silent again and the awkwardness was getting just a little too much for Shilty. Although Adela did not yet know of the plans to sell Little Eden, Shilty, being Shilty, did not keep her mouth shut for long!

"So, when is the elephant in the room going to be discussed?" Shilty asked, as she took a sip of her champagne. "Let's talk about the sale of Little Eden and clear the air, otherwise, we are all going to suffocate to death."

Robert and Lancelot looked aghast that Shilty had mentioned it in front of Adela.

Adela was taken by surprise. "What do you mean the sale of Little Eden?"

Lancelot and Robert hurriedly tried to change the subject but to no avail.

"Mother and I, and our cousin Lucas, wish to sell Little Eden," Collins said finally, after being nudged by his mother several times.

"You know Lucas rather well I hear?" Jennifer said to Adela. "He is a dear boy."

"You've never met him," Robert pointed out.

They all looked at Adela for her opinion. She nearly choked on her halibut. When she had recovered she tried to find the right words. "Lucas is...well...he spends most of his time in Alaska or the wilds of somewhere saving bears or the rainforests. I'm surprised he would wish to sell Little Eden, but perhaps it's because he's never seen it. I would imagine he'll spend the money on protecting the environment." Her heart was sinking as she spoke, and she was desperate to ask how the sale might affect the Star Child Academy, but she didn't want to sound selfish.

"He stands to gain at least two billion pounds from the sale. I should think that would save a fair few black bears and plenty of trees," Lancelot told her.

Adela shook her head in dismay. "I'm sure if you invited him here he would change his mind!" She really wanted to believe it, but she knew that Lucas didn't care for buildings, and he certainly cared more about animals than humans. "You can't really want to sell, Mrs Bartlett-Hart, surely?" Adela asked.

"It is not up to me, is it?" Jennifer replied, moving some sea bass around her plate with her fork and into the langoustine drizzle. "I do not have a say in what happens in the Trust."

"Seems to me you've been saying exactly what you want and that you are just using Collins as your mouthpiece!" India goaded her.

"Collins can do as he pleases," Jennifer said meekly. "If we share the same opinion about selling Little Eden, then all well and good. I am only thinking of my family and what's best for them."

"Oh, stop with your nonsense!" India exclaimed. "How do you define family? Is it only blood that matters? Those who are alive or those who are dead? You're not thinking about Robert, me, Adela or Lancelot and you are certainly not thinking about the Little Eden residents - all of whom are family! It's all your idea and we all know it!"

"Let's not spread blame," Lancelot interjected. "Let's just stay with the facts."

"Hear, hear!" Collins agreed, holding up his wine glass towards Robert. "It's just business, eh Bobby, old chap! You don't want this old place hanging round your neck for the rest of your life. Got to move with the times! The days of aristocratic do-gooders and benefactors are over. Everyone is out for themselves nowadays. Our ancestors didn't have anything better to spend their money on back then. People aren't poor like their used to be. No one needs our help anymore."

"Collins doesn't mean we can't give a bit to charity now and again," Varsity added, trying to smooth things a little. "I like a charity ball as much as anyone else. When I was on the catwalks we did a charity fashion show every year for Africa or somewhere like that."

Robert seethed but kept quiet, not sure if he could hold onto his temper if he spoke.

"We've got to live whilst we're alive. It's time to move on!" Collins said.

"I think..." Varsity began to say, but didn't get any further because Jennifer's dander was up and she waved her fish knife at her.

"You! Keep out of it!" Jennifer scolded her.

Jennifer put her knife down with a clatter onto her plate. "Alright! I will say what I think! My oh-so-venerated ex-husband, Mr Melbourne Bartlett-Hart, left me stuck here with this Trust to look after and two young boys. Your cousin Christabelle's to blame. If she hadn't seduced him with her youth..." Jennifer paused, she hated having to even think of Christabelle. "Off he swans to America (she looked at Adela as if she was to blame for anything related to that continent) and he gave me nothing in return! All I ever got was a pittance of an allowance from the Trust. I've suffered all these years, trying to make ends meet, and I am entitled to my share of the Bartlett-Hart wealth!"

"Father had no personal money," Robert muttered. "And your allowance is hardly a pittance, Mother."

"That's beside the point!" Jennifer retorted. "I have put up with this community," she waved her hand in the general direction of the window and the street below, "These residents, for long enough! I'm sick to death of them begging for help every time they get sick and can't pay the rent. Look at that man the other day - what was his name? He came to the house, at god knows what hour, to ask Robert for one of the alms houses just because he and his wife have both got cancer. If they can't run their shop anymore that's their problem, not ours. All of them - constantly taking from us! It's time to stop this ridiculous babysitting sham once and for all. Robin, Mr Shaft, has assured me that Robert, Collins and Lucas are worth at least two-and-a-half billion each. That doesn't seem like very much to me considering the sacrifices we have all had to make."

"And what do you expect to get?" India asked her. "Half of Collins' and half Robert's share too? Shame you can't lay claim to half of Lucas's money as well!"

Jennifer seethed. She took a large sip from her glass of Montrachet Chardonnay and continued, "You should be talking with my lawyers - with Collins' lawyers I mean, not with me about it. I have no head for business and I don't claim to."

"No one may get any money!" Robert said suddenly. "I have not decided yet whether to sell!"

"You will sell!" Jennifer replied, her face reddening.

"Come on, it's two to one, old chap!" Collins added confidently. "If you challenge us, Shaft, Pencill and Push say there will be no problem getting a legal settlement. You know Father wasn't popular with the establishment after he became a damned hippy. You will have no supporters outside the walls."

Robert looked at Lancelot for reassurance but none came.

"I'm afraid Collins is right," Lancelot agreed. "Your father's way of doing things after the war, was not always appreciated. The establishment always thought he was a commie, you know that!"

"Isn't Little Eden under some kind of preservation order? I mean, surely the government wouldn't want it to be destroyed?" Adela asked hopefully.

"The government are constantly trying to take away our legal and tax privileges," Lancelot told her. "Having our own town is almost like having our own country, and that does not make us popular with, well, with anybody really!"

"I would like to know how much Mr Shaft stands to gain for arranging everything? He seems to be very eager to help you," India said, a little more calmly.

"Never you mind!" Jennifer replied.

"I believe Shaft, Pencill and Push want twenty percent of the profit if it's settled quickly, and forty percent if it goes to court," Lancelot announced.

A gasp went up from everyone - except Jennifer.

Collins looked at his mother in astonishment. "Mother!" he exclaimed. "They want forty percent?" He looked at Robert in desperation. "Come on, old chap, just say you'll sell. Even I don't want Shaft to get his hands on that much!"

"Robert will sell," Jennifer repeated.

"If it goes to court I assure you it will take at least twenty years to resolve," Lancelot told her.

"Whatever do you mean?" Jennifer demanded.

"I will see to it that it costs you hundreds of millions of pounds to fight your case, and that it goes on for as long as possible. I intend to do a 'Jarndyce'[13] on it, and by the end of it all, we will all be bankrupt!"

[13] *Bleak House*, Charles Dickens, 1852-3, Bradbury & Evans

At that, Jennifer threw down her napkin and excused herself to powder her nose. She insisted Varsity accompany her. Varsity returned within a few minutes explaining that Jennifer had a headache and was going home.

The family meal had come to an end!

~ * ~

Robert was getting into the lift as Lancelot caught up to him. "Before you go," Lancelot said. "I have the results of the research you asked for about Melanie Humphreys." As the lift began to descend Lancelot took a folded piece of paper from his pocket and handed it to Robert.

It read:

Little Eden Abbey Magistrates Hearing No. 8149. Presiding: The Honourable Sister Mary J. 21st day of March, the year of our Lord 1878.

Case: Mrs Robert Bartlett-Hart, nee Melanie Humphreys, vs. Little Eden

Verdict: Guilty of murder on three counts; John Quick, Goods Carrier, lately of Dicks Mount; Henry Slight, Pure-Collector, of Balls Green; Mr Leonard Hand, of Swallow Passage, London.

Mr Robert 'Bobby' Bartlett-Hart, husband of the accused, requested leniency of sentence, recommending deportation in a voluntary capacity, with issue. Mr Bartlett-Hart to pay annuity and incur costs of transportation.

Robert looked shocked. "She murdered three men?"

"It would appear that way," Lancelot frowned.

"Good god! No wonder she was deported!" Robert exclaimed.

Lancelot handed Robert another small piece of paper - it was a cutting from the York Herald from 1879:

We learnt this week from our London contemporaries of the greatest excitement in that city, arising from an inquest held at Little Eden Abbey before Judge Sister Mary and an intelligent jury of five, touching the suspicious deaths of three men. The London press has refrained from publishing full details of the proceedings to avoid public gossip in deference to its upstanding and greatly beloved citizen Mr Robert 'Bobby' Bartlett-Hart, who has had the misfortune to be inadvertently caught up in this gruesome affair.

It transpired that the first victim, John Quick, originally of Dicks Mount, was reported missing by his wife, in 1875. Mr Quick's horse and cart were found in Little Eden market shortly after his disappearance, but his body was never discovered.

The suspect, Mrs Melanie Bartlett-Hart, née Miss Melanie Humphreys, was apprehended by a Little Eden patrol officer, P. G. Tips, January of this year, when during a house clearance of Mr Quick's former abode, correspondence of a most lascivious nature was found in a wooden box, which had been hidden under the floorboards of Mr Quick's former bedroom. The letters revealed that several years earlier, Miss Melanie had been secretly married to Mr Quick and had three wretched children by him. The infants had been placed in a foundling hospital.

The death of Mr Henry Slight is also attributed to Miss Melanie, he being a neighbour of Mr Quick. Landlady, Mrs Hettie Buttle, sworn, told the court that she had seen him often with Mrs Melanie and that he had disappeared on the same night as Mr Quick. Mrs Buttle had not reported Mr Slight's disappearance to the authorities as she considered him to have fled the area with Mrs Melanie on the account of her being already married.

In the case of Mr Leonard Hand, of Swallow Passage, his disappearance was discovered on the 1st of January of this year. A housemaid at the Bartlett-Hart residence, Miss Annette Curtin, sworn, said she remembered seeing her mistress, walking out into the Pleasure Gardens around ten o'clock on the evening of the 20th of December last. Miss Curtain reported that her mistress had returned to the house soaking wet and covered with mud. Another servant, a Miss Polly Kettle, sworn, told that, on that same evening she had helped her mistress dispose of soiled clothing on which there were splatters of blood, and to being sworn to secrecy on the matter.

Mrs Melanie was found guilty of the manslaughter on all counts, based on the holy visions of the jury, as well as sworn testimony, as is common practice in Little Eden. It was established that the bodies of the three men were disposed of in the lake but their remains have yet to be recovered.

Mrs Melanie and her three issues, by Mr Quick, are to be deported within the year. Mr Bartlett-Hart is said to be stricken down by the event and may not live to see out the year.

"I don't know if that makes me feel better or worse!" Robert said to Lancelot. "In my past life regression session with Silvi earlier today, I saw that Bobby believed her to be guilty and he was very shaken by the whole thing. I hoped maybe he had been wrong about it all. I still hoped for the best. I'm just glad in this lifetime, as my mother, she can control her temper better or I might be the next one in the lake!"

Lancelot laughed. "Your mother flies off the handle, but she isn't a murderer."

"No, not in this lifetime, but she was in that one!" Robert said. "Sophie's right. Finding out what we did in past lives is not always a good idea. I won't ever be able to think of her just as my mother again. I'll always see Melanie too. It's distressing."

Lancelot nodded in agreement.

"You'd better organise dredging the lake," Robert decided. "See if the three poor chaps are in there. Sophie believes if we find out what happened and can dispel the energy from that past life perhaps it'll stop my mother in this one. Maybe a funeral or a blessing for at least one of them might help?"

Lancelot frowned. "I don't believe in past lives, but I understand the need to lay things to rest. Closure I would call it."

Robert walked home alone and Lancelot took the lift back up to the restaurant to find Adela and India deep in conversation. Adela was shaking her head saying, "Lucas has a good heart, but with him the planet comes first and humans second. No! I correct that statement! All other animals come before humans too. He would rather feed a hungry dog than a hungry human."

Lancelot sighed as he sat down. "How do you feel about the idea of selling Little Eden?" he asked Adela. "Sorry you had it sprung on you so suddenly."

"My opinion doesn't matter really, does it?" Adela said, in a slightly sad tone. "I'm sorry the Star Child Academy won't open now. I guess I'll have to move back to the States. I was looking forward to being here for a long time to come."

"Were you?" Lancelot said and smiled.

"Do you think you might be able persuade Lucas to see sense?" India asked her.

Adela shrugged her shoulders. "I haven't seen Lucas for years, not since his mother's funeral." She thought for a minute. "I might be able to talk to his sister though. Faberge and I still send Christmas cards and we friended each other a while back. She might have some influence over him."

"Anything you can do is welcome!" India said.

"You must promise to keep this a secret from everyone else," Lancelot said seriously. "Only a handful of us know about the sale and if it were to get out…"

"Goodness me yes!" India interjected. "If the residents got to know about it there would be chaos. I dread to think what some of them might do! Their whole lives are on the line and we are hoping to stop all this nonsense before it goes much further!"

Adela nodded in agreement.

"We don't want riots in the streets," Lancelot smiled sadly.

India smiled too, but it was more to do with the fact that she had suddenly noticed how Lancelot was looking at Adela. He was love struck and no mistake! India excused herself for the evening and left them alone together. She chuckled to herself as she went down in the lift. She had not seen Lancelot in love for a long time. She thought for a moment and decided that she had never seen Lancelot in love, ever!

~ * ~

Back at No.1 Daisy Place, Sophie had been in bed for hours, but the chronic fatigue often meant that sleeping at night was difficult, no matter how exhausted she was. She had palpitations and felt waves of fear running through her. She downed some flower remedy, which helped a little, but she still felt agitated. She pulled her jeans on over her pyjamas and threw on her quilted winter coat. She climbed out of her window onto the roof. She looked over London for a few moments - the tops of the tallest buildings illuminated the dark sky. *I need to get away from here*, she thought.

She made her way across the roof terrace and went down the few steps that led her onto Sumona's balcony above the Tea Emporium. It was lit up with white fairy lights and the usually green topiary now looked like huge snowballs. She headed along the balconies and then went down some narrow stone steps, which brought her to just outside Fudge & Bunnies Ice-cream Parlour.

Sophie was caught up in a wave of depression, and when it was this strong there seemed no way out. She did not really know where she was going and found herself heading down Lady Well Walk. She made her way through the Abbey cloisters not even noticing how the canary yellow jasmine flowers shone like tiny stars in the lamp light or how the scarlet berries on the conical holly trees peeked through the white snow. Finally, there she stood at the foot of Hilda-Guards Tower.

Looking up, Sophie could see the 11th Century stone tower looming down over her. The tower, in sunshine and in summer, looks friendly enough. Its four grey walls, making one grey tower, overlook a magnificent garden of flowers. Tonight, it stood silent and still, austere and forbidding in the pale moonlight. The mossy stones were dressed in dusty white frost and no flowers graced the frozen ground, but from a high stained glass window shone rainbows of light onto the flagstones below.

For those in the know, there is always a key hidden under a stone, that unlocks the solid wooden door into the Tower. The vestibule is always lit by safety lights which constantly give off a soft glow, even when the Tower is deserted. Sophie felt a little apprehensive, all alone, late at night, climbing the shadowy spiral staircase as far as the first floor. She stepped into a large, almost empty room. A beam of bright moonlight flooded through the close casement windows illuminating the bare wooden floor boards and the empty fireplace, blackened with age-old soot.

All of a sudden, the clang of the church clock took her by surprise! Twelve doleful dongs reverberated around the Tower. A cloud crossed over the moon and plunged her into darkness. She thought she saw someone at the window - but how could it be? Maybe it was just a trick of the light? Sophie felt a crawling sensation over her skin and the aura of an invisible force creep up behind her. She gripped, in terror, the only thing in the room - the long oak table.

Then she heard someone breathing over her shoulder and she was paralysed with fear. She wanted to scream! To run! She wanted to get away but she could not. Her scream was silent. Her knees weakened, making her cling to the table even tighter. She wanted so desperately to say the Lord's Prayer - to dispel the dark forces from around her - but she found that she could not even recall the first two lines! Her mind was blank! She struggled to recall any invocation of pure white light to banish the unknown spirit from the room. All she could muster was to call out, in her head, to Aunt Lilly.

Within seconds, the sensation of dread was gone and a wave of comfort relaxed her body. She could breathe again.

"Why me?" she whispered. She looked around the room and knew that the spirit had retreated.

"Life is hard enough!" she said to no one. "Never mind you lot out there, scaring the crap out of me on a regular basis. Honestly, I can't go anywhere these days!" She sighed with relief that the light had cleared the evil presence and she would have sat down but there were no chairs in the room.

When she had regained her courage, Sophie wanted to go home, but her feet seemed to want to climb further up the Tower. She wound her way up the stone staircase, passed the next two floors and up into the turret, where the steps became narrower and narrower and the light faded away. Reaching the top, she stepped out onto a flat area of lead roof, which was lit by an old-fashioned coaching lamp, the light from which twinkled across the sheets of unblemished snow, covering the whole roof with a glimmering lustre. There was no sign of human life having been up there, only some tiny, sharply cut, bird footprints scattered randomly around. A stray cat had also padded along the top of the south wall. In the light of a bright moon she looked across the rooftops, which sparkled like millions of tiny diamonds in the moonlight. She could make out the silent shadows of the occasional person walking in the tree-lined streets, and of infrequent cars going slowly by, over on Castle Street. In the distance, the World Peace Centre gave out a cosy, mellow glow from some of its windows, as if lighting the way to sanctuary for a weary traveller.

Sophie shivered as a jet-black crow flew overhead and landed on the very pinnacle of the witch's hat turret. Its loud squawking made her cringe. *Black magic is about*, she thought, but she tried to ignore it.

Moving to the edge of the roof and looking down to the icy ground far below, her body felt light, empty, cold, sharp and numb all at the same time; yet she was also bristling with energy. The frozen flagstones seemed to invite her to join them. She just gazed at the ground beneath and began to notice the thoughts floating in and out of her mind…*there's nothing to live for. You will never be well enough to work again. There is no cure for what you have. No one believes you are ill, they all just think you are lazy and that it's all in your head. No one wants you, you're a burden now. Little Eden is over. You are homeless and penniless. Without the Café, Lucy won't even be able to support you. Everything is lost. Just go.*

The ground began to look as if it was calling her more and more. It was as if the earth itself was holding out an invisible hand to pull her to her death.

Suddenly, she felt her mind switch…*but what about Lucy and Tambo? What if they found me all mashed up on the pavement? They would be devastated. Lucy would blame herself. What if Tambo was traumatised and needed therapy the rest of this life? What about Robert? What if he could save Little Eden if I helped him?*

But, in an instant, her thoughts switched back to despair again…but, how can you help him? You are useless. You are a burden. Everyone would be better off without you to look after as well. Just go home. Go to Aunt Lilly, you'll be safe with her on the other side.

Suddenly, she jumped and let out a piercing scream!

Chapter 15

~ * ~

"What the F**k!" Sophie cried out loud, holding her hand to her chest. "Robert! You scared the crap out of me!"

"Sorry!" Robert said, coming over to the parapet. "What are you doing up here?"

"What are you doing up here?" Sophie responded, her heart still pounding in her ears.

"I asked first!" Robert laughed. "What are you doing up here?"

"I came for a walk. I couldn't sleep!" Sophie said. "You?"

"Same! I noticed the door was open," Robert replied. He peered down over the battlements. "Maybe I should chuck myself off?"

"Don't joke about that!" Sophie said, in tears.

"Sorry," Robert replied, a little taken aback by her reaction. "You okay?"

"I was actually wondering what it would be like to jump off," Sophie admitted.

"Not seriously?" Robert looked shocked and concerned. He quickly put his arm through hers to make sure she didn't attempt anything further.

"I have contemplated suicide a thousand times," Sophie sighed.

"Have you? No, surely not! Really?"

"Yes, really."

"But, why?" Robert frowned.

"Why? Why do you think? I have no life, no career, no future! I've struggled for years to hold down a job through pain and constant fatigue. Now, I can't seem to keep fighting back. I'm so tired of being tired. I don't have the youthful optimism anymore. I can't work enough to earn a living or save for a pension. I'm a waste of space."

"No you are not!" Robert told her, and put his arm around her - partly to comfort her and partly to keep a tight hold of her.

"Really?" Sophie said. "Every day is a struggle, Robert. Chronic fatigue makes even the smallest task a battle! Every morning, when I wake up, I don't know how I will feel from one minute to the next. Sometimes, I am too tired to lift my arms above my head to wash my hair. My body aches and everything is too loud and harsh around me. It's like having 'flu 24/7 but without the snot!"

Robert grinned at her. "See, you can still make a positive out of a negative!

No one wants all that snot as well! Besides, you are getting better," he said hopefully. "You stay awake for several hours at a time now. You couldn't even have walked these few hundred yards from the Café to the Tower when you first came back here last November."

"I can do it today, but I may not be able to do it tomorrow," Sophie explained. "That's the point! It comes and goes. It feels like a life sentence."

"I'm sorry I didn't...I can't understand," Robert said, genuinely concerned. "I can't even begin to imagine what it must be like. You were really going over the edge?" Robert asked, looking down to the ground which seemed so far below.

Sophie shook her head. "Sometimes I stare at the pills, or the knife, or the edge and then I remember Lucy and Tambo, and I used to think of Aunt Lilly too, and all the pain and sorrow it would cause them; and then I can't do it. At that moment something switches in me and I start to come alive again, a fire ignites somewhere inside me, and I think: *I won't let the bastards win*! Whoever they are! And I live to see another day. Tonight, I was thinking about you and if I can help you save Little Eden perhaps I might stay a while longer. That's if you want to save it?"

"What I told you about losing Little Eden, that didn't that push you closer to the edge did it?" Robert asked.

"Yes, it did," Sophie admitted. "But it wasn't your fault. You had to tell us. And it's not your fault what's happening."

"I shouldn't have told you or anyone else," Robert replied. He was mad at himself for having upset those he loved. "We must keep the potential sale a secret from everyone else. You might not be the only one that the news sends over the edge. This is a serious business. I don't think I realised it at first. I think I thought it would all blow over somehow."

"Don't look directly at it and it's not there?" Sophie smiled sadly.

"Dr G says we shouldn't focus on the negative and that we have a choice to see the positive in all things," Robert said.

"Dr G lives in a buddhist centre and before that he lived in a cave in India for twenty years. He gets his food and clothes provided and can spend several hours a day in meditation. Other people do all the practical work for him. Everyone he meets defers to him, worships him even. He doesn't know what it is to live an ordinary Western life. Plus, he has been taught from being a child how to train his mind to cope with emotions, with death, with a simple life. We cannot all give up our lives and become monks...and even if I wanted to, even if I could, the buddhist centre is not a hospital, you have to be able to work for them to live there."

"I suppose you are right." Robert frowned. "But even his way of life is going to end if we sell. There will be no World Peace Centre anymore. I don't want to think about it!"

"To ignore your mother or brother and hope that they will change their minds is the easy option." She looked at him and could see he was reluctant to really face the truth. "You always take the easy route - you know you do! This time, don't you dare put it into one of your 'man' boxes! You have to face your fears, Robert! Too many people are counting on you. You have to be courageous. You must use your sword, as Alienor said."

"A sword these days is not much use," Robert replied. "If I was Richard III, I'd put them both in the bloody Tower."

"King Richard didn't put the princes in the Tower," Sophie remarked. "He tried to stop the Woodvilles from stealing the country's money and they framed him. Ironic really, that you have to do the same for Little Eden now and stop Collins and Lucas running off with the coffers." Sophie thought for a moment and added, "Richard lost the battle in the end, mind you."

"I'm not sure I will win either," Robert replied, looking down and shuffling his feet in the snow.

"Look!" Sophie said to him. "Look at Little Eden! From the north to the south, from the east to the west, this is your land Robert! This is unique! Not in the whole of the world is there a place like this left! It's a true sanctuary, with a true and good leader! This is worth saving, isn't it?"

"Is it?" Robert said, gazing out over the walled town - his eyes hardly noticing anything now. He was starting to feel dazed and numb.

"Don't you want to save it?" Sophie asked.

Robert paused and absentmindedly made a snowball.

"Well? Don't you want to save it?" she repeated.

"It's not relevant any more, though, is it?" Robert moaned, throwing the snowball off the roof.

"What do you mean?"

"This old-fashioned way of going about things - community spirit and aristocratic benefactors - it's not fashionable. It's not politically correct to lead anymore. Aristos are out of fashion. Enough of us get a bad press and we all go down with the ship. Those days are gone. No one wants a king anymore."

"Nonsense!" Sophie replied with passion. "That's what the media say to whip up fear! And, it's what people say when they don't get what they want! History shows us that people want a leader, and in the absence of a good leader - any leader will do. They will put up with tyranny and evil, as long as they are promised personal security and prosperity."

"Don't you think Little Eden is too old-fashioned though?" Robert asked.

"No, I don't!" Sophie replied emphatically. "It's a beautiful sanctuary in a very bad world."

"You make it sound rather grand and noble." Robert sighed.

"Okay then, it's just a village in the middle of London where people still give a shit about each other, the environment, justice and peace!" Sophie responded.

Robert threw another snowball off the roof and it nearly hit the unsuspecting crow, which flew off with a loud squawk. He wanted to drop Little Eden like a grenade before it went off in his hand. "I can't do it!" he suddenly exclaimed. "I can't stop Lucas and Collins from going to court and the judge is likely to let them vote against me."

"Are you giving up before you've even tried?" Sophie asked him.

"I'm tired of being the leader, Sophie, so tired," Robert said in a depressed voice. "I don't even know if I want to save Little Eden. My whole body feels weighted down by the thought of it. If I'm honest - I just can't be bothered!"

They stood for while in silence. They both felt oppressed by the colossal internal weight in their hearts, and Robert felt as if he had been dragged through a hedge backwards. "I feel strange! Suddenly, really, really depressed," Robert admitted.

"I feel as if all hope is lost and we will just walk back down those steps tonight, and you will hand over Little Eden to Collins and Lucas in the morning and that will be that!" Sophie sighed.

They stood together looking out over Little Eden, but they didn't really focus on anything. They felt as if their eyes were clouding over and everything around them felt surreal. Even the strong stone walls around them did not seem tangible any more.

A delicate, white, ring-tailed dove flew by and perched across the street on the top of the old brick dovecote. Then another, and then another, appeared out of the grey sky, as if flying out of the ether, followed by several more. The doves flocked together on the little window perches, their feathers gleaming in the moonlight. Sophie looked up and over to where they were cooing. She felt too tired to speak but found herself saying out loud, "There are no doves in the cote are there?"

"No, not since after the war," Robert said, without looking up.

"Well, there are now! Look!"

"Oh!" Robert exclaimed. But, he could not feel his surprise and he felt unamazed.

"I can hear Elvis singing!" Robert suddenly said. "In my head I mean - not really here on the roof. That song he used to sing, 'If I can Dream'."

"Oh my god, so can I!" Sophie exclaimed. Turning to Robert, her eyes wide and her heart beating faster, she said, "Robert! You're not depressed or sick of being a leader! We are under psychic attack!"

"Psychic attack?" Robert asked.

"Yes!" Sophie replied. She was already starting to feel the energy returning to her brain, and she felt as if the deep depression was lifting a little. "There was an evil presence in the Tower room just before you arrived. Then that crow came, and it was bringing me a warning, but I dismissed it. I couldn't be bothered to look at what it may be trying to alert me to! That's the nature of a psychic attack! It's sent us both to rock bottom, but now, can you feel it's lifting?"

Robert felt his heart racing although he was standing still. He began to feel his courage rising and his resolve returning.

"Oh! I hate psychic attacks!" Sophie lamented. "The trouble is, you never realise you are being attacked. You think it's your own emotions that are getting you down. Lucy always eats too much when she is being attacked by someone, and I always feel as if suicide is my only option. Most people just think it's their own fault, but sometimes it's a work colleague, an ex-lover, or false friend, who is sending them nasty thoughts, which in turn, trigger their inner fears."

Robert thought for a moment; he could feel himself regaining strength and momentum. "How odd!" he admitted. "You're right. I felt as if I had a lead weight inside me, a voice in my head was saying: *Don't fight for what you believe in, it's not worth it.* My mind kept saying: *No one wants you to keep Little Eden, no one values it.* That's so strange! Now, I'm thinking I can't believe I ever had those thoughts! Everyone who lives here values it - to them it's priceless. How could I have even contemplated giving up so easily?"

"We were under attack from the dark forces," Sophie said angrily. "They were playing on our fears. My fear is about my health and future. Yours is about whether to fight against your family and stand up for what you believe in! We talk nonsense when we are under attack." Sophie looked around the roof. "Likely it was Jennifer or your brother."

"My mother or Collins? How could they do that to us? They are not psychic!" Robert said.

"Well, I don't mean your mother has a cauldron in the attic or that Collins is messing about with his magic wand! Being psychic has nothing to do with it. Most people don't understand how powerful their thoughts can be over the airwaves. And when they are supercharged by dark forces, they become really powerful. They can make you physically ill sometimes."

"Like astral bullying?" Robert asked.

"Yes, exactly," Sophie agreed. "People often feel a wave of love from another person who can be miles away. It's just as easy to feel hate, fear or anger coming your way too."

"But how did they get into our heads so easily?" Robert asked her.

"We doubt ourselves too much - it makes us vulnerable!" Sophie replied. "I think we are going to have to be vigilant from now on. Alice, Elijah, Tambo and Blue could be very vulnerable too, as guardians of the portal."

"Let's get you back home," Robert suggested, as it began to snow again. He was not sure whether to believe Sophie or not, but astral bullying did sound plausible to him, and would explain a few things!

As Robert walked Sophie back to the Café, she asked him how his past life regression session had gone with Silvi Swan. "I don't know yet," Robert said. "I felt nothing and I've noticed no great change since this morning. It was like being asleep but not asleep. Like dreaming but not dreaming. I can't describe it really. I knew I was back in time and yet I knew I was in the here and now in Silvi's therapy room." Robert thought for a moment and tried to recall the session. "I felt heavy and relaxed, and it was a bit hard to talk at first. Silvi asked me to describe what I was seeing, but the pictures and feelings were vague."

"Who were you in that lifetime?" Sophie asked.

"I thought you would have known already," Robert smiled. "I was Bobby of course!"

Sophie smiled. "Jack will be jealous of all your women!" She paused and added, "But, maybe not so jealous of the syphilis!"

"Don't tell anyone else, will you?" Robert asked her. "It's a bit embarrassing really."

"About you being Bobby or about the syphilis?" Sophie laughed. "How did you feel, as Bobby?"

"As Bobby, I felt ever so guilty about deporting Melanie, but now I know she was a murderess after all."

"She really did kill someone then?"

Robert nodded. "Lancelot did the research and has found that she murdered three men and they are in the lake apparently. As Bobby, I wanted to protect her, but I just couldn't bring myself to let her off either. I mean it wouldn't have been right for her not to be punished at all, would it? One murder could be considered an accident but three - well, that's serial killer territory. Although I feel that as her husband in that lifetime, I should have taken better care of her."

"Well, I would say that it sounds like the karma is certainly repeating its emotional pattern yet again!" Sophie nodded. "No wonder the dark forces can take such advantage of Jennifer and you! You feel responsible for your mother, not just in this life time, but from when you were Bobby too! You have to learn to stop feeling responsible for her. If you don't, you will reincarnate over and over with the feeling that you have to look after her. You and your mother will be in a never-ending cycle of negative reincarnation."

Robert grimaced. "Oh! Good god! I hope all those other women I was buried with don't show up wanting revenge on me too!"

Sophie laughed. "Your old harem might come back to haunt you still! Who you hurt or who you love in one lifetime may well show up in another!"

~ * ~

When Robert got back to Bartlett Crescent, Shilty Cunningham was waiting for him. She was lying strategically on his bed, wearing lace underwear that was obviously a little too small for her, so that little was left to the imagination.

She seduced him.

And, dear readers, it did not take much effort I can tell you! First, she used her voluptuous and luscious body, and then, when he was relaxed and sleepy, she followed up with her sharp and brilliant mind. Oh! And, a little witchcraft, just for good measure!

"I know it's a shame your friends and the residents will lose their homes, but you would be doing them a favour really," Shilty began to say, "You know what some people are like! They get far too comfortable, and then they miss out on the life they could have had because they are too scared to do anything differently. A fresh start. That's what they all need! When you think about it - you would be giving them their freedom. I always try to see change as an opportunity to do something even better than before."

Robert didn't reply.

"If you didn't have to look after Little Eden you could look after yourself more. You deserve to be happy too." She looked into his eyes and smiled. "We could get married and have the family you always wanted!"

Robert lifted Shilty off him and sat on the side of the bed. He put his head in his hands. Shilty massaged his shoulders, and kissing his neck continued to say, "Why don't we make a clean break of things?" She wrapped her arms around him from behind and whispered in his ear, "Let's go live in the South of France, just as you always dreamed of?"

Robert was about to get up when she pulled him gently back down and kissed him. "We could be happy Robert, away from all this. You wouldn't have to worry about anything; no more meetings and legal headaches. No more people who haven't paid their rent. No more trying to raise money for this and that."

"It all sounds idyllic," Robert admitted, as he let her wrap herself around him again. "You're right!" he said, "I'm not bloody Jesus Christ!"

"Exactly! Just sell Little Eden and be done with it," Shilty whispered as she caressed him.

He kissed her warm soft lips, as if to take strength from them. Robert sighed again saying, "Stella said I should think about the legacy I would leave behind. I want my grandchildren to know I was a good man. I don't want them to think I was driven by greed."

"You are a good man Robert!" Shilty reassured him. "The best man I have ever met. It's not greed on your part. It's the residents who are being greedy - always taking from you!"

Shilty kissed him again and smiled. "I'm on your side, Robert. I just want you to be happy. Let's start a new chapter, just you and me, and leave the past and Little Eden behind us."

Robert fell asleep under Shilty's spell and she lay back on the pillows and smiled to herself in triumph.

~ * ~

The next morning Collins and Varsity were arguing in the kitchen at Bartlett Crescent.

"Damn it Varsity, I've told you before! I don't have any money left this month!" Collins exclaimed.

"But why can't we just put it on credit cards?" Varsity queried, sipping her wheatgrass shake.

"Because, old girl, we have nearly two million pounds on credit cards already and god knows how much in loans, and my brother is too tight to bail us out!"

"Don't blame Robert!" Varsity said. "It was you who promised me I could have anything I wanted if I married you. Well, I want this!"

"Yes, well!" Collins replied, trying to pour whisky from an empty hip flask into his coffee. "I may have oversold myself to you, old girl. You're the only woman I know who takes things so bloody literally!"

"If you can't afford me just say so!" Varsity complained. "You are always saying I buy too many handbags and shoes, but I only bought four pairs at the fashion show. Your mother bought ten last week in that new shop on The Old Kent Road."

She started the blender again. Collins had to shout to make himself heard. "But why do you have to buy them straight off the bloody catwalk? Can't you at least buy them in a shop? That last pair was twenty thousand pounds!" The blender stopped but Collins was still shouting - the last few words came out at top volume - "What were they made of? Solid f**king gold?"

"I'll go right now if I'm so much trouble to you!" Varsity pouted.

"Now look here, old girl," Collins told her. "You know I don't want you to go anywhere! Just wait a few months and we'll have more money than you have ever dreamt of, and you really can buy anything you want, literally! Soon! Just not right now!"

"If the money is coming soon, then what's the harm in spending it in advance?" Varsity argued.

"Come on, old girl!" Collins said, smiling. "Don't pout! You know I can't resist your pout!" He came and put his arms around her waist and pulled her against him. "You love me, don't you?" He lifted her onto the worktop and opened her dressing gown.

"You promised me you would take care of me, remember?" Varsity giggled.

"And I will!" Collins replied, as he looked up at her. "I always take very good care of you, don't I?"

They suddenly pulled apart from each other as Shilty came into the kitchen wearing one of Robert's shirts like a badge of honour.

Robert was doing laps in the pool on the roof, which was gloriously warm in contrast to the freezing snow surrounding it, and he was blissfully unaware of the machinations going on downstairs behind his back!

Collins smiled at Shilty and went to sit in the orangery, hiding himself behind the morning newspaper, with a cup of coffee.

Varsity beckoned to Shilty to join her. "I don't know about you," she said, "But, I don't want them to sell all of Little Eden, do you? I always dreamed of my son inheriting this place. I presume you did too?"

Shilty looked at her in amusement. "I'm not the maternal type," she replied.

"Oh, neither am I," Varsity agreed. "But nannies and boarding schools are a godsend when it comes to children. I have already put our name down for Gordonstoun."

"Are you pregnant?" Shilty whispered.

Varsity nodded and smiled. "I haven't told anyone else yet. I did so want my boy to be a Bartlett-Hart like Collins. But without Little Eden, who are the Bartlett-Harts?"

"This place is a noose around their necks," Shilty replied. "I wouldn't wish the running of this place on my worst enemy. It's a money pit! You know that Robert has no money of his own? He doesn't even take his full allowance. He uses most of it to help the charities. He's a fool when it comes to a good sob story."

"That's what I mean! Exactly!" Varsity replied. "I thought, if Robert could keep the charities then maybe he would agree to sell the rest."

"Maybe? That's not a bad idea!" Shilty said thoughtfully. "Robert might consider that as a compromise and be more likely to sell quickly."

"But Collins said his mother would never go for it. It's all got to be sold," Varsity frowned.

Shilty smiled. "Leave it to me. There may be something that can be done!"

Varsity went to get a shower, feeling confident that she might be able to make both Collins and Robert happy after all, whilst still getting the money she needed.

Collins came into the kitchen area to refill his coffee, and brushing up against Shilty from behind, he let the fingers on one hand stray of their own accord, whilst he filled his cup with the other. Shilty managed to move away from him just in the nick of time as Robert came through the door, looking serious.

Shilty kissed him and whispered, in his ear, "Coffee? Robbie, darling!"

But Robert was in no mood this morning for any kind of shenanigans.

"I have a busy day!" he told her and gave Collins a black look.

"But, last night!" Shilty reminded him. "And this morning! I thought we were..."

"What?" Robert snapped at her.

"Do you want me to go back to Clive instead?" she asked him with a sullen look.

Robert shrugged. "Do what you want Shilty - you usually do. I have bigger things on my mind right now." Robert was surprised at his sudden change of heart regarding Shilty and Little Eden. During his swim he had felt something switch in his brain (just as he had on the Tower with Sophie). He now felt much more confident about wanting to keep Little Eden.

He had not yet, dear readers, equated his sudden subconscious switching to and fro with spells, psychic attacks and also with the past life regression he had had the day before, which was starting to work its magic!

"See you later?" Shilty called to him, as he absent-mindedly left for the office.

Shilty turned around and grinned at Collins, who had gone back to pretending to read his paper. "You see!" she said, sidling up to him and leaning against the table. "I am trying to get Robbie to do what we want, just as I said I would!"

Collins smiled and put down his paper. He began slowly unbuttoning her shirt. Kissing her, he said, "Let's see if there is something I can do that will make you try even harder shall we!"

Chapter 16

~ * ~

Sophie had been asleep pretty much for the whole of the next day, when she was violently awoken by shouting and screaming echoing through the square. She jumped up and looked out of the window but could see no one on the roof. So, she pulled on some clothes and headed downstairs. When she reached the Café it was empty and quiet - the last customers and staff having gone home for the evening.

Suddenly, Tosha came running inside to a backdrop of raised voices and some general yelling. Johnathon Grail followed her a few seconds later, holding a shaking Minnie against his shoulder, and they were followed in by a tearful Linnet. Miss Adela Huggins brought up the rear, on Jack's arm, looking harried and flustered.

"Fetch some water!" Johnathon told Tosha. "And, put some of that flower essence stuff in it you all take around here. Minnie's in shock!"

"I'm absolutely fine," Minnie said, rubbing her bruised elbow and knee. "Luckily, I fell into a pile of snow, which stopped me banging my head too hard against the wall." She laughed - somewhat half-heartedly.

"What on earth happened?" Sophie asked. "What's wrong with everyone these last few days? All this falling over! Was it an accident? Did you slip on the ice?"

Minnie shook her head and looked over at a crying Linnet.

"Make some strong English Breakfast tea would you, Tosha?" Sophie suggested. "With plenty of sugar!"

"I was on my way home," Tosha told her, as she went behind the counter to make the tea. "I not get further than the corner when I see Minnie grappling with a huge man!"

"Grappling?" Sophie asked, intrigued.

"She was attempting a citizen's arrest!" Adela explained proudly. She was in awe of her new friend.

"Please someone, tell me what is going on!" Sophie asked again.

Johnathon took out his phone and started making notes. "Yes. Tell us exactly what happened, and I'll call the police if necessary."

"Adela and I were just one our way back from the gym," Minnie began to say. "Linnet was in her shop as usual and as I - we - came down Rose Walk..."

…"There was a man looking through Linnet's shop window!" Adela interrupted.

"Yes!" Minnie nodded. "The man was standing, looking through Linnet's window, and I recognised him, so I yelled for him to stay put…"

…Adela enthusiastically interrupted again; "She shouted, 'Oy! You! Stay where you are! citizen's arrest!"

"He started to run - so I jumped on him!" Minnie explained (as if that was what everyone did in those circumstances). "And I almost had him too!" She frowned. "But I slipped on some ice and lost my grip. Next thing I knew, he was gone, and I was on my back in a pile of snow!"

"I heard the screams but by the time I got out onto Rose Walk he'd gone," Jack said. "I ran down the passageway, but Castle Street was so crowded I couldn't have made him out, even if I knew what he looked like!"

"She was so brave!" Adela added, gladly taking the cup of tea that Tosha offered her. "What's that saying: Judge me by my size, do you? You should not. For someone so petite Minnie, I wouldn't want to mess with you!"

"Why would someone looking through shop window make you jump on them?" Tosha asked Minnie, handing her a jar of cookies. "Window shopping is normal. Linnet's windows are famous. People come to look in window all the time!"

"He wasn't window shopping!" Minnie responded, reaching out to hold Linnet's hand, who was still in tears. "The man was Marcus Finch!"

Everyone looked at each other in concern. Adela and Tosha just looked puzzled.

"Who's Marcus Finch?" Tosha asked.

"He's Linnet's ex-husband," Sophie said in hushed tones (as if Minnie and Linnet were not supposed to hear, but of course they could). "He's supposed to be behind bars. He was put away seven years ago for nearly killing Linnet!"

"Are you sure it was Marcus?" Johnathon asked Minnie. "I mean, if he's in prison, perhaps you were mistaken?"

"Well, he's escaped or maybe he was let out early for some reason!" Minnie replied, her temper starting to rise at Johnathon's suggestion she didn't know Marcus Finch when she saw him. "It was definitely him! I'd recognise him a mile off. I saw his ugly mug enough at the trial. Believe me, I've tried to forget him: we both have. But, once you have been up close to that bastard, you can never forget him, worst luck!"

Jack put his arm around Linnet, who just could not stop crying and was running out of tissues. "We will find him before he can come back," Jack promised her. "Now, you need to get somewhere warm and safe until we figure out if this Marcus chap is out of prison or not."

"Come upstairs!" Sophie suggested. "You'll be safe here. Lucy and Tambo will be back soon."

"I must get Alice!" Linnet said suddenly. "She's at Elijah's." A look of absolute horror flashed across her face. "What if he has already found Alice?"

"No, I'm sure he couldn't have!" Sophie said reassuringly, but not quite certain of herself. "Does he even know what she would look like at this age anyway?"

Linnet sighed with relief. "No, I suppose not; she was only a few months old the last time he saw her."

"Although, he might have found her through the inter…" Adela began, but then trailed off and said, instead, "No, I'm sure Alice is safe and sound!"

"I'll go and get the kids from the Sprotts'," Jack offered.

Johnathon went off to make his security report and to search for Marcus.

"This is a fine welcome for you, Adela!" Minnie said, as they went upstairs. "These kinds of things hardly ever happen here in Little Eden. You've only been here a couple of days and this is what you witness! I promise, it's generally safer around here than anywhere else in London. It's just psycho ex-husbands that are the problem. Ouch!" Minnie held her side. "I think I hurt a rib or two."

Alice, Tambo and Joshua were brought back to the Café in one piece and went to play in Tambo's room.

Minnie took some arnica to help reduce the bruising, and with the help of some flower remedy and Sumona's blend of valerian and passionflower tea, she finally calmed down.

Linnet however, wouldn't accept any help and did not calm down. In fact, she got progressively more anxious and fearful. "We can't stay here!" Linnet kept saying with wildness in her eyes. "Where can we go? Where can we go?" She kept repeating the words over and over, wringing a tea towel in her hands.

"Come and stay at mine," Minnie offered.

Linnet shook her head. "It's too close! We have to get away! As far as we can!"

"Wait a few hours," Minnie said, trying to calm her down. "If they find Marcus, surely they'll put him away again. He can't have gone far."

"He could be anywhere!" Linnet exclaimed. She started looking around the room as if she expected to see him jump out of the refrigerator.

Sophie felt a shiver down her spine. She had to agree that Marcus could be absolutely anywhere. Although, not in the refrigerator, or at least she hoped not!

"If he hasn't escaped, he might be on parole," Adela suggested. "But then, why would he risk violating his parole?"

"Because he's a f*ckwit!" Minnie replied sharply. "He is stupid and thick and…" Minnie trailed off because it had set Linnet off crying again.

"Until Johnathon reports back, I suggest we all just stay here," Sophie said. "Jack will go for a takeout and we can all be safe up here together."

Johnathon reported back later that evening. "Bad news, I'm afraid," he told them. "Marcus was released three months ago. The police say he would have the right to file charges against Minnie for assault, if we found him. So, we should keep quiet in case Minnie could be arrested."

"I was preventing crime!" Minnie said indignantly.

"There were no other witnesses, so it's your word against his, and you jumped on him!" Jonathon told her.

"So, a crazy bastard can just walk up to his ex-wife and do whatever he likes?" Minnie exclaimed in despair and anger. "A man who has already tried to kill her years before, and been jailed for it, can just turn up wherever and whenever he likes, and she can't even defend herself? You're saying we can't defend ourselves against him?"

Johnathon nodded. "That is the law at the moment. Potential victims have little protection I'm afraid, until they are injured or dead. It's crazy, but that's the way it is; and even here in Little Eden we cannot lock him up for looking through a shop window."

"I saw it!" Adela protested. "I am a witness!" She paused and thought for a moment and then added, "Although I have to say, truthfully, that he was just standing there and Minnie did just jump on him, and if she hadn't slipped on the ice she would have had him in a head lock on the floor. And, I don't know if it was Marcus or not, having never seen him before in my life. Sorry, I guess I wouldn't hold up much as a witness, would I?"

"So, he has to virtually kill someone, or even actually kill someone, before anything can be done?" Minnie said in despair.

"Pretty much!" Johnathon nodded with equal dismay. "But, in Little Eden, we do have some old protection laws that you don't get elsewhere. I'll check with Lancelot, see if we can try and enforce one or more of them. I think the best idea is that we post Cubby Mayhew outside your shop, as a deterrent, during the day. And it would be safer if you can be either here or at Minnie's in the evenings until we figure out what is going on. Maybe we can find Marcus and warn him off."

"If I see him, I'll warn him off alright!" Jack said. "If the evil bastard comes within a hundred yards of the place, I'll…"

…"You'll call me or the police!" Johnathon interjected. "No vigilantes please - or one of you may end up behind bars! I will tell Shooter Graham to be on the alert with the CCTV tonight and get Cubby to patrol the streets. Do you have a photo of Marcus we could have?"

Linnet shook her head. "I took nothing but the clothes I was standing up in when I left. I never went back."

"There may be a photofit of him or a photo of him from the papers at the time?" Minnie suggested.

"I'll check into it," Johnathon said kindly. "Now, just try and relax and get some rest. We will keep you safe."

"Adela, you and Joshua can stay here tonight too, if you'd like," Sophie told her. "Jack will stay with us, won't you Jack?

Jack nodded. He quite liked the idea of playing bodyguard to Adela Huggins! But his daydream was thwarted when Johnathon suddenly said, "I'll take you home Adela. Make sure you are safe."

"Yeah, I'll be safe at home," Adela said. "After all, this Marcus doesn't know me or Joshua. Thank you Johnathon, please take us home." She put her long sleek arm through Johnathon's muscular one and smiled at him.

Jack grimaced in annoyance.

Sophie saw his look and giggled. "You're going to have plenty of competition for Adela, Jacky boy! Better get used to it," she whispered.

"Very funny!" Jack replied and trundled off to see that all the doors and windows were locked.

By nine o'clock Tambo and Alice were ready for bed. "What happened today?" Tambo asked his aunt Sophie. "Why are Linnet and Minnie having a sleepover as well as Alice?"

"Nothing to worry about!" Sophie said. "It's a girly sleepover, that's all! Now, you get a good night's sleep."

Tambo could feel something was not right and asked, “Can we do the bubble? I feel as if I need the bubble tonight.”

Sophie smiled. “Of course we can!”

Tambo lay down on the top bunk and Sophie sat with Alice on the bottom bed. She waited ‘til they were both snuggled down, then she gave them both a rose quartz crystal to pop under their pillows, and then she said in a calm and quiet voice, “Close your eyes and visualise all that I say. By the end, you will fall into a deep and refreshing sleep, safe and sound, and have happy and joy-filled dreams.”

Sophie began to say a guided meditation, in slow, hushed and peaceful tones, which, dear readers, goes something like this:

‘Lying comfortably, feel the pillow beneath your head, let yourself sink down into it…feel the soft blanket over you and snuggle down into your bed…start to focus on your breath now… feeling your chest gently rising and falling……your breath is rising and falling……rising and falling……. feel your breath slowing a little now….rising and …falling…and, as you let your breath reeelax…….your breathing finds its own rhythm and you can let it go……your breath is becoming softer and quieter now, slower and gentler……softly focus upon your feet and feel them getting heavier and heavier……now, your legs…they too are starting to feel heavier and heavier……and now your whole body sinks heavily into the bed…your whole body feels so reeelaxed, so peeeaceful, so still……your shoulders are now relaxing, feel yourself letting go and relax into the bed……now, relax your neck……and finally, feel how your head is heavier than before and feel how it sinks deeper into your soft, comfy pillow……now, imagine that you are sitting inside a giant pink water-lily…it is so huge, it can easily take your weight and you are floating gently, safely and sleepily upon the calm and tranquil waters of the ocean of compassion……you are surrounded by a big pink bubble…inside the bubble is pure love…inside the bubble of love you are safe……now, you begin to drift into sleep and you will awaken refreshed, happy and relaxed in the morning…for now, you are going deeper into sleep…and deeper and deeper into sleep…and deeper and deeper into sleep……you are falling into deep peaceful and joyful sleep.’

Sophie then began to say a beautiful prayer that always helped her and the children to sleep:

Upon the thousand-petalled lotus, here I sit, with you, Great Goddess of Love,
Sailing upon the great Ocean of Compassion.
Safe within the mystic mountain and beneath the sacred tree,
Surrounded by the dolphin's light and the wisdom of the whales.
Here with you I am blessed, I am at peace, I am safe.[14]

Sophie let her voice trail away. The children were in the Land of Nod and she felt much more relaxed too; though a little tired from talking. *If only adults would embrace relaxation and divine energy as easily as kids do*, she thought, the world would be a better place.

Sophie returned to the living room to find Lucy, Minnie and Jack in the conservatory, discussing the day's events.

Linnet had already gone to bed, having passed out from drinking two bottles of Chardonnay to herself.

Suddenly, there was a sharp knock on the conservatory door. Everyone jumped! They looked at each other in fear, as if it might be Marcus himself, but Jack just laughed and went to open the door. "He won't knock on the door!" he told them. "It's Robert."

Everyone breathed a sigh of relief as Robert came in and asked how everyone was. He had heard the news from Johnathon, and had come round to check that Linnet and Minnie were okay.

"Don't you worry!" Robert told Minnie, as he took off his coat and boots. "We will keep you all safe in Little Eden. It is the safest place you could be. I have invoked the old sanctuary laws, Linnet will just have to fill in some paperwork and Marcus will be arrested if he even comes within ten feet of the gates, and I have ordered extra security."

"Thank you, Robert," Minnie said. "I appreciate your help and concern."

"Let's change the subject before I go to bed or I won't sleep!" Lucy suggested. "Anyone got any good news today?"

"I don't know if it's good news, but I found out something today," Sophie said. "Guess who I met in Peony Bow's new shop? Vincent Piccolo!"

"Not 'Vincent 'Rollo' from the chippy?" Lucy asked.

"The very one!" Sophie smiled. "Although, he is quite transformed. As he said himself, quite the ugly duckling into a swan. A bearded, camp and rather arrogant swan mind you!"

[14] *KT King 21st Century Prayers*, KT King, 2015

"Well I never!" Lucy giggled.

"Funny how so many residents find their way home after their travels. It's like some kind of nesting ground around here. They all come back to roost!" Minnie smiled.

"What does that signify now?" Lucy said. "There will be nowhere for anyone to come back to soon." She didn't say anymore, as she remembered that Minnie was still in the dark about the sale of Little Eden.

"You don't think Marcus's reappearance has anything to do with Melanie and the dragon portal do you, old girl?" Robert asked Sophie all of a sudden.

Sophie frowned. "I hadn't thought of that, but now you mention it - yes, I do! I get a creepy feeling that Marcus is linked to Melanie in some way." Sophie suddenly looked horrified and looked at Lucy. "Your dream!" she said. "Alice!"

Lucy thought for a moment. "Alice was dead in my dream. Yes!" Lucy cried out. "Marcus! He might try to harm Alice!"

"Dreams don't mean anything," Jack reassured her. "Besides, we don't even know for sure if this chap Minnie saw was Marcus. It was dark and it could have been a doppelganger for all we know."

"I think we should ask Jimmy to help," Lucy suggested. "If we hold a séance maybe we can talk to Aunt Lilly or Alienor again, and they could tell us what to do!"

"You know I don't like séances!" Sophie replied.

"It's late, we should all try to get some sleep," Jack suggested. "It'll all look better in the morning, it always does."

"We have the Twelfth Night party tomorrow night; that will take the sting out of everything!" Minnie suggested.

Lucy agreed, but she couldn't help thinking that bad things often come in threes!

Chapter 17

~ * ~

The next morning the snow had finally started to melt. During the night, the snowflakes had gradually turned into sleet and then into rain. Grey and brown slush replaced the pure white snow and dark, black water ran through the streets. A cold, wet wind swept around the ginnels and the houses, ominously whirling and calling as it went.

At The Daisy Chain Linnet looked as if she had hardly slept - her eyes were red and sore from crying. She was on edge, still afraid that Marcus might show up at any moment. Cubby Mayhew, one of Little Eden's security guards, was posted at the door, and he stood there all day in the rain, covered from head to toe in his dark green wax cape. He had a good view of all the alleyways in and out of Daisy Place, and he gladly made the most of the free pastries and coffee on offer throughout the day. The day went by without incident, and fortunately, with no sign of Marcus Finch.

Around dinner time, Peony Bow came over to the Café to ask if any help was needed with the preparations for the Twelfth Night Party. Lucy assured her that it was all being taken care of by the monks at the chateau. Adela Huggins was already at the flat getting ready with Minnie, India and Lucy. There were hair tongs, nail varnishes and make-up scattered around; the scent of perfume and wine filled the room. They invited Peony to join them.

Peony smiled. "I'm coming as the Marquise de Merteuil from Dangerous Liaisons," she told them. "I like a little romantic mischief!"

"Ooo, snap!" Sophie exclaimed, with a grin. "Jack is going as the Vicomte de Valmont. Perhaps there is love-karma between you two after all!"

"I may have found my Ace of Cups already!" Peony smiled.

"Your what?" India asked.

"The Ace of Cups is a Tarot card," Sophie explained.

"It means she has found the love of her life," Lucy giggled.

Sophie shrugged. "That doesn't mean it will end well!"

Lucy tushed her sister and wanted to hear more about Peony's romantic encounter.

"I always visualise good things happening to me and they do!" Peony explained. "I asked the universe to send me a man and the very next day, there he was! He saw me struggling with a box and he offered to help. He was so handsome!"

"Who is he?" Lucy asked. "I bet it was Devlin or Johnathon Grail? Or Lancelot?"

"No," Peony said. "He was called Marcus and he is moving here to Little Eden. He said he is looking for an apartment to rent."

"Wait!" Sophie said with urgency, as she flashed a look at Minnie. "Did he say what his last name was?"

"No," Peony replied, "But he sent me the most magnificent bouquet of flowers today. And, he txts me nearly every hour, just to say he is thinking about me! That's why I know he is my Ace of Cups!"

"Hold on! Hold on!" Minnie exclaimed, with fear in her voice. "Describe him to me?"

"Well," Peony began, "He is six foot at least, and has the most gorgeous brown eyes and dark brown hair. He was suited and booted to a tee. Vincent would love him as a customer. Although, no beard. Do you think you might know who it is?"

"You must never see him again!" Minnie declared.

"What on earth do you mean?" Peony responded. "Who do you think it is?"

"Did he ask about Linnet or The Daisy Chain, at all?" Sophie asked.

"No," Peony said, shaking her head.

"Promise me you won't see him or txt him again, until we find out who he is." Sophie looked sternly at Peony and repeated, "Promise me!"

"We have to go and check on Linnet!" Minnie urged Sophie, and they disappeared over the roof terrace to find her.

"Is she always like this?" Peony asked, looking at Lucy.

"I would do as Sophie asks, if I were you," Lucy said with concern. "This Marcus may turn out to be a dangerous man."

Peony laughed and shook her head. "You must have the wrong Marcus. We had such an instant and deep connection. I believe he's my twin flame!"

"I wouldn't bet on it!" Lucy smiled sadly, and suggested Peony go and get her costume.

~ * ~

The scent of hyacinths and narcissus was overwhelming as Sophie and Minnie rushed into the flower shop. They ushered Linnet into the "potting shed" area amongst the ceramic vases, metal flower buckets, reels of tissue paper and rolls of cellophane.

"It's him!" Linnet stuttered. She began to feel dizzy and sick. "It has to be him! I have to get away from here, Sophie! I have to get away! Tonight! Now! This minute. Where's Alice? Oh, my god, my chest is going to explode. Sophie, help me!"

Sophie tried her best to stay calm. "The kids are all at the World Peace Centre getting ready for this evening," she reassured her. "You could both go and stay there for a few days. You will be safe in the chateau with Dr G and the monks."

"I have to get us away from here!" Linnet exclaimed again, now looking as if she were going to pass out.

"It's okay," Sophie told her. "Breathe deeply." They began to take deep breaths together and Minnie found her a chair to sit down on. "Now, put your head between your legs, that's it! Get the blood to your head again. It's a panic attack. I know you feel as if you are going to die but you're not. It's just too much cortisol and adrenalin rushing through your system because your fear response has been triggered. Keep breathing. You are not going to die. It will subside. I promise you."

"What if he tries to kill me again? What if he tries to kill Alice?" Linnet gasped.

"If you go somewhere else he'll find you," Minnie interjected. "He found you here, so he'll find you anywhere, if he wants to. Running is not going to help long-term. We have to find a way to protect you for good!"

"But, how?" Linnet said, bursting into tears. "He always said he'd find me and he has. He won't stop 'til he's killed us both."

"Lancelot will find a way to protect you from him," Minnie told her.

Linnet shook her head in despair. "The law doesn't care."

"Well, most laws are written and decided on by men," Sophie admitted. "That's why you must not let a man bully you into submission, even if the law is on their side. Wrong is wrong and right is right and the law doesn't always know the difference. Minnie is right, if you run away every time, he will always win."

"But what if he's out there now?" Linnet cried. She looked at Sophie with terror in her eyes. "What am I going to do?"

Sophie could feel Linnet's fear coming off her in waves and was almost overwhelmed by it herself, but knew she had to try to stay calm and to think straight. "Okay, look. Cubby is still outside the shop. Right now, you are safe. I suggest you stay at the chateau with Dr G for the next few days: it will be safer there. We just need to keep you and Alice out of harm's way until we figure out how to deal with Marcus."

Linnet nodded and let Minnie help her up off the chair. "I knew this day would come! Now, it has…"

"Let's get you to the chateau," Minnie interrupted, trying to stop Linnet going further into her fear again. "Pack some things for you and Alice. I'll get Cubby to take you."

They packed a few things and Linnet was escorted to the chateau, where she was immediately welcomed, offered a lovely room and all the support she could have hoped for. It wasn't long before the peace and compassion emanating from every inch of the beautiful mansion made Linnet feel as if she was in a sanctuary and safe from Marcus inside its walls.

When Peony returned to the Café apartment with her costume, Sophie tried to warn her again about Marcus as she helped lace her into her extravagant ball gown. But, as Sophie had suspected, Peony was already under the influence of the Ace of Cups and love-karma had her firmly in its grasp.

"It can't be the same Marcus!" Peony insisted, as she let Sophie pull the laces tighter. "Just because it's the same name and they are both tall and dark-haired, that doesn't make any difference. Marcus is a common enough name!"

Sophie tried her best to convince Peony. "Johnathon will arrest him if he sets foot in Little Eden again," Sophie told her. "That won't make it easy for you to build a relationship with him, will it?"

"If he is the same Marcus," Peony replied, a little annoyed at Sophie's implying that she had fallen for a bad man, "He has done his time for his crime and maybe he is reformed. I don't believe anyone is really evil. I believe that we all have good within us. I believe everyone can change. Maybe he deserves as second chance. Everyone must be allowed to start afresh."

"I think Linnet gave him far too many chances when she was married to him," Sophie replied. In frustration, she drew the laces even tighter at the back of Peony's corset.

"He was lovely to me - that's all I know! I'll give him the benefit of the doubt. Besides, I just know the Marcus who was here with me yesterday, would never hurt me."

Sophie despaired, knowing that she could not convince Peony about Marcus at this time. Bloody karma-goggles! Sophie thought to herself. *Why can't we see the truth before it's too late? Love-karma makes fools of us all in the end.*

Chapter 18

~ * ~

With Linnet and Alice safe at the chateau everyone's thoughts were on happier things. The Twelfth Night party preparations continued to build up steam. The ballroom was festooned with white paper garlands, and silver balloons danced on the backs of chairs. Exquisitely carved silver dishes, candelabra and plates of all sizes and shapes, were displayed on white clothed tables which were set out around the edges of the room. Mrs B's Twelfth Night cake took pride of place on the top table. Or at least it did until Cedric got away from Mr T to create chaos all around him. He managed to topple three of the tables like dominos, the last of which hit the top table before anyone could reach out and save the cake. Cedric got himself and several monks covered all over in blue and white frosting!

The cake was hurriedly replaced by an impromptu sushi tower, which was, admittedly, a little unusual, but still very grand! Mrs B managed to push the Twelfth Night bean inside a salmon-skin roll and Cedric's calamity was forgiven.

By eight o'clock the candles were lit, the food was ready and the first guests began arriving, serenaded by Simeon Dander's string quartet. Robert greeted all the guests with glasses of Kir Royale and the buzz of anticipation grew and grew as more and more people arrived.

Lucy and the Café staff all trooped together through the park, looking like a right motley crew! Si and Tonbee were dressed as Neo and Trinity from The Matrix. They were particularly pleased with the swish of their long black coats, but had to take off their sunglasses as Si nearly walked into a park bench! Tosha was Buffy the Vampire Slayer but was now wishing she had put on warmer clothes, and Jack's costume sparkled in the glow of the fire torches which lit the way through the park, and he certainly stood out in the crowd. He was dressed in fine French silk decorated with gold brocade, and even managed to look gorgeous in a white powdered wig. He helped Lucy who was tottering her way along dressed as Marilyn Monroe's Lorelei Lee; although she was starting to realise that it was almost impossible to walk in such a tight dress!

"You all look marvellous!" Robert hailed them from the entrance doors. "Come on! Come in!"

Lucy looked Robert up and down and said, "I can't work out who you are? Are you Dorian Grey? No! I've got it! You're a dapper Dr Watson!"

Robert laughed. "Wrong on all counts, my dear! I'm Algernon Moncrieff from The Importance of Being Earnest and I intend to enjoy myself tonight, in spite of everything that is happening! Let's forget all our cares for tonight and 'Bunbury'[15] to our hearts' content!"

Lucy shook her head. "You're incorrigible!" she said, as she kissed him on the cheek. "Now, where's my champers?"

"Where's Sophie?" Robert asked, when he realised she was not with them.

"You know Sophie can't do big parties anymore because of the chronic fatigue," Lucy told him. "She would be exhausted with all these people and the noise. She's popping in later with Stella, just to see the cake cut and find out who will be king and queen for the night. She wants to check on Linnet as well. I hated leaving her behind, but she insisted we all come and enjoy ourselves."

The double doors to the ballroom were flanked by a champagne fountain on one side and a sparkling water fountain on the other. In the east wing there was a temporary cocktail bar. For those who wanted a quieter evening, a coffee and liqueurs bar was set up in the west wing. Everyone was in party mood and the atmosphere was ramping up. The string quartet gave way to Ginger's band which began to play Disco Inferno!

Tambo had many of his friends there, including Octavia and Finnbar Rodet, who came wearing their ballroom dance outfits. Octavia rarely went anywhere without wearing her ballroom outfit however, so it wasn't really fancy dress! Blue had never seen anyone so completely covered in sequins before and was quite taken with Octavia, following her about everywhere! Joshua Huggins had been lent a Luke Skywalker costume and had already run the battery out in his light sabre. He had also managed to lose himself in the massive network of corridors and rooms, and it had taken Tambo and Alice over half an hour to find him again!

Alice was, of course, her namesake, Alice in Wonderland, and Tambo had chosen this year to come dressed as Legolas from Lord of the Rings. Elijah had decided to be Obi Wan Kenobi. Blue was a little puzzled by the idea of dressing up but he embraced it admirably and with gusto, dressing up as Yoda. Although, he found the costume a little hard to walk in! He waddled about, following his new friends and copying them as much as he could, whilst picking up English words by the dozen. The kids ran about

[15] *The Importance of Being Ernest*, Oscar Wilde, 1895

and hid under tables, danced, chased each other, and by nine o'clock were so excited there was no way they were going to bed any time soon!

Sophie arrived with Stella at about half-past nine, and because of their late arrival, Stella made quite an entrance wearing a pink gossamer ball gown which looked like spun sugar. It was Stella's privilege to start the evening's crowning ceremony which began with the cutting and eating of the Twelfth Night cake. Stella gave a short speech, thanking everyone for coming, telling them that they had raised thirty thousand pounds towards the edible gardens for the new school. She cut the cake, playing along and pretending that it was perfectly normal to present a cake made out of sushi! Everyone waited eagerly to find out who would be crowned king and queen.

"It's me!" Shilty Cunningham shouted. "It's me!" She slinked forward through the crowd in her red satin dress (she was Jessica Rabbit), kissed Robert as she passed by him and went up to the front of the room for her coronation. She sat happily upon her throne, sceptre and orb in her hands. "I declare my king for the evening shall be…" Shilty paused and pretended she hadn't chosen yet, looking around the room. Most of the men hoped she would choose them. Some winked, some smiled, some blew her a kiss to try and tempt her to pick them. Her eyes met Collins' who had just arrived at the back of the ballroom with Varsity and Jennifer. She smirked at him, but then said to the eager crowd…"I choose Robert Bartlett-Hart to be my king!"

Robert, rather reluctantly, went to join her on the podium, and Stella placed a crown upon his head. From his elevated position he caught sight of his brother and his mother and frowned. "I didn't think they would have the nerve to come here tonight," he whispered to Shilty.

"Family is family, Robert!" Shilty whispered back. "This is just a minor falling out: by the end of the night you will all be back to normal." Robert looked at her with a mixture of amazement and contempt, but they both kept smiling and waving to the guests, who bowed and paid homage to their sovereigns - just until midnight of course!

Shilty was, perhaps, the best and the worst choice for such a high position of authority. She knew how to play games all right but didn't really have a stop button. Tage, Johnathon and Devlin cut a fine dash as the Three Musketeers and Shilty demanded they show allegiance to her by bringing her drinks and kissing her feet on a regular basis!

"I think Shilty is in her element," Sophie said, standing away from the crowds on the mezzanine floor with India, Stella, Mrs B and Peony.

"Shilty Cunningham is a woman who takes what she wants from life and I don't blame her!" India replied. "She has more balls than most of the men I have ever met!"

"She copes with life by taking it by the balls - that's for sure!" Sophie giggled.

"I always wanted to have a booty like that! She must be a size fourteen at least!" Peony commented. "Women think it's good being a size eight like me, but men are round her like a honey pot!"

"We always want to be what we are not," Stella mused. "You are all beautiful in your own ways. Men are drawn to honey but that's not saying much - so are flies!" They all laughed, and Sophie went to find out how Linnet was doing.

Linnet had not come out of her room all evening and Minnie had stayed with her. Sophie persuaded Minnie to join the party and have some fun. She promised to facetime Linnet so that she could see everyone's costumes.

Johnathon and Lancelot went upstairs to look in on Linnet about eleven o'clock. She was asleep at last, thanks to the help of Sophie's Bubble Meditation, a hand massage and a couple of herbal sleeping tablets. Sophie was sitting by the window meditating on the fire torches and the hanging lanterns down in the gardens. She greeted Lancelot, whispering, "And which vicar are you? Not the Vicar of Dibley - obviously!"

"I am Father Ralph de Bricassart, at your service ma'am." Lancelot playfully bowed and kissed her hand.

"Ah! How very tragic! And, how very sexy!" Sophie giggled, but then she put her finger to her lips, looking over at Linnet asleep on the bed.

Sophie looked Johnathon up and down and guessed he was a musketeer. "And how is Miss Adela Huggins this evening, my dear Aramis? Has she broken your heart yet?" Sophie teased him.

"I have hardly had chance to talk to her!" he moaned. "Shilty Cunningham has us running around as her servants. But, Adela looks like...well, the goddess she is!"

Lancelot smiled. "She has come as Princess Leia!"

Sophie raised an eyebrow. "Gold bikini?"

Lancelot sighed. "Gold bikini indeed!"

"Oh! Good grief!" Sophie said. "You haven't fallen for her too, have you Lancelot?"

"No! Of course not!" Lancelot said, looking sideways at Johnathon. They exchanged suspicious looks.

"Adela, Adela!" Sophie said, quietly, shaking her head. "To be born so beautiful! I cannot imagine what that must be like. So wise and so kind too. Which of course, are the bits that matter most."

"Right now, in that gold bikini," Johnathon said, "There are bits of her that matter a whole lot more!"

Sophie waved them both out of the room in mock disgust but couldn't help smiling. They started to go back down the stairs, when suddenly, she came running out of the room calling them back. "Come quickly!" Sophie urged them. She beckoned them over to the window. They all looked out but there was no one to be seen.

"I thought I saw a man, a tall man, just now, down there, walking around to the side of the house. It might have been Marcus Finch!" Sophie whispered.

"What makes you think that?" Johnathon asked. "It could have been anyone."

"He was dressed as Zorro. He looked up here - he must have seen the light in the window. It was creepy! He stared me in the face for a few seconds. I felt a shiver and a feeling I can only describe as, well, as if I had seen pure evil. Then, he just disappeared around the corner."

"How would Marcus know Linnet was here?" Lancelot said.

Sophie thought for a moment. "Bloody hell!" she exclaimed, and so as not to wake Linnet, she took them out onto the landing. "I bet Peony told him there was a party here tonight, she may even secretly have invited him. He may not know Linnet is here. He might just be a guest - an unofficial one that is!"

"That could be true!" Johnathon nodded, and looked worried. "I'll check and see if anyone has seen Zorro. Lancelot, go and ask that new girl, Peony Bow, if she told Marcus Finch about tonight's shindig!"

"What is she dressed as?" Lancelot asked.

"The Marquise de Meurteuil!" Sophie told him. "Big white wig, French ball gown, gold and silver, you can't miss her! She did say she liked mischief, but this is 'dangerous liaisons' gone too far!"

After a few minutes Johnathon returned to Linnet's room, bringing Robert and India with him. Sophie unlocked the bedroom door and let them in. India hardly fitted into the room - she was dressed as Scarlet O'Hara -

her large hooped dress was a little oversized!

"You were right!" Johnathon told Sophie. "Peony did tell Marcus about tonight! She arranged to meet him in the garden and let him in through the kitchen doors. He was dressed as Zorro, just as you thought he was; but now we can't find him anywhere! The others are looking for him. Peony insists he isn't the same man as Linnet's ex-husband, but until we are sure we need to get Linnet and Alice somewhere even safer."

"And secret!" Lancelot added.

They all looked at each other. "She could come to the security office," Johnathon suggested. "There's a bunk bed in the cell."

"It's not very comfortable and there will be bad energies lingering from previous occupants. Alice would have nightmares," Sophie replied. "And we don't want to give Melanie any more fear to play with than she already has!"

"Who's Melanie?" Johnathon asked.

"It's a long story," they all said in unison!

"They can come to mine," India offered. "It's out of the way and they can't be seen from outside, so they could move about in relative safety inside the house. Alice loves it there so she would be okay."

"But, we have to get them there without being seen," Sophie reminded them.

"No problem!" Robert said. "I know a way to get them there!"

"I'll go and get Alice from the dormitory," Sophie suggested. "India, you wake Linnet and get their things together. Lancelot, do what you can to find a legal way to get Marcus back behind bars, as soon as possible! And Johnathon, get one of your men to come with us!"

Alice was hard to wake up. She was so sleepy that Robert offered to carry her on his back whilst she clutched her Ewok teddy. Johnathon sent Cubby Mayhew to help them. He was usually dressed in the Little Eden security uniform, but tonight he was dressed as The Flash, in very tight red Lycra and a mask!

They were about to set off when Sophie suddenly stopped them. She took off her daisy pendant and put it around Linnet's neck. "Dr G and I will pray for you as you go," she told Linnet, "This will keep you safe from Melanie, in the astral realms at least, and Cubby and Robert will keep you physically safe from Marcus."

Linnet kissed her and thanked her, with both fear and gratitude in her eyes. They all went down the back stairs and descended a full four floors into the basement.

They made their way through a creaky door into a dimly lit room, which had once been a kitchen. Yellowed peeling paint and a half broken quarry tiled floor made the basement seem somewhat uninviting. Robert led them into another much smaller room, filled with chairs and boxes, old paint tins and various odds and sods. He reached inside a dented safe and located some candles in holders. From an old tobacco tin he took up a box of matches.

"I feel like Wee Willy Winky!" Cubby said, trying to lighten the mood, but no one was able to raise a laugh.

Cubby couldn't see a door out of the basement room and he began to lead the way back, when Robert stopped him. Cubby looked in amazement as Robert fiddled with a brick about half-way up the back wall; as he pushed it, the wall slid sideways to reveal the entrance to a dark, narrow passage. The damp stench woke Alice for a moment and she moaned - then fell back into sleep.

"Where does it lead to?" Cubby asked.

"To India's house - the Colonial House!" Robert replied. "It comes out on Elizabeth's Way."

"Well!" India said in amazement. "Who knew? I'm sure I didn't!"

"You must never ever tell anyone about this passage!" Robert said to them all. "There are passages under Little Eden that go out like the dials of a clock and then crisscross each other. They go far beyond the walls. One comes out near St Paul's and another near King's Cross Station. They were used for espionage in more than one war, and they may be needed again one day. The entrances and exits must remain secret if they are going to be of use in the future. I mean it! Cubby, India, Linnet, do you understand me?"

Cubby nodded and grinned. "Careless words cost lives!" he said. "You can rely on me!"

"And me!" India said.

Linnet nodded in agreement.

The passage was just wide enough for one person to pass down, single file. India took off her large hooped skirt - luckily, she was wearing bloomers underneath, as well as sturdy, black, lace-up boots. Cubby found his rather rotund form was equivalent to one and a half persons and India had to push him through the extra narrow parts. Robert led the way along the gloomy passages and soon they were no longer beneath the chateau but were heading diagonally under the park, towards Hart Crescent. The floor sloped sharply away in places and little streams of water crossed their path at intervals, which they had to jump over to avoid getting their feet wet.

The passageway started to open out as they went further and it became easier to walk along. Then suddenly, they felt the whole tunnel begin to shake all around them and Linnet grabbed onto Alice from behind: but Alice didn't even stir. A noise, as loud as thunder, rumbled towards them and it became louder and louder until it seemed to swallow them up for a moment, but then it passed away into the distance, as quickly as it had come. "That's the tube!" Robert said. "We must be near Eve Street Station - not far now!"

Robert continued to lead the way till finally, they came to a ladder which was fastened to the wall of what looked like a well shaft. "I need something to strap Alice to me with!" Robert said, as they all gathered beneath the circular opening. They tried to think of something but there was little of any use. India finally gave up her bloomers and tied them around Alice and Robert, so that he could climb the ladder with her on his back. India was left in just her corset, frilly knickers and her boots - very cold and slightly embarrassed! "Good job I wasn't going commando tonight!" India laughed.

They climbed, one by one, up the ladder. Cubby let India go before him, 'in case she fell', (which was his excuse - although India had a feeling it was more to do with looking at her bum from below). The well shaft had an iron grid over it that Robert had trouble shifting at first, but he managed to open it in the end. They all clambered out, finding themselves under an azalea bush in the back garden of the Colonial House. "How odd!" India said. "I used to see this manhole cover as a little girl and I wished I could go down it like Alice falling into Wonderland! But Aunt Elizabeth always said never to touch it. I'd forgotten all about it for years and now, here I am, climbing out of it!"

"Come on!" Robert said. "It's only a few yards to the house!"

They made it across the lawn under cover of darkness, and India let them in to her house. She quickly put on a pair of jogging bottoms from her pile of laundry by the back door. "I'm freezing!" India said, as she put on the lights and lit the gas fire, then busied herself putting the kettle on and finding blankets to wrap around Linnet and Alice. "I can't believe Alice has stayed asleep!"

"That'll be Sophie and Dr G's protection prayer no doubt!" Robert said. "I'll txt them that we're safely here."

Alice began to wake up. Linnet cuddled her until she found her bearings. "Where am I?" Alice asked. "Where's Tambo? I dreamt I was in Heaven and Lilly was there," she yawned.

"You can sleep in my sparest of spare bedrooms, Alice!" India said kindly. "The one with the patchwork quilt you like so much!" Alice grinned, then started to fall asleep again. Linnet took her to bed and as she lay down next to her daughter she couldn't help thinking: much good Lilly will do us from Heaven! The dead can't save us now!

Cubby stayed on guard at the house whilst Robert and India returned to the chateau to rejoin the party. They arrived to find that Marcus had been arrested for trespassing. Johnathon had nearly had to lock up Minnie too, mind you! She had been restrained just in time to stop her hitting Marcus over the head with a large, solid silver, candelabrum. A stressed out Minnie was relieved to hear that Linnet and Alice were safe.

Under Shilty's direction, Robert continued to entertain his guests as their king, but he was glad when the clock struck midnight and he could keep a low profile again. Shilty kept her crown on, although she had to stop ordering people around. The band changed to smooth jazz, as the party took on a chilled, more mellow feel.

Shilty wandered around, rather the worse for wear after too much champagne. She found Collins, who was also half-cut, sitting alone in the spirits bar. "You can't ignore each other forever, you know!" Shilty said to him, leaning against the bar and brushing her main assets against his arm. "Who are you supposed to be anyway?" she asked, "A waiter?"

"The name's Bond, James Bond," Collins said, smiling.

"Cheesy, Mr Bond, very cheesy," she replied, and ordered a G & T on the rocks, with a twist.

"You haven't persuaded my dear brother to see reason yet?" Collins asked her, wishing he could remove Shilty's red dress right there and then, but aware that Varsity, dressed as Solitaire, was not far away.

"I think I may have a way to get us all what we want out of this sale," Shilty whispered.

Collins frowned. "I don't know. Robert seems to be resisting Mama more than she expected. You have your wily ways, Shilty," Collins said, "But, it'll take more than huge tits and a blow job to change his mind this time!"

Meanwhile, Adela Huggins had been trying to get Lancelot alone all evening, to tell him of her conversation with Cousin Faberge regarding

Lucas. She finally found him in the coffee bar and sat next to him on the bar stool; he ordered her an espresso. "I spoke to Faberge," Adela told him.

"What did she have to say?" Lancelot asked, rather distracted by Adela's costume (or lack of it, I should say).

"She says she will help you and Robert anyway she can. She thinks selling Little Eden is criminal. She hinted that Lucas is harbouring a grudge against Robert and that's why he has been so easily persuaded to sell."

Lancelot looked sheepish and sighed.

"Does he hold a grudge against Robert?" Adela probed.

"Perhaps!" Lancelot replied. "Perhaps against more than just Robert, but that was more than twenty years ago! None of us have seen Faberge or Lucas since we were teenagers. I would have thought he…" Lancelot tailed off.

Adela continued to tell him about her conversation. "Faberge said we should go out to Canada to see her and she could hook us up with Lucas. Maybe talk some sense into him before it's too late, what do you reckon?"

"Mmmm?" Lancelot replied.

"Don't you think that would be a great idea?" Adela asked him, not understanding why he was so preoccupied.

"A trip to Canada or wherever would be a good idea. Yes. Certainly. I will suggest it to Robert," Lancelot agreed. "You must come too of course."

He downed another coffee and excused himself. He was rather afraid that if he stayed any longer, he would kiss her (and then some) right there in the bar - in front of everyone.

He took his leave and Adela was rather sorry to see him go.

Chapter 19

~ * ~

Two days after the party, Johnathon reluctantly released Marcus Finch from the old castle jail cell. Unfortunately, Marcus could not be kept locked up any longer, but he was banned from entering the walls of Little Eden ever again.

Robert was no nearer to deciding what to do about the sale of Little Eden. He was still sitting on the fence, swaying one way, then the other. Whenever anybody said anything to try to persuade him either way he seemed to change his mind again, and no one knew which side he would fall off onto. He was feeling tired and depressed. Psychic attacks from Melanie and his mother were dragging him into his darkest fears and Shilty was working on him too. Rather than think about what to do, he was hoping that Lancelot was going to perform some kind of legal miracle and rescue him from his dilemma.

Robert was jolted back into focus when various parts of three human skeletons were found in the lake, which had been successfully dredged. They were yet to find out if the bodies were male or not, or how old they were, but they were convinced that, although the skeletons were incomplete, they were looking at the bones of the three men Melanie had murdered all those years ago. Robert breathed a sigh of relief! "I'm sure this will put an end to Melanie's spirit causing trouble," he said to Lancelot. "That past life should be all cleared up now!"

Robert mused over the bones which were laid out on the mortuary table and wondered how a murder from over one hundred years ago could have such an impact on the present. "My mother may change her mind any day now," Robert said with confidence, "And once we visit Lucas and talk some sense into him, it will all be over and done with!"

Lancelot looked at him and sighed - he was not so sure!

Linnet and Alice were still hiding out at India's house, and after another couple of days, Minnie tried to persuade Linnet to come back to her shop and allow Alice to play with her friends again. Minnie had visited them every day and today she was determined to bring Linnet and Alice home.

"Sophie sent you some of Sumona's mixed mint tea; she says it helps clear away a build-up of fear in the body," Minnie said to Linnet. She got the packet out of her handbag and then produced some other bits and bobs.

"Lucy sent you some roll-on lavender and neroli oil from Peony's shop - she said to put it on your temples and wrists, and here, Silvi has sent you one of her aura sprays." Minnie proceeded to liberally spray Linnet with it.

"Stop it, Minnie!" Linnet said impatiently. "My clothes are getting wet!"

"Better that, than being full of fear!" Minnie replied, and continued to squirt the spray around Linnet, and the room in general. "I can feel fear all around you, and every word you say is spikey."

"That smells lovely!" India said. "What's in it?"

"I'm not sure!" Minnie replied. "Silvi uses aromatherapy oils in water, with crystal essences and the energy of Archangel Michael."

"How does she get Archangel Michael into a spray?" India asked. "That doesn't sound plausible to me."

"Sophie would be able to explain it, I'm sure I can't, but apparently it works if you know how!" Minnie replied.

"Do those things really work?" India asked, as she took a closer look at the bottle of spray.

"What things?" Minnie said.

"Sprays, crystals, hands on healing, hypnotherapy. Things like that!" India said.

"Of course!" Minnie replied.

"I tried acupuncture once," India admitted. "I was having the most godawful migraines but it didn't work."

"How many sessions did you have?" Minnie asked.

"Just one," India replied.

"Well, you can't expect it to work then!" Minnie smiled. "Do you think these things are miracle cures?"

"I suppose I did!" India admitted.

"You've got to manage your health on a regular basis, in all sorts of ways. Keep on top of it that's my philosophy!" Minnie suggested. "Miracles are very rare. After all, you wouldn't take an aspirin once and expect it to take away headaches for the rest of your life. If you got another headache a week later, you wouldn't say that the aspirin didn't work, would you?"

"I suppose you're right" India replied, a little unsure that she wanted to be led into a discussion about such things. "Help yourselves to lunch! Where's Alice? There are chocolate brownies for dessert - she loves them!"

As they ate, Minnie tried to persuade Linnet to come home. "Johnathon has invoked the Little Eden Sanctuary Law to make it illegal for Marcus to set foot within the walls. If he does come back here, he can be arrested on the spot!"

Linnet shook her head but Minnie carried on..."There will be new CCTV installed outside your door by the end of today and you can see the screen inside your shop too."

"I can't go back," Linnet said, pushing away her plate - she was too upset to eat anything.

"You have to!" India told her in dismay, shaking her head. "You cannot spend your life afraid of him."

"You don't know what it's like!" Linnet said, her fear turning to anger. "You have no idea what I'm going through! How would you know? I don't know how I can ever feel safe!" Linnet was starting to feel a panic attack coming on. "I can't breathe when I think about it! I can't breathe even when I don't think about it."

"Take one day at a time," India suggested kindly.

"You don't know what it's like!" Linnet cried.

"No, I suppose I don't," India admitted. "But it's what you are going to do about it that counts. I always think practical steps are the best therapy. If Lancelot was here he'd say to keep calm and pray. I vote for keeping calm but not sure praying will do much good." With that, India lifted the dessert plate from beside her saying, "Another brownie, anyone?"

~ * ~

A very frightened Linnet went back to Daisy Place the next day, and Alice finally got to see Tambo and her other friends again. Alice was glad to be out of her home as much as possible. As she put it: Mummy was acting very strangely, and she didn't like it!

Tambo, Elijah, Joshua and Alice had formed a band specially to play at Aunt Lilly's memorial concert, and now they needed to practise every day as the concert was looming large. Their newly formed pop group still hadn't got a name, and they needed to come up with one, as soon as possible.

"We need a name ASAP to put in the programme for the concert!" Tambo said. "They're going to the printers next week."

"I'll ask St Hilda for guidance!" Elijah offered.

"Who?" Joshua asked.

"She's like a saint who looks after me," Elijah told him.

Joshua looked confused. "A who now?"

"Like a guardian angel," Alice told him.

"She isn't real then?" Joshua asked.

"If you mean, is she human, then no, she isn't alive now but she used to be." Elijah explained. "She was a nun and when she died she became a saint. She's not human any more but that doesn't mean she's not real."

"Mama says we all have a guardian angel called Archangel Michael. I have to ask him to help me when I feel scared," Joshua said.

"That's different," Elijah said. "Archangels were never humans."

"Lilly is my guardian angel," Tambo said.

"And mine!" Alice chimed in.

"Is your Aunt Lilly a saint too?" Joshua asked.

"No, Lilly is an angel," Alice explained.

"Can anyone become a saint?" Joshua asked, a bit fixated on the idea.

"I think the Pope has to say if you can be a saint or not," Elijah told him. "But that doesn't mean all saints are real saints."

"How do you know the difference between a real saint and a fake saint?" Joshua asked.

"A real saint doesn't mind what religion you follow or even if you don't go to any church at all," Elijah told him. "They will still support you and comfort you, no matter who you are or where you come from."

"I want to be a saint when I am older!" Joshua said emphatically.

"You can't be a saint until you are dead!" Elijah laughed.

"Well then. I will be one when I am dead!" Joshua replied, with absolute certainty.

Tambo smiled and started to play: *Oh when the saints, go marching in... oh when the saints go marching in...I wanna be in that number...oh when the saints go marching in!...* and they all marched around the room singing, until it descended into silly walks, jazz hands and fits of laughter!

"What about calling ourselves The Saints?" Joshua suggested.

"I think that's been done," Tambo replied.

"What about Otherworld?" Elijah said. "You know, 'cos we are guided from the other world all the time!"

"That's awesome!" Alice exclaimed.

"Righteous," Joshua nodded.

"Otherworld it is!" Tambo agreed.

Tambo came home to find his mother lying on the sofa upstairs looking rather pale. "I'm okay, Tambo!" Lucy reassured him. "Just make me a cup of tea and get me a ginger snap cookie and I'll be fine! I just feel a bit queasy!" Lucy listened to him talk about the name for their new band and the song they were going to play at the concert. She began to feel a little better, but then suddenly, there was an almighty commotion! Linnet burst through the conservatory doors and flew into the room in a total panic!

"Alice is missing!" Linnet cried. "She hasn't come home! Where is she Tambo? Where is she?"

Tambo stood up and looked amazed at the question. He stared at Linnet, whose eyes were flashing like a wild woman's.

"She's at the library," Tambo said calmly. "She went there about half an hour ago."

"She should have come home by now!" Linnet screamed. She ran over to the window in the hope of seeing Alice down in the square.

"She is probably engrossed in a book and has lost track of time. She usually stays there a while anyway," Lucy reassured her.

"You shouldn't have let her go alone! You should have stayed with her, Tambo!" Linnet wailed and began to wring her hands. "I have a bad feeling! Go and find her Tambo! Bring her home! Now!"

Lucy felt a sudden rush of fear through her heart. She had a flashback of her dream about Alice in the coffin and she felt even more sick to her stomach than she had before. "Tambo, go and see if Alice is on her way home from the library," Lucy urged him.

Tambo nodded and went out straight away. It was dark and freezing cold. He was glad of the soft yellow lights flooding the pavements from behind the shop windows. It had begun to spit with rain and he ran as fast as he could down Rose Walk and along Castle Street, and seeing no sign of Alice, he crossed over the road and ran towards the Quaker House Library. He found the place deserted for the evening. He called his mum, and then within minutes, Johnathon Grail arrived, to find Tambo, standing on tip-toe, peering through a small window near the entrance.

The Quaker House was locked and there was no way inside. Johnathon took out his set of master keys and quickly, but quietly, opened the front door. He beckoned to Tambo and put his finger to his lips to indicate that Tambo must stay silent. In trepidation, Tambo followed Johnathon into the vestibule. The floor was laid with slightly shabby linoleum tiles, fortunately, their sneakers made no sound. The musty smell that accompanies public buildings pervaded the air. Blue plastic chairs were stacked in the corner below a notice board, which dangled with public notices, leaflets and cards. Johnathon looked through the thin strips of glass in the double doors which led into the library. He couldn't see any signs of life. The lights were turned out and it was as silent as the grave.

Johnathon slowly opened the door and waved his hand to stop Tambo from following him inside. But Tambo was not to be put off. He followed Johnathon into the library proper and they scanned the room, but they saw nothing and heard no one. It was too dark to see to the back of the hall or through the stacks, but Johnathon was reluctant to turn on the lights. He took out his torch and shone the beam over towards the desk. He sent the light around into the kitchenette which lay behind it, but again they saw nothing.

He was about to turn his attention to the stacks, when Tambo suddenly heard something! He grabbed Johnathon's arm in alarm, and put his hand to his ear to indicate for Johnathon to listen. They stood motionless for a few moments, straining to hear something, and then they both heard the same sound again! It was a low moan coming from behind the desk. Johnathon cautiously made his way around the side of the large wooden counter top and nearly stood on a human hand! He noticed the fingers just in time to avert stamping on them, then he sent the light of the torch along the wrist and was relieved to find it was attached to an arm, which was attached to a shoulder, which was attached to a body. Johnathon swiftly knelt down to see that the body belonged to Iris Sprott, and to find that the moaning was coming from her. At least she was still alive!

"Turn on the lights!" Johnathon told Tambo, "And call an ambulance, quick!"

Chapter 20

~ * ~

Marcus Finch lay down under a blanket, in the back of Peony Bow's Mini Cooper. It was rather a squeeze for a man of six foot two with long legs and a big ego! She drove him into Little Eden, beneath the CCTV cameras, under the cover of darkness. Her love for him had overcome all rationality. Although she knew she was breaking the law, she felt a thrill of rebellious excitement, and most of all, the thrill of being in love. Peony smuggled Marcus into her apartment, on the third floor above her shop, and they spent the rest of the evening and all that night in bed together. Marcus was as passionate and as romantic as Peony had described him to be. She was completely under his thrall by morning. She knew in her heart that the Law of Attraction had brought her everything she had asked for. He was perfect!

After rustling up a brunch of eggs Benedict, Marcus began to tell Peony the sad tale of how Linnet had left him for no good reason, and how she had cooked up the story about domestic abuse, so convincingly, that the police, judge and jury had been completely taken in, and he had subsequently ended up in jail: an innocent man. Justice now needed to be served, and he had to get his precious daughter, Alice, away from Linnet, before she too was poisoned by evil. He relayed to Peony all the poisonous lies Linnet had told about him, but he also explained how he was also able to forgive Linnet. "Jesus found me in prison," he told Peony. "I have been blessed by His grace. There is nothing I cannot forgive with His guidance."

He took a letter from his coat pocket and showed it to Peony, it read:

Dear Marcus

The Lord compels me to write to you my friend. Here in Wisconsin the Lord has seen fit to grant me a humble ministry. Lately I have been called to reach a greater congregation. I have a media deal with NTBC worth millions of dollars. Your abilities and showmanship must be employed to do the work of the Lord. I enclose the documents you will need. Fly into Sawyer Airport and call me from there on the old number.

May the Light of the Lord go with you and God bless you.

Pastor Tilton Swagman

"You're moving to America?" Peony asked him in surprise.

Marcus nodded and smiled. "I want to take Alice with me and you must help me." He saw the disappointment on her face and smiled again. "I will send for you later, my dove."

Peony shook her head. "How can I help you? Besides, you would be recognised on television. The police would find you!"

"Haven't you heard of plastic surgery?" Marcus laughed. "In a few weeks no one will recognise me, or Alice. We have new identities already!" He showed Peony the fake passports that the Pastor had sent them. "When enough time has passed, I will send for you and you can join us."

"I don't know. That sounds impossible!" Peony replied, aghast. "I don't think it sounds like a good idea."

"If it is the Lord's will - nothing is impossible." Marcus replied. "You must always follow the Lord and believe."

"Why not set up a ministry here in London?" Peony asked him.

Marcus took her into his arms, and kissing her, he explained how, due to his stay in prison, no court was likely to grant him full custody of Alice. The only way to take her from Linnet was illegally.

I have to tell you here, dear readers, that whilst Peony maybe prone to being blinded by love-karma (as we all are), she did have a moral compass, albeit deep inside her, which kicked in when kidnapping was on the cards!

Peony protested and refused to go along with such an abominable plan. Marcus took his time to persuade her, and for the rest of the day he used his diplomatic and charming approach. The next day, over breakfast, he changed tack again and using emotional blackmail, he nearly persuaded Peony to change her mind; but not quite! So, in the end, he resorted to a finale of anger and recrimination finished off with a flourish of apologies and kisses. He punched her verbally and emotionally with one hand, and then offered her sweet words and hugs with the other. Over the next two days, whilst he lay low at Peony's, she was on the verge of being convinced by his controlling methods, which wove a stronger and stronger spell as time went on. She was almost convinced that Alice would be safer with him, in America, than with Linnet, whose seemingly good character she highly doubted now.

But when Peony still refused to help him, Marcus lost his self-control and turned grizzly. He started shouting and snarling like a wild beast. The more Peony protested, the more ferocious he became! He lashed out at her. His fist narrowly missed hitting her in the face.

Petrified, Peony tried to escape through the kitchen door onto the roof, but Marcus quickly intercepted her, brandishing the long serrated-edged bread knife that had been left on the worktop. Peony squashed herself up against the fridge to try and avoid the crazy slashing of the blade, crying out in terror as he lurched towards her like a madman. He would have stabbed her straight through the stomach had she not remembered the self-defence moves that Minnie had showed her, and without really thinking about what she was doing, she blocked his arm with hers, stamped heavily on the bridge of his foot and swiftly kneed him in the balls!

Marcus reeled backwards and downwards in pain, which gave Peony time to dodge sideways around the island worktop, and then her survival instinct really kicked in! She grabbed the pasta pan from the night before, still full of water and gloopy pasta, and she threw it at him! He managed to catch it, but the contents flew out, covering him in sticky starched water and strings of stray spaghetti from head to toe. She then picked up the wooden spoon, still coated in tomato sauce, and began beating him around the head with it, but Marcus grabbed her wrist and then, as quickly as he had transformed into 'mad Marcus', he transformed back into 'loving Marcus'. He began apologising profusely. He gently put his arm around her. She began to shake and then burst into tears. Marcus softly caressed Peony's cheek and held her close to him like a child. His tone became soothing. "You shouldn't provoke me by disagreeing with me," he told her and kissed her on the forehead. "We must be in love each other. That was our first 'lovers tiff'. Let's go and make up!"

Peony felt herself calming down a little, but her heart was still racing ten to the dozen and she felt hot and cold at the same time. She shivered as she prised herself, slowly and carefully, from Marcus's embrace and delicately picked some of the pasta strands from his chest and dried his face with a tea towel. Marcus took off his wet shirt and led Peony by the hand into the shower. They stepped under the gushing warm water together. An hour later Marcus lay in her bed, planning his next move, whilst Peony slept in his arms.

Marcus quietly got up, leaving Peony half asleep, and pulled on his jeans and jumper. He had hoped to leave without waking her, but Peony stirred from her doze just in time to see him leaving the bedroom. Peony, afraid he might try to take Alice from Linnet straight away, tried desperately to think how she could stop him from leaving the apartment without setting off his anger. In the end, she thought that agreeing with him was the best idea, and figured that she could warn Linnet somehow, before it was too late. Peony tried her best to convince Marcus that she had changed her mind and would do as he asked. She kissed him as passionately as she could. "Bring Alice here," she suggested. "Then, I will drive you both to the airport tomorrow. That way, they won't see you leave Little Eden."

Marcus smiled, but he was not entirely convinced that she had had a change of heart. Peony wished him good luck as he left via the roof terrace. As soon as he was out of sight, she picked up the phone from its holster and headed off, as fast as she could, down the stairs into Vincent's barbers shop, to see if he was there.

What she didn't know was that Marcus had doubled back and had followed her down the stairs. Before she could reach the bottom, he grabbed her from behind, ripping the phone out of her hand. He threw the phone, and her, through the door and they both shot across the barber's room floor. The shop was deserted, it being a Monday, and there was no sign of Vincent. Marcus picked Peony up off the floor by her hair. Holding her arms tightly behind her back, he manoeuvred her into one of the barber's chairs.

Marcus tied Peony to the leather arm rests using the only thing to hand - hairdryer flexes - and forced a face cloth into her mouth to gag her. She tried to struggle but she could not break free. He was too strong for her, although she did manage to kick him rather hard in the shin! "Bitch!" Marcus exclaimed. "You'll pay for that!" He growled and reached over to the rack of Victorian-style razors, which were hanging beside the chair. He picked up the biggest one he could find. Seeing him brandishing the razor, Peony tried to scream but she could not. She was petrified, paralysed and powerless. Her eyes wide with terror she could feel warm pee trickling down her legs. She thought she was going to vomit and pass out at the same time.

With her eyes blurry with tears, Peony hardly saw Vincent, who had come silently up behind Marcus, brandishing a pair of ceramic hair straighteners.

Vincent had been in the dressing room looking for a new shirt and tie to wear that evening when he had heard Peony come down the stairs. He had been about to come out of the cupboard to greet her, but then had seen Marcus grab her from behind and throw her across the floor. Scared and unsure what to do, Vincent had cowered behind the doors and watched as Marcus tied Peony up. He felt in his pockets for his own phone but realised he had left it on the counter, and Peony's phone was too far away for him to reach without coming out of his hiding place. When Marcus reached for the razor he realised he had to act faster than making a phone call! Vincent knew he had to do something to save Peony - but what? He looked around the small room for a something to hit Marcus with, but there were only expensive shirts and handmade brogues. He picked up one shoe and wondered if it was hard enough to cosh someone with, but the leather was too soft and the shoe far too comfortable to make it a deadly weapon. Looking at the silk ties he wondered if he could strangle Marcus from behind, but hand-to-hand combat did not appeal to him at all. He thought about stabbing Marcus in the back of the heart with a pair of scissors. The only scissors in the cupboard were in a man's shaving kit; he ripped open one of the bags, but then remembering they were nail scissors, and far too small, he dropped them in despair! Even if he had had a larger pair to hand, his stomach churned at the thought of ripping flesh and gushing blood! In the end, he caught sight of a pair of diamond-encrusted, ceramic hair straighteners (worth several thousand pounds), which were hanging up on the wall. In a flash he grabbed them and hoped a good crack to the back of Marcus's head would be enough!

Through her tears, Peony saw Vincent do just that! He whacked Marcus on the back of the head! Or, at least, that was what he was aiming for, but he was a little shy of his mark and hit him mainly on the ear instead. Marcus yelped with pain and surprise! He swung around so quickly, that he almost cut Vincent across the cheek with the razor as he did so! To Peony it looked as if it were all happening in slow motion. She saw the razor blade graze Vincent's beard, taking off the very ends of some of his whiskers in the process, but luckily leaving his face intact, and she saw Vincent move like a ninja and then hit Marcus with the straighteners again, this time, very hard on his left temple. Marcus doubled up to hold his head and with the other hand, he violently pushed Vincent in the chest, which made Vincent lose his footing and he headed for the floor, thudding down onto his back like an upside down turtle. Vincent was too shocked to roll over. Marcus raised his foot and was about to stamp it down on Vincent's face, but the slow-motion action scene paused as they all heard a loud, cheery voice from the lower staircase. It was Mrs B coming up from the perfumery, calling for Peony.

Marcus realised he couldn't take on three people at once, and as quick as lightening he dragged Vincent into the dressing room and locked the doors on him. Then, without a thought for Peony, he scuttled up the stairs and back into her apartment. He headed straight out of the kitchen door and escaped over the roof terraces to Castle Street. As Mrs B entered the barber's she saw no sign of Marcus but let out an almighty scream at the sight of poor Peony, who was still tied to a chair, with soggy wet flannel sticking out of her mouth!

~ * ~

Marcus made it down onto Castle Street. He looked at the clock on Heroes Tower and realised he only had a few minutes to catch Alice alone. He had been stalking her for a few weeks now, and had realised that Alice's most vulnerable time was when she went to the library alone. Alice always took her library books back to the Quaker House on a Monday at four o'clock, and she would spend about half an hour amongst the stacks, choosing another one or two books to read during the week. This was one of the few times she was ever on her own. The library which was for children's books only was open two days a week. Very few people used it these days and Alice liked the peace and quiet. There was a lovely window seat at the back on which Alice liked to sit and flick through the books. Apart from the librarian, Iris Sprott, there was hardly ever anyone else there, especially now, it being school holidays.

Marcus knew Alice was no fool and that she would not talk to him if he approached her as a strange man in the street. He came up with a plan. He would pretend to be a temporary librarian to gain her confidence. Marcus had only a few minutes before Alice was due to arrive. He sneaked into the disabled toilet and waited. Finally, Alice came in and cheerfully greeted Iris Sprott as she handed back her books. She then wandered off to browse amongst the stacks. Iris stamped the books and put them on the trolley. She looked at the clock, and seeing it was indeed four o'clock, she went to make her usual cup of tea.

Marcus snuck out of the toilet and crept up to the front desk. He was about to go around it to attack Iris in the kitchenette, when she turned around and came back out to the desk, carrying her cup of tea. Marcus was sure she must have seen him as he ducked behind the trolley of books, but to his relief she had not. A few moments later, she wandered back into the kitchenette in search of the old Quality Street tin in which she kept some secret chocolate digestives. Marcus took the opportunity to sneak back into the toilet. He started thinking it was going to be harder than he had thought to kidnap Alice! He sat on the toilet seat for a few moments and prayed for guidance from Jesus. A few seconds later a smile crossed his lips as he found his divine inspiration. He put his hand into his jeans pocket and pulled out his wallet. From inside one of the folds he produced a small clear plastic bag containing a white powder. It was ketamine, which he carried at all times, just in case a woman was not being as obliging as he wanted her to be.

He peered through the toilet door and waited for Iris Sprott to leave her cup of tea unattended. He didn't have to wait long, as Iris, having taken only one biscuit from the tin (due to her New Year's resolution of losing three stone), went back into the kitchenette to fetch another. Marcus darted out of the toilet and surreptitiously poured the whole packet of ketamine into her cup of tea. He needed it to act fast. She returned before he could get back into his hiding place, so he quickly bent down in front of the desk, hoping that she would not look over it. He glanced anxiously at the door, because from there, sprawled out on his belly on the floor, he was fully visible, and he prayed that no one would come in. Watching the minutes tick by on the library clock, he grew more and more impatient. Luck was on his side however, and within a few minutes Iris Sprott was wobbling about! She felt extremely tired and dizzy, and a few seconds later she slumped over a pile of books and fell fast asleep.

Marcus quickly removed Iris from her recumbent position. He had a little trouble laying such a bountiful lady down on the floor, and even more trouble pushing her cumbersome form under the counter where she could not be seen. Iris was not the quietest of sleepers and she made a few low grunting noises and let out the occasional snort, which made Marcus anxious that Alice might hear her, so he covered her guttural sounds with his own, pretending he had sinus trouble, reaching for a tissue and blowing his nose every time Iris murmured or groaned.

Marcus willed Alice to come to the desk as soon as possible, but Alice was snuggled on her window seat. Marcus was getting angry with her dawdling and was anxious that someone else might come into the library and uncover his disguise. Eventually, Alice brought two books with her and laid them on the counter. Marcus smiled and picked them up to stamp them. "You look like a clever girl to me. I bet you can read anything!" he said.

Alice smiled at the strange man who was complimenting her ability to read (a skill she was very proud of). "Yes," Alice replied, happily. Where's Mrs Sprott?"

Marcus coughed, "Mrs Sprott had to go early for a dentist appointment. I'm just covering until closing!"

They chatted for a while about Alice's favourite stories, and although Marcus had to disguise a few of Iris' snores from time to time and had to kick her arm back under the counter at one point when it flopped out of its own accord, he had Alice completely beguiled and focused on him.

Alice finally picked up her books and was about to leave, which forced Marcus to say something to keep her with him. "Do you know, you seem very familiar to me - have I met you before?" he asked her.

Alice smiled. "I was thinking the same thing. You look very familiar to me too!"

"Do you go to St Mary's School on Bloomsbury Road?" he asked her.

"Yes!" Alice said.

"Then you will know my son! James Mc...McGovern."

"I don't think I know him," Alice said, a little disappointed not to be able to say she did.

"Perhaps he is a little older than you?" Marcus replied jovially. "But, aren't you the girl who won the Music Prize last year?"

"Yes, that's me!" Alice beamed.

"I knew I had seen you before! Well done you!" He watched with pleasure as Alice warmed to him even more, and he smiled to himself. "I'm meeting James at the sports centre," he told her and then paused and looked at the clock. "Just now, as luck would have it! Why don't you walk me over there and you can tell me all about your music."

"Don't you need to lock up or something?" Alice asked him as they walked out. Marcus thought for a moment and hoped he would be able to find the keys easily. They were by the sink in the kitchenette and as he grabbed them he thanked the Lord for his help.

Near the end of the lane they passed the life-size, bronze statue of an air raid warden blowing his whistle, wearing his metal helmet and carrying a gas mask box slung over his shoulder. Marcus drew Alice's attention to the statue and asked her about it. They stopped to look at it. "It makes me feel sad," she replied. "So many people died in the war, in so many cities around the world. It was called the Blitz here in London. We did about it in school last year."

Marcus smiled. "Look, what is that?" he said, pointing to the ground just behind the statue.

Alice looked down on the grass to where he was indicating, but all she could see were some snowdrops that were poking through the grass, surrounded by small piles of greyish sludge that had not completely melted away. As she peered more intently she could see the outline of a large rusty pair of doors in the ground. Only one was visible, the other was completely hidden by some copper beach hedging which seemed to blend into the colour of the metal plate. "I don't know!" Alice replied, surprised. "I've never seen that before!"

Marcus went to take a closer look and beckoned her over to him. He looked around to check that no one could see them. "Look!" Marcus said again. "I bet it's the entrance to the old air raid shelter." He opened the uncovered door (a little too easily, if you ask me!) and looked down into the pitch-black hole. He encouraged Alice to come and take a look on the pretext of it being of historical interest. As Alice peered over the edge of the opening, she could just make out a short metal ladder and she gasped in delight. She was about to look up at Marcus to exclaim, but before she could, Marcus pushed her over the edge and she tumbled down into the darkness. She screamed, but her sounds of distress were muffled as she fell into the dark hole. She was saved from crashing too hard, onto the cold concrete floor by the old metal ladder which broke her fall. Marcus quickly climbed down after her, pulling the door back over his head.

It was pitch black in the concrete shelter and impossible to see your hand in front of your face. Alice lay on the hard floor, bruised and shaken from her crash landing. Luckily nothing was broken, but she couldn't help crying, from the sheer terror of the fall, more than from the pain. To see where Alice was, Marcus lit his cigarette lighter and she saw his face looming over her like a macabre and dreadful ghoul peering out of the charcoal chasm. "You went with a bang!" he said, holding out his hand to help her up. "You fell in! You worried me for a moment. But, you are okay? Nothing broken, I hope."

Alice looked at him in anger, as well as in fear, but she took his hand all the same. She felt bruised and her leg hurt where she had hit the ladder, but the adrenalin from her fear numbed it a little for now. She was about to say that she had not fallen and that he had pushed her, but looking at his sinister expression, which quivered in and out of the half-light, she was too afraid to say anything, especially anything to contradict him. *He is not the same man from the library.* Alice thought to herself. *Who is he?*

"I'll see if there is another way out!" Marcus told her. "The door came down after me and I don't think I'll be able to lift it back up."

He told Alice to stay where she was, and as he walked away from her, she was plunged back into the all-consuming darkness. She was too frightened to move! She wished she could see the ladder, or even the wall, but she was in the middle of an open space with nothing to protect her.

A few moments passed, then she heard Marcus before she could see him. "Come with me!" Marcus told her in a kindly way, as the flame he was holding came into view. He took her hand and she reluctantly followed him. "I have something to show you and something very important to tell you."

Alice was trembling, and she wanted to scream but she couldn't seem to find her voice. She tried to resist Marcus when he pulled her down a grey concrete corridor, but as she struggled a little whisper of an idea came into her head which said…*Play along 'til you get a chance to escape. Stay calm, play along, play along.* She was a little puzzled by the clarity of this unexpected thought but decided to follow its advice as she had no other idea what to do. So, she let Marcus lead her deeper into the oppressive chamber without struggling anymore.

Marcus had found an old oil lamp hanging on the wall (which seemed a little too full of oil for a place that no one was supposed to have been in for decades!), and the sight of a light emanating somewhere ahead made Alice's heart leap. They suddenly turned a sharp corner and Alice gasped in surprise. Laid out before her was a scene which was quite unexpected!

Alice found herself in a shallow, small room. On the back wall stood a row of life-size wooden statues which formed a screen. Each statue was highly painted and was of a saint. A statue of Mother Mary stood in the very centre of the holy line up, with her arms outstretched, releasing the gift of a pure white dove. Mother Mary had a serene and very beautiful face, yet Alice saw sadness in it and wanted to cry. The other saints looked wretched at first with their faces masked by the deep shadows, but as Marcus lit another oil lamp, which was standing on the altar cloth, the faces of the saints seemed to brighten and glow, bringing some solace to the engulfing gloom. Alice was transfixed by the delicately carved wooden dove in Mother Mary's hands, which began to shine with such angelic softness, it seemed to her that it could almost be real. She felt comforted for a moment but it did not last long. Marcus roughly pushed her towards the altar which stood before the screen and down onto her knees. "Don't be afraid," he told Alice. "I am going to help you. Do you know who I am?"

Alice had guessed that he probably was neither a librarian nor the father of James McGovern, but she did not reply. She didn't really care who he was anymore; she just wanted to get away from him. An oozing presence of evil seemed to exude from his whole body and his words were sharp, like knife blades, in the air. Alice tried to pull away from him. She could sense his insanity thicken into a palpable caress, which began to smoother her body and mind, like a glutinous inky tarmac.

"Pray with me Alice!" Marcus ordered her. Kneeling on the frayed, musty, prayer cushions, he began to pray in earnest. Alice looked at him in total confusion and shock. *Praying is something good, kind, loving people do, isn't it? Not people who push you down holes and lie to you?* she thought to herself. She looked at Mother Mary and she knew, in her pure little heart, that whoever this man was praying to, it was not to Mother Mary. Alice figured that he must believe in some other god. A god that was not compassionate and kind but the total opposite.

Marcus took her cold little hand in his and held it tightly so that she couldn't pull away. On some level he knew her inner light might be stronger than he had bargained for, and he felt the urge to kill her right there and then, but he wanted to possess her as much as he wanted to kill her. He wanted to have control over Alice for longer than Linnet had had. "You have the Devil in you, Alice!" Marcus suddenly said. "Your mother put the Devil in you because she has the Devil in her too. I am here to save you Alice! It isn't too late for you. Jesus will cleanse your soul and you will be free. You are too little and frail to save yourself, but I will save you Alice. I will protect you. I am your father and I love you."

Chapter 21

~ * ~

When Mrs B had untied Peony from the barber's chair and let Vincent out of the wardrobe, she could get very little sense out of either of them for a good ten minutes. They were, both of them, mildly hysterical.

Mrs B had called Johnathon Grail immediately for assistance. It wasn't until Peony had been cleaned up that the whole story of why Marcus had tied her to the chair in the first place was revealed.

Peony confessed to harbouring Marcus, for the past few days, and she told them of his plan to kidnap Alice. "He went crazy!" Peony told Johnathon.

"Crazy doesn't begin to cover it!" Vincent rejoined. "Crazy mother f*cker! Mr Marcus Finch is a sheep in wolf's clothing and no mistake!"

"I think you mean a wolf in sheep's clothing?" Johnathon replied and nodded. "And I think most of us were aware of that from the beginning." He couldn't help but look at Peony with derision for having trusted Marcus. "Now, I need to know where he might have gone."

"I don't know for sure," Peony said, shaking her head as she sipped her mug of sugary tea. "I didn't realise what he was like! I thought…well I thought…"

"Now, now, my love," Mrs B said kindly. "Don't worry yourself. You are not the first person to be taken in by Mr Marcus Finch and you probably won't be the last. I know the type. They have a charm about them and you get easily confused. You hope and hope their nice side is the real them but…"

"Once a nasty bastard, always a nasty bastard," Vincent interrupted.

Johnathon radioed to Cubby and Shooter to stay alert and to road block the gates but then got a call from Lucy and he quickly sped off down Quaker Lane to find Tambo outside the Quaker House. It was then that they found Iris Sprott laid out on the parquet flooring.

After finding Iris but not Alice, Johnathon set up search parties, which grew in number until nearly every Little Eden resident was looking for Alice. Lucy began a sort of unofficial headquarters at the Café. Tosha and Tonbee were providing everyone with copious amounts of hot tea and toasted tea cakes. Outside it was bitterly cold and pouring down with rain. Sludge now filled the gullies, soaking everyone's trousers and shoes. As the residents came and went from the Café, none of them had good news. They hunted everywhere, in every nook and cranny, every alleyway, every attic, every basement. Soon, they were running out of options. Everyone was getting more and more anxious.

"Can't you ask Aunt Lilly to show you were Alice is?" Lucy asked Sophie in desperation. "You could use your remote viewing!"

Sophie sighed. "I'm trying already! All I can see is darkness. I think I'm too close to Alice to see clearly. I'm too worried about finding her - it's clouding my psychic sight. Besides, most evil bastards cloak themselves and make it hard for even the best psychics in the world to locate them. Some people can be kept hostage for years, right under the noses of their neighbours, and are never discovered. I am trying!"

"I'll call Jimmy!" Lucy said. "He's not so close to Alice. He may be able to stay calmer and see more? I bet she is still close by. We have to find her!"

Jimmy Pratt was immediately telephoned and asked to use his psychic investigator abilities to find Alice. He called Lucy back within five minutes, and she almost dropped the phone in her rush to hear the news, but all Jimmy could report was seeing darkness and a statue of Mother Mary. "This Marcus bloke is very well cloaked." Jimmy told her. "Your sister's not wrong! He's a master deceiver. He's pure evil."

"What did he say?" Sophie asked, as Lucy put down the phone. She had a terrified look on her face.

"He only saw darkness and a statue of Mother Mary," Lucy repeated. "He agreed with you, he said Marcus is cloaked and is pure…"

Just then, Jack and Johnathon rushed back into the Café. "There's no sign of her in the Bluebell Woods," they reported.

Lucy told them of Jimmy's vision.

"The church!" Jack exclaimed, on hearing that a statue of Mother Mary had been seen.

"Minnie, Adela and Elijah have already checked the church. Ginger and some of the choir have already checked the Chappelle and the Abbey but they are going through the whole place again now," Lucy told them. "They have even been down to the crypt but there was no sign," Lucy said, looking at the white board; she had put red crosses anywhere that had been searched, so that they didn't double up.

Jack scanned the map. "The Russian Chapel! No one has been there yet! It must be there! Quick!"

"What about the Old French House?" Mrs B suggested. "There's a statue of Mother Mary in the secret chapel there."

"You take the Russian Chapel and I'll take the French House!" Jack told Johnathon, and they both rushed out again.

Lancelot and India burst through the doors just as Jack and Johnathon were heading out. It had started to rain even harder and they were soaked through. "Where next?" India asked Lucy. "No sign of her at the canal. We checked as far as the Pink Pig Restaurant. Noddy and Tage were searching beyond that point. Stella has been looking all over Hart Crescent and the Rainbow Bridge. Devlin says he has checked Binders Lane and he is going to search in the Elizabethan Quarter again with Simeon and Sissy. Silvi and the Rodets told us to tell you that there is no sign of her in Finkle Street, but that they are going to check all the buildings between there and Millicent Way again."

"Jimmy has seen that Alice may be in the vicinity of a statue of Mother Mary," Lucy related to them. They looked at each other and tried to think. "There is that small stone statue at Devil's Gate just by the crematorium!" Lancelot exclaimed and they headed back out into the pouring rain.

"It's hopeless!" Linnet suddenly cried out, from her seat at the back of the Café. She was onto her third bottle of red and was in no state to go looking with the others. "Marcus will kill her, I'm sure of it." She turned a shade of green and rushed to the toilet to be sick.

Sophie went to comfort her.

"We will find her," Sophie reassured Linnet, but Linnet just lay down, next to the toilet, put her cheek to the cold tiled floor and stared into space. She suddenly grasped hold of Sophie's hand, so tightly, that Sophie thought she would break it. "Find her, Sophie! Find my baby!" Then she passed out.

Around nine o'clock, Johnathon really feared that Marcus had taken Alice out of Little Eden without being seen on the CCTV. He called the Metropolitan Police who were willing to be helpful but they had little manpower to spare.

Jimmy Pratt wandered into the Café at about ten o'clock. He had not had any further visions but he did suggest that a séance may help.

"You wanted me to talk to Lilly and Alienor anyway," he said. "We can kill two birds with one stone this way."

"It's worth a shot!" Lucy agreed.

Sophie shook her head. "I don't like séances."

"Come on, Sophie!" Minnie said eagerly. "We have to try everything, don't we?"

"Let's do it here! Straight away!" Lucy suggested and began clearing a table.

"We need somewhere quiet," Jimmy told her. "Somewhere where the veils between the worlds are thinner. It'll be easier to communicate with the spirits."

With that, the phone rang! It was the Reverend Sprott reporting that Iris was recovering well at the hospital. She had suggested a prayer group be set up immediately in the church and was already ringing round, from her hospital bed, to get it organised."

"That'll do!" Jimmy replied.

"What will?" Lucy asked.

"The church! It'll be quiet in there."

"Not with a prayer circle going all night it won't!" Sophie replied.

"Oh, yeah! Suppose not," he agreed.

"The Chappelle might do?" Lucy suggested.

So, as a prayer vigil was being arranged in the church, a séance was arranged in the Chappelle. Lucy, Minnie, a reluctant Sophie and an even more reluctant India, agreed to go to the Sainte Chappelle, to find out if they could contact Aunt Lilly or Alienor, and to ask them if they knew where Alice was.

"Oh, for God's sake!" India exclaimed, as she plonked herself down in one of the chairs that had been placed around the altar. "This is ridiculous! I can't understand how I even agreed to come!"

"I'm not happy about it either!" Sophie agreed. "But, just go with it, India. I'll keep you safe."

"I am not afraid!" India moaned. "I just think this is the most ridiculous way to go about things! Normal people don't rely on superstition to get things done!"

"Who are normal people?" Sophie asked. "British people? Protestants? Atheists? Are they the only normal people? In another country or culture, asking the ancestors or an oracle for guidance, especially in a crisis, would be normal. I have to admit I am with you on séances though, I don't like them in general as they are usually mismanaged and can lead to all sorts of trouble, even years later! Never ever do an Ouija board, no matter how fun it might seem at the time."

"Desperate times call for desperate measures!" Lucy reminded them. "Besides, we are not using a planchette or anything like that - and Jimmy is a professional."

Jimmy swaggered up to the altar. He started to place a camera on a tripod, just to the side of them. "You didn't say he could film this, did you?" India muttered to Lucy. Lucy shook her head. "He'd better not use this in one of his shows!" India replied. "I have a reputation to uphold. I don't want people seeing me on TV taking part in a séance, for goodness sakes! I think I'd better sit this one out!"

"This is why I don't trust him," Sophie whispered to India. "He is a showman first and psychic second."

"I don't trust men who wear black shirts and loafers!" India said, in a matter of fact way, and stood up as if to leave, but Sophie pulled her back down.

"Don't go!" Sophie begged her. "I thought I was going to protect you, but maybe it's the other way around!"

India sighed. "Okay, but I am *not* having my face on TV!" She turned her chair so that she had her back to the camera.

Jimmy lit some candles and then turned off the main lights. It was as if they were suddenly plunged into a very tiny space. The rest of the Chappelle had disappeared into the darkness. He paused a moment, waved his hands around a bit, and then took some Visconte Tarot Cards out of a deep purple velvet pouch and laid them on the altar. The gold leaf on the cards shimmered in the candle light as he cut the deck and made two piles.

"Are you sure you are supposed to have tarot cards in a church?" Minnie asked, a little afraid.

"Shhh," Lucy whispered to Minnie. "You'll put him off!"

"With whom do you wish to communicate?" Jimmy began to say, to no one in particular.

"You know very well we want to talk to Aunt Lilly!" Sophie said impatiently.

Jimmy made them all hold hands and then he closed his eyes. "No, no!" he suddenly cried out. "You are not welcome here!"

"Who is it?" Minnie asked and shivered. The candles flickered all of a sudden and she felt sick to her stomach with fear.

"The room is full of spirits!" Jimmy said, half opening one of his eyes. "A woman in white is trying to get in. Take her away, Alan! Protect my auric space!"

"Who the hell is Alan?" India mumbled to Sophie under her breath.

"That's Jimmy's spirit guide, apparently." Sophie smiled. She was rather amused by Jimmy's theatrical performance.

"She is here! She is here!" Jimmy said. "Come, Lilly! You are welcome! Do you have a message for us?"

A few moments passed and they all stared into the centre of the altar. A silken hush pervaded the chamber. Their minds went blank. Suddenly, a sharp knocking sound startled them all. Minnie nearly jumped out of her skin and yelped like a puppy in distress!

"It came from near the pews!" Jimmy said excitedly, and they all looked over into the darkness. He jumped up, took the camera off its tripod and went to film the front row.

"Aunt Lil is that you?" Lucy said, half laughing. "Don't frighten us all like that!"

"Lilly, speak to Alan! Tell us - where is Alice?" Jimmy said. He began to shake slightly but it was not put on. The transference of one consciousness to another causes the electromagnetic field to vibrate, which in turn, causes involuntary shaking - as a seasoned Quaker will tell you!

Jimmy put the camera back on the tripod. He could hardly hold it steady.

He went back to the altar, as if in a trance like state, and with his hands still shaking, he took the top tarot card and laid it out, face up, in front of himself.

It was the Queen of Swords. "An ancestor comes to speak with us!"

"That must be Alienor or Aunt Lil," Sophie suggested.

Jimmy took another card from the top of the deck and turned it over. It was the Prince of Coins. "A man with power seeks money."

The next card he turned over was The Tower. "Destruction is coming - he will stop at nothing to get what he wants."

"This is getting us nowhere!" India huffed.

Minnie began to get very afraid and the hairs on the back of her neck prickled. "I don't like this," she said. "I think we should stop! There is evil here." She looked around at the others with panic in her eyes. She wanted to get up from her chair and run away, but Lucy kept her hand in hers.

"Don't break the circle, Minnie," Lucy told her. "We must find Alice."

For Alice's sake, Minnie took some deep breaths and Jimmy continued. The next three cards Jimmy pulled were The King of Swords, The Star and The World.

"There will be a battle, not just for Little Eden but for mankind," Jimmy said dramatically.

“I think the war has already started!” Sophie said, exasperated.

“Who will win this war?” India asked him.

“What is he talking about?” Minnie whispered to Lucy. Lucy put her finger to her lips to indicate for Minnie not to ask any more questions right now.

Jimmy took out another card, it was The Fool. “That has not yet been decided,” he answered.

“But...” India began to say, when Jimmy put his hand up to quieten her.

“Lilly is faint. She says she cannot stay in the spirit realms if Robert does not make a choice.” Jimmy dropped his head and then his demeanour seemed to return to his normal swagger. “That’s all I can tell you for now.”

“But...” India tried to say again.

“I have told you what Alan is telling me,” Jimmy said complacently, “I cannot tell you anymore.”

“But, what about Alice?” India asked. “Does Alan know where Alice is?”

Jimmy shook his head. “Nope, sorry. He says Lilly is too faint to help us and he doesn’t know who this Alienor is that you keep mentioning.” Jimmy suddenly put up his hand and added, “Wait, there is one more thing!”

They all looked at Jimmy, hoping it was about Alice, but it was not! “There is a man called Frith - he can help you.”

“Who?” India asked.

“Frith!” Jimmy replied. Everyone looked at everyone else but no one had ever heard that name before.

“We don’t know anyone by that name,” Lucy said finally.

“I’ll leave that one with you!” Jimmy replied and went to turn off the camera.

All of a sudden, Sophie stood up and went as white as a sheet. “They are here!” she said under her breath.

“Who are here?” Lucy asked. The hairs on the back of her neck stood up and she felt a tingling on the top of her head. Minnie squeezed Lucy’s hand, they both had clammy palms and could feel a creeping terror quivering over their skin.

Sophie closed her eyes and shivered. “The three men that Melanie killed - the men they found in the lake! Their spirits are here!”

Chapter 22

~ * ~

Jimmy turned the camera back on and trained it on Sophie. "Where are they?" he asked excitedly.

"Right behind Minnie," Sophie replied.

Minnie jumped out of her seat!

"Can you see what they look like?" Jimmy urged Sophie. He was desperate to capture something supernatural on camera.

"Yes," Sophie responded. "They look bedraggled and are dripping wet. I'm glad I can't smell them."

"I can smell that!" Lucy interjected and gagged. "It's like wet dog meets death!"

As the apparitions of the three men came nearer to the friends they began to transform. "That's better," Sophie said out loud. "They look as they did before they were drowned. Has the smell gone, Luce?"

Lucy nodded. "Yes, thank God. They didn't half pong!"

"Describe them to us, Sophie. What do they look like? Are they young, old, handsome?" Lucy asked her.

"Well the first one…he is shorter than the other two. He has dark hair to his shoulders and he's wearing a burgundy suit. He has a walrus moustache!"

"Ask him his name," Jimmy suggested.

Sophie frowned. "You know I am hopeless at getting names, but I will try!" Sophie asked the first man his name. "He says his name is John. His last name sounds like Vick."

"Could it be Quick?" India asked.

"Oh, yes! Very likely!" Sophie nodded. "The second man…he is taller and really stocky. I wouldn't want to meet him in a dark alley! He has a full beard, which is a bit on the untidy side. I bet there is food stuck in there somewhere! He has very dirty nails." Sophie wrinkled her nose as she focused in on the vision. "He says his name is Henry, but I can't get a second name."

"He must be Henry Slight!" India said, "And the third man?"

"The third man…he is blond haired and clean-shaven. He has a tight-fitting jacket and is wearing a very fine blue silk cravat. He looks as if he has been to the theatre or somewhere like that. He is carrying a cane with a silver top and he has a white rose in his buttonhole. He is smiling at me and bowing down as if to kiss my hand. He is a charmer but I feel he's a bit of a cad!"

"A cad!" India said, with a smile. "I haven't heard that word in a long time!"

They are definitely the three men Melanie murdered."

"His name is…I don't know…he is just showing me his hand. He keeps pointing to it like he is playing charades. What name sounds like hand?"

"It is Hand!" India exclaimed. "It's Leonard Hand! Sophie nodded. "They're telling me they have been summoned here tonight by Melanie."

As Sophie said Melanie's name out loud the side door flew open of its own accord and an unexpected blast of freezing air rushed in, blowing out the candles and plunging them all into pitch darkness.

Lucy screamed and grabbed hold of Minnie, who put her hand over her mouth to stop herself screaming. Minnie's courage was second to none when it came to the living, but the dead, well, they scared the bejesus out of her!

"I don't fancy seeing Melanie again!" Lucy shuddered. "I can smell Lilly's perfume. Lilly is right here with us. Oh God! Please protect us Aunt Lil."

"Don't worry, sis!" Sophie said. "The spirits of Alienor, Lilly and St Hilda are around us. We are protected."

"I assume we have found Melanie," Jimmy said, seeing a large orb float down from the lectern and across his camera screen. He pointed towards the mahogany pulpit.

Sophie could see more of Melanie's spirit than just an orb and she was dressed in her sheer white night gown and was reading aloud from the Bible. *Oh, bloody hell,* Sophie thought to herself, *she's using black magic!*

"What's happening?" Lucy whispered.

"We must form a circle around the lectern," Sophie told the others. "That way we can anchor Alienor's, Lilly's and St Hilda's energy through our bodies and block Melanie's incantations from manifesting."

Minnie was reluctant to move, but India bravely went to stand behind the pulpit; she was not bothered by the astral realms at all.

"I don't like how it feels!" Minnie said, clinging to Lucy's arm. "I feel really scared now."

Sophie intrepidly climbed the steps to the lectern, knowing she would be standing right over the top of Melanie's miasma, and she did not like that idea. She looked down at the huge Bible and saw it was open at Psalm 140.

Melanie was going to use the prayer to whip up evil. Sophie knew she would have to fight like with like and use a prayer in retaliation. The outcome would depend on which of them had the strongest will.

"What are you going to do?" Lucy asked her sister.

Sophie took a deep breath and replied, "Looks like it's going to be a prayer-off between me and Melanie. Wish me luck!"

Sophie took a deep breath and prepared herself. She hoped she would remember the right prayer to say. She did not need to worry, however, St Hilda guided her all the way…

Come, deliver me, Archangel Michael, from the snares and traps of evil.
Silence those who would speak ill or viciously against me, and would accuse me of lies before God.
Release me from their web of deceit, and protect me from the wickedness and mischief of other's tongues and actions.
Let justice conquer all who stand against me and in your holy presence, let those who plot or curse against me, fall into their own net and be gone.
Let them be forgiven as quickly as I am set free.[16]

The prayer of light worked, and Melanie, unable to summon the dark forces as she had intended, suddenly flew down from the lectern and lashed out, trying to strike Henry Slight, who was the closet to her.

Sophie watched as John Quick, who was afraid of Melanie, knelt before St Hilda and asked for forgiveness, hoping it would save him. But St Hilda pointed to Melanie saying, "Forgiveness comes from within yourself and yourself alone. Neither I, nor God, can grant you forgiveness. But I will fill your heart with the Holy Spirit, if you wish it." John nodded, and suddenly, twelve white doves flew out of nowhere, straight through his chest from back to front. John and the doves disappeared into a shaft of white light and were gone.

"Wow!" Sophie said, in a hushed voice. "I've just seen the Holy Spirit in action!"

"I can smell roses," Lucy said quietly.

"I'm getting nothing!" Jimmy moaned, as he looked at his camera screen. "Not even an orb!"

---

[16] *KT King 21st Century Prayers*, KT King, 2015

"John Quick has gone to the other side," Sophie told them.

"Did Melanie really kill John Quick?" India asked Sophie. "Can you find out what happened between them in that past life?"

Sophie asked her spirit guides to show her the story between John and Melanie. Her mind travelled back in time and she could see their life together run through her head as if she were watching a film. Pictures came and went, and she could feel their emotions and sense what they were thinking too. Sophie related the outline of what she saw to the others in hushed tones. "I can see Melanie, she is standing in a Victorian drawing room waiting for someone," Sophie began. "I get the feeling she's at a dance because she's wearing an elaborate evening gown with puffed sleeves and she's holding a large lace fan. She has fresh flowers in her hair. I can hear music in the distance and a feeling of a party going on in another room. Now I can see John coming into the room to meet her. He is smartly dressed, but seems furtive and hurried, as if he shouldn't be there. He kisses her…ooooo…I say, it's very passionate!" Sophie giggled. "I didn't think people were supposed to kiss like that in those days! Now John seems to be proposing to her and she accepts."

Sophie let the film fast-forward, stopping it at the point at which Melanie and John were taking their vows. "They're getting married. It's a bit odd because it's in a room above a London pub, not in a church. I get the feeling it's not exactly legal, but she doesn't seem to mind." Sophie fast-forwarded the film again and then nodded. "They live in a tiny two-room house. I can see Melanie has three children, two toddlers and a baby, and she seems to be sewing gloves for a living. She looks poor and thin. The room she is sitting in is dimly lit and I can feel how cold it is in there. Much of the plaster has come off the walls. It's dingy and smelly and…oh, yuck…there are cockroaches everywhere and rats too! She doesn't look happy."

"Where's John?" Lucy asked. "Why are they so poor?"

"More to the point," India said, "Why did she kill him?"

"Living in squalor with three kids and a bunch of rats - I reckon I would have thought of killing him sometimes too!" Sophie said. "But wait, oh dear…"

"What?" Lucy interrupted.

"John is already married!" Sophie replied. "He has another family. They live in a wooden-clad house near the Thames. I can see his other wife and he has, one, two, three…six more children. They have a bigger, much nicer home. There are curtains at the windows and painted shutters on the outside. His wife is plump and simply but cleanly dressed. He seems to own his own horse and cart. He's a sort of delivery man."

"A bigamist and a white van driver," India laughed. "No wonder she 'done him in'."

Sophie fast forwarded again to see more of Melanie's past life story. "The second drowned man, Henry Slight lived next door to Melanie in that horrible dreary tenement," Sophie whispered. "He found out that John was already married and told Melanie. Henry agreed to help her bump off John!" Sophie frowned and said sadly, "I can see Melanie and Henry at the lake near the chateau in Little Eden. It's a dark night and the London fog is thick in the air. They can move about unseen. They have brought John there in his own cart and he's hidden under some empty grain sacks. John's still breathing but he's unconscious. Melanie and Henry tip his body into the lake together."

"What about Henry?" India asked. "How did he end up dead in the lake too?"

Sophie closed her eyes again to see. "Henry and Melanie have just tipped John into the water; Henry seems to want to kiss Melanie. She pushes him off. He gets angry. Oh no! He is demanding sex in exchange for helping her kill John. Henry is trying to force himself on her. She's struggling to get him away from her!"

"Oh! Poor Melanie!" Lucy said.

"Don't feel too sorry for her - she has just killed someone," Jimmy reminded her.

"So!" Lucy replied. "Should she be raped as a punishment for her crime?"

Jimmy shrugged.

"She was guilty after all," India sighed. "Poor Robert! I think he was still hoping his mother, Melanie I mean, would turn out to be innocent and it had all been a terrible mistake."

Sophie had another look at what had happened that fateful night over one hundred years ago. "Melanie finds a stone beside her on the ground and hits Henry on the head with it!" Sophie grimaced at the frightful scene she was seeing. She was almost overwhelmed by the fear emanating from the pictures, but she tried to detach herself emotionally and just report back what she was witnessing. "He dies within seconds. Melanie seems to panic for a moment and then comes over all calm. She just rolls him into the lake to join John. Then she brushes herself down and takes the horse and cart and drives away."

As she finished her story, Henry's spirit began to disappear into the light, but he did not dissolve as John had done. Instead, he rose upwards to the top of the shaft of light and an elderly man sporting a white beard appeared - he did not look happy with Henry at all. He put some handcuffs on Henry then marched him off into the white mist and was gone.

"I think St Peter came to get him." Sophie said. "That's two down. One to go!"

The third man, Leonard Hand, seemed overjoyed to see Melanie. She did not seem so happy to see him, however!

"Leonard betrayed her," Sophie told the others. "I can see him with her by the lake. She is finely dressed now. She looks as if she has a lot of money. Oh wait! I get it! This is several years after she killed John and Henry and she is married to Bobby Bartlett-Hart now. Leonard is her lover. He promised to run away with her, but he changed his mind at the last minute. That's why I felt he was a cad! Oh dear, poor Melanie! She is devastated! I can see her waiting for him in the moonlight. There is very strong karmic-love between them. It feels so deep and passionate. She really believed he loved her."

"Yes, I can feel it too," Lucy whispered. "There is so much love. So much passion!" Lucy felt an unexpected pain in her chest. "But, so much pain."

"How did Melanie kill Leonard?" India asked.

"Same as Henry!" Sophie replied. "A blow to the head, but this time with a broken branch from one of the oak trees, and then she pushed him in the lake."

"I suppose once you have a winning formula, why change it?" Jimmy chuckled - a little too loudly.

With much persuasion from St Hilda, Leonard and Melanie forgave each other, and he floated upwards into the light. Instead of waiting for Melanie to join him however, he was met by the spirit of another attractive young woman, and he walked off with her, a grin on his face, without looking back.

Melanie, enraged at being rejected yet again, fell back down from the white light portal before she could dissolve into it and began to move about jerkily, in a hideous manner. It was a most unnerving and unnatural sight to see Melanie's contorted body writhing and slithering into itself, as if she were devouring her own being. Sophie watched as Melanie imploded into herself and disappeared into nowhere before anyone could stop her.

Lucy saw the look of shock and then disappointment on her sister's face. "What's happened?" she asked.

Sophie shook her head in despair. "We lost Melanie! She disappeared before we could get her over to the other side. She's still on the loose and madder than ever. But, I don't know where she's gone!"

"Great!" Lucy said, on hearing the bad news. "So all this was for nothing?"

"No! Not for nothing!" Sophie told her. "The spirits of John, Henry and Leonard have been released from limbo and into the heavenly realms tonight. And the more we clear from that lifetime, the better chance we have of getting Collins and Jennifer to change their minds about selling!"

"One question," India said. "If Melanie is now Jennifer Bartlett-Hart, who are these men? Now, I mean, in this present life - in 2012?"

Sophie scanned her psychic mind for information. "I'm being told that John Quick is now..." she paused for a moment to make sure that she had got the right information…"Robin Shaft!" Sophie screwed up her face as she realised who Henry Slight had reincarnated as… "Oh my god, you'll never guess who Henry is now!" she said to the others.

They all looked at her, unable to guess and eager to hear her reply.

"Who?" Lucy urged her.

"Only Marcus Finch!" Sophie replied.

"No way!" Lucy exclaimed. "That explains a lot!"

"Who is the third man, Leonard Hand? Do we know who he is?" India asked again.

"I don't know," Sophie replied. "But I do know something! I know where Alice is!" She went to the door and pulled it open. "Come on!"

Chapter 23

~ * ~

"Alice is in the old air-raid shelter on Quaker Lane! Minnie! Quick, run to the Café and tell the others," Sophie urged her.

Minnie raced off, her being the fittest of them all, and burst through the Café door to find Robert was back from his latest search.

"How do you know she's there?" Robert asked her. "The shelter hasn't been accessed in years."

Minnie was out of breath and had a stitch. She tried to explain, "Marcus used to be Henry Slight...one of the men in the lake...Sophie sent them all to the other side...Henry, aka Marcus, told Sophie...where Alice is!"

"My god! Robert exclaimed, throwing down his coffee. "Damn it! Cubby! Come on!"

The two men sped off into the grizzly night. When they reached the statue of the air raid warden Robert could see that the metal door had been recently disturbed. Cubby yanked it open.

"Shh!" Robert whispered. "I'll go first, you follow, but be quiet!" They climbed down the ladder but being 'quiet' was easier said than done! The metal ladder creaked and groaned as he used the first step. Robert decided to use the sailor's technique and slid down using just the sides. Then Cubby did the same, but he went a little too fast and shot off the end and crashed into the opposite wall!

"Shhh!" Robert told him as he helped him up. They strained to hear any sign that Alice was still down there, but the bunker felt eerily silent. They could see a very faint light coming from beyond the first passage and tiptoed towards the end of the first corridor. Cubby drew his pistol. Robert gestured for Cubby to freeze. Then he signalled one, two, three, with his fingers and together they spun around the corner to surprise Marcus and rescue Alice!

Cubby put his gun down in dismay. They were confronted only by the once majestic statue of Mother Mary, lying shattered into several pieces on the cold grey concrete floor. The oil lamps were still burning but there was no sign of life. They scanned the whole room, but neither Alice nor Marcus were to be found. Robert picked up Mother Mary's head and Cubby picked up her left arm, which was still holding the dove. They gently and reverently laid her dismembered body upon the altar. Disappointed, they took a lamp each and looked in every corner of the bunker, in all the bunk rooms, and corridors, until Cubby finally fell over Alice's library books. "Over here!" Cubby shouted from near the ladder. Robert rushed to see what Cubby had discovered and the two men looked at each other. Their hearts went cold. They feared the worst.

~ * ~

Marcus and Alice had been in the bunker together for several hours. To Alice it seemed like days. Marcus preached and prayed and then preached and prayed some more. He talked about taking her to a safe place in the middle of the night.

Alice went through all the emotions a human can experience and was close to hysterical at times. *I would kill him*, she thought, *If, I was strong enough, or if I had a gun.* She wanted to run away, but she knew there was no way she could get the metal cover off the top of the ladder, even if she made it up that far. In desperation, she looked up at Mother Mary and wondered how she could look down on such a horrible person and still smile. But then, Alice had an idea flash into her head, and she could not believe she had not thought of it before! Alice called out with her thoughts to Lilly for help. *Lilly*, she called silently, *Help me, help me, help me!* She immediately felt a cool breeze waft against her cheek and that was all the sign she needed. She knew that the angels and Lilly were close to her and that they had heard her call.

In her mind Alice heard Lilly's words, *'Pretend to agree with him, gain his trust'*. Alice wasn't too keen on the idea, but the words were repeated over and over, so she gave in to them and as soon as she made up her mind to play along, her tears stopped, and she felt a wave of calmness run over her.

She decided to pretend she was in a school play and that she was a princess captured by an evil king. She had to escape from him by becoming a Jedi.[17] *Good always wins over evil*, she thought. Lilly's voice came into her mind again, whispering, *'Tell him you are hungry and thirsty'*. Alice felt neither, but out loud she said, "Daddy, I'm hungry and thirsty."

Marcus looked annoyed. "You can't be hungry before God. He is all the succour we need."

---

[17] *Star Wars*, George Lucas, 1977, Lucas Film

"Please, Daddy!" Alice pleaded, and then added theatrically and quite convincingly, "Have mercy upon me. I am just a child. I know God wants me to go with you to America, but I can't wait 'til midnight to eat Daddy, it's past my dinner time now."

Marcus seemed taken aback by her words and it mellowed him somewhat. He didn't suspect her motives at all. He always underestimated women and children. He was a little unsure of how to deal with children. He knew that bribery with food worked however, and he saw it as an opportunity to look like the good guy.

"There's a vending machine at the skate park, just down the street, Daddy. It's not far. We could go and see what's in it?" Alice said, as meekly as she could, and looked up at him with her best 'please, please, please' face.

Marcus didn't want to risk her being seen so he told her to stay put and that he would go to the vending machine alone. "I'll be two minutes," he told her. "That's all. Two minutes." He reluctantly left Alice alone and climbed the ladder, exiting surreptitiously onto the grass above.

As soon as she heard the door clang back down, Alice didn't waste any time. She begged Lilly to help her again. "What should I do now?" Alice whispered out loud, looking at Mother Mary again. "What should I do?"

In answer to her question, Alice saw a tiny flash of blue light to her left, followed by a small white floating orb, which appeared from behind the altar and hovered in the air for a few moments. "Lilly, is that you?" she whispered, and she felt in her bones that it was. Alice went to where the orb had been and stood in front of the panel of saints. "Now what should I do?" she asked. Involuntarily, she placed her hands onto the feet of the first saint. As if her hand had a power all of its own, it began moving down the side of the wooden screen and she felt her fingers disappear behind it. She was shocked to find that there was actually a wide gap behind the panel and that it was not the back wall of the chamber after all. She felt the urge to go round the edge and realised that from the front it was an optical illusion. In reality the saints stood proud of the concrete by quite a few inches.

Alice squeezed herself between the wall and the screen. Once she was in the gap, she was plunged into pitch darkness. She tried to keep her courage and slowly shuffled herself along until she fell backwards a little. She didn't like to get so close to the concrete. Its coarse texture and lifeless cement grey colour made her flesh creep. When the short wall came to an end she had popped out of the narrow channel into a deep doorway. She turned around and felt a wooden door barring her way. She tried to open it but found it was locked. Finding her chance of escape suddenly snatched away from her, she nearly burst into tears, but then a wave of lightness came over her and she almost felt dizzy. She remembered a dream she had had two nights ago but had forgotten all about until this moment. In the dream she had seen a locked door in the trunk of a tree. St Hilda had been holding the key, which she gave to Alice just before she woke up.

Quickly, Alice squeezed herself back the way she had come and peered around the corner to see if the coast was clear. Not hearing or seeing any sign of Marcus, she looked up and down the row of saints, willing one of them to be St Hilda. One was St Margaret and another was St Katherine, there was St Oswald, St Aidan and St Olaf. She frantically kept looking until there, thank god, at the other end of the screen was St Hilda, who was carrying a bunch of wooden keys in her hands.

Alice heard the door to the shelter being opened again and she panicked.

With her heart beating ten to the dozen and her stomach feeling as if it couldn't screw itself up any harder, she searched and scratched around St Hilda, desperate to find a key. She frantically scrabbled around in the dust and dirt at St Hilda's feet. Cobwebs covered her hands. She held her breath and tried not to scream when a huge spider crawled over her fingers. She shuddered and tried to tell herself she was on one of those TV shows where celebrities have to endure trials with bugs and spiders and snakes. She told herself, *I can do this, I can do this. Get me out of here!* She pushed her tiny hand as far behind St Hilda's feet as she could, grimacing at the yucky feeling beneath her fingers. Finally, she felt something cold and metallic. It was a key! She tried to pull it out, but it was too big to fit through the gap. She heard Marcus coming down the ladder. She pulled and pulled but it was no use - the key was stuck between St Hilda's ankles.

Alice took a deep breath and let go of the key for a moment. As she heard Marcus approaching down the corridor, she grabbed the key again, and this time it seemed to change its angle slightly, and came out with ease. She took her one chance, and as quick as lightening, she slid herself behind the panel again and slipped into the hidden doorway.

Leaning back against the door, Alice could hear Marcus shouting for her from the chapel. She was afraid to try the key in case he heard the noise.

She hardly dared even breathe and put her hand over her mouth, afraid she might let out a squeak or a sigh. She could hear him calling her name. Then, his angry voice seemed to fade into the distance a little. She was about to try the key when she heard his words become louder again, but this time he was saying her name in a kinder tone. "I'm not angry with you, Alice. Where are you, my dove? I have chocolate and crisps for you. I have a can of lemonade!"

Alice was sure he would hear her heart beating if he came too near the altar. Her blood sounded so loud running through her veins, that it filled her ears with a fast, booming sound, that frightened her almost as much as Marcus did. Alice thought her heart would go pop if it beat any faster and wondered if you could die from your heart exploding.

After a few moments, Marcus started to get angry again. She heard the ladder rattle. She wasn't sure where she got her courage from, but she turned around as quietly as she could and felt about for the lock in the door. She leant her weight against the key and it seemed to turn a little, then it turned so swiftly that she nearly fell through the door as it opened suddenly before her. Still afraid that Marcus would find her hiding place at any moment, she peered into the blackness in front of her. Her heart leaped out of her chest as she heard a loud shout from Marcus, followed by a ferocious growl.

Suddenly, there was an almighty crash! In his fury Marcus had violently smashed the statue of Mother Mary to the floor!

The shock jolted Alice into another memory. This time she remembered the night they had fled from the chateau. *Passageways*, she thought. *Please let it be one of those passageways!* She wanted to walk into the darkness but her knees nearly went from beneath her. The altar room was mysteriously quiet. Marcus had stopped shouting for her and this unnerved her even more because she did not know where he was. She expected his hand to grab her shoulder at any moment.

Alice prayed to Lilly again for help, and with trepidation, she took a few steps forward. She held her hands out in front of her to feel for walls, and realised, after a few steps, that either she was in a very long room or it really was a passageway. She felt to the side and found that the walls were not very far apart. This reassured her that it was indeed some kind of underground corridor, so she kept going forwards. Occasionally, small twinkles of light, like tiny bubbles of fairy dust, danced in front of her. Although absolutely petrified, Alice also felt strangely calm at the same time.

In the back of her mind she could hear Lilly singing the song, 'You're Not Alone' and it was as if a higher part of her brain in her head was at peace and sure of its footing, but the lower part of her brain in her stomach was in fight or flight mode and in a state of pure panic. She paused, feeling too shaky to keep walking. She called out to St Hilda with her mind: *Give me your courage, St Hilda! Give me your courage.* She kept repeating this over and over, and as she did so, she found that she could keep walking after all.

Suddenly, an orb of violet light came floating towards her and hovered in front of her for a few moments before moving to her left and dissolving. Putting her hands out to the sides again, she realised that the walls had disappeared and she couldn't feel anything around her, neither in front nor behind. Her courage failed her again and she wanted to just drop to the floor and cry, but she heard Lilly whispering in her head, 'Follow the light!' Alice did as she was guided to do and after a few steps to her left she could feel the walls of the passageway around her again.

She began to cry silently, tears rolling down her cold cheeks, as she kept walking forward into the all-consuming darkness.

After a while, Alice began to tire. She finally stopped and slid down onto the damp stone floor. *Tambo…Mummy…Jack…Lucy...Sophie…Minnie…* Alice called in her head. *I'm here, please find me. I'm here! I'm down here.* She started to cry and every little noise she heard sent a spike of fear through her body, thinking it might be Marcus come to find her. But then, the atmosphere began to change, and she knew Sophie was with her.

She could feel Sophie almost as clearly as if she were sitting next to her. Sophie! Alice called in her mind. *I'm here in a tunnel! Sophie, please, come and get me!* An orb of white light danced above Alice's head and it floated gently down the passageway a few inches. Alice felt she must follow it. She picked herself up off the floor and followed the orb until it vanished. Alice put out her hands and realised she was in front of a cubbyhole. The wall came up about a foot off the ground and was then recessed, making for a dry seat inside a little alcove. She climbed inside and sat down cross-legged. She felt safe with her back against the wall and hidden from the passageway. Alice laid her head against the back of the inset and let Sophie's voice float through her mind…

St Hilda, St Hilda, St Hilda
You, who love the flowers and the mountains.
You, who love the earth and the skies.
You, who love the oceans and the ancients.
You are my bedrock, my holy water and my sacred fire.
You are my tranquillity, my serenity and my peace.[18]

Sophie's prayer made Alice feel snoozey and she dozed off into a shallow sleep.

~ * ~

Robert and Cubby returned to the Café, from the shelter, with the bad news. Tambo knew Alice was still in Little Eden somewhere and he swore he could feel her nearby. Robert put his arm around Tambo. "We will keep searching," he said. "Why don't you get some sleep? We will have her back here by morning."

Tambo shook his head. His adrenalin was racing too high for him to feel tired. He looked across at some of the searchers who were having a respite, one of whom was Mr T.

Tambo suddenly had an idea. "Cedric!" he cried. "Cedric will find Alice!"

Tambo raced up the stairs, charged out of the conservatory doors and onto the terrace. He hopped over the small wall onto Mr T's roof and barged through his kitchen door. Cedric was asleep in his basket, under the kitchen worktop. Tambo quickly picked up a sleepy Cedric and ran back down to the Café.

"Don't you see!" Tambo shouted, holding up Cedric, who had now started to wake up and look around - a little surprised to be in a different place to where he had gone to sleep.

Lucy shook her head. "I think Cedric is a bit old to be a bloodhound. But it's a nice thought."

Tambo wasn't to be defeated by little things like Cedric walking so slowly these days that it would probably take him most of the evening to make it across the square! He wrapped Cedric in a tea towel to keep him warm and dry. "I will carry him!" Tambo said. "We can go back to the bunker and let Cedric sniff the trail from there."

[18] *KT King 21st Century Prayers*, KT King, 2016

Robert looked at Cedric in Tambo's arms. "Anything's worth a try," he said. "But Cubby and I will go with Cedric. Marcus is dangerous!"

"I don't care! I'm coming to find Alice! Come on, let's go!" Tambo opened the Café door and a huge draught of freezing cold air rushed in. The rain had stopped and the air had become oddly still, as if it was holding its breath in anticipation of what was to come.

"We need to focus where we search," Robert said. "Let me think." He closed the door and Tambo stood, impatiently hopping from foot to foot, whilst Robert planned what to do. Cubby helped himself to another hot buttered teacake, whilst he thought too.

In the quiet of her bedroom, Sophie had been talking telepathically with Alice, but when she heard Tambo racing up and down the stairs, she came to find out what was going on.

"Can't you see anything more?" Robert asked her. "You say you've been talking to Alice, why can't you see where she is?"

"Because there are no landmarks I can go on. She is still underground, its dark, that's all I know," Sophie sighed.

"Think!" Lucy urged her sister. "Is there a smell? Does it feel cold? Damp? Hot? Is it noisy?"

"It is cold, where she is, but I don't think it is just the air or the ground that is cold. I feel as if I'm surrounded by ice-cold water."

The colour drained from Lucy's face - fearing Alice had drowned.

"I feel as if I am under water but not under water!" Sophie added. "Not drowning in it, I mean."

"What does that mean?" Robert asked, a little frustrated.

"I'm under water but not wet. I can't explain it," Sophie replied.

"The lake!" Robert said suddenly. "There are underground passageways under the lake. Perhaps, somehow, they have found their way into the passages."

"Can you get from the shelter into the passages?" Minnie asked.

Robert shrugged, he didn't know all the passageways, but Stella suddenly remembered something. "Wait!" she said. "My mother used to say that in the air-raid shelter, during the war, she was afraid that they might get stuck in there if the German's invaded. But they were told that they could escape, all the way to the Thames, from inside, if needs be."

"Then, there is an entrance to the passages from the bunker? But, where?" Robert looked at Cedric in Tambo's arms. "Maybe Cedric can help us after all!"

~ * ~

Down in the dark, dank passage, Alice awoke from her reverie to the sound of a dog barking in the distance. The yelp echoed through the passages and she recognised it immediately. Cedric? She hardly dare believe it. She thought perhaps she was still dreaming. Then she heard him again and called out, shouting as loudly as she could, "Cedric! I'm over here! Cedric, it's Alice! Cedric! Cedric!"

Alice saw the light of a torch in the distance and her spirits rose with relief. She was going to be rescued at any moment! But then her heart went cold, as the light disappeared, and Cedric stopped barking. "No! Don't go away!" Alice sobbed. "Here, Cedric, I'm here…" her voice tailed off from sheer exhaustion.

Then, just as she was sure that Cedric had gone in a different direction, she heard the patter of his feet and he was right next to her, jumping up and licking her hand. "Oh, Cedric!" she cried, as she cuddled him close to her. "Oh, Cedric!" Alice could hear voices and footsteps approaching. For one awful moment she was afraid it might be Marcus, but then she saw the light from the torch again and it was Tambo's voice she could hear, calling her name. Her heart leapt and her tears were those of relief now.

Tambo had come to rescue her!

Robert and Tambo, both carrying flashlights, turned the corner, where they found a cold and exhausted Alice holding Cedric to her chest. Robert rushed up to her and took her straight into his arms. "Alice! Oh Alice!" he said, as he hugged her. "You gave us a fright! Where have you been?"

She sobbed into Robert's shoulder as he held her to him

Tambo grabbed her hand. "Are you hurt? Are you alright? What happened? What happened to you?" He felt tears welling up in his eyes.

"It's okay," Alice told him. "Sophie and Lilly were with me."

"Let's get you out of here!" Robert told her. "Let's get you home to your mummy!"

He carried her back down the passageway and they headed out towards the surface.

Robert thought it best to take the shortest route back, rather than return to the shelter, where they had left Cubby on guard, and he took them further under the lake. He knew there was an entrance inside Charlotte's Folly.

Sophie had been feeling Alice's fear and was relieved, at last, to get a wave of happiness, and she dared to hope that Alice had been found. She could see Charlotte's Folly in her mind's eye. Grabbing Minnie and reviving Linnet, they headed out through the park towards the stone tower.

The whole park was shrouded in wispy white fog which had descended like a shroud over the lake. It thinned out a little in patches and they could see the edges of the lake and the water lapping amongst the rushes. They arrived at the Folly just in time to see Cedric emerging from the side of a huge fireplace. On seeing Sophie he barked a doggy 'hello' and was followed by Tambo, Alice and Robert. Alice looked in such a state - all covered in black smudges from the passageway walls and floor. Her hair was tangled and streaks of tears marked her cheeks.

"Alice!" Linnet gasped, and ran to her without hesitation.

Tambo ran into the arms of his aunt Sophie and hugged her. Everyone was crying with relief and exhaustion.

"Come on, let's get her back home!" Robert suggested.

"Did you see Marcus?" Minnie asked.

Robert shook his head.

Robert carried Alice, and Tambo carried Cedric, as they all left the Folly together. Walking along the pathway, which lined the edge of the lake, they were under the shelter of a canopy of majestic oak trees. Through a gap in the mist they caught sight of Johnathon and Jack in the distance, who were coming up the path from the opposite direction. But, before they reached them, Robert heard a crackle of branches amongst the trees, as if someone was walking within the woods.

"Shh!" Robert said, and put his hand out to stop Tambo walking on. Robert had a strange feeling that whoever it was moving about amongst the trees was not friendly. Looking at Sophie, she shook her head and flashed him a look to show that she did not trust the presence either. Both of them were right to trust their gut instincts because at that moment, Marcus Finch stepped out into their path!

Marcus had been unaware of their presence due to the shroud of fog swirling all around them. He was a little disorientated, not really knowing his way around the park. He had not found the passageways at all and had, in the end, left the shelter, having presumed that Alice had somehow managed the superhuman feat of lifting the metal door all by her little seven-year old self! He realised that there were people all over the place, obviously searching for Alice, and he headed for the nearest place to lie low in that he knew of - the woods. Although the trees were hardly more than about fifty feet deep at their widest point, he felt as if all sense of direction had left him and had wandered about in a daze. If he had been the sort of person to believe in fairies, he would have sworn they were playing tricks on him!

So, Marcus appeared right next to Robert, and before he even had time to look him in the eye, Robert threw himself at him. Using his best rugby moves, he tackled him with full force, sending them both to the ground with an almighty thud.

The two men hit the grassy bank at such an angle that they rolled down towards the dark water of the lake. Unable to find any purchase on the sodden grass, they both went headlong into the water with a loud splash! They floundered together amongst the gloopy rushes, unable to get a footing on the sandy lake floor. The two men finally struggled to their feet, but without warning, Robert jumped on Marcus from behind, pushing him back underneath the water and holding him down. He was trying to weaken him so that he could drag him out as his prisoner.

As they both struggled in the mire, Marcus realised he needed something to hit Robert with. He desperately felt with his hands along the bottom of the shallow lake, but it was impossible to see anything in the churned-up water. Marcus suddenly felt something metal under the palm of his hand, and he hoped whatever it was, that it wasn't too big to pull up. It wouldn't budge at first, but then the sand gave way and Marcus was wielding, what seemed to be, a metal crossbar from a discarded bicycle. With the last breath in his body he swung it backwards over his shoulder, whacking Robert hard in the face.

Robert took the blow directly across the jaw and it threw him backwards into the water. Marcus stood up, gasping for air, water streaming off his coat like a waterfall. He took the chance to regain his equilibrium and lifted the bar above his head ready to smack its full force down onto Robert again, but Robert grabbed at Marcus' soaking trousers and the bar shot out of Marcus' hand as he tried to stop himself falling. Robert grabbed it and hit Marcus across the head with it toppling him back down under the water.

Robert, still dazed and light-headed, let down his guard for a moment.

Suddenly, Marcus rose out of the water like a sea monster, brandishing a huge stone in one hand. He swung it around like a Titan, cracking it hard against the side of Robert's head, and then Marcus collapsed into the water and seemed to disappear into the darkness.

As blood trickled down Robert's face, he felt someone's arms catch him as he passed out.

Johnathon had arrived just in the nick of time and had plunged into the lake just as Robert took the final blow. It was he who caught Robert and pulled him to safety. Robert was bleeding profusely from his head wound and his jaw was broken. He seemed to drift in and out of consciousness. Johnathon laid him down on the grassy bank and rang for an ambulance whilst Sophie held his hand. Keeping pressure on his head wound, she prayed constantly to Mother Mary to save his life.

Jack, seeing that Johnathon had Robert well in hand, waded into the churned-up, freezing lake to fetch Marcus. He could not find him at first. The mist swirled around the reeds, obscuring everything. Finally, he felt something brush against him and looked down to see Marcus, also unconscious, floating face up in the water. Jack realised that Marcus was still breathing and that he could probably save his life, if he acted quickly. He was about to shout to Johnathon to help him drag Marcus back to shore when something stopped him. All around him everything became quiet and still, as if time had suddenly paused. He could no longer hear Sophie praying, or Linnet crying, or even Minnie talking to Lucy on her phone. All he could hear was the lapping of the water and his own heartbeat. In that split second, Jack didn't exactly decide what to do next - not consciously anyway - he just found himself doing it. He spun Marcus's body over and quietly held him, face down, under the water for a few more seconds. Marcus didn't even struggle, giving his death a kind of quiet grace.

"God forgive me," Jack whispered, as he held Marcus' head under the water, one last time.

Johnathon waded into the lake to find them both. Jack wasn't sure if Johnathon had seen what he had done, but to his relief Johnathon simply said, "It was too late to save him, then?"

"Yes," Jack replied. "Yes, too late."

Chapter 24

~ * ~

Such a welcome awaited the friends back at the Café! All the searchers had assembled to eat bacon butties and to dry off. There was relief and exaltation that Alice had been found safe and sound, but there was also a tinge of sadness. Some people thought that no matter how evil Marcus had been, the loss of a human life was a terrible and regrettable thing. Some people thought that the world was a safer place without Marcus Finch in it, and some people didn't really think about it at all.

Tambo wouldn't let go of Alice's hand, and she even had to drink her hot chocolate with one hand on her mug and the other hand in his! She needed a hot bath and Tambo stood outside the bathroom door, like a sentry guarding his queen. He insisted that Alice sleep over.

Alice didn't want to talk about what had happened just yet. She was too tired and she was starting to feel sore from her fall. She was glad to take arnica and Rescue Remedy® and she willingly let Sophie mend her aura with some Rainbow Rescuer. She also asked Sophie to do the Bubble Meditation with her before bed.

"You can always talk to me or Lucy about anything that you are frightened or worried about," Sophie told her, as she tucked her in. "You know that, don't you? You can tell us or ask us anything, anything at all!"

Alice nodded, as she snuggled down into her deliciously soft feather pillow. "Lilly showed me the way out behind the statues."

"Did she?" Sophie smiled. "Then she really is your guardian angel."

"So are you," Alice said, "You were there too!"

"I was," Sophie nodded. "You are never alone Alice, even when you feel or think you are. There are always angels and fairies with you, and they are just a thought away."

Sophie closed the bedroom door behind her and then lent back against it. *That was a close shave*, she thought to herself. *For some reason, Alice escaped and was saved today.* She thought about what Dr G had said about Alice being a portal guardian and felt a shiver of fear go through her body. *Are all the portal guardians in danger of being attacked, possibly killed? This is getting serious! Too close for comfort. It's one thing when you are fighting the darkness in the astral realms, but another when it starts being three dimensional. What if Robert doesn't regain consciousness? What if the angels are not able to save him? Little Eden will be sold, and the portal left unguarded and there will be nothing anyone can do about it.*

~ * ~

On Russell Street, a rain storm was raging outside the windows of the warm and brightly lit hospital room, in which Robert was lying. Calming music was playing in the background, as smartly dressed nurses padded silently, in soft soled shoes, up and down the corridors, carrying clip boards and whispering to each other in hushed tones. Only the sudden crash of rain against windows gave any indication of the wildness going on beyond its smooth pastel walls and highly polished floors.

In a private room, filled with shiny new machines of the most up to date technology, Robert lay unconscious on billowing pillows and immaculately crisp white sheets. He looked pale yet serene.

A policeman, dressed in a jet black uniform, stood guard on the door. Until Marcus' death was declared an accident, the Inspector of New Scotland Yard wanted Robert under surveillance, just in case he woke up and made a run for it!

Jennifer sat on a plastic chair by his bed, moaning at the cheapness of the decor and asking anyone who would listen, if the price of the treatment was covered by their insurance. She was continually asking an unconscious Robert why it was taking so long for Collins to arrive!

Eventually, Varsity came into the room and Jennifer's face lit up, but her expression immediately soured when she realised that Varsity wasn't with Collins, but that she had Shilty Cunningham in tow instead.

"Where is Collins?" Jennifer demanded. "I've been here half an hour already! Robert could be dead and his brother is not here to see him! Where is he? Did you see that policeman on the door? Treating Robert as if he were a common criminal! It's too much! What if anyone should find out?"

Varsity tried to calm Jennifer down with various platitudes, telling her that Collins was talking with one of the doctors at reception.

Shilty went over to Robert's bedside. She tried her hardest to cry, but in reality found that she felt very little emotion.

Jennifer retold the story of what had happened at the lake to Varsity and Shilty. The story was already second hand, as Jennifer had had it from the policeman, so by the time it reached Shilty's ears it was a far more romantic version of events than had actually happened.

Shilty smiled to herself. Robert being a knight in shining armour sent him up in her estimation. A hero! She thought to herself. *Now, I do like that! It'll be in the papers. When he wakes up we could do an exclusive for one of the magazines.* She squeezed Robert's hand in approval, and was, for a few moments at least, genuinely sad to see him injured and unconscious, but within a few minutes she was getting rather bored.

Twenty minutes later, Collins came nonchalantly through the door.

"Where have you been?" Jennifer exclaimed. "It's hopeless! The nurses don't care and I haven't even been offered a cup of coffee!"

Collins told them that the Registrar did not hold out much hope for Robert, and looking at his brother, lying deathly pale in the bed, he wondered if he would ever wake up. "You know Robert," Collins said. "He might rally round yet, Mother." Although, he was thinking that was what he was supposed to say, rather than actually believing it.

Jennifer screeched, "Don't be ridiculous! He's dying! Look at him! The doctor thinks he is dead already! Oh, my poor boy! No mother should have to watch their child die! And it is very inconvenient. I had a lunch date, which I shall have to cancel now!"

"Go and get Mother a coffee will you?" Collins told Varsity. "In fact, why don't you both go to the coffee machine? I saw one in reception." He gave Varsity some change from his trouser pocket. "That's it, off you both go!"

Varsity didn't want to go, but she didn't like to upset Jennifer anymore than she was already. She carefully led Jennifer out of the room by the elbow, as if she were aged one hundred and three, and on the point of dying herself.

Collins looked at his brother for a few moments and wondered how much the funeral would cost, and how long it would be until he could take full control of the Trust. Then he smiled at Shilty. "Come here, gorgeous!" he said, pulling her playfully off her chair towards him.

"Not here!" Shilty giggled.

"Why not?" Collins grinned.

Shilty motioned her head towards Robert.

"Oh, he can't hear a thing!" Collins said, kissing her. "The doctor said it could be days, weeks even, before he wakes up, if at all!" Collins kissed her neck and slipped his hand down into her ample cleavage beneath her white t-shirt.

Shilty pretended to try and push him away, but she didn't try all that hard. "We mustn't!" she repeated. "Not here!"

Collins carried on groping her and started to undo his zipper.

"Stop it!" Shilty giggled.

Collins was not going to listen to her feeble protestations, but he suddenly found he had to stop his fumbling anyway as the door opened and Varsity returned, with Jennifer, from reception.

"The machine's not working," Varsity told them. Luckily for everyone (or perhaps unluckily, who knows) Varsity's attention was on Jennifer, and she was unaware that Shilty was unceremoniously stuffing her boobs back into her bra, or that Collins was discreetly zipping himself back up.

"This always happens to me!" Jennifer wailed, sitting back down in her uncomfortable chair. "My son is a murderer and now he's dead, and the coffee machine isn't working, and I was supposed to be having lunch with the Moppets."

"There's nothing more we can do here!" Collins said, a little exasperated because he was still feeling horny. "Let's take Mother home. Shilty, why don't you come too?"

"We can't leave Robert all on his own!" Varsity protested. "What if he wakes up and there is no one here?"

Collins shrugged. "I'm sure he can cope. Besides, he isn't going anywhere. Except, maybe, to prison or to Heaven."

"I'll stay with him," Shilty offered, a little reluctantly. But, before anyone could leave, Stella Dew rushed into the room, threw her handbag onto one of the chairs, narrowly missing Jennifer, and went straight over to a sleeping Robert.

"Oh! My darling boy!" Stella whispered over and over to him, as tears rolled down her cheeks. "You are safe, you are in hospital and we are all here. You are safe. You are safe." She looked up at the others, who all looked rather embarrassed by her display of real emotion, but she was not ashamed, not in the least. "How is he? What did the doctor say?" Stella's face was pale with anxiety and fear at the possibility of hearing bad news.

"All we can do is wait and see if he wakes up or not. If he does wake up, we won't know whether he can walk, talk or shit by himself," Collins said grumpily, rather annoyed at Stella's over dramatic show of affection towards his brother. "Personally, if it was me lying there, I wouldn't want to wake up if that's the case, and I'd rather have the plug pulled on me right now!"

Stella ignored Collins and reached over and squeezed Jennifer's hand. "You must be so relieved Robert survived. I am sure he will pull through," she said, sympathetically.

Jennifer shrugged and stood up to leave. "I am! I am Stella dear, I am! But I am so tired with it all! It's all so upsetting! Now you are here, Stella dear, we can go. You will stay with my boy, won't you? I can't bear to see him like this! It's too upsetting!"

"Of course! I will stay till he wakes up. I will stay with him as long as it takes!" Stella replied, and started to rearrange his pillows. She tucked in the already tucked-in bed sheets, smoothing them down the best she could. "You will wake up very soon, won't you, my darling boy? Very soon."

For the next few days, Stella made the hospital her home. Stella was sure in her heart that she must stay by Robert's side, and must not, under any circumstances, leave the hospital. She had a sense of needing to protect him from something, but she wasn't sure what that something was. She also had a morbid fear of Robert dying alone and she dreaded his death with no less fear and pain than a true mother would.

~ * ~

Back in Little Eden, gossip about Robert's critical condition had broken out. Fortunately, no one had gotten wind of the plan to sell Little Eden, but it didn't take long for the conspiracy theories to circulate - thanks to Derren Cox - the local troll from the Tom Thumb Alley tobacconist shop. He claimed that Robert was already dead and that Lancelot was pretending he was alive in order to save Little Eden from falling under the control of his brother Collins. Another theory was the exact opposite: Robert was alive but going to be charged with the murder of Marcus Finch, so Lancelot was going to pretend that Robert had died. That way, he could flee the country to somewhere without an extradition treaty. The man in the hospital bed was a look-alike decoy of course!

After a few more days, the gossip grew old, and instead of the sound of chatter on every street corner, an eerie hush and a slightly creepy silence fell over the small town. The place became almost deserted. The shops and the lanes seemed abandoned. Residents spoke only in whispers. Fear had set in.

One evening, up at the Café apartment, the girls were interrupted by a knock on the conservatory door. Standing outside in the cold were Peony and Vincent.

Peony had been too scared to face Linnet for the last few days, and certainly not on her own, so she had persuaded Vincent to accompany her, just in case things got nasty. Unwelcome as Peony was, English politeness prevailed and Lucy graciously offered them both a cup of tea.

Peony did her best to apologise, but Linnet was so angry with her that she stormed out of the room before Peony could finish her speech. Lucy was just glad that Linnet had not thrown her bottle of red wine across the room - she looked as if she might have done at one point. The cream carpet and sofa would have been a bugger to clean afterwards!

Peony and Vincent sat gloomily huddled together, tucking into a batch of freshly baked and very colourful macaroons, which Lucy had placed on the coffee table for them. Peony, in between nibbling on her macaroons, continued to apologise, "I am so sorry I didn't listen to you!" Peony told them. "You warned me about Marcus and I wouldn't listen! I don't know what came over me. I don't usually do things like that. I'm so, so, sorry."

"I think it may be a long time before Linnet can forgive you," Sophie told Peony.

"But, I need her to forgive me!" Peony moaned, helping herself to more macaroons.

"People don't forgive on cue!" Sophie replied. "You'll have to wait until she is ready."

"But I feel so awful!" Peony lamented. "I mean, how was I to know that he would do such a terrible thing?"

"Perhaps the fact that he tried to murder Linnet seven years ago, and that he had just come out of prison, and that we told you he was dangerous? I think those things might have been the tip off?" Minnie replied, unable to control her anger. Lucy suggested she went to check on Linnet and ushered Minnie out of the room

Peony looked upset again. "But I thought he was reformed!"

"Because he'd found God?" Sophie laughed sarcastically.

"I'm usually such a good judge of character!" Peony said, sadly shaking her head. "You said that, didn't you Vincent, when you first met me, you said, 'You are a good judge of character!'"

Vincent nodded in agreement and sipped his tea.

"Really?" Sophie said in disbelief. "Vincent said that to you did he?"

Vincent glared at Sophie and motioned with his hand across his throat several times, trying to let her know not to say anymore.

"For f*cks sake!" Sophie exclaimed, exasperated. "If you are such a good judge of character Peony, here's something else you should know. Vincent here isn't gay! He's married with two kids and a Doberman pincher."

"Anymore to drink, anyone? Another macaroon? There's plenty!" Lucy interjected, trying to break the tension by offering the plate around.

Peony looked at Vincent in amazement. "You're not gay?" she exclaimed. "But, you are so…"

Vincent looked sheepish and annoyed at the same time. "You bitch!" he said to Sophie, with an extravagant flourish.

Peony was aghast. "Why would you tell me you were gay, if you're not?"

Vincent shrugged and looked daggers at Sophie. "I never said I was gay," Vincent replied. "It's just, I found out years ago that I got hairdressing jobs more easily if I put on the 'act' and it kind of went from there."

"But, why did you lie to me?" Peony asked, still flabbergasted.

"I didn't exactly lie, you just assumed!" Vincent said, in his defence.

Sophie smiled. "Your Law of Attraction is not looking quite so attractive now, is it, Peony? Better be careful what you wish for, in the future!"

Peony burst into tears and Vincent hugged her. "We'd better go," he said, feeling slightly embarrassed and harassed. "Come on, Boo," he said to Peony. "We know where we are not wanted!"

Lucy politely showed them both to the door, but when she came back to the kitchen area and started to clear away the cups, she said to her sister, "You were really cruel to Peony. Vincent is right. You can be a bitch sometimes."

Sophie looked hurt. "Well, she annoys me so much with her 'I bring my own luck!' and her 'I made so and so happen because I wished for it bullshit! Oh, look! I just manifested a new dishwasher! I manifested my own business because I put it on a vision board.' Well! She manifested a right old mess this time!"

"It's a mess alright!" Lucy sighed. "I wonder if Peony will ever be able to trust a man ever again, and I don't think Linnet will ever get over this, or poor Alice!"

"Alice will be okay," Sophie reassured Lucy. "Once the Star Child Academy opens she will start to put this all behind her. She has an ability to forgive that I have never seen so strongly embedded in anyone else. She is a star child, remember."

"Maybe you could take a leaf out of Alice's book and forgive Peony?"

Lucy suggested. "Besides, you would normally say that Peony had no choice in what she did in regards to Marcus. Isn't it bad love-karma that makes us do stupid things in relationships?"

Sophie looked at Lucy who was checking her phone to see if Jimmy had txted her, "Ain't that the truth!" Sophie said and sighed.

~ * ~

A while later, Lancelot arrived, along with India and Miss Huggins, but with no good news about Robert and even worse news about the sale of Little Eden.

"Shaft, Pencill and Push have started court proceedings already!" India said indignantly, helping herself to a glass of Linnet's wine.

"But how can they, with Robert in a coma?" Lucy asked.

"That is exactly why they have pounced!" India replied. She put down the wine. She had an awful feeling that if she didn't watch it, she might end up like Linnet, in a constant state of drunkenness, in order to avoid the stress.

"Robin Shaft persuaded Jennifer and Collins that they could capitalise on Robert's condition, and if he is not compos mentis within sixty days, they can take control of the Trust."

"No way!" Lucy exclaimed.

"Yes, way!" India responded. "The greedy bastards are going to take Little Eden whilst Robert lies there dying."

"He isn't dying," Lucy said, hoping if she believed it, it would be true. "He will wake up, just you wait and see."

Lancelot looked tired and troubled. Miss Huggins passed him a cup of tea, which he gratefully took, although he wished she would offer him more than just a cup of tea. At that moment he would gladly have been drinking in her kisses instead. His mind wandered for a few moments to her soft lips and how he would like to slip open her blouse and run his fingers gently over her…

"Lancelot, didn't you hear what I said?" India asked him.

"Sorry?" he responded, coming out of his reverie and looking at Adela with slight embarrassment, as if she might have read his mind!

"I said, that I think we must tell the residents about the sale before it ends up on Twitter or in the papers. It only takes one person to say the wrong thing and the press will be round here like flies on sh*t," India repeated.

"Yes. Yes!" Lancelot agreed. "We should call a residents' meeting as soon as possible. But, I would rather have something positive to tell them before we do."

The friends all looked at each other, and not one of them could think of how to put a positive spin on the future.

"I think we can work on Lucas," Adela volunteered. "His sister, Faberge, says she is willing to help us."

"If only Robert's Aunt Elizabeth were still alive," Lucy sighed. "None of this would be happening. Why can't Lucas be more like his grandmother? She would never have sold Little Eden - not at any price."

"What I don't understand, is why Lucas got his grandmother's vote?" Adela said.

"She had the right to pass it down through the family and Lucas was the eldest male heir," Lancelot frowned.

"That's just sexist rubbish!" India moaned.

"It doesn't make sense!" Adela said. "I thought Uncle Frith was Elizabeth's eldest male heir. Frith is Elizabeth's oldest child, then his sister Sencha. Lucas is Sencha's son. Surely it should have been Frith or his eldest male child who inherited the vote?"

"Who is Uncle Frith?" Lucy asked.

"I've never heard of any Frith Hudson," India replied, and looked at Lancelot. She could see by the look on his face that he knew something.

"Wait a minute!" Sophie said suddenly, "That's the name Jimmy said at the séance. He said that a man named Frith could help us!"

"What do you know about this Uncle Frith?" Lucy asked Adela.

"Nothing much," she replied. "I never met him and no one ever mentions him. Frith disappeared decades ago, on his sixteenth birthday, and he hasn't been seen since. I know Aunt Elizabeth searched for him for a few years but if she had left the vote to him maybe he could have been found?"

"Is that true?" India quizzed Lancelot.

"All I know about him is that he is legally registered as deceased," Lancelot replied.

"Oh, that's just great!" India exclaimed. "Another dead Bartlett-Hart sent to help us from the spirit world! These days I am starting to wonder which world I am living in half the time!"

"But we don't know for sure that he's dead," Adela said. "That means something, right? He might still be alive, and he might have had children of his own."

Sophie smiled. She had understood the implications. "If we can find Frith, then Lucas has no vote on the Trust!"

"I wouldn't think you could find him after all these years," Lancelot sighed.

"And, even if we did find this Uncle Frith, who's to say he wouldn't mind a slice of a few billion pounds just as much as his nephew Lucas does?" India suggested.

"There is that!" Lucy admitted.

"But, we could use it - the idea of Uncle Frith!" Adela interjected.

"How so?" Lucy asked.

"Well, if we could say to Robin Shaft that we have a new lead and that it's a real possibility Uncle Frith might show up alive, well, they would have to wait until they could prove he really was dead, wouldn't they?"

"Oh, I do like that!" rejoined Lucy.

"But we don't have a new lead," Lancelot reminded them.

"We might have a new lead if we used a psychic investigator," Adela suggested.

"Oh, lordy!" India frowned. "Here we go again."

"I have an idea," Adela said. "What if Lucy's boyfriend Jimmy starts one of his psychic investigations saying that he has a lead on Frith. He could say that Frith came to him in a séance and told him that he was still alive! What do you think?"

"Shaft, Pencill and Push won't buy that," Lancelot said.

"They will if Jimmy was making a TV documentary about it and the press got hold of the story," Lucy suggested.

Sophie nodded. "I don't expect we would find Frith alive, any more than you do, but the more we can chuck at Shaft, Pencill and Push to derail them till Robert wakes up, the better, I reckon!"

"It's worth a try!" Adela pleaded with Lancelot.

"Okay, let's speak to Jimmy and see what's possible. But I can't promise anything," Lancelot conceded.

Adela hugged him and kissed him on the cheek in her excitement!

Chapter 25

~ * ~

A few days later, Sophie awoke from a nightmare in which Robert had been on trial for witchcraft. He had been sentenced to hang on a wooden gallows, whilst men and women, dressed in black and white, shouted hysterically against him. He went silently to his gruesome death without even trying to defend himself, and she could feel herself, like an angel in the sky above him, willing him to speak out against the injustice which had condemned him. But he would not. His neck snapped to the sound of cheering! Although it was just a dream, the emotional residue it left behind swam around in her mind, and she could not shake off the feeling that Robert's silence and inaction in the face of injustice might carry on lifetime after lifetime.

With Robert still in a coma and under suspicion of manslaughter, Sophie was feeling more than a little depressed. She did not hold out much hope of them ever finding Uncle Frith or his off-spring. And even if they did find someone, the likelihood of them being a philanthropist was slim.

She was a little heartened by Alice's courage and recovery, but she couldn't help worrying about Lucy's health and Linnet's drinking. She was on tenterhooks, waiting to see if the Little Eden residents would get wind of the plot to sell the town, which would send the whole community into panic and fear.

Sophie knew what it was like to lose everything, and it was not a situation she would wish on her worst enemy, never mind on her best friends! She had not yet healed from her sudden and enforced change of life direction, and still felt angry and alone. Her chronic fatigue meant that every day was a challenge; so, when things went from bad to worse, her ability to deal with stress was low indeed. She had learnt meditation and various healing methods to help her, but nothing short of a miracle could keep her from feeling suicidal sometimes. She felt useless and helpless, and as for guarding the dragon portal, it seemed real one minute and ridiculous the next!

She mustered all her strength and determination in order to get dressed and go over to the chateau. She walked across the park under the last vestiges of a clear blue sky. The oak trees were aglow with golden shafts of sunset and she wondered, with a sense of dread, where Melanie's spirit was currently hiding out and who else she was trying to convert to the dark side to help her!

Sophie found Dr G and Blue, both sitting in the altar room, meditating. They looked up as Sophie peered in and Dr G beckoned to her to enter. She took off her shoes and walked across the plush carpet, feeling as if this might be the only safe place in the world right now!

Dr G asked about Robert, whilst Blue came and sat on Sophie's knee, wanting to try on her glasses.

"You have come about the sale?" Dr G asked her.

Sophie nodded.

"We found the bodies of the three murdered men in the lake and we helped their spirits over to the other side, but I don't feel it has made any difference," Sophie told him. "I don't think it has put anything to rest. Jennifer has not backed down. She is determined to destroy Little Eden. I still feel Melanie's spirit is strong and that Aunt Lilly's is fading."

Dr G smiled sadly. "Robert's energy is low," he replied. "Your aunt is only able to remain as a spirit guide if he chooses to save Little Eden. That is her purpose, and that is his purpose. He has not yet made a choice. He does not understand that the world depends upon him. He does not believe the dragon portal is real."

Sophie shook her head. "I don't think anyone believes the dragon portal is real. It seems too fantastical - like something out of a sci-fi novel."

Dr G frowned. "It is very real, indeed. Oh, yes, it is!"

"Then we really are all in danger?" Sophie asked aghast. She thought of poor Alice and Linnet and what they had gone through these last few weeks. She thought of Robert, fighting for his life in the hospital, and she began to feel the familiar sense of fear and dread creep up inside her. The astral realm was penetrating the human realm, and what seemed like the stuff of fairy stories was starting to have a very real effect. "You are not afraid for any of us, are you?" Sophie asked him. "You do not value human life enough to care if we survive this 2012 world ascension or not, do you?"

Dr G sighed. "It is easy to kill a light-worker by killing their human body. Indeed it is. When we are human we are at our most vulnerable. Incarnation is a fragile and short experience. Human life is always precious, but it is one small part of a much bigger whole. One must not be so attached to life that it makes one afraid of death. Fear of life and death always brings sadness, grief and suffering."

"I didn't ask for this guardian job, and neither did Robert or any of the children," Sophie complained. She looked down at Blue and dreaded to think what might happen to him. "It's unrealistic to expect us to know what to do. There's no manual, no plan, no map! What's going to happen? How long is this ascension of the planet and humankind going to take?"

"With experiments, no one knows the outcome," Dr G replied.

"Oh, that's just great!" Sophie groaned. "So, no bugger knows what the hell is going on?"

"There is a broader plan," Dr G told her calmly. Although, Sophie was sure she could sense a note of doubt in his voice.

"I don't see the point of ascension," Sophie said. "What difference will it make to the planet or to humans anyway?"

"You wish to stay trapped in the wheel of karma forever?" Dr G asked her.

Sophie shrugged. "Lots of people are not bothered about that. They are only bothered about themselves in this one lifetime. They are too busy just surviving anyway they can."

Dr G sighed. "Survival of the animal body makes us forget the importance of our eternal survival. Humans destroy the planet with nuclear bombs and pollution. They kill and hurt each other because of greed and fear over and over again. Any soul incarnating becomes easily trapped in the karmic cycle of fear. Incarnation is dangerous, especially for star children."

"It's crazy! How are we supposed to break the karmic cycle if karma makes us think that we don't need to break free of it in the first place? It's ridiculous," Sophie replied.

"Compassion is the answer to all your questions," Dr G explained. "Compassion destroys the karma of fear and therefore all our attachments to our human life are destroyed also."

"If no one reincarnated anymore, that would mean no more humans and no more karma," Sophie suggested. "Wouldn't that be just another form of Armageddon?"

"To experience the human world we need karma, this is true, but only the karma of compassion," Dr G said. "In compassionate-karma the star children come, they go, they are free. If they reincarnate, it is a free choice. We must re-build the bridge of compassionate consciousness that has been lost so that humans can be free of the karmic cycle of tribalism, division and war."

"Why must we mere mortals do it?" Sophie asked. "Why don't they send someone like Jesus or Buddha to do it instead?"

"The Buddha Shakyamuni and the Messiah, and many holy beings, were sent into human form to help raise the consciousness of mankind, to help them remember their divine source and help them live a compassionate life, this is true," Dr G agreed.

"It hasn't been working very well then, has it?" Sophie sighed.

"One must follow their teachings," Dr G told her.

"How can we follow the teachings when priests, gurus and leaders pedal fear? They twist the original compassionate teachings to make people afraid, so that they can control them and make them do evil things in the name of God. Those who are afraid of being controlled by religions abandon the teachings altogether and mock anyone who is trying to follow the light, and some people get into all sorts of crazy alternative philosophies instead."

Dr G nodded. "Indeed, there is little left of the pure way, this is true. It is hard to see the compassionate way and even harder to live it. But, do we reject compassion because it is difficult? Do we let fear win because it is easier?"

"I suppose not!" Sophie agreed. "But I still don't see why the job of sorting out fear-karma is left to ordinary people who don't even know what they are doing. It seems like a catch-22 to me."

"Each person must work diligently at their own enlightenment and come to realise compassion within themself," Dr G replied. "The compassion sent to Earth through the dragon portals will help them awaken to their own understanding."

"Like getting an injection of compassion and then taking responsibility for our own actions and motivations you mean?" Sophie asked, "Like taking the red pill or the blue pill?*"

"I do not know of any pills you can take," Dr G laughed. "Each person must choose between fear and compassion, this is the only choice they need to make. This is how the world can change - one person at a time."

"I don't think we have the luxury of time, Dr G!" Sophie retorted. "We have sixty days for Robert to wake up or Collins and Lucas can take full control of the Trust. And then, we are all buggered!"

Dr G reassured her, "You must trust that all will unfold as it should."

Sophie shrugged and pulled a face. She wasn't so sure!

~ * ~

As the days went by, Robert showed no sign of waking from his coma, and everyone was getting more and more despondent. The snow was completely gone and the weather had turned dull, grey and rainy. There was a lack of joy in Little Eden which was the absolute opposite of normal.

Stella still held her constant vigil over Robert at the hospital. She had read to him, sung to him, chatted to him and made sure he had everything he needed. Sometimes, she could hardly hold back the tears, but she tried not to get emotional, in case he could hear her. Sophie joined her as often as she could, and seeing him lying there, unable to respond, both she and Stella began to fear the worst. Their hope and optimism were waning.

On Valentine's Day, Sophie visited him again. She tried to stay strong, but she found tears were rolling down her cheeks and she could not stop them. "Oh, Stella," she said, "I can't bear it. What will we do without Robert? Little Eden only exists because he exists. If they have killed him, we will all sink even further into the sticky web of fear-karma and never get out."

Stella tried to comfort Sophie, but had to fight back the tears herself. "Do you remember when Robert was a little boy and he fell off his horse?"

"Yes," Sophie replied. "The boys were pretending to joust using broomsticks."

"We all thought he might die but it was just a concussion. And the time he fell off the west wall, pretending that the enemy had breached the gate?" Stella continued. "He was out cold for several minutes, and we were all so worried about him. He has always been accident prone, my darling. This is just one of those times, just a little accident - nothing to worry about."

But, Stella began to cry too, she knew this was not the same at all. The pressure of keeping a stiff upper lip had become too much, and floods of tears came pouring out of her heart.

Sophie held onto Robert's other hand in despair, she felt her heart was breaking for the second time in just a few weeks. "Don't leave me to do this on my own," she begged him. "We must defend Little Eden and the dragon portal. I can't do it without you. How can I do it without you? You must come back Robert, you must! Don't leave me here alone."

Suddenly, they heard an unexpected commotion. A rush of paparazzi had congregated at the hospital entrance. Stella went to look out of the window. The journalists had arrived just in time to snap Jennifer, Collins and Robin Shaft, who were coming up the front steps. Jennifer was wearing oversized sunglasses in an attempt to disguise herself, but it only ended up creating the effect of celebrity status and gathered more attention. Flashes were going off nineteen to the dozen, and the reporters were shouting over each other. It wasn't clear what was happening at first. But then, Robin led

Jennifer towards the cameras instead of getting her quickly inside, and gave a statement on her behalf:

"My clients would like to publicly acknowledge that Mr Robert Bartlett-Hart is seriously ill, and they would like to thank all the well-wishers who have been so kind over the last few weeks. My clients feel that the only course of action left open to them is to sell the historic family seat of Little Eden, as soon as possible. This is a regretful and very painful decision for the family who have owned the town for over a thousand years. Anyone who would like information on the purchase should contact Shaft, Pencill and Push, Knightsbridge. There is no further comment at this time."

With that, the three of them disappeared into the foyer letting the automatic doors slide closed in the faces of the reporters. Hospital security staff arrived and ushered them away.

"What is it?" Sophie asked Stella.

"Jennifer is coming," Stella replied. "I don't know what all those journalists are doing here, it's probably nothing to worry about. You'd better go. You know Jennifer doesn't like anyone else visiting."

Sophie left by the back entrance with a feeling of dread inside her. Something was about to blow and she knew it."

~ * ~

That evening at No. 1 Daisy Place, the girls and Jack all sat looking glum in the Café apartment. It was not a happy Valentine's Day for any of them. Jimmy was working, so Lucy felt the sting of rejection, and Sophie had no admirers at all. Jack had wanted to ask out Adela, but Lancelot had got there before him, and he was not in the mood to hook up with any of his usual dates. Lucy decided they should have an impromptu friends Valentine's gathering that evening, instead of a romantic one. She invited everyone, but in the end it was only Jack, Minnie, Linnet, India and Mr T who came over. They all sat around on the sofas eating a takeout from Nico's, followed by Fudge and Bunny's sweetheart ice-cream, but even that could not cheer them up. They had little to say to each other that did not make them all feel even more depressed.

When Lancelot unexpectedly appeared looking dejected, with his dinner jacket over his shoulder and his tie hanging out of his pocket, they all wanted to know what was going on.

"Don't ask!" Lancelot said to them, as they were about to enquire why he was not with Adela at the Assembly Room ball.

"Put the television on," he told them. They asked him why, but he replied, "Just put it on."

A few minutes later the local news started and they were amazed to see Jennifer, Collins and Robin Shaft giving his statement outside the hospital.

"The heartless bitch!" Sophie exclaimed.

"The lying bitch!" Minnie added.

"The stupid bitch!" India finished.

"Now the whole of Little Eden will know. We must call an emergency residents' meeting," Lancelot told them. "There will be panic if they are left without answers!"

Suddenly, everyone's phone started to ring, txts started flying in and Lucy wished she had not looked on Twitter!

Sophie rushed to the window to see if there were any residents in the square. She half expected to see hordes of them brandishing pitchforks, all heading towards Bartlett Crescent to lynch Jennifer and Collins from the nearest tree. She opened the window onto the grim night to get some air. It was spitting with rain and she felt evil whispering amongst the trees. She shivered to her bones.

"This is what we need to do," Lancelot told them. "We'll hold a residents' meeting at ten o'clock tonight and I will give a speech. Tell everyone to tell another five people and it should be all around the town in twenty minutes or less."

"Where though?" India asked him. "If everyone needs to come it'll have to be a bigger venue than the Pump Rooms."

"We could use the stage in the park," Lucy suggested. "It's nearly ready for the concert."

"But what will you say?" Sophie asked. "In the speech, I mean."

Lancelot shook his head and took a spoonful of ice-cream from the tub saying; "I have absolutely no idea!"

Chapter 26

~ * ~

The friends sat around just looking at each other in despair, trying to get their heads around what to do for the best.

Lancelot suggested that they hold a residents' vote. "There is no point in us trying to save Little Eden if the residents are not with us one hundred percent. I suggest we try to pay off Collins and Lucas, and let everyone vote as to whether or not to try and raise enough money."

"How much do you think they will want?" Jack asked him.

"At least two billion each, I would think," Lancelot replied.

"But, that's far too much money!" Lucy exclaimed.

"Doesn't Robert have any money of his own?" Minnie asked. "Can't the Trust just pay them off?"

"The Trust hasn't much cash flow," India said.

Lancelot laughed sadly. "As for Robert, he doesn't even take his full annual stipend. He has nothing of his own."

"It's not just about the money!" Sophie reminded them. "If Robert dies or goes to prison, that would put the Trust firmly under Collins' and Lucas's control. There would be no need for a buy-out. We'd have lost it all anyway."

Lucy burst into tears.

"He won't die or go to prison; it will never come to that, old girl!" Jack said, hugging Lucy. He thought for a moment and then added, "I have some money - only a few hundred thousand - would that help?"

"I have some money saved too," India said. "If we start a fund, perhaps others may follow."

"A Save Little Eden Fund, you mean?" Sophie asked.

"That's a jolly good idea. I could put in a million to start the ball rolling," Lancelot offered.

"I have about fifteen thousand saved, but that's all I'm afraid," Minnie said.

Lucy and Sophie looked at each other and sighed. They were both skint!

"Any money is welcome, but we are still talking drops in the ocean here!" India said. "We need some serious cash!"

"Why don't we ask the other Bartlett-Harts to help?" Jack suggested.

"There are some wealthy Bartlett-Harts around the world," Lancelot agreed. "But they have their own estates and businesses to look after."

"The American side have shed loads of money," Lucy said. "Jennifer is always moaning about how they are billionaires and she is only a millionaire and how unfair it is!"

"They have not been part of Little Eden for hundreds of years, I doubt they would help us now," Lancelot said, regretfully.

"This might sound like a crazy idea," Sophie interjected, "But there might be money beneath our feet - literally - if we could find it!"

"What do you mean?" Jack asked.

"I'm thinking of Genevieve Dumas, who is looking for the gold and booty she stole when she was a highwayman!" Sophie giggled. "Or, highwaywoman, I should say!"

"That's just a ghost story!" Jack said. "There's no real treasure, old girl!"

"Let's keep spirits and ghosts out of this, shall we?" India suggested. "We need concrete ideas."

"Hold on a minute, though!" Jack replied, "If we are moving onto the subject of treasure hunting, there's the gold from the Civil War that was never found. It was supposed to have been delivered here by boat, when the old river still came to Little Eden from the Thames. It could be down in one of the tunnels! I've always wanted to try and find it, but never seemed to have the time. Robbie and I did some scouting around when we were boys, but we found nothing back then. But, that's not to say it's not there somewhere."

"The American family would be our best avenue. They might give us a loan, perhaps?" India suggested.

"But even if they did loan us the money, how would we ever pay it back?" Lancelot reminded her.

India shrugged. She felt as if they were getting nowhere fast! "I just don't think a treasure hunt is a realistic way to go," she protested. "We can't promise the residents they can keep their homes based on some missing treasure that may not even exist."

"Anything is worth a try at this stage!" Sophie said. "There was also treasure from the Abbey that was taken to France at the Reformation. Stella says rumour has it that it went to Chartres. It might be worth a million or two?"

"I think we need some cake!" Lucy said. "I always think better with cake." She went to the fridge and fetched some millionaire's shortbread. She looked at it and smiled at the irony. "I must have known!" She laughed. "I made this earlier but wasn't sure why!" She put out slices for everyone to help themselves to and put the kettle on.

No one had any more bright ideas however, even with the help of tea and cake.

"We will just have to see what the residents think," Lancelot said. "If they want to try and raise the money, then at least we are all in this together."

By ten o'clock, the outdoor theatre in the park was filled to the brim, not only with all the Little Eden residents, but with reporters and strangers too. The drizzle and the biting cold had not deterred them. Rain clouds loomed heavy above their heads and filled the sky with a black swirling menace, and by the time Lancelot stood on the half-built stage, the atmosphere was electric with panic and fear.

Lancelot took the microphone from Cubby Mayhew, who had managed to plug it into one of the amplifiers, and he tried his best to calm everybody down. But, if there was a moment of quiet, it was interrupted again by someone shouting out, which in turn, kicked off a wave of fear and despair. Although the residents were minus pitchforks, there was plenty of hate towards Jennifer and Collins swirling around, which, if unchecked, could have been enough to do someone an injury! Lancelot called for order over and over, but it was a hopeless task. Johnathon Grail and Cubby pushed the crowds back from the stage and managed to stop one of the reporters getting punched in the eye by a resident who was less than pleased at the presence of the press!

In the end, it was India who got the crowd's attention, and it was she who gave the speech, which went something like this:

"This afternoon, some of you may have heard that our town of Little Eden is under threat of sale and demolition."

The crowds jeered and called out obscenities, but India continued…

"To save our town, our businesses and our homes, we must stand together, as a community, as friends - nay, I say- as family!"

The residents cheered and wolf-whistled at that part!

"I tell you now, we need to raise four billion pounds if we are to rest easy in our beds!"

Muttering and chuntering swept through the throng as people shook their heads and frowned over the enormity of the task.

"What if Mr Robert doesn't return?" someone shouted from the crowd.

"Robert will return to us any day now!" India replied with as much conviction as she could muster, but with a stab of doubt in her heart. "But Robert, Lancelot and I cannot save Little Eden alone! We are dedicated to

Little Eden and everything it stands for. We are dedicated to you all. But we need each and every one of you here to stand with us and never give up, no matter how hard the road ahead of us may seem!"

The mood was beginning to change for the better and some people started clapping. India began to find her stride and continued, "Little Eden is the last bastion of independence and sanctuary in Britain! Little Eden is a place where justice is more important than money! Where mutual respect is more important than individual power! And, where peace and tolerance are the most important things of all!"

The crowd went wild at this point, with 'hear-hears' and the stomping of feet, in general approval.

"Our children, our grandchildren, our great-grandchildren - they all need us to stand up against the ever-growing wave of selfishness and greed. We must show the future generations that people can work together to do what is right and that they *will* stand together to do what is right!"

The crowd now roared with gusto and pride!

India put her hand on her heart and said, "I pledge myself, before you now, as a guardian of Little Eden and everything it stands for! Who amongst you will join me to save Little Eden for all the generations to come?"

There was no containing the excitement of the crowd which burst into cheering, whistling, shouting and singing! Some held hands, some high-fived each other, and some started a Mexican wave, which went right around the theatre several times over. India had never felt so alive! It was as if the energy of each and every resident was plugged into her and she was physically buzzing with electrical energy. She felt light-headed one minute yet rooted to the spot the next. She felt as if her whole heart had opened up and an invisible beam of light was pouring out of her into the crowds. She could almost feel the light burning a hole in her chest!

Sophie and Blue, who were standing in the wings, could see the astral beam of white light pouring out of India's heart chakra and into the hearts of all the people. Sophie also caught sight of the spirit of Aunt Lilly, who was standing beside India. She smiled to herself, knowing that Aunt Lil was not giving up either! The crowd, now bathed in a wave of invisible light, became so enthusiastic that some even started waving twenty pound notes in the air!

India realised at once that this was a chance to start the fundraising and she looked around for something to collect money in. She grabbed some yellow workmen's hats, which had been left on the half-made stage, handed them to Tambo and Elijah, Jack and Lancelot, and sent them off into the crowds. In minutes they were back with their hats brimming with notes, coins, rings and watches - someone had even put some diamond earrings in.

The atmosphere became more and more electric as people started climbing onto the stage! Taking the microphone from India they began making pledges of money.

"I pledge a thousand pounds," one resident shouted down the mic.

She was quickly followed by another who called out, "I pledge two thousand pounds!"

Lancelot got out his phone and jotted down who they were and the amount that they promised so that he could collect it later on.

Some of the wealthiest residents hesitated to join in at first, not wanting to part with their money too rashly, but when they saw Stella get up and pledge her life's savings, they were not to be outdone! More and more of them mounted the stage, opening the floodgates. The collecting went on for over thirty minutes, until everyone ran out of steam and out of money!

When most people had finally gone home, Lancelot and India went back to the Café and counted up. There was a massive pile of coins and notes in the middle of one of the tables. Lancelot sipped his cappuccino as he totted up the pledges. Minnie came in to see if they wanted any help. "How much did we get so far?" Minnie asked, as she made herself some hot chocolate.

India looked on her tally sheet. "We have one hundred and twenty million pounds so far, give or take a few!"

"Wow!" Minnie replied. "That's pretty good going for the first day of fundraising!"

India nodded and smiled. "I would never have expected people to be so generous!"

"Don't get too hopeful," Lancelot cautioned. "There's still a long way to go."

"Do you think four billion pounds is do-able?" Minnie asked, as she stacked pound coins up into piles.

India shrugged. "Between me and you, no I don't, but if we can delay the sale by even a few months with the promise of a pay-off, or the threat of finding this Uncle Frith, I will pretend anything's possible right now!"

Just then, Alice and Tambo appeared in their Pjs, holding their hands behind their backs. "We brought you something," Alice said to India, and they both held out their hands, which were full of coins.

"We emptied out our piggy banks," Tambo said, as they poured the shrapnel onto the table.

"Will it be enough?" Alice asked, with tears in her eyes. "I don't want Mummy to lose the flower shop and I don't want Tambo to lose his home."

Minnie felt tears welling up and took Alice's hand. "That is just the amount we needed!" she said smiling. "Just enough!"

Alice smiled and was happy to believe Minnie that everything was going to be alright.

~ * ~

Lucy could not sleep that night and she was not alone in that! She came into the conservatory to get some hot milk and found Jack was still up. He was sitting on the sofa bed watching television with headphones on, his duvet around him and eating popcorn.

She sat down next to him and he put his arm around her. "What do you think, Jack?" she asked him. "Do you think Robert will wake up to find we have raised four billion pounds and we have saved Little Eden?"

"It will take years to come up with even half that amount," Jack mused.

"Don't say that!" Lucy said, feeling tearful.

"Okay, then!" he replied. "Of course it's all going to be alright! Robert will wake up and all will be just fine and dandy, old girl. Don't you worry."

Lucy hit him playfully on the chest, but it was what she had wanted to hear.

She looked at the television. "Isn't this 'It's a Wonderful Life'[19]?'" she asked.

"Yep," he replied.

"It's a sign!" Lucy said, jumping up from the sofa in excitement.

"A sign of what?" Jack asked her, bewildered.

"A sign from Aunt Lilly, silly!" Lucy replied. "This was her favourite film and we watched it every Christmas Eve with her, don't you remember? She always said, 'If life is going badly, we should always remember there is an angel watching over us'."

"Oh, good grief!" Jack said rolling his eyes. "Not more praying and angels!"

Lucy walked up and down the room, trying to think what to do. "It's a

[19] *It's a Wonderful Life*, Frances Goodrich, Albert Hackett, Frank Capra, 1946, RKO Radio Pictures

sign! I just know it is. Aunt Lil is here with us right now! She wants us to do something! I can feel it! But what? What is it, Aunt Lil? What do you want us to do?" She looked up at the ceiling as if Aunt Lil was floating up there somewhere.

Jack ignored her and carried on watching the movie.

"We have to go to the hospital and see Robert!" she said, suddenly.

"In the middle of the night?" Jack replied. "Be serious, old girl. They wouldn't even let us in!"

"Then we will sneak in!" Lucy said, with gusto.

"You're serious!" Jack replied, astonished.

"Yes!" Lucy said. "I know it in my bones! We must go now!"

"You're losing it, old girl!" Jack said. "It's blowing a gale out there and pissing it down too! And, how do you propose to sneak into a hospital?"

Suddenly, Sophie appeared in the doorway looking dishevelled. Her hair was a mess and her pyjamas were skew-whiff. She had just awoken from a vision dream.

Lucy nearly jumped out of her skin when she saw her sister standing in the shadows.

Sophie, half asleep, yawned and said earnestly, "You have to go and see if Robert is okay!"

They both just looked at her.

"Immediately! Now!" Sophie urged. "I had a dream. Stella isn't at the hospital to protect him. Melanie is going to try and kill him. Tonight!"

"It was just a nightmare," Jack told her, as he draped his duvet over her to keep her warm. "It's understandable, with everything up in the air like this. Your fear just got into your dreams, that's all."

Sophie shook her head. "It was too vivid for a dream. It was one of those dreams that isn't a dream, if you know what I mean? It was a vision-dream."

Jack shook his head, but Lucy nodded.

"I dreamt that Alice was in danger and then she was!" Lucy said. "If Sophie dreamt that Robert is in danger, then he is! And besides, I felt we should go too. We must go and see if Robert is alright! Come on Jack, please?"

Jack shrugged, he could see that the two girls would not give it up until he had agreed, and he had learnt over the years that they never gave up. "Okay! Okay!" he said, gesturing with his hands in the air. "I'll go and climb through a window or something! But you two stay here!"

"I'm coming!" Lucy said, adamantly. "And don't try to stop me, old boy!"

Chapter 27

~ * ~

Sophie and Lucy were not wrong about Robert being in danger!

So far, Melanie's spirit had found herself barred from his hospital room by the combination of the power of Stella's love for Robert and the prayer circle, which was still holding vigil 24/7 in the church. But, that evening, due to the residents gathering in park, Robert had been left unguarded for the first time since his accident.

Now that the usual white light was no longer surrounding him, Melanie was able to walk into Robert's room. She sat, invisible and in ghostly form, on the side of Robert's bed, looking down at him with an evil smile.

She was about to force Robert's spirit out of his body when a nurse padded into the room. Melanie was afraid she might be noticed. With the amount of electrical charge running through her from Robert's heart monitor, she was very powerful. But it also made her extra visible to anyone with heightened psychic awareness. Luckily for Melanie, the nurse was oblivious to her presence, and she simply looked at the chart at the end of the bed, checked Robert's vitals, and returned to the door. She paused there for a moment then turned around. She thought she had felt a cold breeze around her, but then decided she was mistaken and left.

Melanie was again preparing to kill Robert when, unexpectedly, the spirit of Marcus Finch appeared out of nowhere, manifesting itself through a cloud of grey smoke.

"You!" Melanie exclaimed. "You bloody idiot!"

Marcus looked sheepish and didn't reply. Melanie screamed at him like a harpie and pointed at Robert. "He is the one who is supposed to be dead. Not you! Look at you! You got yourself killed! Fool! Now I have to find a way to finish him off myself!" She stamped her foot, but it made little difference seeing as she was ephemeral. Melanie sighed, and added a little more calmly, "Do you know how difficult it is to kill a human from the spirit world? Why do you think we use other humans to do it?"

She looked at Marcus and then began to smile. In spirit form, he didn't half look a mess! He had a gash on his head and had several reeds stuck in his hair. His usual handsome face was puffy and gruesome looking. He looked as he had done when he had been Henry Slight: bedraggled and soggy.

"That's the second time you've crossed over looking like a drowned rat!"

Melanie laughed viciously. "You're no use to anyone here - unless you want to haunt your pretty little daughter and that soppy ex-wife of yours?"

Marcus didn't like being bullied, in spirit or in human form, and especially not by a woman! He was about to tell Melanie exactly what he thought of her, when he caught sight of a sparkle of silver light appearing over a bouquet of roses, in the corner of the room, which began to gleam. Out of its aura Alice's face appeared, like the Cheshire Cat![20]

Alice was astral-travelling with Lilly, Alienor and St Hilda, for protection. All of them materialised through the beautiful roses. Only Marcus could see them. They had deliberately cloaked themselves from Melanie and anyone else who might be around.

Alice pointed at Marcus and his heart froze. He thought she was going to curse him. He was so afraid that he cowered behind the heart monitor.

Because Melanie couldn't see them, she looked at Marcus in disgust. "What the hell are you doing? Who is here?" she asked, looking around the empty room.

"There!" Marcus pointed at the glowing women, but Melanie saw nothing.

To his surprise, Alice smiled at him and made a sign of a heart with her hands. She blew him a kiss and from her palms, showering him with iridescent angel dust, leaving him covered in tiny sparkles. His heart swelled with love and for a few moments he gazed at his daughter in awe. A glimmering rose appeared in Alice's hand and she offered it to him. He found himself involuntarily stepping out from behind the monitor and being no longer afraid, he took the flower from her. Even though it was an astral rose, he could smell its exquisite fragrance, and its heady scent made him feel completely at peace. It was an emotion he had never experienced his whole life!

Melanie watched impatiently as she saw Marcus put out his hand and take something that, to her, was invisible. She was even more astonished when she saw him sniff his empty hand and smile. "Fool!" Melanie growled under her breath.

Marcus frowned and finally spoke. "You know what?" he said to Melanie.

"What?" Melanie scoffed.

"I'm sick of all this killing and going round and round in circles. Just going from one life to the next and the next and the next with you! And yes, sick of getting drowned again! This is the last time I'm ever incarnating

[20] *Alice's Adventures in Wonderland*, Lewis Carroll, 1865

with you, bitch!"

At that, a shaft of glittering white light appeared above his head and he began to float gently upwards. He called down to Melanie as he ascended, "I forgive you! I forgive myself! By the grace of God, we are all forgiven!" He had rather expected to see his beloved Jesus as he passed over into the Heavenly realms, but instead, all he saw was a radiant rainbow, into which he seemed to melt, and he disappeared into the brilliancy of pure compassion.

Melanie could do nothing but watch him evaporate.

"Stupid fool!" Melanie mumbled. But she had to admit that she did feel rather sad left there alone, and she had, for just a moment, wondered what it would be like to cross over into the Heavenly realms herself. Her pondering did not last long however and within seconds she was focused back on Robert. If she couldn't have Marcus with her, to be ordered around and to do her bidding, then she would have Robert instead!

Melanie began to suck the life-force out of Robert's body. Robert's heart rate was rapidly decreasing and his physical body was starting to lose its electromagnetic charge.

Suddenly, Melanie became aware of the sound of angels praying, and she finally saw the glowing apparitions of Alice, St Hilda and Lilly in the room. They were trying to create a force field of protection around Robert.

Melanie seethed and before they could stop her, she ripped Robert's silver life-cord out of him.

Robert's ghostly form materialised above the bed. His spirit looked horrified at the sight of his physical body, lying beneath him, fading fast towards death.

He forced his spirit energy downwards, so that he was standing in front of Melanie, and looked her square in the eye. "What do you want from me?" he asked her, in a disembodied voice which echoed strangely around the room.

"I want you to suffer! As I suffered," she replied.

Robert felt his physical body fading even more and he wasn't sure if he had any say in whether he died or not. *Does she have all the power?* he thought to himself. He glanced again at his corpse and he realised that he really was about to die.

Thankfully, the window flew open! Beating rain crashed into the room, followed by Jack and then by Lucy.

"Robert!" Lucy cried, as she rushed to his bedside.

"Jack! Get a nurse! He's dying!" Lucy shouted. "Quick!"

The policeman outside the door rushed into the room to see what was happening. Jack ran down the corridor and grabbed the first nurse he could find.

Lucy began praying to St Therese of Lisieux to save Robert.

The poor policeman didn't really know what to do for the best, so he danced around a bit on the spot, looking useless and in a state of panic.

Jack came flying back into the room, followed by a nurse. "Is he..?" Jack asked, in terror.

Lucy just looked at Jack with horror written across her face.

The nurse twiddled some knobs and raced back out of the room to fetch more help, as quickly as she could.

Lucy knelt down next to Robert's body and took his hand. She could not see Alice, St Hilda, Lilly or Melanie. But she could sense that her aunt was next to her. She could smell her perfume. Lucy felt a shiver of fear run through her as she noticed a tangible grey haze around Robert's body. "There's darkness here!" she said to Jack, with urgency. "But there is also light! Aunt Lil is here. We must do something quickly! Sophie would know what to do! Call Sophie!"

But, as Jack reached for his phone - it was too late!

The heart monitor flat-lined.

Robert was dead.

Jack, Lucy and the policeman just looked at the screen in total silence for a few seconds.

For a fleeting moment Lucy could see the spirits of Alice, St Hilda and Aunt Lilly, almost as clearly as she could see Jack.

"Do something!" Lucy cried, breaking the silence.

In a state of confusion, Jack looked around the room. Usually, playing the hero came easily to him, but there was nothing, literally nothing, he could do to help. He looked around again, as if there might be something he could change, something he could hit, or mend, or fight with. In despair, Jack did something he had never done before - he fell to his knees and he started praying!

In the middle of the room, he prayed as if his own life depended on it! Holy words flooded through him from somewhere high in his consciousness and they consumed his mind. He had not said the Lord's Prayer since he was a boy, and yet in that moment, he knew every word as if it were only yesterday.

Jack's physical energy was so strong, and he combined it so completely with the divine light, that an invisible rainbow shot out of his chest. The blazing rays blasted Robert with a multicoloured bolt of energy.

The hit was so powerful that Robert's spirit expanded instantly, and for a few seconds he was almost too big for the room.

"Fight back!" Lucy begged Robert, not sure if he could even hear her. "Come back, Robert! Don't let them take you! You have a choice! This is not your time to die! Robert! Listen to me! It is not your time! Come back! Now!"

Robert's spirit could hear Lucy, and he could see Jack (who was still kneeling on the ground with the lumionous beam of light emanating from his chest). He could see the spirits of Alice, St Hilda and Lilly and in that moment Robert knew that he was stronger than Melanie. He felt as if he was the very first Robert Bartholemew. He felt the power of the blood line within his soul and he called out to Alienor.

Alienor's spirit parted from Lilly's and appeared at his side. She handed him her sword. It was humming, and dripping with a pink opalescent liquid light, and he took it, this time, without fear. As soon as he had a firm grasp of it he knew exactly what to do!

With triumphant force he ran the gleaming sword through Melanie's ghostly chest. He held it there for a few seconds and she became filled with lustrous rose-gold liquid. She looked horrified by being run through.

"I forgive you," Robert said - and he meant it!

As soon as he forgave her, Melanie's spirit began writhing and wriggling. She was trying her hardest to remove the sword from her chest, but she could not get away. Robert wasn't sure what would happen next, but he had a strong feeling that he must hold the glistening blade firmly inside her heart and keep repeating, "I forgive you."

His words changed involuntarily to, 'By the grace of God, you are forgiven'. This had a wondrous and immediate effect. The sword let out a blinding flash and blasted Melanie's spirit with so much divine light that she began to shrink and shrink in size. She shrank so much that Robert had to kneel down on the floor to keep the sword inside her. As the sword hit the tiles, Melanie was transformed into a baby lamb.

Robert felt shocked and amazed. He swiftly withdrew the blade from the innocent little creature. *Well*, he thought. *I didn't expect that!* The little lamb ran off into the corner of the room and was scooped up by

Alice, who held it in her arms, and it just sat there, benign and tame; unable to hurt anyone, any more.

So that's what they mean by the Lamb of God! Robert mused.

Robert's spirit became aware of his cadaver on the bed and he realised he only had a few seconds left if he was to come back to life.

He bowed to Alienor and then, with his sword still in his hand, and without hesitation, he threw his life force back into his physical body, with such vigour, that he almost gave himself a heart attack!

The heart monitor started beeping like mad and the other machines went crazy, with lights flashing and alarms going off, left, right and centre.

The light bulb above the bed blew out with a crack as loud as a gunshot!

Jack jump out of his skin!

Lucy screamed!

"Bloody hell, Jack!" Lucy cried out, holding her hand over her chest trying to catch her breath! "What prayer did you say?"

Jack just shook his head in disbelief and they both burst out laughing.

"What the hell just happened?" the policeman asked, bewildered. He had felt something go through his body that he could not describe in words. He could have sworn he had seen an angel, with his very own eyes. He sat down in the chair, near the door, and within a few seconds, his mind had rationalised his vision and he decided that he had seen nothing out of the ordinary, after all.

At last, the nurse returned with a doctor, and the two of them raced into the room, followed by several more nurses.

Lucy and Jack were ushered out of the room and were left waiting anxiously in the corridor. They kept trying to peep through the small window in the door, desperate to see if Robert was going to be alright.

Within a few minutes, Robert was breathing on his own and his heart rate was returning to normal. A few minutes later, he began to regain consciousness. Slowly but surely, Robert became more lucid and finally he opened his eyes.

Lucy and Jack were allowed back in. As Robert's slightly blurry vision focused in on Lucy and Jack's smiling faces, he whispered, "Thank you."

"What for, old chap?" Jack grinned. He shrugged off what he had just done, but he had a strange feeling that Robert knew that he had been on his knees praying only a few minutes before. He was so relieved that Robert was back with him that he almost felt like crying.

I think he was crying, dear readers, but he hid it well.

In the astral realms, St Hilda had delivered Melanie (in the form of the little white lamb) into the arms of St Therese. As a lamb, Melanie did not struggle at all. She was docile and calm. She happily allowed St Therese to put her down amongst the green pastures, where other fluffy young lambs were gambolling together, chasing butterflies and generally skipping about without a care in the world.

Just before St Hilda closed the Heavenly portal she passed a tiny silver key to Alienor, then she vanished into the aurora of a rainbow which faded away into nothing.

Alienor smiled. She had been expecting the key. She linked it onto her leather belt, on which she already had many keys of different sizes.

Alienor, Lilly and Alice, now sure that Robert was alive and safe, shape-shifted into pure white doves and flew back to Little Eden. Alice found her way back to her body, which was sleeping on Tambo's bottom bunk, whilst Lilly and Alienor found their way back to their tombs, flying through the walls of the church and dissolving through the flagstone floor, deep into the crypt below.

Alienor showed Lilly the little silver key. "We must keep this safe until Sophie asks for it," Alienor said.

"Robert has passed the first test, but there will be many more to come," Lilly sighed. "Who knows if Robert will make it through to the end? But, I will be with him, every step of the way - if he lets me."

Alienor looked grave and nodded in agreement. "The road is long yet, and there is no surety that the divine light will prevail. Dark days are ahead of us. The dragon portal is vulnerable whilst the Earth and mankind ascend. These are dangerous times. The dark forces will feed people's egos and they will not give up their old ways without a fight. Even those who say they believe in compassion will try to stop us when they are faced with decisions they do not like."

Lilly nodded sadly and made the sign of the cross in front of herself. Then she transformed into a dazzling stream of violet light, and like a tiny whirlwind, she spun herself into her ashes inside the Fabergé egg.

Alienor lay down upon her effigy and sank down inside her tomb, evanescing into her ancient bones.

Chapter 28

~ * ~

On the day of the Memorial Concert, Collins looked anxiously out of the window at the Gatwick runway. "Why aren't we taking off already?" he complained, in exasperation. "It's four minutes past." He downed his whisky and called to the flight attendant for another. The large luxurious cream leather seats should have felt relaxing but today he could not get comfortable.

"I still don't see why we had to drop everything and come away so quickly!" Varsity moaned, as she rearranged her seat. "I had so much planned this week and next week. You always say we should never go to Barbados 'til March."

Collins wasn't listening and kept looking at his watch every ten seconds. "Your phone's switched off, isn't it?" he asked Varsity. She nodded. "Let me check it!" he insisted.

"Yes, I turned it off," Varsity assured him, but Collins took it off her and shook it this way and that, turned it over, and then on and then off again, until he was satisfied that no one would be able to get in touch with them.

"I should never have listened to Shilty 'bloody' Cunningham," he said, under his breath and into his drink. He had a flashback to the night before, when Shilty Cunningham had appeared, unannounced, at his club.

This is a snippet of what had happened:

Since the residents had voted to save Little Eden, and Robert had awoken from his coma, Lancelot had contacted Shilty to enlist her help. As always, Shilty was a willing player, but she was not in the game for nothing! When Lancelot had agreed to Shilty's terms - off she trotted to find Collins.

When she arrived at his Gentleman's Club she found she was barred entry by the Maître d'. "Ladies are not allowed within the inner chambers, madam," he told her, in a haughty manner.

"Really?" Shilty replied. "You can enforce that legally can you? No! I thought not!" She pushed her way past him and tottered up the stairs, flinging open the double mahogany doors into the main smoking room. Collins was sitting in a racing green leather wing chair, drinking old malt. There were a few gentlemen there, and they all looked up from their newspapers in alarm! Standing before them, in a low-cut dress, her fur coat provocatively falling from her shoulders, and wearing impossibly high-heeled shoes, Shilty was an extremely unexpected sight!

Collins stood up and rushed towards her, still carrying his whisky.

"Shilty!" he said, under his breath. He looked around at his fellow club members and whispered, "Ladies are not allowed up here!"

"Don't talk such 19th Century tosh!" Shilty replied, as Collins manhandled her out onto the landing. "I'm surprised Robert allows you to still run this place like something out of the dark ages!"

"You want me to join the Women's Institute to make it equal?" Collins laughed. "What are you doing here?" he asked her, downing his drink.

"We need to talk!" she said. "Somewhere private! Very private!"

Collins smiled. "Really?" In his mind he was about to get lucky! He led her down a burgundy carpeted and heavily decorated corridor, which was lined with portraits of distinguished club members from the distant past. He took her into a small reading room and locked the door. He was sure he was in for an unexpected treat and sat down in a big chair and started to undo his trousers.

Shilty took a cushion and knelt down on it in front of him, resting her hands on his knees. She slid her hands up his thighs and took him gently but firmly in her hands. Smiling up at him, she slowly revealed her breasts, one at a time, from under her vermillion dress and said, in a soft voice, "Now Collins, how about you and I have a little chat?"

"Whatever you say!" Collins smiled, and leaned back in his chair, putting his hands behind his head, ready for pleasure.

"You"…Shilty said, as she caressed him…"You…will accept any deal that Robert puts in front of you…is that clear?"

Collins kept smiling. He was enjoying the glorious sensations rippling through his body.

"You will agree…to whatever Robert wants!" Shilty continued.

"Will I now?" Collins smirked and leaned forward to gaze at her large, soft breasts.

"Yes!" she continued. "You will!"

"And why should I do that?" Collins chuckled.

Shilty suddenly gripped him tightly and he gasped! For a moment he thought she was going to hurt him, but her touch became tender again.

"Because…" she paused and brought him near to climax but then pulled back again… "Because…it's the right thing to do!"

A few minutes later, Shilty licked her lips and stood up. Then, leaning in so she was face to face with him, she looked him in the eye and added,

"And because if you don't, I will tell Varsity what you get up to behind her back!"

Collins suddenly felt very sober and zipped himself up quickly; almost catching himself in his flies as he did so.

"You can't!" he stuttered. He was trying to take in what she was meaning. "Besides, if you tell Varsity, Robert will find out about us and you will lose him!"

Shilty smiled. "We both want money, Collins, and I for one do not intend to wait twenty years and go through all that legal wrangling to get it! I see it this way. You give me fifty million for brokering the deal and you'll be a billionaire within two years. Lancelot is offering to buy you out. No long wait, no court, no costs. You get your money and your freedom and Robert gets to keep his precious Little Eden, so it's a win, win!"

"That's blackmail, or extortion, or something of that sort!" he replied, his mind racing.

"Collins! Darling! It's just a little gift from one friend to another - nothing more than that," Shilty replied. "I mean, if you would rather give Robin Shaft forty percent - then be my guest."

"I'll tell Robert about you and me first!" Collins threatened.

"No, I don't think you will tell him. You don't have the balls. And as for Varsity, it's not just me, now, is it? I wouldn't want her to find out about all the others you play around with as well." Shilty had a wicked twinkle in her eye. She loved life! She always saw it as a constant game of poker. You win some, you lose some: but you always have to take a chance!

Collins felt sick. He really thought he might throw up. "You wouldn't!" he said, trying to read her face. He knew full well that she was right about Varsity. She wouldn't stay with him if she found out he had been sleeping with other women, on a regular basis, behind her back. She was already getting disappointed with him in so many other ways. He couldn't quite make up his mind which he was most scared of - his mother's disapproval, missing out on being a billionaire, or losing Varsity and his unborn child. He didn't like losing in general, and he felt between several rocks and a hard place on this one.

Shilty pulled her fur coat around her. "Rather settle to suit Robert and settle quickly! Then you can walk away with your share, sooner rather than later. And, I suppose you have heard that you might not get a penny if they find your mysterious Uncle Frith."

"Who?"

"Some uncle of Lucas's apparently," Shilty replied. "Lancelot tells me they thought he was dead but turns out he may well be alive and kicking, and if they can locate him, Lucas will have to give up his place on the Trust. Who knows, maybe this uncle will have a soft spot for heritage and old chateaux? I would take the deal on the table and not risk waiting to see if this Frith can be found."

Collins grumbled under his breath and looked around to see if there was anything to drink in the room. He saw a decanter of port, near the window, and poured himself a glass. "When did you become so bothered about Little Eden?" he mumbled.

"Oh, I don't know!" Shilty replied, in a smooth voice. "Maybe I fancy being lady of the manor after all!"

"But it's not up to me!" Collins bleated and turned to face her. He suddenly looked like a naughty schoolboy. "It's Mother who calls the shots!"

Shilty got her phone out of her handbag and started scrolling down the contacts. "Now, where is that number?" She said, out loud, "V…v…ah…"

"Alright!" Collins exclaimed. "Alright! I'll make a deal. Tell Lancelot to put something on the table." He had to admit that being a billionaire in just two years, without a legal fight, trumped his mother's disappointment that Little Eden would not be destroyed as she had hoped after all.

"Good boy!" Shilty said, patronisingly. "Lancelot will be waiting for you at the law offices in one hour." As she opened the door, she suddenly turned back and added, "Now that didn't take much, did it? Just some big tits and a blow job!"

She winked and closed the door behind her.

~ * ~

The plane finally started to taxi along the runway and Collins heaved a huge sigh of relief. When they were airborne he admitted to Varsity that he had signed a deal with Lancelot to wait for a cash sum in place of selling Little Eden.

"You haven't told your mother, have you?" Varsity guessed.

Collins shook his head and held her hand.

Varsity leaned back in her seat and closed her eyes. She felt a sudden wave of nausea come over her at the thought of Jennifer's wrath. She wondered if this was to be just a couple of weeks at their villa or if she might never see London again!

~ * ~

Meanwhile…lying in her oversized bed in Bartlett Crescent, Jennifer watched Robin Shaft button up his shirt.

She was in shock!

Robin had just received a phone call which had caused him to jump out of bed. His surprise soon turned to anger. He threw the phone onto the chair and began getting dressed. He was too furious to speak at first. Looking at Jennifer, lying amongst the peach silk sheets, he felt pure hatred towards her. Without money, she was no use to him, and yet she was the most stunningly beautiful woman he had ever had on his arm - or on top of him, for that matter! In that moment, however, he despised her and desired her, in equal measure. He had to restrain himself from wanting to strangle her, whilst at the same time wanting to thrust himself inside her.

He stormed out - still half dressed - carrying his jacket and tie with him.

Jennifer pulled on her yukata and followed him downstairs. She begged him not to leave and to explain what the phone call had been about.

But Robin Shaft has three very strong principles, from which he never veers, under any circumstances:

1. Get money
2. Get more money
3. Get some more money

He slammed the front door behind him and was gone.

Jennifer sat down on the bottom step of the stairs and stared blankly at the doorway. Dyson came quietly out of the kitchen carrying a cup of tea and he handed it to her, without saying a word. Jennifer absent-mindedly took it from him and sipped it.

Then she burst into tears.

~ * ~

Back at the hospital, Robert had had extensive tests and there was no sign of brain or lasting nerve damage - much to everyone's relief!

The welcome news that Collins had agreed to take the cash payoff helped him feel better much quicker, and whilst he did not like the idea of being a suspect for manslaughter, he was sure that justice would prevail.

Whilst unconscious, Robert had had some amazing and indescribable visions. In fact, you could say, that Robert had been on a transcendental adventure. Out of the confines of his physical body, his consciousness had been able to expand in a way that takes most people years of practice. Robert had seen the universe from the inside out, and he had witnessed Old Father Time holding the solar system in his hands like a child's mobile. He had talked with Mother Mary and Merlin. He had taken tea with the Dalai Lama and Desmond Tutu. He had gone walkabout in the Australian desert and he had ridden on the back of Ganeshe, through forests and up into the snowy mountains. He had travelled through the history of human consciousness, as if he were seeing the whole cosmos from inside a pop-up book.

He had started out lying on a beach. He just gazed out at the ocean and the stars for several days. Then he found a cave, in which there was a pharmacy of coloured bottles and potions, laid out on stone shelves, in front of a shallow pool of water. Once he had dived into the pool, or rather, had been pushed by an invisible hand into it, he had arrived at the edge of into a deep and vast canyon. Slowly, a rainbow bridge had materialised and he had spent several days crossing the enchanted arch to visit various dimensions and timeframes.

The evening that Melanie had nearly killed him, he was back on the beach and a shimmering staircase, made entirely of droplets of water, materialised out of the ocean waves. He climbed the set of ghostly and ethereal steps and found the mystical stairway took him up to a luminous palace, carved out of mist and sea spray. He was faced with monumental gold doors, which seemed so tremendously high, as to disappear into the Milky Way. Once inside, he found himself in an imposing chamber, which appeared similar in design to an immense Gothic cathedral. The floor was so shiny it looked as if it would be as slippery as an ice rink. Vast columns rose upwards into the stratosphere and an imperial golden throne awaited him in the middle of this majestic chamber. He sat for a few moments, before eight glimmering lions walked slowly out from the shadows and sat, like guardians, around his grand seat.

Suddenly, the imperial chair felt as if it were being plunged into the earth like an elevator falling out of control. Energy rushed through his body from head to toe! It was as if every atom in his body was racing into the centre of the planet at an alarming rate.

Just as suddenly as the sensation had begun, it ceased and he came to rest, still sitting on his throne. He realised that he was inside another chamber, similar to the first, only now the gigantic pillars were made of luminescent crystal and they were holding up the centre of the Earth.

A tall wizard dressed in a midnight blue hat and cloak, studded with silver stars and moons, appeared in front of him. The wizard seemed to have been expecting Robert and strangely, Robert felt quite at home. What he was shown there would change his perspective on life forever.

Coming out of the chamber he arrived back on the beach, just as Melanie arrived in his hospital room.

As for the rest, dear readers, you already know what happened next!

~ * ~

Over at the Daisy Chain, Minnie and Alice tried to persuade Linnet to come to the Memorial Concert, but to their dismay they had found her passed out on the living room floor, surrounded by several empty wine bottles. She was too heavy for them to lift, and after a few minutes of trying to roll her over, with no success, Alice finally fetched her a pillow and a duvet and tried to make her as comfortable as possible. She sat on the floor next to her mum for a while, listening to her breathing and occasionally snoring. Then she snuggled down onto her mother's belly, she was so afraid that she was losing her mummy forever and began to cry.

When Linnet finally woke up, Minnie made her some milk thistle and ginger tea, and gave her copious amounts of water and some headache tablets. Minnie helped Linnet shower and then held back her hair as she threw up, put her back into the shower again, and plied her with more liquids.

"You can't go on like this!" Minnie told Linnet, when she was finally able to eat some hot buttered toast and actually listen to her. "It's not just about you!" Minnie lowered her voice, so that Alice could not hear her from her bedroom, where she was getting ready for the concert. "Alice took the worst of it and she isn't acting like it's the end of the world. You mustn't let Marcus get into your head like this! He's dead now! He can't hurt you anymore, but you are hurting yourself and Alice by not letting go."

Linnet began to sob into her tea and toast. "I can't seem to get him out of my head!" Linnet wailed. "He's all I think about. I have nightmares that he is still trying to kill me. They are so real, Minnie, I can feel someone pressing down the mattress next to me and then the duvet seems to move on its own. I can hear someone breathing and I start to panic and it's like I'm paralysed! I try and reach for the lamp but I can feel invisible hands around my neck and sharp finger nails cutting into my skin. I have to scream at myself to wake up! Oh! Minnie, I'm so frightened!"

"Why don't you go and see Silvi Swan for some therapy? It might help," Minnie said, kindly; not really knowing what else to suggest - never having had such night terrors herself.

Linnet sniffed and pulled her hand away from Minnie's. "I had therapy seven years ago and it didn't do any bloody good. Talking about it! Talking about it over and over till I got bored of my own voice! Ten sessions of: What do you think? How does that make you feel? How do you think you'll move forward? Blah, blah, f**king blah!"

"But, you only had ordinary counselling!" Minnie replied. "Maybe you need something more in-depth?"

"What, like lock me up in looney bin you mean?" Linnet said, angrily.

"No! That's not what I mean at all!" Minnie replied, a little frustrated. "I meant inner-child work, past life therapy, post trauma therapy maybe. I don't know what exactly. Sophie would probably say that you need to clear some karma between you and Marcus - that kind of thing!"

"Well, you won't get any of that on the NHS!" Linnet scoffed.

"No, you won't, but Silvi can help you," Minnie replied, pouring Linnet some more tea.

"And where do you suggest I get the money from to go and see Silvi Swan?" Linnet moaned.

Minnie shrugged her shoulders. "I don't know! Maybe if you didn't spend all this money on wine, you'd have enough for some therapy sessions?" Minnie said, impatiently. "And then, there's your gym membership - that you never use! I can think of several things you could do to find the money. You could give up shopping for clothes for a few months whilst you concentrate on getting well on the inside."

Linnet just looked aghast at Minnie and pushed away the rest of her unfinished toast. "You have no idea what my life is like!" she said, with venom. "You! With your vintage dresses and your bunting, and everything so goddamn perfect! You don't know what suffering is! What real pain is!"

Minnie tried to take Linnet's hand again, but it was to no avail. "I only want you to be happy, Linnet, that's all I want," Minnie protested.

Linnet shook her head. "No! What you want is a perfect girlfriend who skips about pretending life's one long tea party! Well, I'm not perfect and I never will be, so why don't you just stop trying to fix me and leave me the hell alone?"

"But, Linnet, I..." Minnie couldn't finish her sentence because Linnet began to yell at her like a banshee.

"Get out! Get out of my house! Get out of my life and take your perfect little tits and arse with you! P**s off! Just f*ck off!"

With that, Linnet pushed Minnie out of the kitchen and slammed the door on her!

Minnie felt as if all she wanted to do was go home and cry. But she knew that Alice needed her right now. She took a deep breath, held back the tears and composed herself. She found Alice, who was dressed in her best outfit and putting on her sparkly shoes. Minnie could see that Alice had been crying and she helped her with the buckle.

"You look like a princess!" Minnie told her and gave her a hug. "You're going to blow them away tonight!"

"Is Mummy coming?" Alice asked hopefully but she knew the answer.

Minnie shook her head. "Mummy isn't feeling well. I'll be there, and Lucy and Jack, and Stella will be there. Sophie is coming to watch you especially!" Alice took Minnie's hand. "Come on! Let's go and find Tambo and the others, and you can have a final practice at the Café!"

Next door, in the Café, Mrs B was baking her heart out, trying to get batches of hot floury scones done in time for the concert. At the grand piano the kids were practising their song and there were only a couple of hours to go before thousands of Lilly's fans would be joyfully celebrating her life.

All day, camper vans and cars had been arriving at the park. Tents had been erected and hordes of people streamed out of the Eve Street underground station, eager to find their place at the open-air theatre. Huge television screens had been erected so that even on the other side of the park you could see the performances and the whole of Little Eden would be able to hear it.

Some, without tickets, congregated along the north walls from where they would get a free show, and some residents meant to listen from their rooftops whilst having a rather chilly barbeque and a few drinks with family and friends.

The buzz of excitement was becoming infectious, but India had more serious matters on her mind! She had decided to make the most of the hordes of spectators and had turned it into a fundraiser for the Save Little Eden campaign. She had the intention of squeezing every last penny from the crowds by the end of the evening! She had roped in Peony (who was still trying to make amends) and Vincent, Eric and Iris Sprott (who was fully recovered from her ordeal), Silvi Swan, Devlin Thomas, Tage, Sumona and all the Café staff. Even Mr T had ventured outdoors to collect money (with Cedric in tow, of course).

Stalls had been set up around the park, selling hot drinks and wondrous snacks, and as always, Fudge and Bunny had their ice-cream cart at the ready. Mrs B, along with Tosha and Tonbee, would be serving from Lilly's retro cream tea caravan which they often used in summer when tourists flooded the Peace Park.

Mrs B was covered in flour by the end of her baking session and the Café smelt divine! "It's such a shame Robert will miss the concert!" she lamented to Lucy, as she filled baskets full of soft warm scones. "He will be so sorry not to be there. He loved Lilly so."

Lucy thought for a moment as she spooned clotted cream into a huge silver bucket. She pondered and a cunning plan formed in her mind!

By seven o'clock, the crowds were gathered and the bands were doing their last sound checks. Luckily, it was a clear night and the weather had suddenly turned mild for a winter's evening. A warm wind had begun to blow - one could almost have said it was the middle of May rather than February!

And, there were some unexpected shenanigans going on at the hospital…

Johnathon distracted the policeman by calling him, on a false pretext, to reception, whilst Jack surreptitiously crept down the shiny corridor and into Robert's room. A minute later, Cubby nodded the all clear as he pressed down on the fire door bars, and Jack fled out of the hospital pushing Robert in front of him in a wheelchair!

Once outside, Robert was so happy to feel the fresh air again. He felt really alive! And he was unbelievably happy to be so. He had awoken from his near death experience knowing that his life's purpose was to save Little Eden and to guard the dragon portal. He knew that the next thousand years of human history would depend upon whether Little Eden was kept safe or not. He was determined never to waste another day trying to please his mother. The veil of karma had been lifted and he saw her for what she really was. He was no longer inclined to excuse her behaviour just because she was his mother. Little Eden was his destiny and he would see it through no matter what. He was no longer afraid of death. He had seen Heaven and he was humbled to the core by his existence. He knew that his life on Earth was just one moment in time and he had to use it wisely.

As Jack sped across the car park and out onto the street the two boys felt seventeen years old again as they laughed at the ridiculousness of their situation!

Further up the road, hidden around the corner, Stella opened the back of Jack's van and helped Robert climb in. Jack folded up the chair and quickly closed the doors behind them. "Drive!" Jack shouted to Minnie. They shot down the street, reaching the crossroads just as the traffic lights turned to amber, but without hesitating, Minnie whipped the steering wheel round and took a sharp left. In no time, they sped through Queen's Gate and into the sanctuary of Little Eden.

Back at the hospital, Johnathon lay in the bed, taking Robert's place. In the low light of the room, both having dark hair and being about the same height, to the casual observer - like the policeman outside the door - there was no reason to suspect that it wasn't Robert peacefully asleep!

The friends arrived just in time to hear Tambo and Alice's band, Otherworld, open the concert and perform their song, 'A Thousand Years'. Robert was wheeled backstage and his heart sang at the sight of so many residents, loyal fans of Lilly's and close friends, who were all gathered together in Little Eden that night. Sophie came and placed her hand on his shoulder and smiling up at her he took her hand in his and kissed it affectionately.

"Look at them all!" she smiled. "All here because they loved Lilly!"

Alice, Joshua, Tambo and Elijah wowed the crowds with their amazing performance and the applause went on nearly as long as the song had done! Alice rushed off the stage and into Minnie's arms. "I wish we could go and do another one right away!" she said, jumping up and down. Lucy high-fived Tambo and Iris hugged Elijah. Adela Huggins swung Joshua around in her arms. They were beaming with pride at the talent and hard work of their children and had been really surprised how good they actually were!

"I think I had better take your musical talent more seriously now!" Iris admitted to Elijah. "You can have a new guitar for your birthday, no matter what your pa says, to be sure!"

"And, can I have a bigger drum kit?" Joshua asked his mother. Adela smiled. "We'll see," was her reply. She winked at Lancelot, who lifted Joshua onto his shoulders so that he could see the next band playing on the stage.

Ginger came up to congratulate the kids and to hurry Tambo into his gospel choir outfit. Alice sadly watched Tambo walk away and she felt very alone all of a sudden. "I wish Mummy was here," Alice said, looking around hopefully, but there was no sign of Linnet. Then, she caught sight of Robert, who was positioned, in his chair, just behind one of the backstage pillars and she screamed with delight! She ran up to him and jumped onto his lap.

Robert held her tightly and kissed her cheek. "We are one step closer to saving Little Eden," he told her. "I'll make sure it'll be here for another thousand years."

Sophie, reluctantly, headed back to Daisy Place, to get out of the crowds and the noise. She felt drained to her bones. She wanted to sleep for a week and all of her body ached from head to toe. Her heart was filled with sadness that she could not stay for the rest of the concert and be with her friends. But, unexpectedly, Stella and Mr T caught up to her, just as she turned onto Eve Street.

"You can't be alone tonight!" Stella told her. "Come, we'll sit on the porch swing together and listen to the rest of the concert."

Cedric yelped in agreement. Sophie smiled as she picked him up and cuddled him. "I think Aunt Lil would have been proud of the children tonight," she said to them both. "We can't lose Little Eden, we just can't." She looked across the street at the Bookshop, tears welling up in her eyes. "We mustn't let anyone take this away from us."

The concert continued for the next two hours and it was a great success! Not least because India had managed to raise another few thousand pounds. She shook the collecting bucket she was holding and smiled at Robert. "We are going to make it!" she told him. "Even if it takes me every day for the next two years - I will find the money!"

Robert smiled sadly and wished he could believe her.

"There's always the possibility of Uncle Frith!" Lucy reminded them.

"And the buried treasure!" Jack interjected.

"That's if the inquest..." Lancelot was about to remind him that they were not out of the woods just yet, but Adela stopped him with a (and I might say, dear readers, long overdue), kiss!

Back up on the roof of Daisy Place, Sophie had fallen asleep on the porch swing, under the patio heater, wrapped up in blankets. Stella and Mr T sat next to her and Cedric had curled up on her lap, keeping her legs nice and toasty. All of a sudden, she awoke to feel the presence of her Aunt Lilly all around her. She was overwhelmed by a tingly sensation and the feeling of deep inner comfort, that only an angel can bring. She looked at Stella and Mr T, and she sighed. The future seemed still so uncertain and so dangerous. She knew the war for the dragon portal had only just begun.

How she longed for Aunt Lilly to walk through the conservatory doors right now, carrying a cup of tea and humming a tune as she always used to do. *Please, Aunt Lil*, Sophie wished, *Come back to life and tell me this has all just been a bad dream.*

But, of course, she could not.

Stella also felt Lilly's presence and she patted Sophie's arm whispering, "Listen, my darling".

On the night air, the dulcet tones of Ginger and the gospel choir floated over Little Eden. As Sophie looked up at Venus, hanging bright in the night sky above, she heard her aunt's voice in her mind whispering, *'No matter what happens, never give up, never give in!'*

A white dove came to perch on the chimney across the way and Sophie saw Lilly's shining apparition, smiling at her from the doorway, as they listened to the last song of the evening... 'From a distance'...

The End

Daisy Place
Recipes
Little Eden

Hello, dear readers,

KT asked me to pop a handful of recipes in the back of the book, so that you can nibble as you read! I've chosen some of my easiest tasty treats for you to try at home.

Hoping you enjoy them, my loves,

Mrs B x

Mrs B's top tips for a great bake…

When I go shopping, my loves, I always try to buy what I need less than a couple of days in advance. As my mother used to say to me, 'Patricia, she'd say, that what's fresh, tastes the best!' But you can use whatever you have in the cupboard, as long as it's not gone stale, and it'll still turn out just fine!

I know not everyone can afford Organic and Fair Trade products, but if you can manage it, you will be helping build a web of love and care around the world. When I'm baking, I always do it with love. I thank the animals, for giving up their goodness to feed us, and everyone who helped get the ingredients from the fields to my table. Baking always reminds me that we all depend on each other in some way or another! Finally, I always make a wish, as I pop it in the oven, that whosoever eats it, will feel a little happier for having enjoyed a treat that day.

Exact measurements are the key to a good bake, so make sure you have some scales, measuring spoons, and a measuring jug. Your oven might not be exactly like mine, so experiment a little to find out if your oven bakes quicker or slower. You might need to turn it up or down 10 degrees, or take things out a few minutes sooner or later.

If you sieve your flour at least twice, this will get lots of air into it and create a lighter bake; and fresh free range eggs will add a richer taste. When making anything spongy, leave your butter and eggs out of the fridge, so that they are at room temperature when you start.

To make my recipes you'll need: a wooden spoon, a spatula, a teaspoon and a tablespoon, (or measuring spoons) a sieve, a big mixing bowl, a jug and a cooling rack (you can use the top of a grill pan). You'll also need a cake tin, a shallow baking tray for brownies, a muffin tin and muffin cases, a round pastry cutter, some baking parchment and have a skewer or clean knitting needle handy, so that you can check if things are done in the middle!

Oh, and this is a tip I learnt at school; always have a bowl of hot soapy water ready from the start, so that if things get sticky, it's easy to wash it off as you go along.

I'd love to see your bakes! Pop a photo of your creation on our Facebook group, Little Eden, and share your bakes with other readers and with us at Daisy Place! I hope you enjoy baking, my loves. Never be afraid to try something new!

Love Mrs B x

For more recipes from Book One come and visit us at
ktkingbooks.wordpress.com

Arval Bread

Arval Bread was traditionally presented to guests at funerals in England and is given out at Lilly's wake in Chapter 4. It can vary from region to region, and is often more like cake than bread. At the Café we always use this recipe, which is rather like the Welsh Bara Brith cake. I was given this recipe by my father's best friend Peter Johnson, who came from North Wales.

If you like fruit cake you'll love this one, as it's moist without being dense, and fruity without being boozy. This is a one bowl recipe so it's easy peasy, my loves.

You'll need to start it the day before you want to bake and eat it, but don't let that put you off. This is only because we soak the fruit in tea for 24 hours. You can soak it for less time if you are in a hurry, but the longer the better.

Oven: 170 C (fan) gas
Time: 1 ½ hours
Tin: Loaf tin - 20cm long, 12cm wide, 9cm deep (2lb) Grease and line with baking parchment. If you don't have a loaf tin you can make a round or square cake instead.

Ingredients:
455g dried mixed fruit (you can include peel, it'll make for a more piquant taste)
½ pint black tea (I like to use Lady Grey tea, but everyday tea is fine too)
Pop the fruit into a bowl or jug and pour over the hot tea. Soak the fruit in the tea over night or for 24 hours. Do not put in the fridge, just cover and leave on the side.

455g white self-raising flour
255g dark or light brown sugar
1 large egg (beaten)
1 tablespoon golden syrup
2 teaspoons mixed spice

Method:

Sieve the flour (twice) into a large bowl. Add the other ingredients and stir with a wooden spoon until all combined together.

Pour your mixture into your lined tin and make sure it is evenly distributed.

Bake at 170 degrees C for 1 hour 30 minutes, but check with a skewer or knitting needle at about 1 hour 20 minutes; if it comes out clean it is done. The top of the cake will be risen and cracked. Only take it out of the oven when the skewer comes out clean.

Serve whilst still warm with custard or cream. It is delicious served cold too, with butter or just on its own.

It'll keep for at least a week in an air tight container and in the freezer for at least a month. I often cut it up into slices to freeze, so that we can take out smaller amounts when we need them, and they defrost quicker too!

Stella's Carrot Cake and Ginger Cookie Muffins

In Chapter 8 Stella offers Robert one of her all-time favourite bakes; carrot cake and ginger cookie muffins. This recipe was given to me by a dear friend, David Sparke, who likes to experiment with baking and often adds his own little twists!

I use Lucy's Ginger Snap biscuits (see recipe) but if you don't have any of these or don't have time to make them as well, you can use any ginger biscuits you have in.

Oven: 170 C (fan) gas
Time: 25 minutes
Tin: 12 muffin tin
Quantity: 12 large muffins

Ingredients:
200g white plain flour
1 teaspoon baking powder
½ teaspoon bicarbonate of soda
2 teaspoons ground ginger
¼ teaspoon sea salt
100g soft light brown sugar
2-3 medium sized eggs (beaten)
200ml sunflower (or vegetable oil of your choice)
200g peeled and grated carrots (approx. 2 small carrots)
100g chopped walnuts
170g ginger biscuits crumbled up into small pieces.

Method:
Sieve the flour, baking powder, bicarb', ginger and salt into a bowl.
In a separate bowl put the sugar, eggs and oil and stir with a wooden spoon until all combined.
Add the mixed wet ingredients to the flour mix and combine them well.
Stir in the grated carrot, walnuts and crumbled biscuits but do not over mix.
Spoon into muffin cases, filling nearly to the top. Bake at 170 degrees for 25 minutes. Check with a skewer or knitting needle; if it comes out clean they are done.
Put onto a cooling rack for 10 minutes.
Serve whilst still warm with crème fraiche (the slight tartness compliments these muffins perfectly) or any topping of your choice. You can enjoy them cold as well, my loves, and they make a nice breakfast muffin.
They will keep for at least a week in an air tight container, and in the freezer for at least a month.

India's 'slightly healthy, but still very squidgy' Brownies

India gave me her recipe a few years ago and we all love them; especially Alice and in chapter 19 India makes them for her to help cheer her up. They are delicious warm with ice-cream and strawberries, but you can use any fruit on the side that you like! They are quite rich, my loves, but you can cut them smaller if you prefer and have them as brownie bites.

Oven: 160 C (fan) gas
Time: 25 - 30 minutes
Tin: 8 inch square cake tin (lined with baking parchment)
Quantity: 9 medium sized, 12 smaller

Ingredients:
150g dark chocolate, melted in a bain-marie
4 tablespoons natural cacao or cocoa powder
3 tablespoons of hot water
1 teaspoon vanilla essence
120ml sunflower oil (or vegetable oil of your choice)
2 tablespoons date syrup
2 eggs beaten
100g light muscavado sugar
50g coconut sugar
65 - 100g walnuts chopped into small pieces (these are optional, chose your amount to taste)
50g - 100g milk chocolate chunks (these are optional, chose your amount to taste)
65g white self-raising flour
½ teaspoon bicarbonate of soda

Method:
Melt the dark chocolate in a bain-marie.
Mix the cacao powder with the hot water to make a smooth loose paste.
Put all the wet ingredients, sugar, nuts and chocolate chunks into a bowl and mix together.
Sift the flour and bicarb' into the other ingredients and gently fold together until all the flour has disappeared.
Pour the batter into lined tin (it will be silky and fairly loose) and bake at 160 degrees for 25-30 minutes.
You might have to experiment with your timings, my loves, depending on your oven. You don't want to over bake them as it takes away the fudgy gooeyness. Your skewer should come out with fudgy bits on but not liquid. If it comes out totally clean you may have over cooked them

a bit but they will still taste lovely!
Cool in the tin for 10 minutes, so that they continue to cook, then place them on a cooling rack. Serve hot or cold.
They will last about 5 days in an airtight container (if you can resist them that long!). You can freeze them and they'll be fine for a month. You can re-heat them as well.

Lucy's Ginger Snap Cookies

Lucy loves ginger cookies and she likes them crunchy! In Chapter 19 they help settle her stomach; ginger being good for digestion and nausea.

This recipe was given to me by my old friend and chef, Mr Michael Brattan. When I was younger, a group of us used to go, each year, to see the Trooping of the Colour, and we'd take a picnic to St James Park. One year Mike brought these delicious biscuits with him. Everyone was sorry he had not brought twice as many, and he had to make them every year after that!

Oven: 170-180 C (fan) gas
Time: 14 minutes
Tin: flat baking tray lined with baking parchment
Quantity:12 medium sized

Ingredients:
115g unsalted butter
3 tablespoons of golden syrup
425g white self-raising flour
115g dark brown sugar
115g brown muscovado sugar
2 tablespoons ground ginger
1 teaspoon bicarbonate of soda
1 teaspoon vanilla essence
1 large egg (beaten)
100g crystalized ginger (chopped into small pieces)

Optional ingredients:
100g dark chocolate, melted, to coat or drizzle over cookies or as chips to add into mix.

Method:

Melt the butter in a pan and add the syrup. Set aside to cool.

Mix together dry ingredients and make sure to sieve the flour and bicarb' and break up any lumps of sugar.

Add the vanilla essence to the beaten egg.

Then, add the egg/vanilla and butter/syrup to the dry ingredients and thoroughly mix together. Add the crystalized ginger (and the chocolate drops if you are using any).

The mixture will seem very dry and crumbly, but don't panic, my loves. It will come together as a dough in your hand.

Take small amounts at a time (about the size of a golf ball for medium sized biscuits) and roll into a ball. Place onto baking parchment on the baking tray.

Squash down each ball to about 1cm thick. You may find the biscuits look crumbly around the edges but this is fine.

Bake at 160 degrees for 14-16 minutes. Your biscuits will look golden brown on the surface when done.

Take out and put onto a cooling rack.

The biscuits will remain soft for a few hours and then harden. You can drizzle melted chocolate over them or dip them in melted chocolate at this point.

They will last about 5 days in an airtight container. You can freeze them and they'll be fine for a month. I like to make a batch and freeze them, then Lucy can take some out of the freezer when she wants them.

Just a word of caution, my loves, if you have problems with your teeth - be careful, these are very crunchy indeed. You can dunk them in your tea to soften them if you need to!

The mixture also makes a great crumble topping!

Mrs B's scrumptious Scones

We serve scones every day at the Café with our afternoon teas. I do love a good scone! I make plain scones because traditionally fruit scones are not served with cream. My recipe uses icing sugar and a little lard. This makes for a lighter, slightly shorter bake which sets off the jam and cream to a T.

Scones are best eaten fresh out of the oven so that the cream melts as it ‘kisses’ the scone. When the girls were little, they always use to say that the cream, or the butter, ‘kisses’ the scones and it ‘melts with love’.

I try to get everything ready before I start, including my parchment and baking tray. Also, I try to keep my hands and the ingredients as cold as possible throughout. Have some flour to dip your hands into for when they get sticky, and scatter flour on the worktop to put the dough onto when cutting out.

My scones only take 5 minutes to make and 9 minutes to bake, so you can whip up a small batch anytime you like!

Oven: 220 degrees C (fan)
Time: 9 minutes
Tin: a flat bottomed baking tray, lined with baking parchment
Quantity: 6 medium sized - 6.5cm round cutter, 10 small - 5.5cm round cutter (use a fluted edge cutter - if possible).

Ingredients:
200g white self-raising flour
1 heaped teaspoon baking powder
1 pinch of finely ground sea salt
40g unsalted butter or margarine (cold and chopped into very small pieces)
10g lard or shortening (cold and chopped into very small pieces)
20g white caster sugar
5g white icing sugar (powdered sugar)
140ml full fat milk (cold)
A splash of milk (cold) - to use as a glaze

Method:
Double or triple sift the flour, baking powder and salt into a large bowl. Add the chopped fats. Rub them into the flour, with your hands, to make a breadcrumb like consistency. If you tap the bowl a few times, it brings any bigger pieces to the top and you can rub them in again. Give the whole lot a good stir when all crumbs are roughly the same size to make sure any free flour is fully mixed in.
Sift in the sugars. (Icing sugar is often lumpy, when it’s been in storage, and needs sifting).
Add half the milk and use a dull bladed knife to help you combine the

ingredients together. It'll look very dry but not to worry. Add the rest of the milk, slowly and combine again until the dough gets very sticky. You'll need to flour your hands and the worktop.

With your hands, bring the dough into one big ball. Try to handle the dough as little as possible, my loves, just gently bring it together and treat it with care.

Put it on the worktop and pat it down (do not roll with a rolling pin) to the depth of about 3cm (The scones will almost double in height when baked).

Take your cutter and dip it in some flour.

Do not twist the cutter as you push it through the dough, as this will seal the edges of the scone and you want to have a crispy outside. Dip your cutter in flour after each scone. Cut out as many as you can from the dough.

Bring together the remaining dough and pat down again and cut out more circles. Do this till there is nothing left to cut from.

Place them on your lined tray with spaces in-between (your scones won't spread outwards very much but you want to get the hot air all around them).

Using a pastry brush, lightly sweep some milk over the top of each scone.

Bake at 220 degrees for 9 minutes.

If you have an oven that is hotter at the back, you may need to turn your tray half way through, and if you have an AGA you will know what to do!

When ready, they should be slightly golden and have a crust on the top.

Remove the scones from the sheet immediately and put on a cooling rack so that the bottoms don't go soggy.

Serve as soon as possible (preferably within 30 minutes) with your choice of toppings.

You can freeze your scones once cooled. Let them defrost first, then you can refresh them in a low oven for a few minutes or in the microwave for a few seconds.

For more about Afternoon Teas come and visit us at the blog:
ktkingbooks.wordpress.com

~ * ~

Dear Readers,

Thank you for reading Little Eden Book One, I hope you enjoyed it and are wondering what happens next!

There are so many questions still to be answered....will Robert be found guilty of manslaughter and thrown into prison? Will the friends raise enough money to pay off Collins and Lucas? Will Uncle Frith be found dead or alive? Will Lancelot and Adela take it to the next level? What will be revealed in Book Two? Keep an eye out on social media for the next instalment.

Join me on social media @KTKingbooks and don't forget to visit KTKingshop on Etsy.

If would like to know more about ME/CFS and for everything Little Eden including links to the songs throughout the book visit my blog at ktkingbooks.wordpress.com

Please consider leaving me a book review on Amazon or Goodreads as reviews mean the world to me and help spread Little Eden to others who have not found it yet!

Thank you KT xx

Dear Book Club Readers

I'm so thrilled you are going to be reading Little Eden in your book club. Please get in touch and let me know where you are and a bit about yourselves and your group.

Why not bring your bakes along to your book club meeting? India's brownies and Lucy's cookies are especially yummy and easy to take with you!

I hope you enjoy reading Little Eden.

Love KT xx

Here are some question suggestions to get you started…

- How did the book make you feel when you first started reading it?
- Did you fall in love with Little Eden? If you could live there where would you set up your home?
- Which characters did you identify with the most? If the novel was a film or TV adaptation who would you cast in the roles?
- Would you try to save Little Eden or would you take the money? Do you think the natural environment is more important than Little Eden?
- Did you feel there were plot twists and cliff-hangers? Did the switching between time-lines add to the storytelling? Which parts of the story stood out to you and why?
- Did you believe in the supernatural elements or did you think they were fictional? Have you ever had a psychic or supernatural experience of your own?
- Did the novel touch on any social issues which are close to your heart? Did the book change your opinions about anything or anyone?
- Did Sophie having chronic fatigue make her less of a heroine? Do you want to know more about ME/CFS now?
- Did you like the addition of the map? Did you use any of the wiki-links? Did you listen to the sound track on KT's blog? Did you try any of Mrs B's recipes from the back of the book? Have you looked at or bought anything from the Little Eden Etsy shop on line where you can buy the crystals and handmade jewellery inspired by the novel?
- What did you think of the ending? Would you read the sequel? Would you leave a review on the site you bought your copy from? What would you say in your review and why?

47929901R00157

Printed in Poland
by Amazon Fulfillment
Poland Sp. z o.o., Wrocław